# RIDING THE NIGHTMARE

*Look for these exciting Western series from bestselling authors William W. Johnstone and J.A. Johnstone*

*The Mountain Man*

*Luke Jensen: Bounty Hunter*

*Brannigan's Land*

*The Jensen Brand*

*Preacher and MacCallister*

*The Red Ryan Westerns*

*Perley Gates*

*Have Brides, Will Travel*

*Guns of the Vigilantes*

*Shotgun Johnny*

*The Chuckwagon Trail*

*The Jackals*

*The Slash and Pecos Westerns*

*The Texas Moonshiners*

*Stoneface Finnegan Westerns*

*Ben Savage: Saloon Ranger*

*The Buck Trammel Westerns*

*The Death and Texas Westerns*

*The Hunter Buchanon Westerns*

*Tinhorn*

*Will Tanner, Deputy U.S. Marshal*

# RIDING THE NIGHTMARE

# WILLIAM W. JOHNSTONE

**AND J.A. JOHNSTONE**

## PINNACLE BOOKS

Kensington Publishing Corp.

www.kensingtonbooks.com

PINNACLE BOOKS are published by

Kensington Publishing Corp.
119 West 40th Street
New York, NY 10018

Copyright © 2022 by J.A. Johnstone

PUBLISHER'S NOTE
Following the death of William W. Johnstone, the Johnstone family is working with a carefully selected writer to organize and complete Mr. Johnstone's outlines and many unfinished manuscripts to create additional novels in all of his series like the Last Gunfighter, Mountain Man, and Eagles, among others. This novel was inspired by Mr. Johnstone's superb storytelling.

All Kensington titles, imprints, and distributed lines are available at special quantity discounts for bulk purchases for sales promotion, premiums, fundraising, and educational or institutional use.

Special book excerpts or customized printings can also be created to fit specific needs. For details, write or phone the office of the Kensington Sales Manager: Kensington Publishing Corp., 119 West 40th Street, New York, NY 10018. Attn. Sales Department. Phone: 1-800-221-2647.

PINNACLE BOOKS, the Pinnacle logo, and the WWJ steer head logo Reg. U.S. Pat. and TM Off.

First Printing: October 2022

ISBN-13: 978-0-7860-4888-5
ISBN-13: 978-0-7860-4889-2 (eBook)

10 9 8 7 6 5 4 3 2 1

Printed in the United States of America

# CHAPTER 1

"There's hell in Thunder Canyon!"

The excited shout made everyone in Fiddler's Green turn their head toward the entrance, where a man had just slapped the batwings aside and rushed into the saloon.

"What the devil is that rannihan going on about?" asked Biff Johnson, the former cavalryman who owned Fiddler's Green. Biff had named the place after an old cavalry legend that said every man who had answered the call of "Boots and Saddles" would journey after death to an idyllic meadow with a tree-lined creek on one side, where he would be able to sit in the shade and visit with all his former comrades. Biff had made his Fiddler's Green into something of an idyllic spot, itself, seeing as it was the finest saloon in the town of Chugwater, Wyoming.

"Why dinnae ye ask him what he's on about?" suggested Duff MacCallister, who was sitting at a table with Biff, Elmer Gleason, and Wang Chow. The latter two worked for Duff on his vast ranch, Sky Meadow, at least technically speaking. In reality, Elmer and Wang were more like members of the family.

Biff nodded. "I'll do that." He pushed to his feet and started toward the agitated newcomer. Several men had gathered around to ask him questions.

Biff's powerful voice cut through the hubbub. "Pinky Jenkins, what do you mean by bursting in here and yelling like that? Can't folks enjoy a peaceful drink in the middle of the day without having their ears assaulted by your cater-wauling?"

Jenkins stared wide-eyed at him. "But Biff, there's hell in Thunder Canyon!"

"Yes, you said that. But what are you talking about?"

"Avalanche!"

That raised even more of a ruckus in the saloon. Duff stood up, went over to join Biff, and asked, "Was anyone hurt in this rockslide, d' ye ken?"

Jenkins turned his bug-eyed expression toward Duff. "It was more 'n a rockslide, Mr. MacCallister. The whole derned mountainside came down on the canyon! Closed it up, clear from one side to the other!"

"How do you know that?" asked Biff.

"I seen it with my own eyes!"

Biff grunted. "Then you can give us more details, or at least you should be able to."

"I reckon I can," Jenkins said. His tongue came out and swiped across his lips. "But the ride into town sure made me dry, Biff. I could prob'ly talk a whole heap better if my speakin' apparatus was lubricated some."

Biff glared, but it was all Duff could do not to laugh. Pinky was a decent wrangler and ranch hand, when he rattled his hocks long enough to actually work any. He had an inordinate fondness for Who-Hit-John, too, which meant that he had worked for most of the spreads around Chugwater at one time or another, sticking for a spell before he got drunk and did something to get himself fired. He was a colorful but amiable local character. Duff wasn't surprised Pinky would try to cadge a drink or two before he spilled whatever news he happened to have.

"Come on over to the bar," Duff told him. "'Tis happy I'll be to buy you a drink."

"I'm much obliged to you, Mr. MacCallister."

Duff put a hand on Jenkins' shoulder and steered him over to the hardwood. He nodded for the bartender to pour a drink. As the men pressed around him, Jenkins picked up the glass, threw back the whiskey, and licked his lips again.

"That helped a mite," he said, "but—"

"Tell the story first," Duff interrupted in a firm voice. "Perhaps then 'twill be time for another drink."

Jenkins nodded. "Yeah, sure, I reckon that makes sense. I was ridin' close to Thunder Canyon, thinkin' I might mosey up to Longshot Basin and take a look around. But thank goodness I wasn't in any hurry, because if I'd been in the canyon when that avalanche came down, I'd be dead now, sure as hell! I'd be on the bottom of thousands and thousands o' tons of rock."

Longshot Basin was an isolated valley some twenty miles northwest of Chugwater, Duff recalled. Although it was a large stretch of range with decent but not outstanding graze, no ranches were located there. The land was still open to be claimed because the basin was surrounded by sheer cliffs and there was only one way in or out: the trail through Thunder Canyon, a narrow slash in the rugged landscape.

Now, according to Pinky Jenkins, that trail was closed, meaning Longshot Basin was cut off completely from the rest of the world.

Elmer and Wang had joined the crowd gathered around Jenkins.

Elmer asked, "What started the avalanche? Rocks don't usually go to slidin' for no reason."

"That is not necessarily correct," said Wang. "A stone can be in perilous equilibrium and on the verge of falling for a lengthy period of time before it finally does so under the impetus of some force too miniscule for human senses to perceive."

Elmer squinted at him. "If you're sayin' what I think you're sayin', there still has to be *somethin'* that starts the ball rollin' . . . or the rock, in this case . . . even if it's too puny for us to feel it."

"Oh, I felt it, all right," Jenkins declared. "It was an earthquake, boys! Are you tellin' me you didn't feel it here in town?"

"I didn't feel any earthquake," Biff insisted. "In fact, I'm starting to wonder if maybe you were drunk and imagined the whole thing, Pinky."

"No, sir!" Jenkins looked and sounded offended at the very idea. "I was sober as a judge. More sober than some judges I've seen. Until the one Mr. MacCallister just bought me, I hadn't had a drink in three days." He looked a little shame-faced as he added, "Couldn't afford one. I'm stone-cold broke. That's the reason I was headin' up to Longshot Basin. I thought I might comb through those breaks and maybe turn up a few strays I could drive back to their home ranches. Figured I might get me a little, what do you call it, finder's fee that way."

What Jenkins said made sense. Even though no ranches—not even any little greasy-sack outfits—were located in the basin, from time to time a few cows wandered up through Thunder Canyon and got lost in the rugged breaks that filled the basin. Rumor had it a sizable number of wild critters lived there, descendants of stock that had gone in but never came back out.

"I still don't think there was any earthquake," said Biff, shaking his head. "They have them up in the northwest part of the state, around what they've started calling Yellowstone Park, but there aren't any around here."

"Dinnae be so fast to think that, Biff," spoke up Duff. "Now that Pinky mentions it, earlier this morning when we were loading supplies onto the wagon, I thought I felt the earth shiver just a wee bit under me boots." Duff's broad shoulders rose and fell in a shrug. "I said nothing about it because I was nae sure I felt it or not."

"You did," declared Wang. "I felt the same faint motion of the earth."

Elmer frowned at them. "Well, I sure didn't. How come you never mentioned it, Wang?"

"It seemed of little importance at the time. Simply an inconsequential geological . . . hiccup."

"Not so inconsequential, to hear Pinky tell it," Duff said. "An avalanche big enough to close off Thunder Canyon is pretty major."

One of the townsmen said, "Aw, nobody lives up there. What does it matter whether anybody can get in or out of Longshot Basin? Nobody gives a damn about that place."

Duff shrugged again. "Perhaps not. Go on with your story, Pinky."

Jenkins licked his lips again, but when Duff didn't offer him another drink and neither did anyone else, he continued. "The ground shook and scared the bejabbers outta me, and then I heard this big ol' roar. Thunder Canyon sure lived up to its name! It was like the biggest, loudest peal of thunder anybody ever heard. When I glanced up at Buzzard's Roost, it looked like half the mountain was comin' down. I never seen anything quite as . . . as awe-inspirin' as all that rock tumblin' down into the canyon and throwin' up a cloud of dust higher than I could even see! I tell you what, the ground shook some more when all that rock landed in the canyon. It sure as blazes did! And then . . ."

Jenkins' voice trailed off as he licked his lips again.

Elmer exclaimed, "Oh, hell, give him another shot o' whiskey!" He dug a coin out of his pocket and tossed it on the bar. "I'll pay for it this time." He waited until Jenkins had downed the whiskey, then growled, "Now get on with the story."

"Sure, Elmer. Don't rush me. As I was sayin', that avalanche made a terrible racket and kicked up the biggest cloud of dust you'd ever hope to lay eyes on, and the whole thing spooked my horse so bad, it was all I could do to keep it from runnin' away with me. But I was far enough off that I knew I was safe, and I wanted to see what things looked like when the dust cleared.

"Well, sir, what I saw was a wall of rock a good twenty feet high, stretchin' all the way from one side of the canyon to the other! Ain't no tellin' how far up the canyon it runs, neither. But it plugged that canyon up just like a cork in the neck of a bottle, ain't no doubt about that!"

Duff, in his explorations of the countryside after he had come to Wyoming and started his ranch, had ridden through Thunder Canyon and into Longshot Basin a couple of times. He recalled that the canyon was approximately forty yards wide. It would take an enormous amount of rock to close off the passage, but from the way Pinky Jenkins described the avalanche, he supposed it was possible.

"Anyway," Jenkins went on, "once I'd seen what had happened, I lit a shuck for town. Figured folks here would want to know about it."

"And you figured the story was worth a few drinks," said Biff. He shook his head and chuckled. "I suppose you were right about that."

"I'd just as soon never see anything like that again," Jenkins intoned solemnly. "For a minute there, it was like the world was comin' to an end." He closed his eyes and shuddered. When he opened them again, he continued.

"And witnessin' somethin' like that . . . it sure does leave a man with a powerful thirst!"

Pinky Jenkins continued repeating the story as long as the men standing at the bar with him kept buying drinks. Duff, Elmer, and Wang went back to the table where they had been sitting with Biff when Jenkins came bursting in to Fiddler's Green. Biff remained at the bar, keeping an eye on Jenkins.

Duff and his two companions had come to Chugwater earlier in the day to stock up on supplies. Their loaded wagon was parked down the street in front of the general store, ready to be driven back to the ranch. Because most folks around there knew the vehicle belonged to Duff, it was unlikely anybody would bother the wagon or the goods in the back of it.

And Duff MacCallister, for all of his mild, pleasant demeanor, was *not* a man anyone who knew him set out to get crossways with.

Tragic circumstances in his Scottish homeland had prompted him to immigrate to America. After spending some time in New York, he had headed west, eventually winding up in Chugwater and buying a ranch not far from the town. He had named the spread Sky Meadow, after Skye McGregor, the beautiful young woman he had loved and planned to marry, before she met her death at the brutal hands of Duff's enemies. Duff had avenged that murder, but vengeance didn't return Skye to him, so he had put that part of his life behind him and established a new life on the American frontier.

A tall, brawny, powerful man with a shock of tawny hair, Duff was a formidable opponent in any hand-to-hand battle, whether with fists or knives. He was a crack shot with pistol or rifle. But the quality that really made him deadly was an icy-nerved calmness in the face of danger. He never panicked, never lost his head and acted rashly. And if forced into a fight, he never quit until his opponent was vanquished, one way or another.

Because of all that, Duff had a reputation as a man not to tangle with. But he was also known as the staunchest, most loyal friend anyone could ever have. In times of trouble, he never turned his back on someone who needed his help.

As it turned out, after leaving Scotland under those heartbreaking circumstances, he had made quite a success of his new life in America. The newly acquired ranch had a gold mine on it, a mine no one had known about except Elmer Gleason, the colorful old-timer who had been hiding in the mine and working it in secret when Duff bought the place. Duff had befriended Elmer, and even though legally the mine belonged to him since it was on his range, he had made Elmer an equal partner in it. Elmer also worked for him as the foreman of his crew of ranch hands.

That crew had grown as Duff expanded the operation into raising Black Angus cattle, the first stockman in the area to do so. The effort had been successful and quite lucrative. Duff shipped Black Angus not only back east to market but also to other ranchers who wanted to try raising them.

The other man sitting with Duff in Fiddler's Green was Wang Chow, a former Shaolin priest in China who had been forced to flee his homeland, much like Duff. In Wang's case, the Chinese emperor had put a bounty on his head after he killed the men responsible for murdering his family. Duff had "rescued" him from a potential lynching, although it was likely that Wang, with his almost supernatural martial arts skills, could have fought his way free from the would-be lynchers. Just as in Elmer's case, that encounter had led to a fast friendship with Duff. They were a nigh-inseparable trio.

When they had finished their beers, they left Fiddler's Green, with Duff giving Biff a casual wave as they headed out. Biff just nodded, looked at the crowd still surrounding Pinky Jenkins, and sighed.

"Biff's a mite aggravated," commented Elmer, who had noticed the same thing.

"Aye, but as long as those fellows are buying drinks, I think he has little to complain about," Duff said. "Still on the same subject, I thought I might take a ride up to Thunder Canyon so I can have a look at this natural disaster with me own eyes." He had ridden his horse Sky into Chugwater today, so there was no reason he had to return to the ranch with Elmer and Wang.

"You reckon it's as bad as ol' Pinky made out it is?" asked Elmer.

"I dinnae ken. That's why I wish to have a look for meself."

"Thunder Canyon and Longshot Basin are a considerable distance from Sky Meadow," Wang pointed out. "Even if Mr. Jenkins' claims are correct, they have no bearing on our lives."

"Nae, 'tis true they do not," agreed Duff. "Just mark it up to curiosity."

"Sure, I don't blame you for that," Elmer said. "We'll see you later, Duff."

As Elmer and Wang climbed onto the wagon seat, Duff untied the team from the hitch rack in front of the store. Skillfully, Elmer took up the reins, turned the team and the wagon, and headed for home.

Duff was about to untie his horse so he could swing up into the saddle, when a voice said from behind him, "Not so fast there, Duff MacCallister."

# CHAPTER 2

Duff turned his head and looked over his shoulder. A very pretty young woman with blond hair tumbling around her head and shoulders stood on the boardwalk and regarded him with a stern expression on her face.

Duff saw the good humor lurking in her blue eyes, though, so he wasn't surprised when a smile suddenly appeared on her lips.

"Did you really think you could come into Chugwater and then leave again without even saying hello to me?" she asked. The smile took any sting out of the question, which could have been taken as a reprimand.

"Sure, and I planned on stopping at the dress shop on me way out of town," Duff told her.

"Well, we'll never know, will we," said Meagan Parker, "since I spotted your wagon earlier and knew you were in town."

"Been keeping an eye out for me, have ye?"

She laughed. "Don't get a swelled head. Yes, I looked out the shop's front window every now and then to see if the wagon was still here, but I had other things to do, too, you know. My world wouldn't have come to an end if I'd missed a chance to see the great Duff MacCallister."

"But ye *are* glad to see me?"

"Of course, I am," she said, her voice softening. "You know that."

"Aye, 'n 'tis pleased I am to lay eyes on ye, too. Were we not in the middle of town, in broad daylight, I might lay a kiss on ye, as well."

Meagan sighed dramatically. "I suppose we should maintain some sort of decorum."

"I suppose," Duff said, "but 'tis not easy."

The romance between Duff and Meagan had begun pretty much at first sight, even though that moment had been in the middle of a gunfight and Meagan had been warning him of some lurking killers about to open fire on him. Since then, they had gotten to know each other very well, developing a relationship built on passion, trust, and genuine affection.

Meagan operated a successful dress shop in Chugwater, sewing dresses of such beauty and elegance that ladies from all over the territory hired her to add to their wardrobes.

She was also a partner in Duff's ranch, Sky Meadow, having loaned him some money when he was in financial straits. He could have paid back the amount many times over since then, but Meagan preferred to leave things the way they were, with her having a percentage interest in the herd of Black Angus.

Duff suspected that was because the arrangement gave her an excuse to visit the ranch from time to time, and also to accompany him when he delivered stock elsewhere. She was a partner, after all, so why not go along on those trips?

Most folks who knew them figured they would get married someday, but for now, they were both happy with the way things were and saw no reason to change the easygoing relationship.

An idea occurred to Duff. "Did ye finish those other things ye were working on at your shop?"

"As a matter of fact, I did."

"Then ye have no pressing business at the moment?"

Meagan shook her head. "No, I suppose not. I mean, there are always things that need to be done . . ."

"I'm taking a ride up to Thunder Canyon. Why dinnae ye come with me?"

"Thunder Canyon?" Meagan repeated. "Why are you going all the way up there?"

"Dinnae ye hear the commotion earlier when Pinky Jenkins came riding into town?"

"No, I didn't. Pinky Jenkins is a pretty disreputable character, isn't he?"

"He's known to be, at times," admitted Duff. "But he brought a very interesting tale with him today." He filled her in on the story Jenkins had told about the avalanche closing off Thunder Canyon.

"My goodness, it sounds like quite a catastrophe," Meagan said. "Do you think he was telling the truth?"

"He seemed mighty sincere, and he insisted he was nae drunk when it happened." Duff shrugged. "So I thought I would go and take a look for meself, and now I'm for inviting you to come along."

"Could we ride up there and be back before nightfall?"

"Oh, I think 'tis likely."

"Would I have time to pack a little food? I've been busy today and didn't stop for lunch, but I have a loaf of bread and some roast beef I could bring along, as well as a bottle of wine."

"'A jug of wine, a loaf of bread, and thou'," Duff quoted. "To my way of thinking, Omar Khayyam had it right, but I'll not pass up a chance to put that old saying to the test!"

\* \* \*

Meagan wanted to change into more suitable clothes for riding, so while she was doing that, Duff rode to the livery stable and had the hostler bring out the horse she kept there. Duff saddled the mount himself to make sure everything was the way it should be. Where Meagan's safety was concerned, he took no chances.

He mounted up and rode to the dress shop, leading her horse. Carrying a small wicker basket with a clean white cloth draped over its contents, she was just coming outside when he got there. Even her denim trousers and a man's shirt made the clothes look good on her. Her blond hair was tucked up under the brown hat she wore.

They rode for about an hour and then stopped on a grassy, tree-shaded hill to enjoy the simple but delicious picnic lunch Meagan had packed. Duff enjoyed the wine, too, although he preferred coffee, tea, beer, or a good Scotch whiskey, for the most part. But not surprisingly, the company made everything better, as when they stretched out on the grass and lingered in each other's arms for a while, sharing kisses.

Then they rode on, following a faint trail Duff knew led to Thunder Canyon and beyond that to Longshot Basin.

Buzzard's Roost, the mountain that reared its ugly peak just southwest of the canyon, was visible for quite a few miles before they got there. Even though they rode steadily, it didn't seem as if they got any closer to the mountain. It still loomed ahead of them, tantalizingly out of reach.

To the northeast lay a vast, high tableland bordered by sheer cliffs that formed the other side of the canyon. Those cliffs curved around to merge with the lower slopes of Buzzard's Roost and completely enclose Longshot Basin. It was an impressive geographical barrier. A man might be able to climb the cliffs in a few spots, but a horse couldn't, and getting a wagon over them was downright impossible. Duff had never been atop that sprawling mesa and didn't know anyone who had.

Finally drawing close enough to see they were approaching Buzzard's Roost and an even more obscure trail veering off to the left, they reined in at that spot to allow the horses to rest for a few minutes.

As they dismounted, Meagan pointed to the path, which would have been easy to overlook, and asked, "Where does that go?"

"I could nae tell ye, lass," Duff replied with a shake of his head. "I remember it from the last time I rode up this way, but I did nae follow it. From the looks of it, it either leads up onto Buzzard's Roost or, more likely, peters out somewhere betwixt here 'n there."

"It must go *somewhere*," said Meagan, "or else no one would have come along here to make such a trail."

"Aye, what ye say is reasonable. I'll ask Elmer about it. He'll ken the answer if anyone in these parts does."

They rode on, their route curving around the base of Buzzard's Roost until they came in sight of Thunder Canyon.

Or rather, where Thunder Canyon had been. Duff pulled back on Sky's reins as he saw that the excitable wrangler had been right. The mouth of Thunder Canyon was completely blocked by a jumbled mass of rock—a pile of boulders that ranged in size from a few feet in diameter to huge slabs of stone the size of a house. Meagan came to a stop beside him, and they both sat there, staring at the impassable barrier.

"That's incredible," she said in a hushed, awed tone. "I'm not sure how far it goes up the canyon, but it would take weeks to dig through that."

Duff shook his head. "Ye could nae dig through it. Ye

would have to blast a path with dynamite, which might cause even more rockslides. 'Twould be a job requiring months of hard labor. Maybe even years."

"And what's on the other side? Just an empty basin?"

"Aye. And you're looking at the reason why 'tis empty. Everyone in these parts knew that if such a thing ever happened as has occurred today, Longshot Basin would be cut off from the rest of the world."

A little shiver went through Meagan. "I'm glad I'm not on the other side of that."

"That goes for me as well, lass."

"What do you think caused it?"

Duff tilted his head back and stared up at the rugged slopes of Buzzard's Roost rising above them. He could see the long, fresh scar in the mountainside where hundreds of tons of rock had pulled loose and roared down into the canyon.

"Pinky Jenkins claimed 'twas an earthquake, and Wang and I felt it, too, although in Chugwater the effect was small enough that I was nae sure I hadn't but imagined it. Wang agreed with Pinky, though, and I trust his senses."

Meagan gazed intently at the devastation and said, "It's magnificent, in a way, isn't it? And yet, at the same time, I hate to think about how small it makes me feel. Humanity is really insignificant in the face of nature, isn't it?"

"Nae," Duff answered without hesitation. "If 'twere no humans to appreciate and be impressed by nature, what good would it be, I ask ye? The tallest, most majestic mountain . . . more majestic than ol' Buzzard's Roost here . . . would be nothing without human eyes to gaze upon it. Does anything truly even exist without someone to take note of it?"

Meagan laughed. "Why, Duff, you're becoming quite the

philosopher. You must have been sitting out there at the ranch thinking deep thoughts."

"Nae, not really. But a man's mind *does* take strange turns now 'n then, when he's out riding the range alone."

They sat in their saddles for a few more minutes, drinking in the awe-inspiring sight in front of them, then turned their mounts and headed away from Thunder Canyon. The aftermath of the huge avalanche was impressive, but once you'd seen it, you'd seen it, Duff mused.

"You don't have to ride all the way back to town with me," Meagan said. "It would be out of your way. You should just cut back across country to the ranch."

"I would nae do that, leave ye to ride all the way back to Chugwater unaccompanied."

"Really, Duff, I'm not a helpless little child." Meagan patted the smooth wooden stock of a Winchester carbine that stuck up from a saddle sheath strapped under the right stirrup fender. "I'm not unarmed, either, and you know I'm a good shot."

"'Tis true," Duff admitted. "But ye would nae rob me of the chance to spend more time with ye, would ye?"

Meagan smiled. "Well, when you put it that way . . ."

Duff would have continued the enjoyable banter, but at that moment, from the corner of his eye, he spied movement off to their right. Turning his head to take a better look, he saw two riders angling toward them. After a moment, he realized the horsebackers were following the trail he and Meagan had seen earlier.

Meagan was to his right, between him and the pair of riders. Quietly, he said, "Move around here on the other side of me, lass."

"What? Is something wrong, Duff?"

"Nae, not that I ken, but yonder are a couple of strangers,

and I'd be more comfortable if 'twas between you and them I was."

"Oh." For a second Meagan looked as if she might argue the matter, but then she slowed her mount, let Duff pull ahead of her, and swung around to his left.

"'Tis glad I am now that I dinnae let ye go on to Chugwater by yourself," he commented.

"You don't know those men mean us any harm."

"I dinnae ken they *don't*."

It was entirely possible those riders were as wary of Duff and Meagan as Duff and Meagan were of them. As they drew closer, Duff got the impression the men hadn't been stalking them since the strangers were making no effort to conceal their presence. They had been following the other trail, and it could well be coincidence their route was going to intercept that of Duff and Meagan.

However, he could also tell the men had noticed them. One of them drew a rifle from its sheath and rested the weapon across the saddle in front of him. Duff did likewise, his movements casual and unhurried to show that he wasn't afraid, merely cautious.

Neither party slowed until they were about thirty feet apart. Then all four riders reined in.

Now that he could get a good look at them, Duff confirmed the two men were strangers to him, but at the same time, something about them seemed vaguely familiar. Since they were riding in the direction of Chugwater, the same as Duff and Meagan, he thought maybe he had seen them in town before. He had a good memory for faces.

And these two faces were memorable, in their way. The man who edged his mount slightly ahead of the other horse and rider was lean, with dark beard stubble covering the cheeks and chin of his lantern-jawed face. His eyes had what seemed to be a perpetual squint so pronounced Duff wondered how he could see through those narrow slits.

Duff knew the man could see him, though. He could feel the cold regard of that stare, almost like a snake was watching him, ready to coil and strike.

The man wore black trousers and a black coat over a white, collarless shirt buttoned up to the throat. His black hat had a flat brim and a slightly rounded crown. Duff spotted the walnut grips of a revolver under the man's coat, worn on the left side in a cross-draw rig with the butt forward. He was the member of the duo who had pulled his rifle out and had it balanced across the saddle in front of him.

The other man was much larger, with ax-handle shoulders, a barrel chest, and a head like a block of wood that seemed to sit directly on his shoulders with no neck. Dark, shaggy hair hung out from under a shapeless hat with a ragged brim. His bulk stretched the fabric of a patched, homespun shirt. His whipcord trousers were stuffed down in the tops of well-worn boots. He didn't have a rifle, but what looked like an old cap-and-ball revolver was holstered on his right hip.

Duff moved his horse a little to put himself more squarely between them and Meagan then nodded and said, "Good afternoon to ye, gents."

Neither returned the greeting. The man in black said in a flat voice, "What are you doing out here?"

Before Duff could say anything, the other man asked in a rather high-pitched voice, "Hey, Cole, is that little fella a woman? Look at the way his shirt sticks out in the front."

"Shut up, Benjy," the man in black snapped without looking around at his companion. He kept his reptilian gaze fixed on Duff and went on. "I asked you a question, mister. What are you doing out here?"

"'Tis open range hereabout, is it not?" Duff responded. "My friend and I are in the habit of riding where we please, as long as we're not trespassing."

The big man called Benjy got even louder as he said, "Damn it, Cole, that's a woman ridin' that other horse, I tell you. She's wearin' pants like a man, but she ain't no man."

"Benjy—"

"I'm gonna get her and take her home with me!" Benjy dug his boot heels into the flanks of the big horse on which he was mounted. The animal sprang forward. Meagan let out an involuntary cry of alarm and pulled her horse to the side. Duff jerked his horse to the right as Benjy started around him, trying to get in the big man's way.

The man in black whipped his rifle to his shoulder and fired, the sharp crack of the shot echoing over the rolling landscape.

# CHAPTER 3

Duff was about to lift his rifle and return the fire, but he paused when he saw the battered old hat fly off of Benjy's head. Benjy yelped in alarm, hauled back on the reins with one hand, and clapped the other hand to the tangled thatch of dark hair on his head.

"Damn it, Cole, you like to blowed my brains out!"

"I'm not a good enough shot to hit that small a target," Cole snapped, a wry response that brought a ghost of a smile to Duff's lips even in this tense moment. "Now get back over here."

"But you know what Pa said about us needin' women!"

"I know it, but that don't mean you can just grab any gal you see and do whatever you want with her."

Benjy's lower lip stuck out in a childish pout. "Ought to be able to," he said in a sullen voice.

"Get over here," Cole snapped again.

Muttering, Benjy turned his horse and retreated. Duff kept his rifle ready as his gaze flicked back and forth between the two men. He felt an instinctive distrust for Cole, and clearly, Benjy was slow in the head and unpredictable.

"I appreciate you calling him off, mister," Duff said to Cole. "I dinnae like trouble unless 'tis absolutely necessary."

"It might still be necessary," the man replied with another

trace of the dry humor he had displayed a moment earlier. "But my brother misunderstands things sometimes, and I didn't want him getting hurt."

Duff wouldn't have guessed that the two men were brothers; any family resemblance was slight. He said, "I dinnae mind telling ye, my friend and I rode out here from Chugwater to take a look at Thunder Canyon."

"You mean where Thunder Canyon used to be."

"Aye," said Duff, although Cole hadn't framed it as a question. "A man brought word into town about the avalanche, and I wanted to see the results for meself."

"Thunder Canyon is gone. It'll never be open again. When that earthquake hit, Buzzard's Roost jumped like it was on the deck of a ship in a rough sea."

"Ye were out here when it happened, then?" asked Duff.

Benjy said, "I thought the world was endin', like Cousin Willie talks about when he goes to preachin'."

Duff didn't know who Cousin Willie was, any more than he was familiar with these two. "You fellas must live in these parts."

Cole inclined his head vaguely toward the mountain. If somebody had settled up there, that would explain the faint trail heading in that direction.

Duff didn't believe in prying into another man's business, so he didn't press for a more detailed answer. "'Tis sorry I am for the misunderstanding. "My friend and I will be moving on now."

Cole regarded him intently for a moment, then said, "You're Duff MacCallister, aren't you?"

"Aye. We have nae met, have we?"

Cole shook his head. "We've never been introduced. But I've seen you in Chugwater and heard talk about you. There aren't that many Scottish immigrants around here."

"More than ye might think."

"Maybe . . . but none who wind up in trouble as often as you do."

Duff shrugged. "'Tis a fair observation, I suppose. Trouble does seem to have a way of finding me."

"Not today. You can go on about your business, and so will we."

"Aye, sounds like a good plan to me."

Cole turned his horse and jerked his head. "Come on, Benjy."

The big man tried one more time, saying, "That gal sure is pretty, Cole. You can marry her if you want. Just 'cause I saw her first don't mean I have to lay claim to her."

"I'm not marrying anybody today," said Cole. "Get your hat and let's go. Don't make me tell you again." He heeled his mount into a jog onto the main trail and rode toward town without looking back, clearly expecting Benjy to follow his orders.

Still muttering, Benjy hesitated only a couple of heartbeats before riding over to where his hat had landed when Cole shot it off his head. He dismounted, clapped the hat on the thatch of dark hair, and then followed his brother. He glanced back over his shoulder at Duff and Meagan a time or two, then concentrated on catching up with Cole.

Duff turned to Meagan and saw that her face was a little pale, but anger glittered in her eyes.

"The gall of that . . . that big ox!" she burst out when Cole and Benjy were no longer in earshot. "To think that just because I'm a woman, he can carry me off and do whatever he wants with me, even force me to marry anybody against my will—"

"That was never going to happen," Duff assured her. "We would have seen to that."

"You mean you would have protected me." Meagan sounded like she didn't particularly care for that idea, either.

"Nae, I mean I would have shot the one called Cole, and if I dinnae have time to deal with Benjy, I'm for thinking ye would have drilled him with that carbine of yours."

"You're damned right I would have," she snapped. "Before I'd let him or anybody else just grab me and carry me off."

Duff looked back along the faint trail and then raised his eyes to the imposing bulk of Buzzard's Roost that loomed over it. He tugged a couple of times at the lobe of his right ear, then scraped his thumbnail along the line of his jaw as he frowned in thought.

"The question is," he said, "where in the world would they have carried ye off *to?*"

"Oh, hell," Elmer Gleason said as he put down his fork and stared across the table at Duff. "Those boys were a couple of the Hardcastles, and they caught you right there where the Nightmare Trail starts!"

"The Nightmare Trail?" Duff repeated. His forehead creased in puzzlement.

He and Elmer were sitting at the table in the kitchen of the ranch house at Sky Meadow. Wang, who could cook American food as well as Chinese, had just placed plates full of fried steaks and potatoes in front of them and taken his own seat next to Elmer. Duff had been telling his friends what had happened that afternoon when he and Meagan rode out to look at the aftermath of the avalanche in Thunder Canyon. He had left out the part about the picnic lunch and the kisses, but he had told them about the encounter with the two strangers.

"Who are these Hardcastles ye speak of?" Duff went on.

Elmer shook his head. "A bad bunch, that's for durned sure. Nobody really knows how many of 'em there are or where they came from, although I've heard rumors they're from the Ozark Mountain country down in Arkansas. *'Way back* in the Ozark Mountains, if what I've heard is true. There's a whole slew of brothers and uncles and cousins and who knows what all."

"They're ranchers?"

Elmer snorted. "They live somewheres up on Buzzard's Roost. Nobody knows exactly where. You couldn't run much stock to speak of up there."

Wang said, "Perhaps they devote their efforts to agriculture."

"Farmin', you mean? Hell, you can't raise crops on the side of a mountain any more than you can raise cattle."

"'Twould seem, then," said Duff, "there's only one other alternative."

"Yeah," Elmer said, nodding. "They're owlhoots. They ride off from time to time to rustle some cattle or rob a bank or a train, then go back to their hideout on Buzzard's Roost. Ever'body knows that."

"I had no idea," Duff said. "This is the first I've heard o' the Hardcastle clan." His eyes narrowed. "From the sound of what you say, though, there be highwaymen like them back in Scotland."

"I have never heard of them, either," said Wang. "Why is that? Duff and I have both lived in this area for several years. Why has there been no mention of these Hardcastles?"

"I reckon because they've been layin' low for a spell," Elmer said. "Ever' so often, one or two of 'em will come into town for supplies, but they're careful not to cause any trouble in Chugwater. They always have been. They do all their desperadoin' somewheres else, so they'll have a place to come back to between jobs."

Duff nodded. "That makes sense, I suppose. And if they

live in such an out of the way place as Buzzard's Roost, 'tis nae likely most folks would ever run into them."

"That's the truth. Anybody who knows about the Hardcastles is careful to stay far away from 'em. What did you say the names were of the two you and Meagan run into?"

"Cole and Benjy. They said they be brothers."

"Cole Hardcastle has a rep as a fast gun. You may not have heard of him, but I'll bet a hat your cousin Falcon has, since he travels more in them circles. Now, as for Benjy . . ." Elmer shook his head. "Him I don't know, never heard tell of. It don't surprise me, though, if he's a mite slow in the head, like you said." Elmer made a face. "One of the rumors about the Hardcastles is that, uh, there's been some, uh, inbreedin' goin' on over the years. On account of it not bein' easy to find gals willin' to marry up and live with a whole clan o' outlaws."

"Well, given what Benjy said about them needing women wherever 'tis they live, that makes sense."

"It's a good thing you didn't let 'em carry Meagan off to that hellhole."

Duff chuckled. "If they had, they might've found they had bitten off more than they expected."

"It ain't funny, Duff," Elmer said. "Years ago, before you lived around here, when the country was settled sparser than it is now, some women and girls went missing ever' once in a while. They never did find out what happened to 'em. But there was always rumors that the Hardcastles took 'em and forced 'em to marry up with some of the bunch. Some of those gals may still be up there on Buzzard's Roost. If that big galoot Benjy's got his eye set on Meagan, he might come back and try to get her."

"He would nae bother her right there in the middle of town, surely."

"Prob'ly not . . . but to tell you the truth, I wouldn't put *nothin'* past the Hardcastles."

Duff frowned as worry stirred within him. He knew Meagan didn't plan to leave Chugwater tonight, and she hadn't said anything about going anywhere in the near future, either. But she rode out to Sky Meadow by herself sometimes, and she liked to ride other places as well. Maybe it would be a good idea for him to go to town tomorrow, pass along Elmer's warning, and advise her to stay put for a while, he told himself.

Of course, telling Meagan Parker *not* to do something was often like waving a red flag in front of a bull. She had seen what a brute Benjy Hardcastle was, though, so she might take the situation—and the potential threat—more seriously than usual.

Something else occurred to Duff. He said to Elmer, "Ye called that trail the Nightmare Trail. Why? It did nae look like the stuff o' nightmares to me."

"Maybe down there on flatter ground, it ain't. But up there on the side of the mountain . . . Well, I'll tell you, Duff, 'bout fifteen years ago, when this part of the country was first startin' to really open up, a party of sodbusters came along who decided they were gonna homestead some claims in Longshot Basin."

Duff shook his head. "'Tis not good farming country, from what I've seen."

"Not that good for farmin' nor raisin' cattle, neither one," confirmed Elmer. "But it wouldn't be impossible to do either o' those things, and you know how sodbusters are. The most ambitious, starry-eyed, optimistic in the face o' stark reality bunch anybody ever saw. They believed they could do it, and so they set out to do it.

"But they decided not to go through Thunder Canyon to

get there. Mind there was still some Injun trouble in those days, so the leader of those sodbusters got the idea they'd just go *around* the canyon, since that's where the savages had jumped several folks. Somehow, he'd found out there's a trail leadin' up onto Buzzard's Roost and on across and down into Longshot Basin."

Wang asked, "Such a trail actually exists?"

"Oh, yeah. Duff saw one end of it. It's a hard go, but you can get into the basin that way . . . if you're lucky."

"But those homesteaders didn't make it," Duff guessed.

"One fella in the bunch got back to Chugwater," Elmer said. "The story he told will give you a pretty good idea why folks started callin' it the Nightmare Trail. You see, it's so narrow only one wagon can follow it at a time, and even at that, there's barely room for the wheels. If you're sittin' on the seat and lean out just a mite and look down, you can't see no ground underneath you. Just a few hundred feet o' empty air."

"I'm not afraid of heights, but ye make the prospect sound quite unappealing," said Duff.

"Yeah, it'd sure as hell give me the fantods, too. Anyway, the Nightmare Trail ain't just narrow. It's steep, and to make things even worse, sometimes rocks fall from higher up on the mountainside. There were five of those sodbuster wagons. One of 'em went off the trail, got tangled with the wagon behind it, and took that one down with it. The remainin' three spread out more, but a couple of 'em went off, anyway, one at a time. And then a boulder come along and knocked the fifth one off. The only hombre who survived was on that fifth wagon. Young fella. He saw the rock comin' and jumped clear just in time, but he lost his whole family, Ma and Pa and brothers and sisters. And he said that even though he couldn't be sure about it, he thought he caught a glimpse of somebody movin' around up higher, before that boulder came smashin' down."

"The Hardcastles," Wang said.

Elmer shrugged. "That's what some folks figured. No way to prove it, though. More pilgrims tried to use the Nightmare Trail after that." The old-timer shook his head. "None of 'em ever came back, and we never heard tell of anybody makin' it through, neither. After a while, nobody would even try it anymore. The Nightmare Trail belongs to the Hardcastles, plain and simple."

"It bids fair to boggle me mind that such things have gone around here and I've not heard of them in all this time," said Duff.

"Well . . ." Elmer looked a little embarrassed. "I reckon some of that is because folks got outta the habit of talkin' about the Hardcastles. Nobody wanted to tempt fate, I suppose you could say. They didn't want word to get to the Hardcastles that anybody had been gossipin' about 'em, because there was no tellin' how they'd take it. They might decide to ride to town and burn the place to the ground. Nobody'd put it past 'em."

"If you speak too often of a demon, it may appear to remind you why it is unwise to do so," Wang said.

Elmer nodded emphatically. "Yeah. That."

"The two I saw looked like they might be trouble, but not demons," Duff said. "And I'll not be afraid to speak of them."

"Yeah, Duff, but you ain't like normal folks. You're a MacCallister. You're used to standin' up to bad hombres. Most folks just want to be left alone . . . and for the demons to steer clear of them."

"And I cannae blame them for that," Duff agreed. He smiled. "We got so carried away with talking that we're letting this fine dinner Wang prepared for us grow cold. Dig in, lads."

"Now you're talkin'," Elmer said. "I ain't lettin' no Hard-castles spoil my appetite."

No sound was heard in the kitchen then except the faint scrape of knife and fork on plates and chewing as the men ate, interspersed with occasional slurps from coffee cups. Duff put the outlaw clan out of his thoughts.

At least, he tried to. But as he sat there and ate, he admitted to himself his curiosity was up. He couldn't help but wonder what lurked at the other end of the Nightmare Trail.

# Chapter 4

Meagan Parker's dress shop on Clay Avenue in Chugwater was a neatly kept, two-story building with her living quarters on the second floor above the shop. Two staircases, one inside the building and one outside, led up to the living area. Like most Westerners, Meagan seldom locked the door to her home, although she was in the habit of locking the shop's front door to keep thieves from wandering in. The door that opened from the outside staircase's landing was unlocked when she went to bed that night.

In the town where she made her home, Meagan didn't expect any trouble. And if anything *did* happen, she kept a .32 caliber Smith & Wesson double-action revolver in the drawer of the small table next to her bed, with all five chambers in its cylinder loaded. The three-inch barrel didn't provide much accuracy beyond ten feet or so, but in the close confines of her bedroom, she believed the weapon was accurate enough.

She had fired it numerous times, as well as other, heavier revolvers. It was what spending time with Duff MacCallister did for a girl, she had told him once. It made her more proficient with firearms. She'd been teasing him, of course, but that didn't make the statement any less true.

Meagan believed her nerves were good, but ever since

the encounter that afternoon out near Thunder Canyon, a shiver had gone through her every now and then. She remembered the undisguised lust in the dull eyes of the giant called Benjy. If Duff and the other man hadn't been there, if Benjy had caught her out there alone, he could have carried her off as his prisoner, and there was no way of knowing what he might have done.

Actually, there *was* a way, she corrected herself one of the times that thought crossed her mind—but she didn't want to experience it.

Tonight, after she had put on her long white nightgown and sat for several minutes at her dressing table brushing out her thick blond hair, she had opened the drawer in the nightstand and peered in at the revolver. The faint gleam of its nickel-plated finish in the lamplight was reassuring. She left the drawer open as she blew out the lamp and climbed into bed.

As she tried to go to sleep, she told herself to think about something pleasant. She'd always heard doing so would bring good dreams. So she thought about the picnic she and Duff had shared that afternoon, and the delicious way it felt to sprawl on his broad, muscular chest with his arms around her as their lips and tongues merged in one sweet, heated kiss after another . . .

She drifted off to sleep with that warm feeling filling her.

Meagan had no idea how long she had been asleep when she woke up with a hushed gasp and an undeniable sensation that something was wrong.

Her eyes opened, but other than that, she didn't move, didn't do anything to give away the fact she was awake. She lay there with all her senses on high alert.

It was dark enough in the bedroom her eyes didn't do

her much good, but two of her other senses did. She heard a faint creak as a floorboard shifted under someone's weight, and she smelled the unmistakable scent of unwashed human flesh. Somebody was in the room with her, all right, someone who hadn't bathed in quite a while.

Slowly and carefully, she lifted her right arm from the bed where it lay beside her. She poised herself for a second, keeping her breathing steady so as not to warn the intruder, and then lunged toward the side of the bed as she reached into the open nightstand drawer where the Smith & Wesson rested.

Even in darkness, her instincts guided her unerringly. She had just closed her hand around the little revolver's checkered, hard rubber grips when what felt like a bear trap slammed shut on her wrist.

Meagan cried out in pain. She realized it was a huge hand that held her, not the steel jaws of a trap, but that didn't stop it from hurting. She felt another hand brush her face. The intruder was searching for her mouth, so he could shut off any more noises. Meagan jerked her head away from his groping touch and screamed as loud as she could.

At the same time, she writhed in the bed and tried to pull her gun hand free of his grasp, but his enormous strength kept her from succeeding.

She knew the man had to be the dull-witted giant called Benjy whom she and Duff had encountered that afternoon. He hadn't listened to his brother and had come after her, anyway. She didn't know how he had found her, but just about everybody in Chugwater knew her, so she wouldn't have been difficult to locate. All Benjy had to do was ask questions until he found somebody willing to answer them.

"Aw, now, settle down, gal. I don't want to hurt you none."

The high-pitched, childish voice confirmed the intruder's identity. Meagan drew in a breath so she could scream again, but Benjy had continued to flail around with his other hand and luck landed it on her face. His palm, which tasted and smelled dirty, closed over her mouth and nose, shutting off any sound she might try to make.

It shut off her air, too, Meagan realized a moment later. The deep breath she had taken just before he grabbed her gave her a little time before she got desperate, but that wouldn't last long.

"Stop fightin'," he rasped at her. "I just want to take you back with me so's we can marry up. Cousin Willie, he said he wouldn't do no more weddin's for them who was too close kin, and we ain't got nobody else left. I'll take care of you and treat you real good and pet you like you was just a purty little rabbit—"

Terror had grown stronger and stronger inside Meagan as Benjy rambled on. Since she couldn't scream or even breathe with his hand over her mouth and nose, she did the only thing she could. His grip on her wrist was making her gun hand go numb, so while she still had some feeling in her fingers, she jerked the Smith & Wesson's trigger.

The barrel wasn't pointed toward Benjy. The .32 caliber slug thudded into the wall of Meagan's bedroom, but the gunshot was loud enough, and the muzzle flash bright and shocking enough, Benjy cried out in surprise and jumped backward. He took his hand away from her face, but kept hold of her wrist with his other hand.

Meagan had had the presence of mind to squeeze her eyes shut when she fired the shot, so the muzzle flash hadn't blinded her. When she opened her eyes, they were still adjusted well enough to the darkness for her to make out Benjy's massive shape looming over her. In her thrashing around, she had kicked the covers off of her. Her nightgown was bunched up around her hips, so her legs were free. She lifted the right one, drew back the knee, and rammed the heel of her foot into Benjy's groin.

Where she estimated his groin would be, anyway, and judging by the shrill shriek he let out, she was right. He let go of her wrist, too, as he staggered backward and bent forward to clutch at himself with both hands.

Meagan's gun hand had barely any feeling in it as she sat up in the bed. She couldn't force her muscles to work the way she wanted them to. Clumsily, she transferred the Smith & Wesson to her left hand. During her practices with Duff, she had shot some with her left hand. She wasn't very good with it, but at this range, she didn't have to be. She thrust the double-action revolver at Benjy and triggered it twice more.

She didn't know if she hit him or not, but he turned and charged out of the bedroom, his heavy footsteps sounding like a bull stampeding across the floor in the sitting room. The door leading to the outer staircase's landing slammed open.

Not the sort of woman to cower and hope things would turn out all right, Meagan leaped out of bed and ran out into the sitting room. The door was open. Hearing thuds and grunts and groans, she raced to the door and stepped onto the landing, holding the .32 in both hands now.

She was in time to see Benjy topple down the last couple of stairs before coming to a stop at the bottom. He rolled over and groaned again as he came up onto his hands and knees. Meagan thought she could have drilled him at that moment, since he was a pretty big target and it was brighter in the light from the moon and stars.

She held her fire, though, as he struggled to climb to his feet. She didn't want to kill him unless she had to . . . but if he started back up the stairs, she wouldn't hesitate to plant the last two slugs in his broad chest, as soon as he was close enough that she couldn't miss.

Instead of trying to climb the stairs again, Benjy turned and stumbled away in the shadows. At the top of the stairs, Meagan heard a strange sound.

Was he *crying?*

She supposed it was possible. She had kicked him in a sensitive area, and she might have wounded him with those last two shots, after all. She was kind-hearted enough to hope she hadn't injured him fatally.

But if she had, he had brought it on himself, her more pragmatic side reminded her. Duff never lost any sleep when he was forced to kill someone who had it coming, and Meagan wasn't going to, either.

The darkness swallowed up Benjy after he had gone only a few steps toward the alley behind the buildings on Clay Avenue. Meagan could hear him as he continued to stagger away. Those sounds dwindled and finally disappeared. He was gone, and she didn't think he would be back tonight.

"Meagan, are you all right?"

The voice came from the street, a few steps away from the bottom of the staircase. She looked in that direction and saw Biff Johnson standing there, a shotgun in his hands.

"A fella came into Fiddler's Green and said he heard shooting from down here," Biff went on. "I figured I'd better check on you."

"Thank you, Biff," she told him. "I'm fine."

That was almost true. Her heart still pounded in her chest, and her right wrist ached dully where Benjy had squeezed it. But other than that, she was unharmed.

And she was standing in the moonlight in her nightgown, she realized. It had fallen back down to its full length and was a conservatively cut garment that didn't reveal anything except part of her calves, but it still wasn't proper attire for a lady standing in full view of anybody who came along the street.

"What happened?" Biff asked. "Was that you who did the shooting?"

"Yes," she admitted. "Someone got into my living quarters and was rummaging around." *That was putting it mildly,* she thought, but she didn't really want to go into detail. "I fired a couple of warning shots and frightened him away."

Biff grunted. "Should've drilled the son of a— You're sure you're all right?"

"Yes, I'm certain."

Biff tucked the shotgun under his arm and said, "Better lock your door when you turn in again. Chugwater's getting too blasted civilized, and you know what *that* means. Too many people who can't be trusted."

"I will, Biff. Thank you."

He nodded and went on his way. Meagan stepped back into the sitting room of her quarters and closed the door. The key was already in the lock. She turned it and pulled it out of the keyhole.

She hoped again that Benjy wasn't hurt too bad, and then scolded herself for being so soft-hearted. But that was her, and she couldn't change it.

She went back to bed, but not before reloading the Smith & Wesson. Quite a while passed before she dozed off again.

Cole Hardcastle sat up sharply in bed, a gun leaping into his hand as if by magic. He had the muzzle pressed up under the chin of the man who had just touched his shoulder before he realized it was his brother, Benjy.

"D-Don't shoot, Cole," Benjy stammered. "It's just me. And I'm already shot."

Cole's brain was so fuzzy from rotgut whiskey it took him a moment to grasp what his brother was saying. Then he took the gun away from Benjy's throat and exclaimed, "Shot! You say you've been shot?"

"Yeah. I don't reckon it's too bad, though. It hurt a lot worse when I got kicked in my private parts."

The woman in the bed beside Cole stirred and mumbled sleepily, "Wha . . . wha's goin' on?"

Like Cole, she had had quite a bit to drink, and after they had sated themselves with some clumsy coupling, both had gone to sleep with a candle still burning on the night table in the tiny room. The table was the only piece of furniture other than the sway-backed bed.

Still naked, Cole swung his feet to the floor and stood up. The candle burned, although the flame was guttering like it might go out soon. Its flickering glow revealed Benjy standing there with a shame-faced expression and blood on the left sleeve of his homespun shirt.

"Is that the only place you're shot?" asked Cole.

"Yeah, I think so."

"You don't know?" Cole said, before realizing that, yeah, it was entirely possible Benjy might be ventilated somewhere else without being aware of it. Cole didn't see blood anywhere else on his clothes, though.

The soiled dove, whose name Cole couldn't recall, gathered the sheet around herself with a modesty that seemed totally misplaced under the circumstances. Or maybe not. Because she said to Cole, "You're the only one who paid. He can't be here—"

"Shut up," Cole said.

The gun had been under the pillow. He set it on the night table next to the candle and reached for the bottom half of his long underwear, which he'd draped over the footboard with the rest of his clothes. As he pulled on the underwear, he asked his brother, "Who shot you?"

"Uhhh . . ." Benjy looked at the floor.

"Did you not see 'em? Were you bushwhacked? You *did* stay in your room like I told you to, didn't you, Benjy?"

Benjy didn't say anything, just shuffled his feet.

Cole sighed in exasperation. "Where'd you wander off to?" he demanded.

Clearly embarrassed and reluctant to admit what he'd done, Benjy said slowly, "I . . . I, uh, went lookin' for that gal—"

"What gal?"

"The one we saw out on the trail. You know, the real pretty one who was with that fella who talked funny."

Cole couldn't keep himself from rolling his eyes. "Oh, hell, Benjy! What were you thinking?"

Benjy's lower lip trembled. A sob escaped from him. "I'm sorry, Cole," he wailed. "But you had a gal, and I wanted one, too. And that one with all that yella hair, she'd be a good one to take home. You know I need to be married up, and Cousin Willie said he wouldn't let me get hitched to Della."

"That's because Della's our sister, you damned fool!"

The rebuke just made Benjy cry harder.

The soiled dove stared at the two of them and said, "What kind of a family are you two from, anyway?"

Cole whirled toward her with such a fierce expression on his face that she cried out, cringed against the headboard, and clutched the sheet tighter around her nudity.

"Don't you go talking bad about our family," Cole told her. "We do the best we can."

"I . . . I'm sure you do," she managed to say.

"It ain't as bad as my brother makes it sound." Cole

glanced at Benjy. "Hush up that bawling. Take your shirt off and let me see your arm."

The wound was just a graze along Benjy's forearm, bloody but not serious. The bottle of rye on the night table had about an inch left in the bottom of it. Hating to waste it, Cole dribbled a few drops on the wound. Benjy howled like a kicked dog.

"Hush! You'll wake the whole house."

"I'm sorry, Cole. I don't do nothin' but make trouble."

Cole shook his head. "No, it's my fault, Benjy. I should've let you stay in here so I could keep an eye on you."

"Not without him payin'—" the soiled dove began.

Cole jabbed a finger at her. "I'm not gonna tell you again to shut up. This is between my brother and me." He turned back to Benjy. "Put your shirt on. We're heading home."

"At night? We can't ride the Nightmare at night."

"No, but we can make camp out there where it starts up the mountain, so we'll be ready to move when the sun comes up. Go get your gear out of the other room and come right back here. Don't go anywhere else."

Benjy bobbed his head. "All right, Cole. I promise." He left the room.

As Cole started getting dressed, the soiled dove said, "I'm sorry, honey. I shouldn't have said those things I did. Do you have to leave right now? You paid for all night."

"It's better if I do." He picked up the bottle, which still had a swallow in it, and tossed it to her. She let go of the sheet to catch it. "Here. You can finish that off and then get yourself some sleep for a change."

"That doesn't sound too bad." She tipped up the bottle, and the last of the Who-hit-John slid down her throat. "You come back to see me next time you're in town, all right?"

"That may be a while." Cole buckled on his gun belt and reached for his hat. "After my brother's little fandango, it might be a good idea for us to stay out of Chugwater until folks forget what happened."

"You know that girl he went after?"

"I don't know her name, but earlier today, she was with that MacCallister hombre. Duff MacCallister."

The soiled dove's eyes widened. "A real pretty girl with blond hair?"

"Yeah."

"That's Meagan Parker. Owns the dress shop here in town. Everybody figures her and Mr. MacCallister will get married one of these days. You think your brother hurt her?"

Cole bit back a groan. He hadn't thought to ask Benjy if he'd done any harm to the girl. "I hope not."

"You'd damned well better hope not. Because if he did, Duff MacCallister will come after the both of you . . . and I don't reckon he'll stop until you're dead."

# CHAPTER 5

A week passed before Duff rode into Chugwater again, accompanied once more by Elmer and Wang. While his friends parked the wagon in front of the store and went inside to see about getting more supplies, Duff rode straight to the dress shop, dismounted, and looped Sky's reins around the hitch rail in front of the building.

"I'm told the prettiest girl in town can usually be found here," he called out heartily as he walked in and the little bell over the door jingled as if his presence needed any more announcing.

An attractive, middle-aged woman standing in front of the counter at the rear of the shop turned and smiled at him. "Why, thank you, Mr. MacCallister," she said. "I just wish Elmer Gleason could be halfway as gallant and charming as yourself."

Duff stopped short in surprise and fumbled for words for a second before saying, "Ah, 'tis sorry I be, Vi, but 'twas not ye to whom I was referring—"

Violet Winslow laughed, and Meagan, who was standing on the other side of the counter, joined in.

"That's all right, Duff," Violet said. "We all know who you meant."

"But if you could have seen it, you'd have to admit the expression on your face was priceless," added Meagan.

"Aye, more than likely. You ladies should be ashamed of yourselves for teasing a poor, defenseless man."

"You're wearing a gun," Meagan pointed out. "I'd hardly call you defenseless."

"A Colt .45 is no defense against the tongues of two smart females."

Violet walked toward him and said, "Take some advice from one of those smart females, Duff. When you're already in a hole, stop digging." She looked back over her shoulder with a smile and added, "I'll see you later, Meagan."

"Goodbye, Vi."

Violet Winslow owned Vi's Pies, a small but popular restaurant that was justly famous for the wide variety of delicious pies she baked. She had been keeping company with Elmer Gleason for quite a while, and the citizens of Chugwater assumed they would tie the knot someday, just as Duff and Meagan would. Although it was also a commonly held belief that Vi was probably too good for an old reprobate like Elmer. On that score, however, Vi's opinion was the only one that counted.

When she was gone, Duff went to the back of the store and placed both hands on the counter. "I did nae mean to interrupt—"

"You didn't," Meagan assured him. "We were just visiting."

Duff looked around the store. "No customers hiding behind dress dummies?"

"No, we're alone."

"Well, then, in that case . . ." He leaned over the counter, Meagan leaned forward from the other side, and their lips met in a tender kiss that lasted as long as it could in that slightly awkward position.

When they both straightened, Meagan said, "It's good to see you again, Duff."

"The feeling is mutual, to be sure."

"You haven't run into any trouble since the last time you were in town, have you?"

"Nary a smidgen." He chuckled. "Do ye not believe that a week can go by without some sort of hell popping?"

"You have to admit, that does seem to happen fairly frequently wherever you are."

"Perhaps. But in this case, I have nary a thing to report except the usual work that goes into running a ranch."

"I'm glad to hear it." She turned to several bolts of cloth stacked on the counter. "Let me put these away, and then we can talk some more—" She stopped short as she picked up the bolts. A look of pain passed over her face, there and gone so quickly anyone less observant than Duff might well have missed it.

He saw it, though, and didn't hesitate in plucking the bolts out of her hands. "What's wrong? I could see that picking these up hurt you."

"Oh, it's nothing," Meagan replied with a slight edge of irritation in her voice. She glanced down at her right hand. "This wrist has been a little sore lately."

Duff looked, too. The blue sleeve of her dress had white lace bordering the end of it, but enough flesh was visible for him to see her skin had a faint discoloration to it. He set the bolts of cloth aside and took her hand gently, cupping his fingers under her wrist. "What happened here?"

"It's nothing," Meagan said again. "If I tell you, you'll just get upset."

"I'm well on me way for to being upset right now, lass. Did ye hurt yourself somehow . . . or did someone hurt you?"

Meagan hesitated a heartbeat longer, then sighed. "Do

you remember those two men we met out on the range the day we rode up to Thunder Canyon?"

"Of course, I remember. Two members of the Hardcastle clan."

Meagan shook her head. "I don't know their names, other than Cole and Benjy. But that's who I'm talking about."

Duff recalled he hadn't seen Meagan since Elmer had filled him in on the Hardcastles and the Nightmare Trail, which explained why she didn't know their last name. He asked, "Did they come here to your shop?"

"Just the big one. Benjy. That night, he found out where I live and got into my quarters upstairs. I'd gone to sleep, but I woke up with him skulking in my bedroom."

"Why, the devil ye say! What happened?"

Meagan's chin lifted. "He grabbed me, so I kicked him where it hurts and took some shots at him with that .32 I keep in the nightstand drawer."

Duff stared at her for a second, then threw his head back and laughed. "Aye, 'tis a fierce lass ye be! If I dinnae ken already that ye have a bit of Scottish blood in ye, I'd know it now!" He grew serious again. "Did ye kill him?"

"I don't think so. I certainly hope not. He left under his own power, after he fell down the outside stairs trying to get away. I haven't seen him since."

"Did ye find much blood in your room?"

She shook her head. "Only a few drops on the floor. That's another reason I don't think he was hurt too badly."

"But ye put the fear o' God in him, 'tis a brand-new Stetson I'll be wagering on that." Duff reached over the counter and rested a hand lightly on Meagan's shoulder. "Ye say that sore wrist is the only injury ye suffered?"

"That's right. He grabbed it and squeezed it hard enough to bruise it. That's all, though."

"'Tis lucky," said Duff.

"Lucky for me?"

"Aye, but mostly for Benjy Hardcastle. If he'd done worse to ye, I woulda been for hunting him down and having a few words with him."

"He's a head taller and eighty pounds heavier than you, Duff, and you're a big man."

"Size matters less when justice is on your side."

"That's a nice sentiment, but I'm not sure how true it always is." Meagan changed the subject slightly by continuing. "You obviously know more about those men than you did the last time we spoke."

"Aye, Elmer told me quite a bit about them."

"I have a pot of tea on the stove in the back. I'll pour some for us, and you can tell me about it."

"I dinnae want to interfere with your business."

Meagan waved a hand at the empty shop. "There isn't any, right now, and if someone comes in, we can always pause in our talk."

Duff couldn't argue with that. Meagan fetched cups of tea for them, and they sat at a small table with two chairs tucked into a rear corner of the store. Husbands sometimes waited there while their wives shopped.

While they sipped their tea, Duff told her what Elmer had explained to him about the Hardcastle family and the so-called Nightmare Trail.

"And they live somewhere up on that mountain?" she asked.

"So Elmer claims."

"It didn't look like a very hospitable place to me."

"The Hardcastles are not a very hospitable clan."

"How many of them are there?"

Duff's broad shoulders rose and fell. "I doubt if anyone knows, other than them."

"Well, I've lived in Chugwater longer than you have, and this story is new to me, too." Meagan shook her head. "It's amazing how many secrets can lurk underneath the surface in a community."

"Everybody has their own story, and 'tis often more complex than anyone would dream."

"There you go, philosophizing again."

Before Duff could say anything else, rapid footsteps sounded outside the shop. He sat up straighter and let his right hand drift toward the Colt on his hip, thinking someone might be about to burst into the shop for some reason. But the footsteps kept going without slowing down. A yell sounded in the distance.

"My, that sounds like some sort of commotion going on," Meagan commented.

"Aye," Duff said as he came to his feet. "And with Elmer and Wang in town, 'twould probably be a good idea if I found out what it is."

Earlier, after parking the ranch wagon in front of Matthews Mercantile, Elmer and Wang had gone inside and found Fred Matthews behind the counter at the rear of the store.

The merchant grinned at them and said, "Most folks don't come in for supplies but once or twice a month. You boys show up nearly every week. It must be my sparklin' personality that brings you in."

"Or perhaps it is that I prefer fresh produce and meat for my cooking, and so does Mr. Kirby," replied Wang, referring to Red Kirby, the old puncher who did the cooking for the ranch crew in the bunkhouse while Wang prepared most of the meals for himself, Duff, and Elmer. "We will also visit Mr. Mullins, the butcher, and Mr. Wyatt, the greengrocer, before we depart today."

"But while we're in town," Elmer added, "we might as well pick up some more flour, sugar, tobaccy, and ammunition." He took a piece of paper from his shirt pocket, unfolded it, and placed it on the counter, revealing a list of several items written in his laborious scrawl. "There you go."

Matthews picked up the list and nodded. "I'll have one of my clerks start gathering these goods for you."

He was just turning away when the sound of quite a few hoofbeats came through the open front door, along with the creaking of wagon wheels and the rattle and jingle of harness.

Matthews frowned and said, "Sounds like a bunch of wagons just pulled up out there."

Elmer nodded to Wang. "Let's go see."

By the time they reached the high front porch that also served as a loading dock, a hubbub of voices had arisen. Some of Chugwater's canine population had taken note of the newcomers and arrived to greet them with loud barking. Elmer stood on the store's porch with his feet spread and planted solidly and his thumbs hooked in his belt as he took in the scene. Beside him, Wang's stance was more casual, but he was equally alert and observant without appearing to be.

Eight wagons were lined up along Clay Avenue, the first two parked in front of Matthews Mercantile and the others arrayed behind them, all pointed north. Some had mule teams hitched to them; others were pulled by oxen. Each wagon had a man and woman on the driver's seat, and kids ranging from toddlers to mostly grown teens peering from the wagons or running around and playing with the dogs.

The man on the seat of the first wagon wrapped the reins around the brake lever, said something to the woman beside him, and then climbed down from the vehicle. He turned toward the store.

Elmer guessed the stranger was in his forties or fifties. He was tall and solidly built, with broad shoulders and a barrel chest pressing out against an old-fashioned linsey-woolsey shirt. Suspenders held up canvas trousers tucked into high-topped boots. The man's face was craggy and deeply weathered and tanned under a shock of white hair that stuck out from under a broad-brimmed brown hat. He wasn't wearing a gun, but Elmer noticed a rifle lying on the floorboards of the driver's box where it would be handy.

The man came to a stop in front of the porch, looked up at Elmer, Wang, and Fred Matthews, who had joined them, and said in a deep voice, "Hello, men. This is Chugwater, isn't it?"

"Right the first time, friend," Matthews replied. "Something we can do for you? If you're in need of supplies, you can find just about anything you need right here at Matthews Mercantile."

"I'm obliged to you for that offer, but right now I'm just looking for information. What I find out will determine whether we need any more supplies."

Elmer was about to tell the man that he'd come to the right place—a general store was one of the best sources of both factual information and gossip—but before he could say anything, Wang nudged him in the side with an elbow.

At that same moment, a man said angrily, "Hey, watch where you're goin', you little . . ."

Elmer turned his head to look toward the rear of the wagon train, where Wang had already detected trouble brewing. He saw several men on horseback. One of them was struggling to control his mount, which danced around skittishly. A young, redheaded boy was on the ground nearby, and so was one of the dogs. The yapping seemed to make the horse even more nervous. Both boy and dog were in danger of being stepped on.

A young woman, with hair as bright as the boy's, jumped down from the rear wagon and dashed toward him. "Teddy! Get away from there!"

The man on the horse pulled viciously on the reins, finally bringing the animal under a semblance of control. He fumbled at the gun on his hip and said, "I'll shut that damned dog up!"

"No!" the boy cried. He leaped toward the rider and waved his arms. "Don't hurt him! He ain't doin' nothin'!"

The man on horseback cursed, jerked his left foot from the stirrup, and kicked the boy in the chest, sending him flying backward. The dog's barking got even more frenzied as the man pointed his gun at the animal and his finger tightened on the trigger.

# Chapter 6

Before the man could fire the gun, he cried out in pain. His fingers opened and the weapon slipped out of his grip and fell to the dirt. The man clutched his arm to his body and looked down at his wrist, where a shiny, five-pointed metal star was lodged in his flesh.

Wang had thrown that *shuriken* with unerring accuracy as he raced along the line of wagons, having leaped down from the store's porch when he saw what was about to happen. One of the other riders yelled a curse and clawed out his gun, but he had barely cleared leather before Wang leaped onto a wagon wheel, pushed off from it, and launched himself, feet first, at the man. The double kick smashed into the man's chest and knocked him clean out of the saddle.

Wang rebounded, caught himself on his hands when he landed in the street, and flipped upright again.

By then, Elmer had charged down the street, too, and pulled the short-barreled Colt Peacemaker that had been stuck behind his belt at the small of his back. He covered the other two riders and said, "If you boys was thinkin' of slappin' leather, I don't reckon it'd be wise."

The redheaded girl caught the youngster around the shoulders and pulled him away from the confrontation.

"Lemme go, Becky!" he yelled. "That mean ol' son of a gun was gonna shoot that poor dog!"

"I know," she told him, "but he doesn't look like he's going to shoot anyone now. He's hurt, himself."

It was true. The man had jerked the metal star out of his wrist and thrown it on the ground. The wound was bleeding more freely now. "I need a sawbones!" he said. "I'm fixin' to bleed to death!"

"No, you are not," Wang said as he bent to retrieve the shuriken from the dirt. "I was careful to avoid any major blood vessels with my throw, so you are in no danger of dying from that injury. The same may or may not be the case when it comes to nerve damage, however. That may have been unavoidable, so you may not regain full use of that hand." Wang's expression didn't change as he continued. "Of course, this entire incident *could* have been avoided, had you not threatened to shoot the dog, or kept your mount under control in the first place."

The man's face twisted in an ugly snarl as he looked up from his bleeding wrist at Wang. "Why, you dirty Chinaman! You talk to me that way? Boys—"

"Take it easy, Blackledge," said one of the two men Elmer was covering. "That old pelican's got the drop on us, and he looks like there's enough bark left on him that he wouldn't mind shooting us."

Elmer grinned. "I sure wouldn't. I wouldn't mind it one damn bit." He nodded to the redheaded young woman. "Beg pardon for my language, missy."

The white-haired man from the lead wagon strode up and ordered sternly, "Becky, take Teddy and get back in your pa's wagon."

"Yes, sir, Uncle Waylon," Becky said. She tugged the boy toward the wagon.

The dog followed them, wagging its tail, blissfully unaware of the violent commotion to which it had contributed.

"He likes me!" the boy said. "Can I keep him?"

"We'll talk about that later," Becky told him.

The man Wang had kicked off his horse had been lying in the street, only half-conscious. He groaned and stirred and sat up as his wits returned to him. He started to reach for his gun.

But a boot toe prodded his hip and a voice said, "I would nae be doing that if I was you, mister." The tall figure of Duff MacCallister loomed over him, casting a shadow that covered the man in the noonday sun. Duff's hand rested on the butt of his .45.

"What in blazes is going on here?" asked a voice that rang with authority. Jerry Ferrell, the marshal of Chugwater, hurried up with a shotgun in his hands. His deputy, Thurman Burns, followed him, also toting a double-barreled street sweeper.

"These people attacked me," cried the wounded man. "That Chinaman threw some kind of funny knife at me and cut my wrist. He was tryin' to kill me!"

"And then that old-timer threatened to shoot us," one of the other men added as he pointed at Elmer, who lowered his gun now that officers of the law were on hand.

Marshal Ferrell ignored that complaint and addressed the man with the bleeding wrist. "Mister, if Wang wanted to kill you, I promise you, you'd be dead by now."

"You know that stinkin' Chinaman?"

Elmer said, "I'm bettin' he's had a bath since you have, sonny, if you want to talk about stinkin'."

Duff stepped back a little and motioned for the man he was standing over to get up.

The man did so, although not without some effort, and once he was upright, he rubbed his chest where Wang had kicked him, which caused a grimace. "I think I got some broken ribs."

"Just bruised, more than likely," Duff told him. "Go over there and join your friends."

"What I want to know," Ferrell said, "is what started this ruckus. Elmer, you talk."

With his free hand, Elmer rubbed his grizzled chin. "I didn't rightly see the first of it, Marshal. When Wang and me come out on the mercantile porch there, the wagons were already stopped in the street and these four fellas were ridin' past. Them dogs were all stirred up, and that fella's horse got spooked. Then a little shaver from one o' the wagons run at 'em, tryin' to get the dog, I reckon, and that redheaded gal tried to chase *him* down, and then the fella on the horse got mad and kicked the boy and said he was gonna shoot the dog, and he pulled iron and that's when Wang took a hand."

"But you didn't see much," the marshal said dryly.

"Only what I just told you."

Fred Matthews spoke up from the porch, saying, "Elmer's got the straight of it, Marshal. That's the way it happened."

The white-haired stranger said, "That's how it looked from my vantage point, as well. I apologize for the part my people played in this incident, Marshal."

"Does anybody care that I'm still bleedin' here?" asked the wounded man. "Are we gonna sit around and palaver all day?"

"I can lock you up and the doc can tend to you in a cell, if you want," Ferrell snapped. "I'm getting to the bottom of this before anybody wanders off." He turned back to the white-haired man. "Who are you, mister?"

"Waylon Spencer is my name. I'm the captain of this little wagon train." A wave of his hand took in the eight vehicles. "All these folks are kin of mine. We'd just driven into Chugwater and stopped at the mercantile. Didn't intend to cause any trouble."

"I'd say welcome to Chugwater, but you probably don't feel very welcome right now." Ferrell turned to the wounded man. "How about you? I've seen you and your friends around town a few times lately, but I don't know you."

"I'm Dave Blackledge," the man answered sullenly. He inclined his head toward the other two mounted men. "That's Killeen and Warnock. Fella the Chinaman knocked off his horse is Jake Lamb. I don't know why you're givin' us trouble. We didn't do nothin' but defend ourselves."

"Yeah, I'm sure that twenty pound mongrel dog was a real serious threat to your life."

Blackledge's face flushed with anger. "The way my horse was actin' up, he coulda throwed me, and I coulda broke my neck. I was within my rights to make the damn dog leave me alone."

"Watch your mouth around ladies," Ferrell warned him. He looked around at the whole group, clearly considering his options. After a moment he went on. "All right, nobody's getting locked up. Blackledge, the doc's house is three blocks up the street, on the right. Go get that wrist tended to. Your friends can go with you, and then all of you go on about your business. I don't want to hear about you being mixed up in any more trouble."

"Wasn't our fault," Blackledge said with a surly scowl. "What about my gun?"

Deputy Burns had picked up the weapon and started to give it back, but Ferrell gestured for him to wait.

"Pick it up at my office in the morning," he said. "With your gun hand hurt, you don't need it right now, anyway."

Blackledge looked like he wanted to argue, but after a moment he turned his horse and rode slowly toward the doctor's office. Lamb climbed back onto his horse, making pained faces as he did so, and he and the other two followed Blackledge.

Elmer sniffed and commented, "Them four look like hardcases to me."

"You might be right, Elmer," Ferrell agreed. "When I get back to my office, I'll go through the reward dodgers I have on hand. They're probably not wanted around here, though, or else they wouldn't be so casual about showing their faces." The marshal looked at Duff and went on. "I'm a mite surprised you weren't in the big middle of this."

"Elmer and Wang had everything well under control by the time I arrived," said Duff. "All I had to do was issue a word of warning to one of those fellows."

Ferrell nodded and addressed the white-haired man. "Are you and your people just passing through Chugwater, Mr. Spencer?"

"Actually, we're planning to settle not too far from here," Waylon Spencer replied.

"Homesteaders, are you?"

"That's right."

Ferrell frowned. "I wasn't aware of any land in the area being open for homesteading right now."

"Well, according to the maps I've seen, it's another twenty miles or so from here," said Spencer. "That's one reason we stopped in Chugwater today, so I could check the directions with you local folks and find out exactly where we're supposed to go and how much farther it is."

"This place you would be for to settle," Duff said. "Does it have a name?"

Spencer nodded. "It's marked down on the map as Longshot Basin."

"Longshot—" Elmer choked off the startled exclamation.

Spencer frowned at him. "That's right. Is there something wrong with that?"

Duff said, "Mr. Spencer, I hate to be the one to tell ye this, but ye cannae be settling in Longshot Basin. Ye cannae even get there anymore."

The woman Spencer had left on the driver's seat of the first wagon said in a worried voice, "Waylon, what's that man talking about?"

"I don't know, Edith," Spencer said. "But I'll find out." He looked intently at Duff. "The map shows a suitable route for wagons into the basin through Thunder Canyon."

"Aye, and until a week ago, that trail was rough but passable. But an avalanche has closed off the canyon."

The people on the wagons were listening closely to this exchange. At Duff's words, some of the women cried out in shock, and a few men muttered curses or questions. Even the children had fallen silent and were watching and listening. Most of the dogs had wandered off, the novelty of the wagons' arrival having diminished. The redheaded boy, Teddy, was on one knee, petting the black and white cur Blackledge had threatened to shoot. Becky stood beside him, one hand on his shoulder.

Into the strained silence that followed Duff's words, Spencer said, "Closed the canyon off . . . completely?"

"Aye," Duff replied as gently as he could. He could tell these people were having their hopes and dreams smashed right in front of his eyes. "No one will be traveling through Thunder Canyon any time soon, if ever."

"Waylon, what are we going to do?" wailed the woman on the wagon seat.

"Blast it, Edith, I don't know," Spencer snapped. "But don't carry on so. There's got to be a way . . ." He looked hopefully at Duff.

"I have a ranch not far from here. Sky Meadow," Duff said. "There's plenty of room for ye and your people to camp for a time, Mr. Spencer. Until ye can figure what ye should do next."

A man on one of the other wagons said, "Do you have land you could sell us for farming?"

"Nae, I'm afraid not. I raise Black Angus cattle and fine horses, and I need all my range for my stock. But 'twill be fine for you folks to stay for a spell and rest up after your journey."

"Can you take me to Thunder Canyon, so I can have a look at it for myself?" asked Spencer.

Duff was about to tell the man that wouldn't do any good, but then he nodded and said, "Of course." He figured Spencer might need to see it with his own eyes before he could accept the disaster had overtaken his plans.

"I . . . I don't want to put you out, Mister . . . ?"

"MacCallister. Duff MacCallister." He extended a hand. "And it will nae put us out at all. Will it, Elmer?"

"Nope," Elmer replied in a hearty tone. "If there's one thing we got at Sky Meadow, it's plenty o' room. I'm Elmer Gleason, Mr. Spencer, Duff's foreman. And this short-growed hunk o' Oriental mischief is Wang."

Elmer shook hands with Spencer, and Wang gave him a formal bow.

"It is an honor, sir, but you should be informed the principal source of mischief at Sky Meadow is Elmer, not my humble self."

"Well, I'm just grateful to both of you for stepping in when you did." Spencer sighed. "As bad as things have turned out, I reckon it could have been even worse if you boys hadn't done what you did."

"Are you talkin' about those hardcases?" Elmer made a scoffing sound. "Don't you worry about them. They ain't gonna bother you no more."

* * *

The wagons were still parked in front of Matthews Mercantile when Blackledge, Lamb, Killeen, and Warnock emerged from the house where the doctor's practice and living quarters were located. Some of the men, women, and kids were still hanging around the vehicles, but the lawmen were gone, and the Chinaman and the old-timer were no longer in sight.

Blackledge's right wrist was bandaged, and that arm was in a sling. After cleaning up the blood, the medico had confirmed the wound looked messier than it really was.

"But an inch the other way with that shuriken, and you could have bled to death quite easily," Dr. Urban had said as he bound up the injury.

"You know that Chinaman?" Blackledge had asked.

"Of course. Nearly everybody around here knows Wang, as well as Elmer Gleason and Duff MacCallister." The doctor looked around at the four men. "Honestly, if you had trouble with those three, you came out of the encounter remarkably well."

Thinking back to the encounter as he looked down the street at the wagons, Blackledge's eyes were narrow, hate-filled slits.

"Come on, Dave, let's get a drink," said Warnock. "I reckon we could all use one."

"Yeah, I guess," Blackledge said.

Jake Lamb looked at him shrewdly. "You're thinkin' about gettin' even with that bunch, aren't you, Dave? Not just the Chinaman and his friends, but those pilgrims, too."

"You heard what the Chinaman said. My hand may not ever work right again."

"The sawbones seemed to think it will," Killeen piped up.

"Yeah, but he don't know for sure. And even if it does, it hurt like hell. Don't your ribs hurt, Jake?"

Lamb rubbed his chest again. "Yeah, but the doc said they ain't broken, just bruised. They'll heal up."

# CHAPTER 7

Later that afternoon, the ranch hands who were at Sky Meadow's headquarters instead of out on the range, stared in surprise as the wagons rolled in.

Duff, riding alongside the lead wagon, pointed at a grove of trees a couple of hundred yards away and told Waylon Spencer, "Ye can park over there, Mr. Spencer. There's good shade, and 'tis not far from the creek, so ye and your people can fetch water any time ye need it. The creek has ne'er gone dry in the time I've been here, so I don't believe we need to worry about that."

"We're much obliged to you, Mr. MacCallister," said Spencer. "I know I told you that before, but it's true. I don't know what we'll do in the long run, but at least we have a place to stay tonight."

"There be no hurry for ye to leave," Duff assured him. He pulled his horse a little to the side and let the wagons roll on past him.

Waylon Spencer and his wife Edith had the lead wagon, befitting Spencer's position not only as the captain of this wagon train but also as the patriarch of the extended family traveling with him. Spencer and Edith had two grown sons, Grady and Robert, and a daughter, Evelyn. The three children were married and had families of their own, and each family had a wagon.

The next two wagons belonged to Spencer cousins, Samuel Quinn and Ezekiel Kelly, and they had wives and families, as well. Waylon Spencer's younger brothers, Burl and Leon, drove the final two wagons. Burl was a widower, and he had no living children, but his two grandchildren were traveling with him—the redheaded teenager Becky and young Teddy. Leon and his wife had two sons in their late teens, grown men for all intents and purposes.

Duff had been introduced to all of them before the group left Chugwater. He was pretty good with names and faces, but with the family resemblances and the number of people in the wagon train—thirty, in all—he knew he might have trouble remembering who was who.

Not that it really mattered, he reminded himself. He would extend the ranch's hospitality to these folks for as long as he reasonably could, but sooner or later they would have to move on. He had started thinking already about other possible destinations where they would be able to homestead.

Elmer and Wang brought up the rear of the procession in the ranch wagon. As the big immigrant vehicles swung to the right toward the grove of trees, Elmer pulled the team he was handling to the left so he and Wang skirted around them.

Thad Sinclair, one of the cowboys who'd been standing in front of the barn watching the wagons, walked over to meet Duff and asked, "What's going on, Mr. MacCallister? Who are those folks? Are we startin' a new town out here or something, and they're the first settlers?"

Duff laughed as he reined in. "'Tis full o' questions ye be, Thad. Nae, there'll be no town here. Those folks are our temporary guests, that's all." He crossed his hands on the saddle horn and leaned forward to ease his muscles. "They were on their way to settle in Longshot Basin."

"Oh," Thad said as his eyes widened. "If they've been on the trail, they didn't know about the avalanche in Thunder Canyon."

"Not until they were told in town." Duff shook his head. "'Twas a surprising and saddening development for them. I extended Sky Meadow's hospitality to them until they can figure out what to do next."

"Well, that was mighty generous of you, Mr. MacCallister. I'll let the other boys know what's goin' on. I'm sure they're as curious as I was." The young puncher frowned slightly. "They won't get in the way of the work we're supposed to handle, will they?"

"I can nae see how they would." Duff turned his horse and nudged it into motion toward the house again. Elmer and Wang had reached it already while he paused to talk to Thad Sinclair.

A short time later, Red Kirby came to the house with a worried look on his weathered old face. "I ain't expected to cook for all them pilgrims who showed up, am I?" he asked Duff as the two of them stood on the front porch.

"Nae, they have their own supplies and will build a cooking fire where they're camped, I'm sure," Duff told him.

"It ain't that I mind the idea so much," Red said. "I've rustled vittles for round-up crews that big. I just figured if that was the case, I'd best know about it, so's I could prepare."

"Just carry on as usual, Red. Our visitors should not disrupt life here at Sky Meadow in any fashion."

Red nodded and headed back to the cook shack near the bunkhouse. For a moment, Duff gazed toward the trees where the eight wagons had stopped so they formed a rough circle. Making up his mind, he went down the steps and started toward the temporary camp with his long-legged stride.

Waylon Spencer saw him coming and walked out to meet him.

"Are ye settling in all right, Mr. Spencer?" Duff asked.

"We are, indeed. It's a very good campsite, just as you said, Mr. MacCallister."

"Why dinnae ye call me Duff? Be there anything else ye need?"

Spencer shook his head. "Only a home. Duff, are you absolutely sure there's no way we can get our wagons through Thunder Canyon?"

"I wish I was wrong, but 'tis certain I am. Tomorrow, ye can borrow one of our saddle mounts, and the two of us will take a ride up there so ye can see it for yourself."

"I think that's a good idea," Spencer said, nodding. "It's not that any of us doubt what you're saying. Don't think that for a moment. But I believe the others will be able to accept it better if they hear it from a member of the family. I hope so, anyway."

Duff clapped a hand on the older man's shoulder and said, "We'll head out first thing in the morning."

"You ever done much horseback ridin', Mr. Spencer?" Elmer asked as he and Spencer walked into the barn the next morning. Duff had asked Elmer to pick out a good horse for the wagon train captain and saddle it.

"Not in recent years, but when I was a younger man, I rode a lot. Sometimes pretty hard and fast, too."

Elmer gave Spencer a shrewd look from the corner of his eyes. "You're a mite younger than me," Elmer observed, "but not a whole heap. I'd say we're pretty much the same generation."

"That's right."

"Would I be too far off in guessin' that that hard, fast ridin' you done might've been durin' the Late Unpleasantness about twenty years ago?"

Spencer shrugged and said, "It might've been. I'm in the habit of not talkin' much about what I was doing twenty years ago. When folks ask me about those days, I generally tell them that I disremember."

Elmer grunted. "Matter of fact, I'm sort of in the same habit."

Elmer had ridden with a band of Confederate irregulars during the Civil War. Some had considered them nothing more than a gang of outlaws, not fighting for a cause as much as they were for the opportunity to loot and pillage. Unfortunately, there had been some truth to that. Elmer wasn't proud of everything he had done in his life, but at the same time, he knew he hadn't been nearly as bad as some. He had tried to hang on to at least a few shreds of honor and decency.

That time wasn't anything he really cared to discuss. If Waylon Spencer felt that way about his own experiences during the war, Elmer was perfectly willing to go along with it.

"So you can handle a horse and don't need a mount so old and gentle it's about to be put out to pasture," he went on.

"No, I don't," said Spencer. "In fact, if you have a horse with a little bit of spirit, that would be just fine, Mr. Gleason. Been a while since I've gone for a ride on a high-stepping animal."

"I got just the thing for you, then, Mr. Spencer. But seein' as how we're agreed we're roughly the same age, how's about we make it Waylon and Elmer?"

Spencer grinned. "I'd like that just fine . . . Elmer."

A few minutes later, Elmer had put one of the spare saddles on a sturdy brown gelding and had the horse ready to ride. Duff had already saddled the horse he was going to ride and left it tied to one of the front porch posts while he talked to the hands in the bunkhouse, giving them their assignments for the day. Normally Elmer would do that, but Duff had told him to give Spencer a hand, instead.

As they met up at the house, Duff took note of the fact that Spencer wasn't wearing a gun or carrying a rifle. "'Twould be better if ye were for being armed where we're riding today, Mr. Spencer."

"Is there Indian trouble around here?" Spencer asked with a frown.

"Nae, there's been very little trouble with the natives in this area in recent years. But 'tis the frontier, after all. A fellow never knows for certain what he might run into."

"I haven't used a handgun in many years. I never was much good with one, anyway. But we can go by the wagons and I'll get my old Henry. It's a good, dependable weapon."

Duff nodded. "That will be fine." He looked at Elmer. "We should be back by midday. Early afternoon, at the latest."

"If you ain't, me and Wang will come lookin' for you."

Elmer understood what Duff meant. They were heading into an area where another encounter with some of the Hardcastles was possible. Duff was still angry with Benjy Hardcastle because the massive young man had hurt Meagan. If he ran into Benjy or any of the Hardcastles, he wouldn't be in the mood to walk soft.

Not that Duff would go looking for trouble or would resort to violence without a good reason. Elmer knew that. As far as he was concerned, Duff was too durned peaceable for his own good sometimes. But if he and Waylon Spencer didn't return to the ranch when they should, Elmer and Wang would know what to do.

Duff and Spencer rode to the grove next to which the wagons were circled. Spencer dismounted and climbed into his wagon to get the Henry rifle. While Duff was waiting, little, redheaded Teddy Spencer trotted past, trailed by the black-and-white mongrel that had been rescued from a bullet in town the day before.

Teddy stopped short and turned back to gaze up at Duff. "Gee, Mr. MacCallister, you sure are tall! When you're sittin' on that horse, it looks like your head reaches clear up into the sky!"

Duff laughed, then commented, "I see ye brought a new friend with ye from Chugwater."

"Yeah." Teddy reached down and scratched the dog's ears. "The deputy said he was just a stray, so I could have him. I decided to call him Bandit, on account of those black patches around his eyes. They look kinda like he's wearin' a mask, don't you think?"

"Aye," Duff agreed. "'Tis a good name for him."

The boy and the dog both cocked their heads to the side a little as they gazed quizzically at Duff. "Whereabouts are you from, Mr. MacCallister? I don't reckon I've ever come across a fella who talks quite as funny as you do."

Teddy's sister Becky had walked up behind him in time to hear him ask that question. "Teddy, what a rude thing to say!" She blushed as she looked up at Duff. "I'm sorry, Mr. MacCallister—"

"Nae, lass, dinnae worry about it," he told her with a grin. "I hail from the highlands in a far-off land called Scotland. 'Tis on the other side o' the great Atlantic Ocean."

"I've read about Scotland in books," Becky said, sounding a little wistful. "I don't suppose I'll ever get to see it for myself, though."

"You must've had to travel a really far piece to get here," Teddy said.

"Aye, that I did." Duff thought about the long journey that had taken him from Scotland to Wyoming, a journey filled with tragedy and danger, but one that brought many good moments as well. It had ended with him in a place where he had the best friends he had ever known. Though he missed the people he had known in Scotland, Sky Meadow was home now, and he knew it was the place where he'd always been meant to be.

"Are you ever goin' back?" asked Teddy.

"Perhaps someday, to visit. But right now, I'm very happy to be here . . . right where I am."

Becky said, "I'm glad you're here, too, Mr. MacCallister. I . . . I don't know what we would have done without your help." Her green eyes were shining with gratitude and maybe something else, Duff realized as he met her gaze. A bit of hero worship, perhaps . . . or it might be something even more than that.

He'd been about to tell her to call him Duff, but he decided it might be better if she continued to think of him as *Mr. MacCallister*. That would serve as a reminder to her that he was considerably older than she was and gratitude was the only thing she ought to be feeling for him. And that wasn't even necessary, since he was glad to help.

Waylon Spencer came back with his rifle, slid it into the sheath strapped to the saddle on the horse he was riding, and swung up onto the animal's back. "I'm ready if you are," he told Duff.

"Be seein' ye," Duff told Becky and Teddy as he raised a hand in farewell. He turned his mount and headed north as Spencer fell in alongside him.

"I hope my great-nephew wasn't bothering you," Spencer commented as they rode.

"Nae, he's a fine broth of a lad."

"He's high-spirited. Quite a handful. The same could be said of his sister."

"I recall the lass referred to you as Uncle Waylon yesterday, but 'tis really your great-niece she's for being?"

"That's right," Spencer said. "My brother Burl lost his wife and their son and daughter-in-law to the same fever a few years ago. Terrible thing. Becky and Teddy were sick, too, but survived, thank the Lord. Burl took in the youngsters, of course. There were other members of the family who would have done that, but since he's their closest relative, he believes it's up to him to provide for them. He's done a good job of it, as far as I can see."

"They both seem like fine children," said Duff, referring to Becky that way and thinking maybe Spencer wouldn't worry Duff thought of her as a young woman—which, of course, she actually was. He had no interest in her that way and didn't want anybody thinking he might.

Sky Meadow fell behind them as they angled toward the northwest. It wasn't long before the craggy range of peaks where Buzzard's Roost was located came into view on the horizon. Duff pointed out the distinctively shaped mountain, then said, "Thunder Canyon is just to the northeast of it, with Longshot Basin lying beyond. Ye did nae *buy* the land in the basin, did ye? I believe 'tis still open range, legally speaking."

"That's right. Before we left our homes back in Ohio, I wrote to the Wyoming state land office in Cheyenne and asked for help locating suitable land for homesteading. Longshot Basin was the only option they gave me."

"That does nae sound right," Duff said with a frown. "Wyoming is a big state, and 'tis hardly full up, now is it?" He waved at the grassy, rolling hills around them.

"No, it doesn't appear to be," Spencer agreed. "But this

is a cattle state. That's what I was told. Most of the range is needed for the herds of cattle being raised on the large ranches. There's really not much room for farmers."

Duff nodded slowly, not in agreement but to show he was listening and considering what Waylon Spencer said. The older man was right about the importance of the cattle business in Wyoming. It was the driving force behind just about every other economic activity. Without it, the state would be devastated.

He could just imagine some clerk in the land office in Cheyenne, unsympathetic to idea of more "sodbusters" coming in, responding to Spencer's letter and directing the group of immigrants to Longshot Basin. It would be a good joke on those farmers, and once they saw how much work would be required to make a living there, they might just turn around and go back where they came from.

Now, of course, they couldn't even reach Longshot Basin, let alone make a living from it, and going back where they came from might not be an option.

Curious about that, Duff said, "I imagine you and your family spent most of what ye had getting here, didn't ye, Mr. Spencer?"

"Yes, we did," Spencer replied with a sigh. "We sank our life savings into this move."

"Ye said ye come from Ohio?"

"That's right."

"And ye had farms back there, did ye?"

Spencer nodded. "Yes. And we were doing all right, I suppose. But my brothers and I . . . we, ah, decided it was time to strike out for somewhere new . . . and my cousins Samuel and Ezekiel wanted to come along, too, so . . . here we are."

Duff was watching Spencer as the man spoke, but when Spencer finished his response, Duff turned and looked straight ahead again. He didn't want to stare and make Spencer uncomfortable.

Something about the older man's face, some tone in his voice told Duff Waylon Spencer wasn't being entirely forthcoming with him. Maybe there was more behind the family's decision to come to Wyoming than a simple desire to pull up stakes and try something new.

However, even if that turned out to be the case, it was none of Duff's business. He wasn't one to pry into other folks' affairs. So, if there *was* a secret, Spencer and the others could keep it to themselves . . . as long as it didn't bring trouble down on Duff or any of his friends or his ranch.

If that ever happened, the truth *would* become Duff Mac-Callister's business.

# CHAPTER 8

At mid-morning, they came to the faint trail that veered off to the left toward Buzzard's Roost. Waylon Spencer pointed at it and asked, "Where does that go?"

"I've ne'er followed it, so I dinnae really ken," Duff replied. Technically, that was true. According to Elmer, the trail led to the Hardcastle clan's stronghold somewhere up on the mountain, but Duff didn't know that for a fact. Neither did Elmer, for that matter. It was more hearsay, gossip, and speculation.

Duff's eyes followed the trail for a moment. It was visible for a mile or more as it wandered up the sparsely timbered lower slopes of the mountain. *The Nightmare Trail*, Elmer had called it. The route didn't look nightmarish from down where they were, but up higher, it would be a different story, Duff supposed.

At the same time, he was checking to make sure none of the Hardcastles were in the vicinity. He wasn't afraid of them, but it never hurt to keep an eye out for potential trouble. He didn't see anything moving, except for a small bunch of antelope in the distance.

Spencer spotted the animals, too, and said, "What beautiful creatures. This is really magnificent country any way you look, isn't it?"

"Aye, 'tis. Or at least, it can be. Plenty of less hospitable places around, though, if ye know where to look for them."

"What about Longshot Basin? Have you ever been there, Duff? What kind of place is it?"

"I've ridden up there a couple of times," Duff replied honestly as they rode on. "Since it's open range, I thought I might want to run some of my stock on it someday, although 'tis a bit far from my home ranch for to be doing that. There's grass and water, aye, but 'tis hardly the best graze I've seen for cattle. Sufficient, at best."

"What about for growing crops? How's the soil?"

"Rocky in places, not bad in others. There are a lot of gullies and little ridges that make the terrain difficult for plowing. But 'tis not like that everywhere. The basin is about two miles wide, I'd say, and five or six long, with quite a variation in the landscape."

"It sounds like there would be plenty of room for eight families."

"Oh, aye. And enough decent land that ye could put in crops, if ye were willing to work hard enough. But how productive they would be, I cannae say. The only way to find out would be to try it and see."

"Which we can't do, because we can't get in there anymore," Spencer said heavily.

"Aye, more's the pity." Duff reined in and pointed. "And there's the reason why."

They had come within sight of the former mouth of Thunder Canyon. Following the avalanche from their distance it was difficult to make out where the entrance had been. If a man didn't know what he was looking for, it would appear to be a long, unbroken ridge that lay to the north.

Spencer shook his head and said, "I don't see it."

"I'm not for being surprised. We'll ride closer, and then ye should be able to see what happened."

They moved on, and when they were near enough, Duff was able to point out where the canyon walls and the gap between them had been. As they approached the insurmountable barrier, Spencer shook his head again and said in an awed voice, "That must have been some rockslide."

"Aye. A cowboy named Pinky Jenkins was up here when it happened, and he said it seemed as if the entire world was about to end."

Spencer looked over at Duff. "What caused it?"

"An earthquake. Jenkins said the ground shook and jumped under his horse's hooves, and that was when a big chunk of the mountainside came crashing down. I believe him, because we felt the same tremor back in Chugwater, although 'twas not nearly as powerful by the time it reached that far."

"Humans like to think of themselves as being in charge of things, but then nature does what it wants, and there's not a blasted thing we can do about it."

Duff chuckled. "A lady friend of mine likes to josh me about being philosophical, but I'm for thinking ye actually are, Mr. Spencer."

"I don't know about that. It's just common sense to realize there are a great many things in life over which we have no control."

"Aye. So we'd best do a good job with the things we *can* control."

"Now there's some philosophy for you," Spencer said with a nod.

They turned their horses around and rode away from Thunder Canyon.

"I wish I could have gotten a look at Longshot Basin, at least," commented Spencer. "Although I suppose looking at it and knowing that I can't get my family there would just be torturing myself, wouldn't it?"

Elmer had mentioned the Nightmare Trail led eventually to the basin, and Duff knew the route was too dangerous for wagons. However, two men on horseback probably could make it without much trouble.

*Not much trouble other than the Hardcastles*, Duff reminded himself. Supposedly, the Nightmare Trail led to their stronghold, as well. He and Spencer would have to ride past the clan's home to reach the basin. Duff didn't know how they would react to that, but probably not well. And the trip would serve no purpose. Those thousands of tons of rock would still be blocking Thunder Canyon.

Those thoughts went through Duff's brain in a split second, following his momentary impulse to take Spencer over the perilous trail and let him have his look at the basin. It was too dangerous and there was no point to running the risk, so he didn't say anything about it.

Passing about half a mile away from the base of Buzzard's Roost and not yet to the point where the trails intersected, Duff spotted a flash of light from the thin growth of trees on the lower slope. The sun had reflected on something metal, and Duff's instincts suddenly shouted a warning at him—only one thing it was likely to be.

The next instant, he heard the flat, sinister hum of a bullet cutting through the air close by his head, followed instantly by the distant crack of a rifle.


Cole Hardcastle sat with his legs stretched out in front of him, crossed at the ankles. His back was propped against a tree trunk, and his hat was tipped forward so that its brim shaded his eyes while he dozed. He was taking life easy, which he supposed wasn't the reason Cousin Willie had sent him and Benjy and Ferris out there, but the other two were keeping watch on the trail. Besides Cole sort of considered the job a waste of time, anyway.

Nobody was going to bother the family. Folks around those parts knew enough to steer clear of the Hardcastles. Hell, nobody in Chugwater even *talked* about them anymore. Nobody wanted to risk getting on their bad side.

That was just fine with Cole. The less he had to deal with people, the better.

He was almost sound asleep when the shot made him bolt upright and jerk his head up so hard his hat fell off. As he came to his feet, he blinked and looked around stupidly and dropped his hand to the butt of the gun on his hip. "What the hell!"

His startled gaze lit on the other two men standing nearby. Benjy was staring and sort of shaking his hands back and forth, worried like. Ferris stood beside a tree with the barrel of his rifle resting in the fork of a low branch. A thin wisp of smoke still curled from the rifle's muzzle. He looked over his shoulder at Cole with a frown on his mean, pinched face and said, "What?"

Cole gazed past his cousin, down the slope, and out onto the rolling plains southeast of Buzzard's Roost. Two men on horseback were out there, maybe half a mile away, racing their horses toward a little swell in the ground.

"Did you just take a shot at those riders?" Cole demanded of Ferris.

"I told him not to," Benjy spoke up. "I said they wasn't doin' nothin'—"

Ferris snapped, "They were pokin' around where they got no business bein'. Thunder Canyon's closed since that avalanche. Nobody's got any reason to come 'round Buzzard's Roost no more. If they do, they're lookin' for trouble. You know what Cousin Willie said, Cole. He said we got to keep an eye out for anybody who wants to cause harm to the family."

That was a long speech for Ferris, who generally had trouble putting half a dozen words together.

Cole picked up his hat, raked his fingers through his dark hair, and clapped the hat on his head again. "Willie didn't say to shoot at anybody we saw. Just that we needed to keep an eye on them."

"He said they didn't need to come pokin' around out here." Ferris let out an ugly laugh. "After I nearly ventilated one of 'em, those two won't . . ." He kept talking but Cole tuned him out.

Cole had watched the two riders disappear over the distant rise. They had been slowing their horses as they crested the rise, though, and he figured he knew what they were going to do next.

Ignoring Ferris's boasting, he grabbed Benjy's arm. "Get behind those trees and keep your head down," Cole told his brother. "Now!"

As Cole shoved Benjy toward cover, Ferris said, "What are you—" then yelped and dived to the ground as what sounded like a flock of angry hornets buzzed around the three men. Ferris yelled, put a hand to his left ear, and brought it away bloody. "They shot me!" he howled. "Shot my ear plumb off!"

*That isn't quite true*, thought Cole as he pressed his back to one of the trees and tried to make himself as narrow a target as possible. The bullet had nicked the top of Ferris's ear. He was bleeding like a stuck pig, but Cole thought most of his cousin's ear was still intact.

"You're all right," Cole told him over the distant popping and crackling of rifle fire. "Just dumb as hell. What'd you think those two pilgrims were gonna do?"

"I figured they'd wet themselves and run off." Ferris whimpered as he added, "My ear hurts."

"You're liable to hurt a lot worse if you don't keep huggin' the ground. Raise up much and you'll catch a bullet in your thinkin' box."

Cole's muscles jerked a little each time he heard a slug thud into the far side of the tree he was using for cover. Those boys out on the other side of that rise had repeaters. Considering the amount of lead they were throwing at the trees where Cole and his brother and cousin had been posted, they must have emptied them and reloaded them at least once. They were bound to stop shooting sooner or later, though.

That thought had just crossed Cole's mind when the rifles fell silent. *What will those hombres do next? Watch for any sign of movement up here, and if they spot it, cut loose their wolves again?*

"Cole, what are we gonna do?" asked Benjy.

"Just stay where you are." Cole was glad to see Benjy had stretched out on his belly behind one of the trees and was keeping the trunk between himself and those distant shooters. If he didn't get up, he was safe enough, but getting him to follow orders or do anything predictable was a challenge.

Something crashing through the brush in the other direction caught Cole's attention. He peered that way but couldn't make out anything through the growth just yet. After a moment, he heard hoofbeats and knew a rider was approaching. "Who's that?"

"Willie Hardcastle," came the reply in a powerful, stentorian voice honed and strengthened by years of preaching the Gospel and bossing the Hardcastle clan.

"Stay back, Cousin Willie!" yelled Benjy. "They's shootin' at us!"

Willie ignored that. He kept coming and burst out of the undergrowth a moment later, a tall, spare man on horseback. He wore a dark suit, collarless white shirt, and black hat. The outfit made him look like a preacher, which was exactly what he was . . . part of the time. Graying, rusty red hair stuck out from under the hat, and he had a close-cropped beard of the same shade on his angular jaw.

"I don't hear any shooting now," Willie said from the saddle of the rawboned black horse he was riding. He stared at his three younger relations with eyes the same shade as chips of ice, and just about as chilly.

"They've stopped," Cole said, "but there's no tellin' when they'll start up again."

From where he lay on the ground, Ferris moaned. "Cousin Willie, I'm shot!"

"I see the blood," Willie said. "How bad are you hurt?"

Without waiting for Ferris to exaggerate about how his ear was shot off, Cole said, "He just got nicked a little. Looks a lot worse than it really is."

"That's easy for you to say!" Ferris yelled at him. "It ain't your ear that's shot off!"

*Well, he got it in, anyway,* thought Cole. Luckily, Willie knew Ferris as well as he did and didn't put much stock in the dramatic claim.

Willie asked, "What's going on here, and who started it?"

"That'd be Ferris," said Cole. "Two hombres were riding by out there, not payin' any attention to us, so Ferris figured it'd be a good idea to take a potshot at them."

"Just two men?" Willie frowned. "I figured from all the shooting I heard that it must be a posse after us."

"Nope. Just two men ridin' along and mindin' their own business."

Ferris said, "Cousin Willie, you told us not to let anybody come snoopin' around!"

"Those men didn't start up the Nightmare Trail?" asked Willie.

"Well . . . no, I don't reckon they did. But they might've—"

Cole said, "They took cover and started shootin' back, just like you'd expect."

Willie turned a glare toward him. "What I'd expect is for you to keep a better eye on things, Cole. You're the oldest and have a lot more sense than these two."

"Hey!" Ferris said.

Willie ignored that and went on. "What were you doing when Ferris started lining up that shot?"

"Well . . . I was sitting under a tree," Cole admitted reluctantly. "I, uh, I reckon I might've dozed off a little."

"So you didn't know what Ferris was doing until he pulled the trigger."

"No, sir, I didn't."

"Yes, I expected better of you than that." Willie sniffed and turned his wrath back toward Ferris. "And you should know better than to do anything like that without asking somebody first."

"But I thought—"

"Thinking isn't your strong suit, Ferris, and you know it." Willie gazed out across the plains and sighed. "I don't see anybody moving out there now, and they've stopped shooting. Get up and get your horse, Ferris. Head on back to the dwelling place and get one of the women to patch up that ear of yours. Cole, you and Benjy continue standing watch here. Just don't doze off again before someone comes to relieve you later."

"I won't, Cousin Willie," Cole promised. "After all this uproar, I'm not exactly sleepy anymore."

Willie grunted. He waited until Ferris was mounted, and

then the two of them rode off through the trees and brush, heading higher on the mountain.

Benjy said, "Who do you reckon those two fellas who shot at us are, Cole?"

"I don't have any earthly idea," Cole replied, trying to keep a tight rein on his anger and irritation. None of this was Benjy's fault. Like Cousin Willie had said, it was his responsibility to make sure nothing went wrong, not Benjy's or Ferris's. "Probably just a couple of fellas who rode up here to gawk at what used to be Thunder Canyon. Most folks have never seen what an avalanche like that can do."

"I hope I never see one," Benjy said as he climbed clumsily to his feet. "Just listenin' to it was bad enough. I never heard anything so loud in all my borned days as when all them rocks started slidin' and tumblin' down the mountain." He glanced out from the trees and suddenly pointed excitedly. "Hey, there they go!"

Cole looked where his brother indicated and saw two small figures on horseback receding into the distance. The men had peppered the lower slope with lead, and now they were rattling their hocks back toward Chugwater.

Benjy said, "I'd still like to know who they are and why they were here."

"It don't matter," snapped Cole. "They're gone, and that's the end of it."

"What in the world was that about?" Waylon Spencer asked once he and Duff had put enough ground behind them to feel safe from any more bushwhackers' bullets.

"I dinnae ken," Duff said. That answer was true as far as it went, but in reality, he had a pretty good idea who had fired that shot at them.

If the Nightmare Trail weaved its way up the mountain

reasonably straight from the portion of the trail visible down where he and Spencer were, the shot had come from there. That meant the man who had pulled the trigger was almost certainly a Hardcastle.

*Probably Cole*, Duff mused. According to Elmer, Cole had a reputation as a gunfighter, and Duff had seen the man's cold-eyed stare himself. Cole Hardcastle was a killer, so it wasn't surprising he might be a bushwhacker, too.

But Duff and Spencer hadn't been very close to the Nightmare Trail when that bullet whipped past them. Maybe Cole wanted to keep anybody from going up the mountain and intruding on what the Hardcastles considered their domain, but even if that was true, it didn't justify shooting at Duff and Spencer.

"Other than you and Elmer and Wang, it doesn't seem very friendly around here," Spencer said. "First that ruckus in town, and now somebody tries to ambush when we were just riding along peacefully."

"I suppose they had reasons that made sense to them."

"Do you think we got him when we shot back?"

"No way of knowing without riding up there," Duff said, "and I dinnae think 'twould be a very good idea."

"No, I don't, either. And I wouldn't really know what to hope for."

Neither did Duff. He didn't like being shot at, and if anyone was foolish enough to do that, they usually got what was coming to them. But if he and Spencer had killed one of the Hardcastles, it might mean war with the reclusive, violent clan . . . and Duff didn't see that working out well for anybody.

# CHAPTER 9

Duff advised Waylon Spencer it might be best not to say anything about the ambush to the other members of his group.

Spencer agreed. "I wasn't planning to mention it. My wife's a worrier, and there's no point in giving her something else to fret about. She's already beside herself from worrying about what we're going to do next."

"I'm for hoping I can do something about that," said Duff. "Tomorrow I'll ride into Chugwater and send a wire to the state land office in Cheyenne. When the railroad arrived, so did the telegraph line, so we can reach out to the world now. We need to find ye another place to homestead, and if that does nae do any good, I can get in touch with some other friends of mine at the capital."

Duff didn't mention those friends of his occupied positions of power in Wyoming's government, reaching all the way up to the governor himself. He was confident he could get to the bottom of the problems plaguing the Spencer family.

The ambush had delayed them a little, so it was early afternoon by the time the two men reached Sky Meadow. As they rode up, Elmer walked out of the barn to greet them.

The little boy, Teddy, and the dog, Bandit, trailed after him. Clearly, they had attached themselves to the grizzled old-timer.

Elmer lifted a hand. "Howdy, Duff. Wang and me was just fixin' to start thinkin' about what you said. We'd have come lookin' for you fellas in a while if you hadn't showed up."

"Well, we're back," said Duff. "Any problems while we were gone?" He would tell Elmer about the ambush later.

Elmer shook his head. "Nope, it's been quiet here."

Teddy piped up, saying, "Uncle Waylon, get Elmer to tell you about the Nightmare Trail."

Elmer made a face and shuffled his feet uncomfortably as Duff frowned.

"What've ye been saying to this youngster?" Duff asked quietly.

"And what's this about a Nightmare Trail?" Spencer wanted to know. Duff could tell that the older man's curiosity wasn't going to be turned aside. Elmer had said more than he should have to the boy, and there was no taking it back.

Still, Duff figured he had to try. "'Tis nothing, Mr. Spencer. Just a bad trail up in the mountains that nobody uses."

"Elmer says it leads to Longshot Basin!" said Teddy.

Spencer's eyes widened in surprise as he turned his head to look at Duff. "Is that true?"

Duff sighed and said, "Why dinnae ye come over to the house? I'll wager that Wang's kept some food warm on the stove for us. We can eat, and I'll tell ye about the Nightmare Trail." He shrugged. "Ye've already seen one end of it with your own eyes, so I cannae very well deny that it exists."

"That little trail we saw out there on the way to Thunder Canyon?" Spencer guessed. "Close to where we got shot at?"

"Shot at!" Elmer exclaimed, and Teddy's eyes got big,

too. Despite Duff's intentions, everything seemed to be spilling out into the open.

Spencer pointed a finger at Teddy and told him, "Don't you say anything about what you just heard, boy. You understand me? Especially not to your sister or your Aunt Edith."

"I swear, Uncle Waylon. I won't say nothin'."

Duff figured that Teddy meant the promise . . . but whether or not he'd be able to keep it was probably another matter entirely. Secrets had a way of being revealed. So maybe it was better in the long run to get everything out in the open.

As Duff had predicted, Wang had kept some fried chicken, potatoes, and greens warm for the two men. They sat down for a late lunch in the ranch house kitchen. Elmer poured himself a cup of coffee from the pot on the stove and joined them, as did Wang with a cup of tea. Teddy had been sent back to the wagons with another admonishment from Spencer not to talk about what he had just overheard.

Elmer said, "I'm sorry I flapped my jaw too much, Duff. That little fella's full o' questions and talks a mile a minute. We was just palaverin', and I mentioned the Nightmare Trail without thinkin', and from there he just wouldn't take no for an answer. He had to hear all about it."

"Ye told him about the Hardcastles?"

"Well . . . not in any great detail, you understand. I just said there was some unfriendly folks who lived up yonder on Buzzard's Roost."

Spencer said, "That's the mountain next to where Thunder Canyon used to be, isn't it? Am I understanding this right, Duff? There actually *is* a way to reach Longshot Basin?"

"Not for wagons," Duff replied firmly. "'Tis too dangerous to even consider."

"And none of us have ever actually been over it," added Elmer.

Spencer looked back and forth between them. "So you don't really *know* whether wagons can travel over it."

Elmer shrugged. "The last folks who tried, their wagons all went off the side of the mountain. They all died, 'cept for one fella. Ain't no way it's gotten any better since then. And that ain't even takin' into account the Hardcastles."

Spencer frowned. "Who are they?"

Duff said, "More than likely, it was a Hardcastle who took that potshot at us. There's a whole clan of them living somewhere up there on Buzzard's Roost. They're said to be outlaws and killers, and 'tis certain they dinnae want anyone traveling over the Nightmare Trail."

"But you said that whole area is open range," Spencer protested. "They don't own the trail, do they?"

"Nae, I suppose that's true—"

"Then legally they can't stop anybody from using it."

Elmer said, "The Hardcastles don't care about what's legal and what ain't. Like Duff said, they're outlaws. They do what they please, and the hell with the law or what anybody else wants." The old-timer shook his head. "You don't want to cross them, Waylon. You really don't."

"If that's a viable way to Longshot Basin, I don't see that we have any choice."

Duff leaned forward in his chair. "I'm going to find ye some other suitable place to homestead—"

"But why do we need some other place? You said yourself, Duff, there's plenty of room in Longshot Basin and the soil is good enough to support crops."

"I also said I dinnae ken how productive those crops would be."

"Well, that's a chance a farmer takes anywhere," said

Spencer. "We can improve the land. My family and I have never shied away from hard work."

"'Tis the Hardcastles ye should be shying away from."

Spencer protested. "You don't know it was one of them who shot at us. It could have been anyone. We never saw who fired that rifle."

"About that," said Elmer. "Somebody tried to ventilate you fellas?"

Duff filled him in on the ambush attempt and the way the two of them had retreated to a nearby rise and returned the fire, raking the area in the trees where the bushwhacker had been.

Elmer nodded and said to Spencer, "I agree with Duff, Waylon. That had to 've been one of the Hardcastles. Nobody else would've been up there, and they're sure contrary enough to do such a thing."

"Maybe it was just a warning shot," Spencer suggested.

Duff said, "At that range, as close as the bullet came, it was no warning shot. The fellow meant to hit us. And even if it *had* been a warning shot, would ye not be wise to heed the warning?"

Wang said, "That does not sound like you, Duff."

"What do ye mean by that?" Duff asked with a frown.

"Never in the time I have known you have I ever seen you turn your back on trouble."

Duff shook his head. "I'm not turning me back. If 'twas just the danger of the trail itself, or just the danger of the Hardcastles, I'd be for exploring the idea. But ye put the two together, and the risk is too great that innocent people will be killed. I dinnae want that."

"None of us do, either," said Spencer. "But sometimes, especially when you're trying to make a new start in life, you have to take some chances."

"You're talking about your family, man."

"I know that."

"And there be alternatives—"

"Where?" Spencer interrupted him. "The letter from the land office said Longshot Basin was the only available range."

Duff slapped a hand down on the table. "Whoever told ye that was lying to you. I dinnae know why, although I can guess. But there are other places ye can settle, if you'll just give me time to look into the matter."

"We've spent a long time getting here already. We're worn out from traveling, Duff. We need that new home, and we need it now."

Duff's forehead creased. He thought Spencer was being unreasonable, but he had to admit the man knew his own family better than any outsider could. And once again, a little tingle in his brain told Duff there might be more to Waylon Spencer's determination than was readily apparent. He had a hunch Spencer would be completely close-mouthed about whatever that was, however, so it probably would be a waste of time pressing him about it.

Nor did Duff care for what Wang had pointed out. Duff had never hesitated to help people, even when it was dangerous, but on most of the occasions in the past, that danger had been to Duff himself. In this case, women and children needed to be considered, and that made everything different.

Spencer went on. "I don't want to seem ungrateful, Duff. Lord knows you've done plenty for us already, helping us in town and then opening your ranch to us like this. But I know where that trail starts now. I can talk it over with my brothers and sons and cousins. If they all vote that we should give it a try, I don't see what else we can do."

"Ye could be making a big mistake if ye do. You'll be putting your whole group at risk."

"We've been at risk ever since we left Ohio."

Trying to talk Waylon Spencer out of something once he'd made up his mind was like ramming his head against a stone wall, Duff sensed. The man's expression was full of stubborn determination as he looked across the table.

"How about this?" Duff said, trying to come up with something that would keep Spencer from acting too quickly or rashly. "Why not let Elmer and me take a ride up there and find out for sure what you'll be facing if ye go through with this? We can scout the trail and make sure 'tis even passable all the way to Longshot Basin. For all we ken, it may have collapsed somewhere along the way."

Elmer said, "Uh, Duff . . . you're talkin' about ridin' right into the Hardcastles' bailiwick and darin' 'em to shoot us."

"Not necessarily. Ye said yourself nobody goes up there anymore, so there's no way of knowing what they'll do. Perhaps the ones who were so trigger-happy in the past are no longer running things on Buzzard's Roost."

Elmer was visibly struggling to control his reaction to that idea. Finally, he burst out, "But they shot at you just a couple hours ago! They're loco and kill-crazy, Duff. You know that."

"Somebody shot at us. We dinnae ken who 'twas." The more Duff thought about what he had suggested, the more he liked it, at least within reason. If he could keep the Spencer party at Sky Meadow for a few days, it would give Wang time to ride to Chugwater and send the wire Duff would give him. A response might come from Cheyenne before Duff and Elmer got back from exploring the Nightmare Trail.

Frowning, Waylon Spencer said, "I don't like the idea of you risking your life again on our behalf, Duff. It's our responsibility to protect ourselves. Besides . . . and I mean no offense by this, I assure you . . . you and Elmer might come back and tell us the trail is impassable whether it is or not."

Elmer's face darkened. He drew in a deep breath and said, "Are you claimin' that we'd come back and *lie* to you?"

Hastily, Spencer shook his head. "No, of course not. I shouldn't have said that. I apologize. I just don't think you should run the risk alone. One of us should go with you. That way, whoever it is can bring back a first-hand report on the trail conditions."

That actually wasn't a bad idea, Duff realized. "Are you volunteering for the job, Mr. Spencer?"

"No . . . No, I think it would be better if I stayed here with the rest of the group, just in case there's any trouble."

And why would he sound almost like he was expecting trouble, Duff wondered?

"My son Grady should go with you," Spencer continued. "He's an excellent rider and a good shot. And he's cool-headed. If there was any sort of problem, he could keep his wits about him, I'm sure."

"What'll he think about you volunteerin' him?" asked Elmer.

Spencer smiled. "I believe he'll consider it an opportunity for a grand adventure. Grady's never been one to turn down a chance for that. When he was younger, he would take off hunting and camping for weeks at a time. Now that he's married and has a couple of young'uns, he's had to settle down a lot. I'm sure he still gets those old, restless urges, though."

"If he agrees to come with us, ye and the others will wait here until we get back?" Duff said.

Spencer nodded. "Yes, I think that would be all right. I suppose it *does* make a lot more sense to scout the trail first, before we start trying to follow it with all those wagons."

"'Tis settled, then. We'll go and talk to Grady right now, and if he's agreeable, he and Elmer and I will start for Buzzard's Roost in the morning."

Elmer said, "I can't help but notice you was mighty quick to volunteer *me* to come along on this loco errand, Duff."

A grin spread across Duff's face. "Why, I'm for knowing that ye never pass up a chance for an adventure, either, Elmer."

"Yeah, that's right, I guess." Elmer sighed. "Damn it."

# CHAPTER 10

As his father had predicted, Grady Spencer was not only willing to accompany Duff and Elmer on their scouting mission, he was eager to do so. He had the red hair that cropped up in some members of the family, although his was a darker shade than that of his second cousins Becky and Teddy.

When Duff and Waylon Spencer laid the proposal before him, he nodded and said, "First thing in the morning, is it? I'll be ready!"

His wife, an attractive young blonde named Leticia, put a hand on his arm and said, "Are you sure that's a good idea, Grady? It sounds like it might be dangerous."

Duff wasn't going to take anybody with him who wasn't fully aware of the risks, so he had explained to Grady not only the possible perils of following the trail but also the potential threat of the Hardcastle clan. Grady didn't seem bothered by either of them.

"Aw, Tish, there's always gonna be something dangerous," the young man said. "We knew that when we started out here. We could've got jumped by Indians or washed away in a flooded river or picked up by a cyclone. None of those things happened, did they?"

"Well, no," she admitted. "But that still doesn't mean you have to tempt fate."

"For what it's worth, Mrs. Spencer, your husband will be with Elmer and me," Duff said, "and we're pretty experienced hands out here on the fro. tier, if I do say so meself. Elmer's been in all kinds of scrapes the past forty years. Fought in the war, went to sea, and traipsed from the Rio Grande to the Milk River. He always came through fine."

"If he's survived all that," Leticia Spencer said, "I would think the odds would be running against him by now."

Duff frowned. "Well, I never thought of it that way . . ."

The young woman pointed to two toddlers sitting on the ground nearby and playing. They were twins and had inherited their mother's fair hair.

"You're not just a husband, you're a father now," she reminded Grady. "You have responsibilities you didn't have when you were a younger man."

"But . . . but . . . blast it, Tish . . ."

She folded her arms over her chest and stared at him solemnly.

Duff had a pretty good idea what was coming, even before Grady sighed and turned to face Duff and his father.

"I'm sorry, Pa, Mr. MacCallister. I reckon I'd better not go, after all."

"If you're sure, son," Spencer said.

A new voice said, "We'll do it, Uncle Waylon."

Duff looked over his shoulder and saw two young men standing there. Clearly, they had been listening to the conversation. He recognized them as the sons of Leon and Hannah Spencer, which made them Waylon Spencer's nephews. Walter and Oliver were their names, Duff recalled after a moment. Walter was tall and slender, with a shock of light brown hair, while Oliver was shorter and stockier, with the same sort of dark red hair as Grady, only in tight curls.

"How old are you lads?" Duff asked.

"I'm nineteen and Oliver's seventeen," Walter said.

"We're full-growed, pretty much," Oliver added.

"And we can ride and shoot."

"And we're not afraid of anything."

Waylon Spencer said, "Now hold on. You'd have to ask your ma and pa—"

"When you were our age, Uncle Waylon, you were off fighting in the war," Walter pointed out. "Did you ask Grandma and Grandpap before you enlisted and went off to fight the Rebs?"

"Well, no, because everybody else my age was joining up, and it was the right thing to do—"

"Helping the family's the right thing to do now, too. And I apologize for interrupting you, Uncle."

Spencer looked at Duff and shrugged. "They're good youngsters. And they're right about being able to ride and shoot. All the Spencer men can do that. It comes natural to us."

Duff turned the idea over a few times in his mind, then looked at Walter and Oliver and asked, "Will the two of ye agree to do as you're told? If we run into any trouble, all our lives might depend on you following orders from meself or Mr. Gleason, without any hesitation or asking questions."

"We swear that we will, Mr. MacCallister," Walter said.

Oliver raised his hand and added, "Swear."

"I suppose 'twould be all right, then. Do ye have saddle mounts?"

Both young men shook their heads.

"No matter," Duff went on. "We have plenty of horses here at Sky Meadow. We can spare a couple from the remuda. How about rifles?"

"Just, uh, single shot squirrel guns," said Walter.

"We have extra Winchesters, too, and some Colts if ye'd care to pack them."

Both of them looked eagerly at Spencer.

"Can we, Uncle Waylon?" asked Walter.

"I suppose if you're going through with this, you should be well armed," Spencer said. "Just be careful. If you were to shoot yourselves or each other, your mother would never forgive me!"

News of the plan spread swiftly through the camp. Duff figured it would be the subject of much discussion around the campfire that evening. It was possible that by morning, things would have changed again, depending on whether or not Hannah Spencer decided to put her foot down and forbid her sons from going along on the scouting mission.

Evidently that didn't happen. Walter and Oliver showed up at the ranch house before sunup, while Duff and Elmer were still eating breakfast.

"We're ready to go," Walter announced.

"Sit down and have a cup of coffee," Duff invited. "When we're done, we'll see about arming the two of ye, then we'll pick out some horses."

The young men were chattering and full of excitement about the adventure on which they were about to embark. Duff recalled what he had been like at that age, and evidently the same sort of memories were going through Elmer's mind.

The old-timer chuckled and leaned over to whisper to Duff, "Full o' piss and vinegar, ain't they?"

"Let us hope this trip does nae take too much of it out of them."

After breakfast, they went into Duff's study, where almost one entire wall was taken up with gun racks. One rack held several Winchesters, but a different type of rifle next to them caught Oliver's eye.

"What's that?" he asked Duff as he pointed at the weapon.

"'Tis a Martini-Henry Mark II," Duff replied. "The rifle carried by the British Army, of which I was a member for several years. I was part of the Black Watch, to be precise, the Forty-second Regiment of Foot. The Martini-Henry is a good, dependable rifle. Single shot, breech-loading, reliably accurate."

"Is that the very rifle you carried when you were in the Black Watch?" asked Walter.

"Nae, I found one in Cheyenne and purchased it after I settled here at Sky Meadow, as a memento of me army days, I suppose ye could say. How a Martini-Henry got from Africa or Afghanistan or wherever it was carried into action by some Tommy, all the way to Cheyenne, Wyoming, I cannae say. The same is true of that pistol there, next to the Colts. 'Tis an Enfield Mark I. Not a bad gun, but the very devil itself to reload quickly and efficiently, especially when ye be under fire. I dinnae like to go against me roots, but I have to say that in a battle, nothing beats a good Winchester and a Colt."

"Who's that fella Tommy you mentioned?" Oliver wanted to know.

Duff laughed. "Tommy Atkins, lad. 'Tis a catch-all name for British soldiers all over the world. I've heard it said the name comes from a poor soldier in the Thirty-third Regiment of Foot many years ago named Thomas Atkins who was grievously wounded in battle. The Duke of Wellington was in command, and when he went among the wounded men to commiserate with them, Tommy Atkins assured the duke it was all in a day's work, just before he passed on. The duke decided then and there that the lad's name would always be remembered, and so it has." Duff shrugged and added, "Whether 'tis true or not, I dinnae ken, but it makes a good story. We Scots have gone from cursing the Tommies to numbering ourselves among them, since fate was against us that terrible day at Culloden and we failed to put James back on the throne."

Walter said, "I don't have any idea what you're talkin' about, Mr. MacCallister, but I reckon I could listen to you spin yarns all day."

"We've no time for that now, lad, but perhaps we can talk more along the trail. Pick out your guns."

Each of the brothers took a Winchester and a Colt revolver. Duff filled the loops in spare gun belts with cartridges and then handed a box of .44s for the Winchesters and .45s for the Colts to Walter and Oliver with instructions to put the extra ammunition in their saddlebags.

With that taken care of, they headed for the corral to pick out horses. There were plenty of good saddle mounts at Sky Meadow. Relying on advice from Duff and Elmer, Walter decided on a rangy roan gelding while Oliver picked out a sturdy dun. The young men saddled their own mounts and snugged the Winchesters into the scabbards lashed to the saddles.

Duff was impressed by the way they handled those chores themselves and made sure everything was done properly.

Then all four of them rode to the grove of trees where the wagons were parked. The whole group of immigrants was assembled to bid farewell to them. The men shook hands all around and wished them well.

Hannah Spencer hugged each of her sons and then looked sternly at Duff and Elmer. "I'll be expecting you to bring my boys back safely to me."

"'Tis my full intention to do so, madam," Duff said. "Having gotten to know Walter and Oliver a bit better, I can say they both be fine young men, and 'tis certain I am they'll acquit themselves gallantly, happen we should encounter any problems."

"I'd rather you didn't run into trouble."

"Aye, and I'm for feeling the same way, ma'am. Never ye doubt that."

With their farewells said, the four riders headed north toward the spot where the Nightmare Trail began. Before they went out of sight, Walter and Oliver looked back over their shoulders a time or two at the wagons. Duff could tell they were a little nervous. They were excited about going on an adventure, of course, but at the same time, they were riding into the unknown. Neither of them had ever been tested in battle. They might believe they knew how they would react in the face of danger, but until that happened, they could never be sure.

And there was always the chance that they wouldn't return from this journey. Not alive, anyway.

To distract them from thinking about that, Duff said, "Ye wanted to hear more about my time in the Black Watch. I can tell ye about the battles we fought in Egypt, some years ago."

Walter nodded eagerly. "Yes, we'd love to hear about that."

"And if I run out of stories, Elmer can always tell ye about his time at sea and his battles with the Malay pirates and the time he visited the infamous tobbo shops of Siam."

Elmer frowned. "Now, Duff, you know good an' well there's some o' those stories that ain't fit for the innocent ears of impressionable young fellas like Walter and Oliver."

"Oh, no, we want to hear them, Mr. Gleason," Oliver spoke up instantly. "We're not really that innocent."

But they were curious about anything lurid and exciting, like all young men, thought Duff. Between him and Elmer, they ought to be able to spin enough yarns to keep Walter and Oliver from dwelling on the dangers that might await them along the Nightmare Trail.

They just needed to be careful that none of those wild tales ever got back to the boys' ma, he warned himself.

The sun was still an hour from its midday zenith when they reached the beginning of the Nightmare Trail. Duff signaled a halt and lifted a pair of field glasses to his eyes, following the trail as it began its winding path up the wooded slope at the base of Buzzard's Roost.

While he was doing that, Elmer pointed out various landmarks to their young companions, including the ugly, misshapen crag itself that loomed over them and dominated the landscape. "If you take a gander up there at the peak, you can see it looks a mite like a buzzard's head, and the way the mountain spreads out around it, it's like a buzzard perched on a branch, just waitin' for somethin' to die so's he can have hisself a feast."

Oliver said, "It just looks like a mountain to me, Mr. Gleason. I can't really see that it looks like a buzzard."

"Neither can I," Walter agreed.

"Well, it looked like that to somebody, sometime, and he's the fella what named it. Over west of here a ways, you got the Grand Teton Mountains, which was named by a French hombre who claimed they reminded him of, well, uh . . . a lady's bosoms."

Walter and Oliver grinned at each other.

"I've seen them Grand Tetons plenty of times, and I never once would've thought about that, I reckon, if I didn't know the story of how come they're called by that name," Elmer went on. "So I guess it's all in the, uh, whatcha call it—the eye of the misbegotten."

"I think it's the eye of the beholder," said Oliver.

"Yeah, that would make more sense, wouldn't it." Elmer glanced over at Duff. "See anything?"

Duff lowered the field glasses. He had followed the trail's twists and turns as high as he could before the trees and the irregularities of the terrain shut it off from his sight.

"Nae. No reflections from gun barrels or field glasses they might have. The Hardcastles may have sentries posted, but if they do, they're staying well out of sight."

Elmer rubbed his grizzled chin. "Ain't nothin' we can do except push on and hope for the best."

"Aye." Duff nudged his horse into motion once more. For the first time, he actually followed the faint trail that veered off to the left, instead of staying on the main trail leading to Thunder Canyon. That trail remained in sight to the right as the four men headed toward Buzzard's Roost.

"Maybe you'd better tell us some more about the Black Watch, Mr. MacCallister," Walter suggested with a trace of nervousness edging back into his voice.

"Nae," said Duff. "'Tis not the time for storytelling, lad. From this point, all of us need to stay as alert as possible to our surroundings."

"But don't just stare straight at the trail ahead of us, or at the mountain," Elmer added. "Keep your eyes movin'. Sometimes you see more from the corners of 'em than you do from whatever's right in front of you. You see somethin' movin' up yonder on the slope, or catch the sun glintin' off something, don't panic and don't make a big show of it. Just say somethin' calmly to Duff and me about what you saw. Understand?"

"We sure do, Mr. Gleason," Oliver said. "If we're being watched, we don't want to give away that we're aware of it."

"Aye," Duff said. "That might stampede the watchers

into doing something, while they might be content to just keep watching if they dinnae ken we know they're there."

"It's not just riding and shooting and fighting, is it?" asked Oliver. "You have to *think* in order to survive out here, too, don't you?"

"Aye, lad. And if ye know that, 'tis a good lesson ye've learned already."

They moved on, drawing closer and closer to the spot where the trail entered the trees and began to climb.

Walter commented, "I can tell it gets a little rougher ahead, but it doesn't look like much of a nightmare."

"Ye have to get considerably higher before it becomes nightmarish. That be what I assume, anyway, since I've never been over the trail meself."

"Me, neither," said Elmer. "I've heard folks talk about it, though. The trail covers about four miles before you get to the spot where it starts down into Longshot Basin. The first couple of miles ain't bad, but the next two is where things get dangerous."

"What about the part that goes down into the basin?" Walter wanted to know.

Elmer shrugged. "I've heard tell it ain't too bad. A little steep, but if you've got wagons with good brakes, they can manage it. And it's wide enough you ain't always in danger of fallin' off. The trick is just makin' it that far."

"We can do it," Oliver said. "We have to be able to do it." His voice held a note of finality that once again set off warning bells in Duff's brain. This journey involved more than a group of immigrants looking for a new home. Duff wondered if he might not be able to worm the facts out of Oliver and Walter. That wouldn't be a very nice thing to do to people he was trying to help, but he *was* putting his life and Elmer's on the line for them. Looking at it a different way, they had a right to know what they were getting into.

Though that probably could wait.

As they were about to enter the trees, Duff said quietly, "Look sharp now, lads. Keep your eyes open."

With grim and serious expressions, Walter and Oliver nodded their agreement.

At that elevation, the pine, spruce, and fir trees were all tall and impressive. The forest and the underbrush seemed to close in around them. The rolling plains to the east were still visible through gaps, but more and more the four men were closed up between green walls.

"I don't reckon I ever saw anything like this before," Walter said with a touch of awe in his voice.

"Me, neither," Oliver put in. "We've seen plenty of trees and some thick forests, but not like this. There are so many trees you could cut them down for lumber for a hundred years and not be able to tell any difference."

"Dinnae ye believe that for a second, lad," Duff told him.

"And never underestimate the way folks can come into an untouched wilderness and change everything," added Elmer. "Usually not for the better. Folks used to say there were so many buffalo out here you could shoot 'em for their hides for a hundred years and not even make a dent in 'em. I've seen piles o' hides taller 'n houses down in Kansas about fifteen years ago. But all that killin' *did* make a dent in 'em. The herds are just a shadow of what they once was. Another few years of slaughterin' 'em at that pace, and the buffalo would've been gone for good. It may still come to that."

"I hope not," said Oliver. "We saw some buffalo when we were crossing Kansas and Nebraska. They were so huge and fierce-looking they were frightening, but they were also majestic, in a way. Too majestic to just wipe them out."

"The Injuns agree with you. That's one reason they fought so hard to keep the white men from floodin' in here the way they did, with the wagon trains and the railroads. At the same time, things were gettin' so crowded back east folks had to have more room to spread out, and there's no denyin' civilization has a few good things to say for itself. Reckon it's a battle that won't never be over, the struggle between the way things used to be and the way they're gonna be, and most folks, all they can do is keep their heads down and hope that them and theirs come through it all right."

"You make the future sound pretty bleak, Mr. Gleason," Walter said.

"Nope. Not bleak. But not easy, neither. Anybody who thinks life is gonna be easy is just foolin' theirselves."

While Elmer was talking, Duff was looking around. The skin on the back of his neck had started to prickle a few minutes earlier, a warning something wasn't right up ahead.

But he didn't see anything, no matter how intently his eyes searched the trees on either side of the trail, which had widened out until there was room for all four of them to ride abreast. Duff was about to tell the others to rein in and let him take a look out ahead of them on his own, when one of the pine boughs overhanging the trail suddenly moved a little.

Duff's head jerked up in time to see a figure leap out of the tree and crash into Walter, driving him off his horse. A split second later, a second attacker dived from the branches, tackled Oliver, and knocked him out of the saddle, as well.

Duff and Elmer pulled their Colts but couldn't risk any

shots. The four shapes were tangled up on the ground like a knot of battling wildcats.

A rifle cracked somewhere close by, a slug ripped through the branches above their heads, and a voice called out commandingly, "Drop those guns, or the next bullet goes through one of you!"

# Chapter 11

Duff stiffened in surprise. Not at the fact that they'd been attacked; he'd expected that they might run into an ambush. What surprised him was that the voice issuing that order belonged to a woman. And that wasn't all.

As Elmer stared at the violently struggling figures rolling around on the ground, he exclaimed, "Hell's bells! Those are *gals!*"

It was true, Duff saw. Even though it was difficult to make out the details because of all the thrashing around and the dust it raised, he could tell the attackers who had leaped from the tree where they had been hidden were female. They wore men's shirts and trousers, but as they strained against Walter and Oliver, the curves under the shirts were obvious. Also, long hair tumbled around their heads and shoulders.

"I'm not gonna warn you again!" The shout came from the woman who had spoken earlier. "Throw down those guns!"

"Nae," Duff replied as he lowered his Colt. He slid the revolver in its holster and went on. "We'll put them away, but ye'll not be disarming us." He nodded for Elmer to pouch his iron, as well.

Elmer looked like he didn't think that was a very good idea, but he did as Duff ordered.

"If that is nae enough to satisfy ye, I suppose you'll just have to shoot us," Duff told the unseen rifle-wielder.

"Don't go givin' her ideas," Elmer muttered. "She sounds mean enough to do it."

"I heard that, you old pelican!"

Elmer snorted. "Old pelican, is it! Come on out and put that rifle down, gal, and I'll teach you to respect your elders. I'll put you over my knee and whale some manners into you!"

"I'd like to see you try it!"

Meanwhile, the fracas in the trail continued. The horses Walter and Oliver had been riding, made skittish by the shots and the humans rolling around near their hooves, danced back to give the combatants more room.

Walter, who was a mite on the scrawny side, wound up on the bottom, lying on his belly with a dark-haired girl on top of him. She had her left arm looped around Walter's neck, holding him in place, while she used her right hand to grip Walter's right wrist and twist that arm behind his back.

"You best give up," the girl told him, panting a little from her exertions, "or else I'll pop that arm right outta your shoulder socket."

A few yards away, Oliver, who was built sturdier, was having better luck. He planted his right shoulder in his opponent's belly, wrapped both arms around her waist, and surged to his feet with her draped over his shoulder. Her upper half hung down his back; her legs were in front of him, and he had to twist back and forth to avoid her feet as she kicked at him. She pounded at his back with her fists, but he was able to shrug off those blows.

"Settle down!" he told her. "Settle down, or I'll dump you in that sticker bush over there!"

"You wouldn't dare, you no-good . . ."

What followed was a stream of profanity so colorful it made Duff and Elmer glance at each other in surprise again, all of it delivered in a voice that sounded like a little girl, although the curly-haired blonde's body, clearly displayed in the tight shirt and trousers, was that of a full-grown woman.

"I warned you." Oliver stumbled toward the briar thicket at the edge of the trail.

The blonde screamed. "Don't you dare!", then heaped more obscenities on his head.

Oliver grunted with the effort as he heaved her from his shoulder into the brush. She screamed again.

"Della!" shouted the dark-haired one who had Walter pinned to the ground. "Look what he done to Lydia! Shoot him!"

The woman who stepped out of the bushes on the other side of the trail and kept a Winchester pointed toward Duff and Elmer was older than the other two, but she probably wasn't much past twenty. She was a blonde, too, with the same sort of curly hair as the one called Lydia. She had an old, broad-brimmed felt hat pushed back on her head with the fair hair spilling from under it. Like the other two, she wore a man's shirt and trousers. Her forearms, revealed by the shirt's rolled-up sleeves, were deeply tanned, and so was her face. The rifle was rock-steady as she covered Duff and Elmer with it.

"Lydia brought her troubles on herself," she said. "If she'd called me some of those names, I would've thrown her in the brambles, too." To Duff and Elmer, she said, "You'd better tell your friend to give. Ginny'll bust his arm if he don't, sure as hell. And tell the other one to stay back!"

Duff lifted a hand and gestured to Oliver, who was about to go to his brother's aid. He could make a guess as to who these female hellions were, but he wanted to be sure and perhaps find out more information from them. "Go ahead and surrender, Walter."

"N-no!" the young man cried. "I won't— Ahhh!"

His captor had heaved on his arm again, putting even more pressure on the bones and sockets.

"A-all right." Walter gasped. "I give up!"

"That's better," the girl called Ginny told him. She let go of his arm so he could pull it back around in front of him, but she continued to kneel on him with her right knee planted firmly in the small of his back. She pushed back several strands of hair that had fallen in front of her face and added, "Don't you try nothin' else. You'll be sorry if you do."

"I'm already sorry I ever laid eyes on you," Walter said.

"That's enough of that," said Della. "Ginny, go help Lydia."

"I don't trust this here rascal." Ginny punctuated her comment with a hard slap to the back of Walter's head.

He yelped in surprise and pain.

"If he tries anything, I'll shoot him," Della said.

Duff said, "Ye might want to be thinking twice about that, lass. Nobody's badly hurt yet, but that could change mighty quickly."

"You're right, but it won't be us getting hurt," Della snapped.

"I would nae be so certain of that I dinnae believe that ye could take care of both me and Elmer before one of us got you."

"Again, don't give her no ideas," Elmer said under his breath.

Della frowned curiously at Duff. "What's your name?" she demanded. "And why do you talk so blasted funny?"

"I'm called Duff MacCallister. And since I was raised in Scotland, to my ears 'tis ye who sounds funny."

"MacCallister." The creases in Della's forehead deepened. "I think maybe I've heard of you. Are you any kin to Falcon MacCallister? I *know* I've heard of him."

"Falcon is me cousin, and a good friend, to boot."

"He's also known from one end of the frontier to the other as a gunfighter. How about you, mister? Are you as slick on the draw as your cousin?"

"Falcon's the fastest I've ever laid eyes on."

"You didn't answer my question."

Duff's broad shoulders rose and fell. "No, I dinnae. But since I have no interest in shooting anyone at the moment, it does nae matter, does it?"

"You don't want to shoot me?"

"Nae, Miss Hardcastle, I do not."

"How do you know who I am?" she asked sharply.

"'Tis said no one lives up here on Buzzard's Roost save the Hardcastle family."

While Duff and Della were talking, Ginny had been reaching carefully into the briar thicket and trying to disentangle Lydia from the thorny creepers. She had finally gotten the blonde loose enough for Lydia to pull free the rest of the way and stumble out of the stubbornly clutching growth. She had blood on her hands and face from a number of scratches, and her shirt was ripped in several places, creating gaps that revealed swathes of creamy female flesh. With fury twisting her face into a murderous scowl, Lydia stomped toward Oliver.

"I'm gonna kill that dirty, low-down—"

"Ginny, grab her and hang on to her," Della said. "We've had enough fighting until we sort this all out."

Ginny caught hold of Lydia's left arm and stopped her from charging at Oliver, who regarded the pair of them warily. Walter was on his feet straightening his clothes and slapping at them to get the dust of the trail off as he glared at the two girls a few yards away.

With that conflict at a momentary stand-off, Della returned her attention to Duff and Elmer. "What are you doing up here? You wasn't invited."

"I was nae aware an invitation was required to travel on a public trail."

"This trail ain't public. It's the Nightmare Trail, and it belongs to the Hardcastles, just like the rest of Buzzard's Roost."

"Your family holds title to the entire mountain and the foothills around it?" Duff asked with a skeptical raising of one eyebrow.

Della glared over the Winchester's barrel. "You said it yourself. Ain't nobody else up here but us Hardcastles. That makes it ours. Nobody else wants the mountain or this trail."

"Once, perhaps, but 'tis no longer the case. With Thunder Canyon closed, probably for good, there be no other way in and out of Longshot Basin."

"And what the hell's your interest in Longshot Basin?" Della shot back at him.

From the corner of his eye, Duff saw Walter opening his mouth and figured the youngster was about to answer Della's question with the truth. That might not be a good idea, Duff thought. He caught Walter's eye and gave a tiny shake of his head, a signal for Walter to keep quiet. Duff hoped Della hadn't noticed the gesture, but if she had, they'd just have to deal with that later.

"'Tis said the basin has some decent graze, and I was thinking that I might run some of me stock up here. I have a ranch, ye ken, with a large herd of Black Angus cattle."

Della regarded him intently for a second, then said, "I think I've heard of your ranch, too." She jerked the Winchester's barrel in a curt gesture that took in Elmer and the two brothers. "Who are these rannies?"

"My foreman, Elmer Gleason," Duff said with a nod toward the old-timer. "And two of my ranch hands, Walter and Oliver Spencer."

More than likely, the Hardcastles didn't know anything about the Spencer wagon train. There was a good chance Duff could get away with that deception. If he could make Della believe his only interest in Longshot Basin was in using it as grazing land, the girl might be more likely to let them go. The idea of a bunch of immigrant wagons making use of the Nightmare Trail probably would meet with more resistance.

Lydia had pulled a bandana from her pocket and was using it to wipe blood from the scratches on her hands and face. "The mountain's our home. You ain't welcome anywhere around it, includin' Longshot Basin. You understand that, you big ugly ape?"

Under his breath, Elmer said, "Well, at least big ugly ape ain't as bad as what she called you before."

Duff ignored that. "Legally speaking—"

"The only law in these parts is Hardcastle law, mister, Della interrupted. "And you've broken it by ridin' up here uninvited. Only one thing to do now."

"And what might that be?"

She raised the Winchester to her shoulder and sighted over the barrel. Duff tensed as he realized she was aiming right at his head.

"You're coming with us," said Della. "It'll be up to Cousin Willie to decide what to do with you."

Duff shook his head slowly. "We'll not be going anywhere with ye, lass . . ." His voice trailed off as he heard the unmistakable sound of more Winchesters being levered in the brush around them.

"I think you will," Della said with a smug smile. "And this time, you'll go ahead and drop those guns, all four of you, whether you want to or not."

"Duff . . . ?" Elmer said quietly.

"It seems we have no choice," replied Duff. Carefully, with his left hand, he reached across his body, eased his Colt from its holster, and tossed the gun onto the trail.

With a sigh of resignation, Elmer followed suit with his Colt. Duff told Walter and Oliver to do likewise. The two young men were every bit as reluctant as Elmer to disarm themselves, but they did so. With an unknown number of enemies pointing rifles at them from the brush, they really had no choice, as Duff had said.

Lydia started toward the guns lying in the trail, but Della said quickly to her, "Stay back and let Ginny gather them up."

Lydia glared at her. "What, you don't trust me?"

"The temper you've got, you're damned right I don't. You might decide to shoot these fellas, and that's not gonna happen unless Cousin Willie says so."

"I don't know who Cousin Willie is," Elmer muttered to Duff, "but I sure as blazes hope he's in a good mood."

When Ginny had gathered up the four revolvers, Della told her to bring them over to her. "Set them down on the ground there, then go and get their rifles," Della said. "Start with the big hombre first."

Ginny nodded and walked over to Duff's horse, edging up to it carefully. She reached out to grasp the sheathed Winchester, stretching her arm away from her body.

Duff hadn't really had a plan, but now that it was clear Della wasn't going to let them go, he was quick to take advantage of an opportunity when it was presented to him. His hand shot out and wrapped around Ginny's upper arm. He heaved up as she cried out in surprise. She was a solidly built girl and not easy to lift like that, but Duff packed a lot of power in his broad shoulders and muscular arms.

"Hold your fire!" yelled Della. "Hold your fire!"

The Hardcastles couldn't risk a shot with Duff and Ginny so close together. He pulled her onto the horse's back in front of him, wrapped his other arm around her waist to jerk her against him, and then looped his left arm around her throat. She writhed in his grip, but she was no match for his strength.

"Mister, have you gone loco?" Della said. "We can still shoot your friends."

"Aye, and I can snap this girl's neck in the blink of an eye, too, which is exactly what I'll do if ye harm any of us."

Della glared darkly at him. "You wouldn't dare! We'd just shoot you down if you did."

"Aye, but poor Ginny here would still be dead."

"You'd do that to a defenseless girl?"

"The rest of ye dinnae seem so defenseless," Duff replied coolly. "Perhaps it evens out."

Della continued scowling at him. Elmer sat on his horse, expressionless, like a cat waiting to see what was going to happen before deciding which way to jump. Walter and Oliver both looked nervous, and Duff hoped they wouldn't do anything foolish.

Of course, he was a fine one to be thinking that, he told himself, after the reckless play he had just made.

Della shook her head and sneered. "You're not going to kill her."

That was true. Duff didn't even like manhandling Ginny the way he had. Holding her so intimately like this made him uncomfortable. But Della didn't know any of that, and although she was putting up a defiant front, she had to be worried about how far he would go.

"Here's what you're going to do," he told her. "First, call all the others out where I can see them."

"Go to hell."

"I can choke the lass to death. She'll die a lot more slowly and painfully." He tensed the arm around Ginny's neck, enough for Della to see but without really increasing the pressure all that much. It was enough to make Della exclaim, "Wait, wait!"

"Do as I said," Duff told her calmly.

Della glared daggers at him for a few more seconds, then lowered the Winchester and called, "All the rest of you, get out here!"

Three more young women in men's clothing, all in their late teens like Ginny and Lydia, emerged from the brush and brandished rifles. They all looked like they wanted to fill Duff with lead. Two were brunettes; the third had reddish blond hair.

"Is that all of them?" asked Duff. He reminded Della, "You'll be wagering this girl's life on the answer, ye ken."

"That's all," Della said. "If you don't believe me, you can go to blazes."

"All rifles on the trail, there in the middle, and then back away from them."

Della sighed and told the others, "Do what he says."

She went first, bending to set her Winchester on the ground. The other three did likewise, then all backed away as he had ordered.

"Walter, Oliver, get those rifles, and retrieve all our Colts."

The youngsters hurried to do so. They took the weapons back to where Duff and Elmer sat on their horses.

"Slip my gun back in its holster," Duff told Walter. He didn't want to let go of Ginny, even with one hand, to pouch the iron himself.

Following Duff's orders, the boys handed the Winchesters to Elmer one by one. The old-timer took each rifle and worked its lever until all the rounds in it had been ejected. Walter and Oliver picked up the cartridges and stuck them in their pockets.

"Now take the empty rifles and throw them in the same briar patch where Oliver tossed little Miss Lydia there," Duff said.

That characterization set Lydia's temper to blazing again. She spewed curses and started forward, but Della grabbed her from behind and held her.

"As long as they have Ginny, they've got the upper hand," Della told the younger blonde. "But it won't always be that way."

"'Tis not going to change for a while," said Duff. "Miss Ginny will be coming with us."

"You really *are* loco! We're not gonna let you carry her off and do God knows what to her."

"No harm will come to the lass as long as no one tries to stop us. I give ye my word on that."

"Where are you going to take her?"

"We're still headed for the same place we were before ye ambushed us—Longshot Basin."

Elmer said, "Uh, Duff, shouldn't we turn around and light a shuck for the ranch? If we go on to Longshot Basin, this crazy bunch'll still be between us and home."

"Aye. But I'll not be turned away from me goal that easily." Duff looked at Della again and went on. "We mean you and your family no harm, Miss Della. Miss Ginny will come with us to Longshot Basin and then back to where this trail meets the Thunder Canyon trail. We'll let her go there and be on our way. Do we have a deal?"

Della's chin jutted out defiantly. "And if I say no?"

Duff sighed. "Then it appears someone will have to die. Perhaps a number of someones. 'Twould be most regrettable, but at times there be no other choice."

The two of them traded hard stares for a long moment. Then Della jerked her head in a nod. "All right. You can ride on to Longshot Basin, have your look around, and then ride back out on the Nightmare Trail. Nobody'll bother you. But know this, Mr. Duff MacCallister. You've made enemies of the whole Hardcastle clan today. And if anything happens to Ginny . . . I'll hunt you down and kill you myself."

"I believe ye would."

"Damn right I would."

"Or make the attempt, at least." Duff shifted his grip on Ginny so he could grasp the reins in his right hand, As long as ye keep your word, nothing will happen to the girl. I gave ye *my* word on that, and I meant it." He nudged his mount forward with his knees. "Now step aside."

The five Hardcastle girls moved to the edge of the trail so Duff, Elmer, Walter, and Oliver could ride by. They were living, breathing examples of the old saying about how, if looks could kill . . .

Especially from Lydia. Her ire was directed specifically toward Oliver, who had tossed her in the briars.

As he rode past her, she said, "I'm gonna carve your liver out, fat boy. You better not ever go to sleep again, 'cause if you do, I'm gonna be there, and I'll kill you. Slow and painful-like."

"That's enough, Lydia," Della snapped. "Let them go on their way. There'll be another day . . . and then they'll all be sorry they ever ventured up the Nightmare Trail."

# CHAPTER 12

Once the four from Sky Meadow had followed the trail around a bend, so they were out of sight as well as earshot of the Hardcastle females, Elmer said, "That Della gal was right about one thing, Duff. I'm already sorry I took this *pasear* up the Nightmare Trail."

"Look at it this way," Duff said. "There's been no real harm done so far."

Walter said, "Speak for yourself, Mr. MacCallister. That girl walloped the heck out of me a few times while we were wrestling around."

Ginny turned her head as much as she could with Duff's arm around her neck and glared over at Walter as he spoke.

Duff took that as an opportunity to ask, "If I let go of you, girl, will ye promise not to start fighting again?"

In a strained voice, Ginny said, "You can . . . go straight to . . . Hell, you—"

"Now, taking that attitude is nae going to accomplish a blessed thing, lass. You'll be traveling with us for a while, and ye might as well be comfortable while you're doing it."

Ginny didn't respond for a moment. Then she said, "All right . . . I won't . . . try anything . . . Just . . . let me breathe again."

"Your word on it?"

"My . . . word."

Duff lowered his left arm away from her throat but kept his right wrapped around her waist. As Ginny drew in several deep breaths, he said, "I never had tight enough hold to keep ye from getting air. 'Twas careful I was about that."

"Yeah, I guess I wasn't in any danger of suffocating," Ginny conceded grudgingly. "But you did threaten several times to break my neck. I was so scared—"

"Ha!" Walter broke in. "I saw your face. You weren't scared. You were just mad enough to chew nails, like that wildcat sister of yours."

"Shut up, string bean. Anyway, Lydia ain't my sister. She's my cousin."

"What about Della?" asked Duff.

"Me and her are cousins, too."

"And the other girls?"

"A couple of them are sisters. We've all got lots of cousins."

"How many of you Hardcastles are there living on Buzzard's Roost?"

Ginny looked askance at Duff and said, "I ain't tellin' you nothin' else, mister. How many of us Hardcastles there are ain't none of your business. Just know there's plenty to settle your hash." She pushed at his arm. "And you be careful how you're touchin' me."

Elmer said, "Duff's arm is well south of improper, missy. In case you ain't figured it out yet, Duff's a gentleman, and you're the luckier for it."

"Gentleman!" repeated Ginny. "He near jerked my arm out of its socket when he pulled me up on this horse."

Walter said, "That's what you threatened to do to me, so I reckon maybe you had it coming."

Ginny ignored him. "And he threatened to kill me!" She

frowned and looked back at Duff, again. "You weren't going to do it, though, were you? It was all just a bluff."

"Fortunately for us all, your cousin Della decided to be reasonable," Duff told her. "So, thankfully, things never reached that point."

Ginny shook her head. "No, you wouldn't have done it. I can see that now. If Della had just stood her ground, you'd still be our prisoners." She paused. "You will be again, before this is all over. You just wait and see."

"But dinnae ye ken, there's no reason for your family to be enemies with me and my friends?"

"The whole world is enemies with the Hardcastles," Ginny said darkly. "And nothin' will ever change that."

Duff wasn't going to waste any more time or energy arguing with her. For one thing, he suspected she was right. But he wished that weren't the case. According to Elmer, the Hardcastles were outlaws. Cole Hardcastle was a gunwolf, a killer. All that might be true. But it wasn't Duff's job to bring any of them to justice, at least not at this point.

If the Nightmare Trail was passable for wagons all the way to Longshot Basin . . . if the Hardcastles would allow Waylon Spencer and his wagon train to pass over Buzzard's Roost unmolested . . . Duff was willing to live and let live with the owlhoot clan. Even after Benjy Hardcastle had terrorized and injured Meagan. That would be a difficult pill to swallow, but Duff would do it, for the sake of keeping the peace in the area.

As they rode, Elmer kept checking their backtrail. "I don't see no signs of anybody comin' after us," he reported. "We should've brought their horses with us, Duff."

"I thought about it, but not knowing how rough the trail is farther up, I decided it might not be a good idea. 'Twill take them a while to fetch those rifles out of the brambles."

"Yeah, but they'll get 'em sooner or later," Elmer said

gloomily. "And they've probably got extra ammunition. When we head back, we're liable to ride right into another ambush."

"Not as long as Miss Ginny is with us."

Walter said, "Better hang on to her, Mr. MacCallister. She's squirmy as a cat, and pretty strong, for a girl."

"Strong enough I didn't have no trouble makin' you holler calf rope," Ginny said with a contemptuous snort.

"You just took me by surprise, that's all."

The scoffing sound Ginny made in response to that claim was even more full of scorn.

The trail became steeper the higher they went. The trees closed in more on both sides until they were forced to ride single file. Duff went first with Ginny, followed by Walter, Oliver, and then Elmer bringing up the rear. Wagons could still get through, Duff judged, but in some places, men might have to use axes to trim back the branches before the vehicles could pass. Some of the turns were pretty tight, too. It wouldn't be easy, but it could be done.

When the trees began to thin out, Duff knew they were reaching higher altitudes. As they went around a bend, the vegetation retreated on both sides, giving way to a steep slope that was all dirt and bare rock. Duff reined in and waited as the others emerged from the trail through the trees and joined him on the open stretch about fifty feet wide.

On the far side of the clearing to the left, an almost sheer rock wall reared up a hundred feet or more. To the right, open air fell away, revealing just how far they had climbed. They were higher than Duff had realized. The pine-dotted slope to the right wasn't as steep as the rocky one to the left, but if anything ever started tumbling down that incline—be it man, horse, or wagon—it would fall for a long way before reaching the bottom. A long, fatal way . . .

And directly in front of them, acting as a dividing line

between the two slopes was a ledge that angled sharply upward. Dotted with rocks, it was barely wide enough for both pair of wagon wheels to fit on it.

They all stared at it for a long moment before Duff said, "And there, lads, is where the Nightmare Trail truly begins."

Della cursed, jerked her hand back, and sucked at the drop of bright red blood that had appeared on her index finger where a thorn had pierced it.

Behind her, Lydia said, "Why don't you let me crawl in there and get those rifles? I'm already scratched up."

"That's why," Della told her. "It wouldn't be fair. Anyway, I'm the oldest. I was in charge." A bleak note entered her voice. "It's my responsibility. My fault those damned varmints trespassed on our mountain and carried off Ginny."

One of the other girls, the strawberry blonde called Patsy, said, "Why don't we see if we can find a long, broken branch we could use to fish those rifles outta there?"

That was actually a pretty good idea, thought Della. She nodded. "Go and look for one. Junie, you help her. Iris, go fetch the horses, so we'll be ready to follow those men once we've got our guns again."

"What do you want me to do?" asked Lydia.

"We really ought to clean up the worst of those scratches."

Lydia scoffed at that idea. "They ain't that bad. Hurt like hell, that's all. I reckon they've already stopped bleedin'."

"Well, yeah, I suppose they have. But we get back to the home place, I'll get a bottle of Cole's whiskey and clean 'em, just to make sure they don't fester."

"Why, that'll sting like fire! And Cole might not like you takin' his whiskey."

"A little sting's better than lettin' 'em get infected. And I ain't scared of what Cole likes or don't like."

That was true, anyway. A lot of the cousins were leery of Cole because he had such a reputation as a gunfighter and was rumored to have killed close to twenty men. Della knew her oldest brother had indeed shot men down in gunfights, but she figured the number he'd killed was considerably lower than that. Cole, for all his reputation, was a cool-headed sort and never let himself be pushed into a fight unnecessarily. Any time he pulled his gun, it was because he didn't have any other choice. He had to defend himself or another member of the family.

No Hardcastle would stand by and allow another Hardcastle to come to harm. Might as well ask 'em to stop breathing.

But Della wasn't scared of Cole. She was the baby of the family; he was almost fifteen years older than her. Benjy was eight years older. There had been six children in all, but the one between Cole and Benjy had died in childhood, and so had the two between Benjy and Della. Della knew the names of all the dead ones because she'd seen them written down in the big family Bible with the tattered edge black binding, and she could read enough to recognize names when she saw them, but she didn't think about them much. She didn't remember any of them at all. They'd passed on before she was old enough to recall anything about them.

Life was hard, Cousin Willie always said. The Good Lord made it that way on purpose, so as to strengthen folks and help them make it through all the travails of this earth before it was time to give up the ghost and ascend to the rewards waiting for them in heaven.

Cousin Willie had a lot to say about what the Good Lord intended, as if the Old Fella had called him aside and explained it all to him, but he seemed not to have been listening very hard to the parts about how a man shouldn't steal or kill. Or maybe those parts just didn't apply to the Hardcastles.

Or the parts about the lusts of the flesh, Della thought wryly. There was always a lot of drinking and carrying on around the home place. Sometimes when the boys came back from one of their jaunts, they brought gals with them, gals they had taken from some settlement they'd raided. It was rough on those prisoners, sure, but they got used to living at the home place and most even grew to like it, and that cut down on the fooling around between cousins, which Cousin Willie said was permissible but not good for the family in the long run, and so far he'd been stern about brothers and sisters not marrying up, *ever*, which was good. Della didn't like the way Benjy eyed her sometimes.

Benjy was all right; slow in the head, sure, and he sometimes hurt people because he didn't realize how strong he was. But he wasn't deliberately mean. He wanted what he wanted, though, so Della was careful around him and had been for a good number of years now.

All those thoughts were spinning around in her head while she waited for Iris to get back with the horses and for Junie and Patsy to find a branch they could use to fish those rifles out of the briar patch. That was Della's biggest problem: her brain just never seemed to stop whirling and whirling. On the outside, she had the same cool, icy-nerved calm Cole exhibited, but inside she was always thinking and wanting more and wondering what it would be like to leave the home place and go out and see what else was in the world. Cole and the boys got to do that, at least, even though they had to rob banks and trains and such while they were at it and sometimes have shoot-outs with posses. Della would be willing to run that risk, just to be able to *do* something.

But of course she couldn't. She was a girl, and Cousin Willie said it wasn't seemly for girls to be outlaws.

Damn it all, anyway.

"How about this?" Patsy asked as she came up holding a long, gnarled branch with a natural crook at one end where a smaller branch had grown out but broken off.

"Hand it here," said Della. "I'll give it a try." Since the thorny growth was a little thinner, she got down on one knee low to the ground, and started snaking the branch toward the nearest of the Winchesters.

"Once we get the rifles," said Lydia, "are we goin' after those varmints?" She added a few more colorfully obscene descriptive phrases.

"I don't know," Della muttered as she tried to hook the stub of that smaller, broken branch through the rifle's trigger guard. "We might ought to go and tell Cousin Willie what happened."

"The hell with that!" Lydia exclaimed. "He didn't want to let us gals stand guard in the first place. If we tell him those men got past us and, even worse, took Ginny with 'em, he'll never let us do anything again except sit around the home place and cook and wash and make babies."

"Don't talk about makin' babies," muttered Della. "You ain't old enough even to be thinkin' about that."

"The hell I ain't!"

As reluctant as Della was to admit it, Lydia might have a point. It hadn't been easy talking Cousin Willie into letting her and her girl cousins take a turn guarding the Nightmare Trail. He'd be a lot more likely to let them keep doing it if they proved they were able to deal with trouble.

"Yeah," she said as she finally hooked the rifle and started dragging it through the brush toward her. "Yeah, we're goin' after 'em."

* * *

"That's not even wide enough for a wagon!" Oliver exclaimed as he stared aghast at the ledge.

"Yeah, it is, but there sure ain't any room for leeway," Elmer said. "Get just a little too far over to the right, and your wheels on that side'll drop over the edge. Once that happens, there ain't no stoppin' it. The whole wagon tips over and goes a-tumblin' down that slope. Time it gets to the bottom, it'll be busted into a million pieces, and most likely, so will anybody who was ridin' on it. A fella *might* survive the fall if he was able to grab hold of a tree or a bush before he fell too far, but the odds against that'd be mighty high."

"So how can we take the wagons over that?" asked Walter. "It's a death trap!"

Duff winced. He hadn't wanted the Hardcastles to know what their actual goal was, but with what Walter had just blurted out, it was too late to keep that a secret.

Ginny confirmed it by turning her head to look at Duff as she said, "I thought you were talkin' about drivin' cattle over the Nightmare Trail into Longshot Basin."

"Oh, shoot!" Walter said as he realized what he'd done. "I'm sorry, Mr. MacCallister."

"Dinnae ye worry about it, lad," Duff told him. "The truth was bound to come out sooner or later." He went on to tell Ginny, "We still mean no harm to ye or your family, lass. All we're trying to do is see whether or not 'tis possible to take wagons over this route so these lads and their family can homestead Longshot Basin."

"Homesteaders!" Ginny's lip curled. "You mean sod-busters. Dirt farmers."

Oliver said, "Farming's an honorable way to make a living. Folks wouldn't eat if there weren't farmers."

"'Tis true," said Duff. "The days of most people growing all their own food are coming to an end. People in the cities, especially, rely on farmers and ranchers for beef and produce."

Ginny shook her head. "Seems to me like a miserable way to live. And we sure don't want a bunch of sodbusters livin' as close to us as the basin." She scowled at Walter and Oliver. "If that's what this is about, you and the rest of your bunch ought to go back where you came from. Or to Hell. I don't care which one!"

"That's enough," Duff told her. He walked his horse forward. "Come on. We'll take a closer look at that trail."

The others followed. They reined in again where the ledge began. It didn't look any more promising, close up.

"Seems to me there's only one safe way to get the wagons through," Elmer said. "Folks'll have to walk, since it'll be too risky to ride. The men and boys can lead the teams, goin' mighty slow-like. Somebody else will have to follow along behind each wagon, watchin' the wheels on the right-hand side all the time. If they ever stray too close to the edge, it'll be up to whoever's followin' to yell out a warnin'. Then the leaders can pull the team back a little closer to the wall on the other side."

"That might work," said Duff. "Especially if the wagons are spaced out, so if one happens to go over, it will nae take any of the others with it."

"And the fellas who are leadin' and followin' will have room to jump out of the way," Elmer added.

Ginny snorted. "You fellas are plumb loco to even think about takin' wagons over the Nightmare Trail. You'd never make it, even if Cousin Willie and the others would ever allow such a thing!"

"Why do you hate us?" Walter asked her. "We never did you any harm. All we want is to find a new home and be left alone."

"The whole world hates the Hardcastles," she replied,

echoing something she had said earlier. "Always has. We didn't start it."

Oliver said to his brother, "You're wasting your time talking to her, Walt. She's crazy, just like the rest of them."

Ginny laughed, but it wasn't a pleasant sound. "You'll find out just how crazy we are. You never should've throwed Lydia in that briar patch! She'll get even with you if it's the last thing she ever does."

Oliver swallowed hard, clearly troubled by Ginny's words.

Duff brought the subject back to the reason they were there. "'Tis all well and good to make plans for taking the wagons through, but 'twill only be possible if the trail doesn't get any narrower and hasn't collapsed anywhere up ahead. If we're going to see about that, we had better be moving."

He took the lead again. The trail was plenty wide enough for them to ride single file. Duff stayed close to the left-hand wall. Ginny didn't appear to be the least bit nervous, he noted. That wasn't really surprising. If she and her family lived higher up on the mountain, she probably rode this trail fairly often. She would be accustomed to it.

Walter and Oliver certainly weren't. They kept glancing apprehensively toward the edge. Elmer was careful to stay as far away from it as possible, too.

The ledge curved and climbed along the mountainside. There were no switchbacks, which was good. That would have made the trail almost impossible for wagons to negotiate. Duff thought about it and realized if the Hardcastles lived up there somewhere, they must have been able to get wagons, or at least carts, through in order to bring in the things they needed to live. They might have hewn their dwellings out of stone, but they would still need furnishings, food, other supplies . . .

As they approached a bend around a jutting shoulder of rock, Duff felt Ginny's muscles tense. Something must be waiting for them up ahead, he thought, and she was expecting it. An ambush, maybe? More guards?

He didn't know, but the only way to avoid whatever it was would be to turn around and go back the way they had come from. Duff wasn't willing to do that. He hadn't found out what he wanted to know yet. Besides, turning tail just wasn't something MacCallisters did. Never had been, never would be.

He kept his horse moving steadily up the sloping trail. They reached the bend, followed it around . . .

And then he pulled back on the reins, bringing his mount to a stop, as he saw what lay ahead. Another trail opened up in the left-hand wall, angling off between high, sheer cliffs, rising at an even steeper slope as it led up farther than Duff's eyes could follow.

He didn't need to be able to see the top to know where it led.

The Hardcastles' stronghold.

# CHAPTER 13

As Ginny's shoulders sagged, Duff felt the anticipation go out of her and said, "'Tis disappointed ye are, lass. Ye must've expected some of your relatives to be waiting for us here."

"It could've happened," she muttered. Then she stiffened again and drew in a deep breath.

Duff's free hand clamped over her mouth before she could make a sound. "Ye were about to scream and hope someone up above heard you. I cannae let that happen. Will I be forced to gag ye? Because I can if I need to."

Ginny sat taut and stubborn for a couple of seconds, then she seemed to deflate again and shook her head. Duff loosened his grip on her mouth enough for her to mumble, "I won't scream."

"Ye promise?"

"I promise," she said.

"And how likely are ye to honor your word when 'tis given to someone who isn't a Hardcastle?"

He felt as much as heard her teeth grinding together in frustration and anger. "Fine," she managed to say. "I give you my word, and I'll keep it even though you're not a Hardcastle."

"I hope ye dinnae prove me foolish for believing you," said Duff as he took his hand away from her mouth.

"I don't need to scream. You'll get what's comin' to you later. Nobody crosses the Hardcastles and gets away with it. Not ever."

"Always a first time for everything, lass," he told her as he got his horse moving again. He half turned to gesture toward the others, indicating they should take it slow and easy . . . and quiet. He didn't know how far the sound of hoofbeats would carry in the thin mountain air. If the Hardcastle stronghold was within hearing distance, he didn't want to alert them someone was passing by.

Ginny kept her word; Duff had to give her credit for that. She didn't make a sound as they rode past the cleft in the mountainside. Because they had to go slowly, several nerve-wracking minutes passed before the riders went around another bend, out of sight of the opening.

Even though the danger was less, their pace was still slow. Nobody wanted to get in a hurry on a trail like that one. Haste led to carelessness, and carelessness led to death. Time dragged by. It was well after noon. They wouldn't make it back to the camp at Sky Meadow before dark.

Duff knew it would be a terrible idea to follow the trail back around the mountain after darkness fell. They might have to spend the night in Longshot Basin. Water wasn't a worry as they had plenty in their canteens, and there was a creek in the basin as well. And Wang had packed enough provisions in their saddlebags for them to stay out overnight and not go hungry.

But by nightfall, the rest of the Hardcastles would know someone had dared to intrude on what they considered their domain. Not only that, Ginny had been kidnapped. At least, her family would look at it that way. Elmer had been right. Duff and the others should have lit out for home when they had the chance. His resolve—or call it what it was, he mused, *sheer stubbornness*—might have created a trap from which there was no escape.

But at least so far, the scouting mission itself had been a success. The ledge remained wide enough for a wagon to travel over it, if barely, and it hadn't crumbled away anywhere. The trail's surface was mostly rock and very solid.

The change in orientation was subtle enough he didn't notice it at first. Then he realized they weren't climbing anymore. The ledge was level, and after another quarter-mile or so, it began to slope down gradually. Rocky shoulders rose to the right of the trail, cutting off the view in that direction. Walter and Oliver relaxed a little, since they could no longer see how dizzyingly high up they were.

The trail curved around another bend, and suddenly, like it had just dropped down from the sky, Longshot Basin opened up in front of them, sprawling out left and right. Duff reined in.

The others came up alongside him and Ginny and stared in silence for a long moment.

Oliver finally found his voice and said, "It's beautiful."

Duff wasn't sure he would go that far. Longshot Basin was rugged, no doubt about it. The basin was a couple of miles wide and maybe five miles long, and from that elevation, he and the others could see just about all of it.

Sheer cliffs ranging from eighty to a hundred feet tall ringed the entire basin, except for a fifty-yard-wide gap near the southern end, well off to the right from where Duff and his companions had emerged. That was Thunder Canyon. Clearly the end of the canyon where they were was still open; the avalanche hadn't filled it the entire way.

That didn't really matter. No matter how deep the plug was at the other end, the canyon was closed. It was a box canyon now, terminating where the avalanche had dumped hundreds of tons of rock.

Areas of rougher terrain—gullies, ridges, mounds of rock—ran roughly north and south through the basin, as if at some point in the distant geological past, giant hands had pushed on each side of it and forced the earth to fold and bulge to relieve that immense pressure.

The areas in between those breaks were relatively flat and covered with grass, scrub brush, and a few trees. A line of darker green wandered across the basin at an angle from northwest to southeast. The thicker vegetation was where the creek ran, bubbling up from springs under the cliffs and flowing across the basin before it plunged back underground where it reached the other side.

The areas of open ground between the breaks were wide enough for fields with enough room each of the families in the Spencer wagon train could have their own good-sized farm. How productive those farms would be, Duff couldn't say . . . but to folks who had nowhere else to go, settling here would be worth a try.

Walter said, "You know, I'll bet if we could get in here, build some cabins, and get crops in, we could take our time working on the rockslide in the canyon. We might be able to clean it out and use that as the way in and out of the basin without having to go back over this trail."

"That's just a crazy dream," Ginny said, sneering at him. "That canyon'll never be open again."

"You don't know that," he told her, his eyes flashing with anger. "We don't know how thick the barrier is."

"Enough rock came down it sounded like the world was shaking itself apart. Don't be a damned fool. You'd never get through it."

"It's not being a damned fool to hope for something to work out."

"If you think my family's ever gonna let you go back and forth over the Nightmare Trail, then a damned fool is *exactly* what you are, beanpole."

Instead of sitting there and letting them squabble, Duff started forward. "Come on. Let's have a closer look at the rest of the trail."

The ledge descended the cliff in front of them. It wasn't any wider, but it wasn't as steep as it had been while climbing onto Buzzard's Roost. Anybody bringing wagons this way would still have to exercise great caution while descending, to prevent runaways, but he thought it could be managed without too much trouble. It took them almost fifteen minutes to reach the bottom of the trail where it opened out into the basin proper.

They rode into it toward a small ridge about a quarter of a mile away. Walter reined in after they had gone a couple of hundred yards. The others halted, too, and watched as the young man dismounted, hunkered on his heels, and reached down to dig his fingers into the soil.

"Walt's got a real good touch for growing things," Oliver explained. "He's checking to see how good the dirt is."

Walter brought up a handful of earth, let some of it trickle out through his fingers, then rubbed them together to check the consistency. He lifted his hand to his nose and sniffed the soil, then took a pinch of it and put it on his tongue.

"What the devil is he doin'?" Ginny laughed and called out jeeringly. "Instead of beanpole, I'm gonna start callin' you dirt eater!"

Walter dropped the rest of the dirt and stood up, brushing his hands together to get rid of any clinging particles. "You can get an idea of what's in dirt by tasting it. There's nothing crazy about it. And this is pretty good dirt, I think."

"I'll take your word for it."

Walter swung up into his saddle again and said, "Come on, Ollie, let's take a look around." He glanced at Duff. "That's all right, isn't it, Mr. MacCallister?"

"As far as I ken, we're alone in this basin," said Duff. "Except for some deer, antelope, maybe some rabbits, and wild cattle, descendants of stock that strayed up here and never left. If ye run into any of those cows, best ye give them a wide berth. They will nae have learned to be wary of human beings, and many of them will have a mean streak. They might well charge ye if you crowd them."

"We'll be careful," promised Oliver.

The brothers rode off, gazing around wide-eyed and chattering to each other.

Ginny snorted. "Fools. You're all pathetic fools."

"I could gag ye, you know, if 'tis determined ye are to keep heaping vile calumnies on our heads."

"I don't know what . . . vile calumnies . . . are, but if you want to hear some cussin', you should hear Lydia go at it."

"We heard," Duff assured her.

"Oh, she can get a lot worse than that. She tries to hold it in around Cousin Willie, though. He don't cotton much to folks cussin'."

"This Cousin Willie, he's the patriarch of your family?"

"The what?"

"The leader," Duff said. "The father of the clan."

Ginny shook her head. "Cousin Willie ain't nobody's father. He never married up nor had any kids. He says he's too devoted to doin' the Lord's work to bother with that. But he's the boss, sure enough. He's the one who led the Hardcastles up here from the Ozarks twenty years ago, 'fore I was born."

Duff leaned his head toward the mountain. "Ye've ne'er lived anywhere but here, on that crag?"

"That's right, mister. You talked about how those sod-busters need a new home. Well, they'll be intrudin' on *our* home if they settle here, but you don't seem to care about that."

"But your family dinnae farm nor ranch in the basin. There dinnae be any reason why the Hardcastles and the Spencers cannae be neighbors."

Ginny sniffed. "Hardcastles got to have some elbow room. Besides, if it gets all *civilized* up here"—contempt dripped off the word—"how long do you think it'll be before somebody gets the idea that we ain't good enough to stay around these parts? They'll want to run us out, just like folks down in the Ozarks got together and run Cousin Willie and the others outta there."

"Vigilantes, that's what you're talkin' about, ain't it?" Elmer said.

"Bunch of meddlin' sons of guns who wouldn't mind their own business, that's what I'd call 'em."

"And they didn't take it kindly when your kinfolks robbed and killed and run roughshod over ever'body. I expect *that's* what really happened."

Ginny glared at him. "You can just go jump on a stump, you old pelican."

"That's enough of that," Duff said. "Let's ride on over to the creek and have a look."

It was a decent-sized stream, ten feet wide and a couple of feet deep, with cottonwoods and aspens shading the banks. The area along the creek seemed to be the prettiest-looking country in the entire basin.

"Now, this ain't bad," Elmer said as they reined in beside the stream.

Ginny squirmed a little and said, "Lemme down."

"Why?" Duff asked her.

"So I can go in those bushes over there and tend to my personal needin's, if you've got to know."

Instantly, Duff was embarrassed. He felt his face warming as he said, "Ye promise not to run off?"

Ginny waved a hand at their surroundings. "Where in blazes am I gonna run to? It's near a mile to where the trail outta here starts. I reckon you wouldn't have any trouble chasin' me down before I could get there."

"Aye, 'tis true enough, I suppose." Duff still had his arm around her waist. He leaned over and helped her slide off the horse. "We'll be keeping an eye on that brush, though, so dinnae try sneaking off."

Ginny just glared at them for a second, then stomped off toward the bushes.

"One time when I was a boy," Elmer said, "I decided I was gonna trap me a bobcat."

Duff chuckled. "I think I have an idea where this story is going."

"Yeah, I bet you do. I trapped that bobcat, all right, and then went to haul him out by the tail. After I grabbed on, I didn't want to do nothin' but let go again, but he weren't havin' none of it. I'm startin' to get the same feelin' about little Ginny gal there."

"Her fangs and claws have been pulled."

"Yeah, well, give her half a chance and she'll grow 'em right back, mighty quicklike."

Duff didn't doubt that.

He looked around, checking the height of the sun in the sky, then said, "This would nae be a bad place to make camp tonight."

"You figure we ain't gonna be able to make it back over the mountain before nightfall?"

"I dinnae believe it likely."

Elmer rubbed his chin. "And we don't want to be stuck up there on the Nightmare Trail after dark."

"'Twould be awfully dangerous, I'm thinking."

"More dangerous than waitin' here for the Hardcastles to come after us?"

"We have a hostage, as uncomfortable as it makes me to say such a thing."

"Yeah, but is a hostage really a hostage if there's no chance in hell you're gonna hurt 'em?"

"They dinnae ken that."

Elmer shrugged and said, "That depends on how much they've heard about Duff MacCallister. You've got a reputation in these parts as a pretty upstandin' sort of hombre."

Duff didn't comment on that, but he looked around and said, "Speaking of Miss Ginny, I cannae see or hear the brush moving around over there anymore. Perhaps one of us should check on her."

"I'll do it. Better an old pelican take a chance on interruptin' a gal at a bad time than a strappin' young fella."

Elmer dismounted and let his horse's reins dangle as he started toward the brush.

"All right, gal," he called as he approached. "Time to come on outta there. You've had enough time to take care of whatever needs takin' care of."

No response came from the bushes. Duff frowned. Elmer hesitated and looked back over his shoulder. Duff spread his hands, indicating that he didn't know what the older man ought to do next.

Elmer drew in a deep breath, blew it out, and said, "All right, gal, if you don't want to come out, I'm just gonna have to come in there and get you. If there's any reason I shouldn't, you best sing out right now."

Still nothing. Elmer cast one more apprehensive glance at Duff, dragged in another deep breath, and reached out to part the brush with his arms so he could step into the thicket.

In a blur of motion, Ginny exploded out of the growth, and before Elmer could stop her, she used both hands to swing the rock she had found somewhere. The stone smashed into Elmer's head and sent him careening backward with blood streaming down his leathery face.

# CHAPTER 14

Elmer's feet got tangled up, and he sat down hard. Ginny dropped the rock and leaped after him. She bent down and snagged his gun from its holster.

Duff was in motion, charging his horse forward, covering the intervening space in little more than the blink of an eye. He launched himself from the saddle in a diving tackle aimed at Ginny.

She was raising the gun in both hands but couldn't bring it to bear before Duff crashed into her. The impact knocked her backward. She held on to the Colt, but her arms flew up in the air as she jerked the trigger, and the bullet flew harmlessly into the wide blue sky.

The next instant, Ginny landed on her back with Duff on top of her. His weight on her forced all the air out of her lungs and left her gasping. He reached up, wrapped his hand around the Colt's cylinder, and twisted the weapon out of her grasp.

His plan was to pin her down and subdue her while she was still stunned, but she recovered quick enough to lift a knee sharply into his belly. He figured she was aiming at his groin and missed, but the blow was still painful enough to make him grit his teeth and double over.

With his face within reach, she clawed at it with both hands. Her fingernails raked down his cheeks and might have done some real damage, but they'd been bitten off short. At least she didn't try to gouge his eyes out. That was something to be thankful for.

Duff tossed Elmer's gun well out of reach and grabbed Ginny's wrists. He needed to check on Elmer but couldn't do that as long as Ginny was fighting. She might even try to recover the Colt or snatch up the rock she had used to wallop Elmer.

"Stop fighting!" Duff told her. "Stop that, I tell ye!"

She spat in his face and yelled, "Go to hell!"

He was reminded of the bobcat Elmer had been talking about a few minutes earlier. The analogy was sure proving to be an apt one.

Forced to do something he didn't like to do, Duff let go of Ginny's left wrist, balled his right hand into a loose fist, and clipped her on the jaw with a short, sharp blow that rocked her head back against the ground. He wouldn't have done that, even under duress, if he hadn't been worried about Elmer being badly injured.

Ginny's left arm fell beside her and onto the ground as did her right arm when Duff let go of that wrist. He stood up and whistled for his horse. Sky trotted over, and Duff removed the coiled lariat from the saddle and worked quickly, rolling Ginny on to her belly, and tying her wrists together. Then he ran the excess rope down to her feet so he could wrap bonds around her ankles, too.

She regained her senses and started screaming and yelling curses and trying to kick. Ignoring all that, Duff grasped her firmly and finished looping the rope around her ankles several times before he pulled it tight. He stood up and surveyed his work. She was hog-tied well enough. All she could do was writhe and squirm a little, and not much of that.

Satisfied Ginny couldn't cause any more trouble for the moment, he hurried over to Elmer, who was lying on his back where he had fallen. The old-timer was moving around a little, and as Elmer let out a groan, Duff felt a surge of relief. At least his friend was still alive.

Elmer's eyelids fluttered open as Duff dropped to a knee beside him. His gaze was unfocused, though, as he muttered, "Wha . . . wha' happen . . . ?" He winced and lifted a shaking hand to his forehead, where blood still oozed from a cut surrounded by a swollen area turning purple.

Duff caught hold of Elmer's wrist with one hand and rested the other on his shoulder to hold him down as he tried to sit up.

"Take it easy there, Elmer. Ye got a mighty potent wallop on the head."

Elmer sagged back slightly. "You're tellin' me. Feels like this skull o' mine is busted plumb open."

"It may feel like that, but I can assure ye the damage is nae that bad. Ye've got a cut and a bruise, but other than that, I think you're all right."

"Did a horse kick me? I can't quite remember . . ."

"'Twas not a horse, but rather Miss Ginny."

"That gal?" Elmer exclaimed. Once again he started to sit up, only to have Duff hold him down gently. "No girl ever laid me out like that!"

"This one did. Dinnae worry. She's tied up now."

"Wasn't worried," Elmer said in a surly voice. "She, uh, must've took me by surprise."

"In truth, 'tis exactly what happened. Ye were going to check on her, and she was lying in wait in the brush. She found a rock somewhere and used it to strike ye in the head."

"Yeah, I'm startin' to remember now. She come outta there about as fast as a dang rattlesnake. I didn't have a chance to do anything before she clouted me. You got her tied up, you say?"

"Aye."

Elmer grunted. "Good. Help me sit up."

"Perhaps ye should rest a bit longer."

"No, I want to sit up. I know I'll be a mite woozy-headed at first, but I don't like layin' here like this."

"All right, then." Duff got his arm around Elmer's shoulders and carefully eased him into a sitting position. "We'll need to get that cut cleaned up—" He stopped as a swift rataplan of hoofbeats sounded nearby. Keeping his left arm around Elmer's shoulders, he moved his right hand closer to the butt of his Colt.

A moment later, Duff relaxed as he spotted the two riders hurrying toward them. He recognized Walter and Oliver Spencer. While they were exploring the basin, the brothers must have heard the single shot Ginny had gotten off and were coming to see what had happened.

There was also a good chance some of the Hardcastles had heard it up on Buzzard's Roost, too, thought Duff. In the long run, it probably didn't matter. More than likely, Della and the other girls had already alerted the rest of their family about what had happened.

Walter and Oliver pounded up and reined in. They gazed wide-eyed at Elmer with his bloody head and Ginny hog-tied on the ground nearby.

After a moment, Walter said, "I'm not sure what happened, but we probably should have trussed her up like that from the start."

Ginny raised her head enough to glare at Walter as she screeched, "Go to hell, dirt-eater!"

Oliver dismounted and led his horse toward Duff and Elmer. "How bad are you hurt, Mr. Gleason?"

"I'll be all right," Elmer said with a slightly shaky wave of his hand. "A mule kicked me in the head once. Compared to that, this ain't that terrible."

Walter nodded toward Ginny. "She did that, I reckon?"

"Aye," said Duff. "She found a rock and took Elmer by surprise. It will nae happen again."

"Durn right it won't." Elmer scowled. "I'm gonna be keepin' my eye on you all the time, gal."

She proceeded to spit curses that would have done her cousin Lydia proud.

Duff ignored the tirade and said to Walter and Oliver, "You fellows keep a watch for trouble. I'm going to clean up that cut on Elmer's forehead." He went to his horse and fetched a small, silver flask from one of the saddlebags.

Elmer's eyes lit up at the sight of it. "I know you brung that good Scotch whiskey along strictly for medicinal purposes, Duff, but don't you reckon a little swig would be justified, under the circumstances? I mean, it'd settle my nerves and maybe help this poundin' in my head."

"A swallow, that's all," Duff said as he pulled the cork from the flask and handed it to Elmer, who took it and lifted it eagerly to his lips.

Duff allowed him to take a little more than a swallow, but then he gently disengaged the flask from the old-timer's grip and used the whiskey to wet a corner of his bandana. He used the cloth to wipe away the blood around the wound.

"'Tis not too bad," he said. "I think the lass must have fetched ye a glancing blow. 'Twas fortunate she did nae stove in your head."

"Well, it felt like that's what she done."

Duff carried a small amount of first-aid supplies in his saddlebags. He had some clean cloth he fashioned into a bandage, wrapping it around Elmer's head and tying it in place.

"I ain't gonna be able to wear a hat for days," the old-timer groused.

"I expect ye can. You'll just need to be careful putting it on." Duff asked Walter and Oliver if they had seen any signs of trouble.

They shook their heads, and Walter said, "We've been watching this end of the trail. From here, we can't see where it comes out at the base of the cliff, but it's visible higher up." He pointed to illustrate what he was saying. "And nobody's come along there. That's the only way in here."

"Aye. And the only way out."

Oliver said, "Do you think we might be able to climb over those rocks in the canyon, Mr. MacCallister? I mean, I know we can't take our horses that way, but if we had to, isn't that a possible escape route?"

Duff considered the suggestion and then nodded. "'Tis possible. 'Tis been long enough since the avalanche that the rocks should have settled by now and will nae be shifting around anymore. But if we were to do that, we'd still be a-foot and a long way from anywhere . . . except the Hardcastle stronghold."

"Oh," Oliver said. "Yeah, we'd still be in a pretty bad fix, right?"

"Indeed we would. Right now, our best bet still seems to be negotiating with the Hardcastles to let us leave the same way we came in."

From where she was tied up on the ground, Ginny said, "Cousin Willie'll never let you do that. You've invaded our home and attacked us. You're all gonna die. It's just a matter of time."

Duff saw the way Walter and Oliver paled slightly at the threat. He said, "Dinnae ye be so sure of that, lass. Your family may value your life more than you think they do."

"They'll know you won't kill me. And even if they thought you might, they still won't let you get away. Defendin' the family is more important than anything else."

"We'll see." Duff swung an arm toward the ridge a couple of hundred yards away. "For now, we'd best be about finding a good place to fort up. I'd thought to make camp here at the creek, but now I believe we need higher ground."

He went to Ginny's side, reached down to take hold of her, and lifted her to her feet, where she balanced precariously.

"Walter, bring your horse closer. Oliver, help me lift the lass."

"No!" Ginny cried. "You ain't puttin' me on the dirt-eater's horse! Anything but that!"

"Don't worry," Walter told her. "I won't bite you."

"I'm not worried about that," she fumed. "I'm just embarrassed to be seen on the same horse as a sodbustin', dirt-eatin' beanpole!"

"'Twill not be for long," Duff told her. He and Oliver got on either side of Ginny, took hold of her arms and legs, and lifted her so they could drape her facedown over the back of Walter's horse, directly in front of the saddle.

Walter grabbed hold of the waistband of her trousers with his left hand and rested the right, which also held the reins, between her shoulder blades. "I've got her," he told Duff and Oliver.

"You don't got anything," Ginny said through clenched teeth. "And you watch where you put them hands!"

"Be a gentleman, Walter," said Duff, trying not to grin.

"Sure," Walter agreed. "Even if she's not exactly a lady."

Climbing to his feet, Elmer shook his bandaged head gloomily and said, "Boy, you're just diggin' yourself a deeper hole. Whatever you say, you can bet a brand-new hat that gal ain't never gonna forget it!"

# CHAPTER 15

Della stiffened as she heard the distant shot. It came from the basin, she was sure of that. She reined in, and the other girls brought their mounts to a stop behind her.

"Did you hear that?" Lydia said. "Those dirty, no-good skunks just shot Ginny! They killed her!"

Della jerked her head around and snapped, "We don't know that. Maybe she got her hands on a gun and killed one of them."

Barely breathing, she waited for a flurry of more gun-shots that would signify an actual battle between Ginny and her would-be captors. Outnumbered four to one as she was, she might be able to down one of the varmints, maybe even two, but she wouldn't stand much of a chance against the whole bunch. One of them would get her, for sure.

But there were no more shots. Just the one, the echoes of which faded away quickly. Della heaved a sigh of relief. It was still possible something bad had happened to Ginny, but Della figured she stood more of a chance than if it had been the other way.

"Della, what do you reckon happened?" asked Patsy. "You really think it was Ginny who fired that shot?"

"I don't know," Della answered honestly. "But I still plan on finding out . . . *and* on getting her back safe and sound."

Lydia said, "You don't know if we can do that. She could be dead already."

"If she is, none of those men will ever get out of Longshot Basin alive."

"That's mighty big talk." Lydia's upper lip curled in a sneer. "But so far, that's all you've done, cousin. *Talk.*"

Della turned her horse and crowded it against Lydia's mount. Her left hand flashed up and cracked across the younger girl's right cheek. Lydia cried out in surprise and pain.

"I'll snatch you bald-headed if you talk to me like that again," Della said. She leaned closer, causing Lydia to flinch a little. "You understand me? I'm older than you, and I'm in charge here."

"Sure, I . . . I understand," Lydia said. "I'm sorry, Della."

"You better be." Della turned her horse again and pretended not to hear the curses Lydia muttered under her breath, since she had demonstrated she wasn't going to take any sass. Della didn't have to do anything else about it . . . yet.

But if Lydia continued being defiant, there might come a showdown between them, one of these days. Maybe today.

"Come on," Della said, kneeing her horse into motion again.

A few minutes later, they came to the narrow path that veered off the Nightmare Trail and climbed to the home place. Della called another halt and peered up that passage as she thought about what she ought to do next.

"We ought to go tell Cousin Willie what happened," Iris said. "And we left the other end of the trail without anybody watchin' it."

Iris wasn't a Hardcastle, at least by name; her mother had married a Peabody, who was only a cousin by marriage. She had Hardcastle blood, though. Problem was, it was thinned out considerable, which meant Iris tended to do what she was told and had a habit of wanting everybody to like and approve of her, instead of the usual Hardcastle attitude of figuring the whole world could go to hell.

"That would be a good job for you, Iris," Della decided. "You ride on up to the home place and break the news to Cousin Willie and the others. The rest of us will go on after that damn MacCallister and his friends."

A look of apprehension appeared on Iris's face. "Cousin Willie will be mad. Ferris and some of the others will be, too. You remember, Ferris didn't trust girls to stand watch. He'll say we proved him right."

"Not if we get Ginny away from those varmints and kill them," argued Della. "Yeah, we let the family down a little. That's why we've got to make it right."

Patsy spoke up. "I agree with Della."

"So do I," Junie added.

The others all looked at Lydia, the only one who hadn't weighed in on the subject. She scowled and said sullenly, "Yeah, I reckon we better go along with what Della says."

Lydia didn't like agreeing with her, thought Della, but even she knew it was the right thing to do in those circumstances.

"It's settled, then," Della said as she lifted her reins. "You go on up to the home place, Iris."

"Cousin Willie's gonna want to send some of the boys to help you," Iris warned.

"To take over, you mean. Tell him not to. The four of us can deal with the problem, can't we, girls?"

Lydia, Patsy, and Junie all nodded.

"I ain't *tellin'* Cousin Willie anything," said Iris. "He don't take kindly to havin' his decisions challenged."

"Well, just make sure he understands we got this situation under control."

Iris sighed. "I'll try. But that's all I can promise."

If that was the best she could do, Della would take it. She jabbed her boot heels into her horse's flanks, called, "Come on!" to the others, and headed on up the Nightmare Trail.

Elmer didn't like having to have assistance, but he was still shaky enough from the wallop on the head that Duff had to help him up into the saddle.

"Another swig or two of that Scotch might be enough of a bracer to get me back to normal," Elmer suggested once he was mounted.

"'Tis best we save as much of it as we can," said Duff. "In case we need it again for medicinal purposes, ye ken."

"Yeah, yeah, I reckon," Elmer grumbled.

After filling their canteens, the little group splashed across the creek and started toward the ridge. Ginny had given up on wriggling around and lay quietly across the back of Walter's mount. Tied as she was, she could keep her head up, so it was unlikely being carried that way would make her sick.

She wasn't happy, though. She said in a cold, bitter voice, "You fellas are gonna be sorry you ever rode up here. You should've just left us alone."

"It wasn't our idea to come to this part of the country," Walter told her. "Somebody in the land office in Cheyenne said we should settle in Longshot Basin. That's what the letter he sent to Uncle Waylon said."

"Well, if you'd had the sense God gave a goose, you could've asked around once you got to Chugwater and found out Longshot Basin ain't any place for sodbusters."

Duff said, "I had that very discussion with the leader of the group, lass. 'Tis determined they are this be the place for them."

"They're wrong," Ginny snapped.

Oliver said, "I still don't understand why you're so strongly opposed to us homesteading here. Your family doesn't use the basin. We're not going to bother you. We just want to be left alone to lead our lives."

"That's the way it always starts. But then you'll get all high and mighty and decide you can't have a family of no-good hillbillies livin' up on the mountain, and you'll try to run us off."

"I really don't think that would ever happen," Walter told her.

"You just don't know. Civilized folks always have to ruin things for everybody else. That's just the way it is."

Thinking back to his own wild highland ancestors, a small part of Duff could almost agree with her. But there was no stopping the spread of civilization and the rise of progress—if progress it truly was. People needed to learn how to deal with change. Things were never going to stop changing.

The ridge was fairly steep but rough enough the horses had no trouble picking their way to the top. It was fairly level for about fifty yards before falling off in another rugged slope. Duff led the group through a fairly thick stand of pines to a clearing. "This will be a good enough spot to camp. We can see for a good distance in all directions. 'Twill have to be a cold camp, I'm afraid. We dinnae want to announce our presence up here."

"We'll have to post a guard all night, too," Elmer said.

"Aye. But with three of us, that shouldn't be too hard."

"What do you mean, three? There's four of us, Elmer pointed out."

"Normally I would be counting on ye to take a shift, but not after that wallop on your head. Ye need your rest."

Elmer snorted. "Hogwash. My head hurts some, but it

ain't all that bad. I can carry my weight. Don't you doubt that for a second."

"I'm not doubting it, but head injuries are tricky things. I dinnae want to take a chance on it."

Elmer grumbled a little more, but he didn't press the argument. Duff and Oliver lifted Ginny down from Walter's horse. Duff loosened the section of rope connecting her wrists and ankles, and they were able to prop her up in a sitting position against one of the tree trunks. Then Duff looped the extra rope around the tree and tied it well out of Ginny's reach.

"You can't leave me like this," she said. "It ain't fair. My hands have already gone numb. I'm never gonna be able to use them again."

Walter said, "You mean you won't be able to try to kill someone, like you did with Mr. Gleason."

"I wasn't tryin' to kill him. I just wanted to knock him down and grab his gun."

"And if ye had succeeded, what would ye have used the weapon for, I'm wondering?" asked Duff.

Ginny glared at him. "I would've shot you."

"Aye, that seemed to be your intention." Duff's voice became brisk with command. "Walter, tend to the horses, but leave mine saddled. Oliver, take your rifle, stay at the edge of the trees where you'll be mostly out of sight, and keep an eye on the trail. Elmer, sit down on that log over there and take it easy."

Ginny said, "And what are you gonna do, big man? Torture your poor, defenseless girl prisoner?"

"Defenseless?" repeated Walter. "Ha!"

Duff said, "Before it gets dark I'll take a ride up to Thunder Canyon and find out exactly what the situation is there. 'Twouldn't hurt to know."

"I'll watch the gal and make sure she don't get up to any

mischief," Elmer said from the log where he had sat down. "I can manage that much, anyway."

"We'll see about that, you old pelican," Ginny snarled at him. "We'll just see."

Elmer frowned. "Don't you ever get tired of bein' unfriendly?"

"Why would I ever want to be friendly with a flea-bitten old mossback like you?"

Duff left them wrangling and went to explore more of Longshot Basin while there was still some light.

Once he had ridden a trail or explored a place, Duff had a good memory for where he had been, so he didn't have any trouble finding the northern end of Thunder Canyon. The sun was low enough in the western sky gloom was filling the canyon between its sheer rocky walls.

When it had been open all the way, Thunder Canyon had run about half a mile through the rugged tableland. Duff had covered only a couple of hundred yards when he began to see the beginnings of the avalanche's aftermath. As he weaved his way through the piles of smaller rocks, they became taller and the chunks of stone larger. The gaps between them narrowed. Finally, the fallen rock became an impenetrable wall that rose forty or fifty feet above him as he reined in and studied it in the gathering shadows.

A man could indeed get out of the basin this way, as Oliver had suggested. It would take a pretty agile hombre, but it could be done, climbing from rock to rock and then, once atop the barrier, jumping from one boulder to another.

Doing it would be pretty dangerous, though. The rocks had settled and weren't likely to shift, but some might be perched precariously enough it could happen. If a man slipped down into a gap and then the rocks moved . . .

Duff didn't like to think about what kind of shape a luckless fellow would wind up in. It wouldn't be pretty.

Satisfied he had learned all he could from his reconnaissance, he backed his horse until he had room to turn the animal around and then headed out of the canyon, toward the ridge where Elmer and the others were waiting.

Overhead, the sky was shading to deep blue. It wouldn't be long until the stars began to pop out.

Della raised a hand to signal a halt, then said, "We'd better wait here for a spell."

"Why would we want to do that?" Lydia asked. "Those varmints still have Ginny. There's no tellin' what they might be doin' to her!"

"If they haven't hurt her already, they're not going to. MacCallister's been around these parts for a while. He's got a big ranch, and folks think he's an upstanding sort. He wouldn't take advantage of a woman. He wouldn't want to risk his friends findin' out about it."

Lydia snorted. "You sound mighty sure about that."

"I'm older than you," Della said, narrowing her eyes at her cousin. "I know more about men than you do."

Lydia glared at her in the gathering dusk. "Well, what about the other three?"

"That old-timer's full of bluster, but he seemed a decent sort. And I'm betting the two younger ones are too scared of Ginny to try anything."

"You're doin' a lot of betting, but you're not the one who'll lose if you're wrong."

Patsy spoke up. "You ought to give Della the benefit of the doubt, Lydia. Like she said, she's the oldest."

"Oldest don't mean smartest," snapped Lydia.

"That's true," Della allowed. "But for now, I'm in charge

of this bunch, and I say we wait here for a little while. The sun's down and it won't take long for night to fall. They won't be able to see us if they're keeping watch from down in the basin."

The women were in the cut between the mountainside on the left and the rocky shoulder that rose on the right. Not far ahead, the Nightmare Trail dropped down into Longshot Basin. Della wanted to take their quarry by surprise, and they couldn't do that if the men saw them coming.

MacCallister had a reputation as a canny one, and a good fighter. He'd be expecting trouble. He would have found a place to fort up, and he would be standing guard or having one of the others do it.

But Della had grown up on Buzzard's Roost and spent hundreds of hours exploring Longshot Basin. She knew her way around better than MacCallister ever could.

Hardcastle females weren't encouraged to wear dresses and play with rag dolls. Some did, of course, but some, such as Della, had been able to ride almost before they could walk, and as they grew up, learned to handle ropes and guns and horses as well as any of their brothers and male cousins did.

Because of that, she had hunted all over Longshot Basin. Cole had taught her to shoot, and although she would never be able to match his speed and accuracy, she was a better than fair hand with pistol and rifle, and liked to think her nerves were cool and steady.

The only real way to test that was in a fight, and Della had never been in a serious gun battle. She believed she would acquit herself well if it came to that . . . but there was only way to actually *know* she would, and that was to live through it. To smell the powder smoke and hear the bullets whipping past her and come out the other side of that baptism of fire.

The four young women dismounted to let their horses rest while they waited. Della listened intently but didn't hear any more sounds coming from Longshot Basin. Quite a while had passed since that single gunshot. Despite the confidence she had displayed, she was worried about Ginny.

Finally, the heavens faded from deep blue to black. Millions of stars appeared, casting enough silvery light for Della to see the trail in front of her. She took hold of her horse's reins and said quietly to the others, "Come on. Lead your horses, and take it slow and easy. We don't want to make a lot of racket and warn MacCallister and the others, and we sure don't want to fall off the trail."

"I sure hope Ginny's all right," muttered Lydia as she fell in behind Della. "It's takin' us too damned long to find her and rescue her from those no-good sons o'—"

"We'll find her," Della cut in. "MacCallister probably made camp not far from the bottom of the trail. In fact, I know a good place pretty close, and it wouldn't surprise me a bit if that's where they went. We'll check there first."

"And if they're there?" Lydia pressed. "How do you figure on playin' this, Della?"

"We get Ginny away from them first," said Della. Her voice hardened as she added, "After that . . . all bets are off. It was their choice to ride into Hardcastle country. Shoot to kill."

# CHAPTER 16

Meagan Parker locked the front door of her dress shop from the outside. She had stayed late to finish a dress she was working on but had promised to stop by Vi's Pies for supper and a visit with Violet Winslow. The café was close, so it wouldn't take long to get there.

Despite that, Meagan paused on the boardwalk to take a good look around. Ever since Benjy Hardcastle had invaded her living quarters, she had been a bit more cautious in her general attitude toward her surroundings. Not frightened, really; Meagan wasn't the sort to get spooked by much of anything. Just . . . careful.

Not only that, but the .32 caliber Smith & Wesson double-action was nestled in the bag she carried. If Benjy showed up to menace her again, she would be ready for him. She wouldn't hesitate to use the gun.

She didn't see anything unusual as she looked along Clay Avenue, Chugwater's main thoroughfare. Matthews Mercantile was still open, light spilling out through its front door over the high porch and loading dock where a couple of farmers' wagons were tied up. R.W. Guthrie's Building Supply and Freight Company was still doing business, too, and of course Fiddler's Green, the Wild Hog Saloon, and the City Café had horses tied at the hitch racks in front of them, as well. A couple of men plodded along on horseback, and pedestrians strolled here and there. Nothing out of the ordinary for early evening in Chugwater.

Satisfied with her survey of the town, Meagan turned toward Vi's Pies, where the windows were lit up with a warm, cheery yellow glow from inside.

She paused as she heard a low, rumbling sound. Could that be thunder, she wondered? Not likely, since the sky had been clear all day except for a few tiny white clouds floating here and there. Meagan didn't think there had been time for a storm to move in since sunset.

Holding her bag in her left hand and her right close to the opening at the top so she could reach in and wrap her fingers around the Smith & Wesson's grips if she needed to, she listened to the rumbling grow louder. She recognized it. Those were hoofbeats she was hearing. The hoofbeats of a fairly large number of horses.

The glow from numerous windows illuminated Clay Avenue well enough for Meagan to see the group of riders as they reached the far end of the street. The mounted men came on steadily, not slowing until they neared the center of town.

The man slightly in the lead raised a hand and the others reined in, almost in unison. They stayed where they were, some of the horses pawing a little at the ground, while the leader walked his horse slowly forward and angled toward the left side of the street.

Meagan stiffened as she realized the man had spotted *her* and was riding right toward her. She thought about turning and walking quickly to Vi's Pies but didn't want to be rude so she stayed where she was. But she *did* allow her hand to stray into the bag. The hard touch of the revolver's butt was reassuring.

Although approximately twenty hard-bitten looking

strangers were sitting their horses in the middle of Clay Avenue that little .32 caliber popgun wouldn't mean much if they had come to Chugwater looking for trouble.

She shouldn't be getting ahead of herself like that, thought Meagan. Just because they were unshaven and covered with trail dust didn't mean the newcomers meant any harm. They'd been riding hard for a while, obviously, but they might be just passing through on their way somewhere else.

As the leader brought his horse to a stop in front of her, Meagan figured she was about to find out.

He nodded and pinched his hat brim politely as he smiled. "Ma'am, would this charming settlement happen to be Chugwater?"

Well, so much for the hope they were just passing through, she thought. "Yes, it is." Since he hadn't asked anything else, she didn't volunteer anything.

"My name is Kingman," he said. "Thomas Kingman. *Major* Thomas Kingman."

"Major," Meagan said, nodding. He seemed to be waiting for more of a response, and her natural politeness wouldn't allow her to ignore that. "My name is Meagan Parker."

"Mrs. Parker?"

"Miss."

"It's an honor and a pleasure to meet you, Miss Parker."

Thomas Kingman had given his rank as major, but he wasn't wearing an army uniform. Like his companions, he was dressed in civilian garb. In Kingman's case, it was gray trousers tucked into high-topped black boots, a black coat over a pin-striped shirt, and a flat-crowned black hat. He wore a holstered revolver with plain walnut grips.

The other men were a mixture of types. Most sported

range clothing like cowboys, but a few in tweed suits and derby hats looked like they would be more at home in a city.

All were armed, most with one gun but some with two, and Meagan saw rifle butts sticking up from sheaths strapped to their saddles.

She was keen-eyed and quick-witted and took in all of that with a glance. More than once, gangs of outlaws had ridden into Chugwater, bent on robbery, destruction, and murder. At first, she had thought these strangers might be the same, but she revised that opinion—or at least reserved judgment on it—as she realized, like Thomas Kingman, all the men were middle-aged and had a weary look about them, as if they had been riding for a long time and were worn out. She saw none of the hotblooded young firebrands who gravitated toward owlhoot gangs.

Of course, that was no guarantee of anything. They could still be bent on trouble. However, Meagan didn't allow any of the apprehension she felt creep into her voice as she asked, "What brings you to Chugwater, Mr. Kingman?"

"Major Kingman," he reminded her.

His friendly smile was meant to take any sting out of the correction, she thought.

He went on. "I suppose that's a bit of an affectation of mine. I haven't been an actual major for quite some time. Not since the end of the Late Unpleasantness, to be precise. Still, old habits die hard, especially when they're engrained in a man by the stress of combat."

He was well-spoken, obviously well-educated, as so many officers in the war had been. Meagan had been too young at the time of that great conflict to remember anything about it, but she had heard Elmer Gleason and Biff Johnson speak of it often enough, both men being careful to gloss over the more unpleasant details of their service.

"As for what brings us to Chugwater, Miss Parker,"

Kingman continued. "We're looking for some acquaintances of ours. Do you know if a party of immigrants has passed through here in recent weeks? Most of them with the last name . . . Spencer?"

The shadows were thick as Duff approached the camp on top of the ridge, and he wasn't surprised when he heard Oliver call out, "Who's that? Don't come any closer!"

Not wanting the youngster to spook and pull the trigger, Duff reined in immediately and replied in a low but clear voice, "'Tis me, Oliver. Duff MacCallister."

"Oh." Oliver sounded a little ashamed of himself. "Come ahead, Mr. MacCallister."

As Duff walked his horse forward, Oliver stepped out from behind a tree and pointed the rifle he was holding toward the ground. "I didn't mean to do anything wrong," he said.

"And just what is it ye think ye did wrong?" Duff wanted to know. "Ye were protecting the camp, just as I charged ye with doing. Seems to me ye were just doing your job."

"Well . . . thanks. I've been trying to keep a good watch."

"Any sign of trouble?"

"Not one. It's almost like nobody else is around for a hundred miles."

"Aye, it may seem like that, but 'tis not the case. Those Hardcastles may not have tried anything yet, but they're not far off, ye can be certain of that."

"I won't let down my guard," promised Oliver.

"I know ye won't. I'm going to check on Elmer and the others now."

"I'll be here," Oliver declared.

Duff rode on. A few minutes later he came to the clearing where the others were. Full night had fallen, but the

stars provided enough illumination for Duff to see Walter
and Elmer as they stood up to greet him.

"What did you find?" Elmer asked as Duff swung down
from the saddle. "Is the canyon blocked as completely as it
looks like from the other side?"

"Aye. As Oliver suggested earlier, a man might be able
to climb out over the rockslide, although he'd be risking his
life to do it. No wagons or horses will be going through
there for a long time, if ever." He unsaddled his horse and
tied the animal where it could graze, then went on. "I talked
to Oliver. He said there'd been no trouble."

Duff nodded meaningfully toward the tree where Ginny
was tied. His eyes had adjusted to the darkness and he could
make out the way she sat with her head slumped forward,
as if she were asleep.

"It's been quiet," Walter said, then added, "Eventually."

"I heard that, dirt-eater," Ginny said, proving she hadn't
dozed off after all. She lifted her head and went on. "You
deserve every cuss word I've thrown at you."

"Why?" asked Walter. "Just because I want my family to
have a home?"

"Because you want to take away *my* family's home."

"But that's what's so loco about this whole thing. We
don't! I mean . . . sure, your family may have a reputation
as, well, being on the wrong side of the law, but that's none
of our business. We'd rather just live and let live."

"You say that now," Ginny muttered, "but it wouldn't
stay that way."

"How do you know, if you never give us a chance?"

Ginny turned her head away and didn't say anything.

After a moment, Elmer told Walter, "You're wastin' your
time, son. You ain't ever gonna talk sense to any of that
Hardcastle bunch."

Walter sighed and nodded. "I'm starting to think you're right, Mr. Gleason. It's like arguing with a stone wall."

Duff asked, "Have ye eaten anything?"

"We were waitin' for you to get back." Elmer went to the saddles, which had been placed on the ground after being taken off the horses, and started digging in the saddlebags.

"How's your head doing?" Duff asked him.

"Still hurts a mite, but not bad." Elmer straightened with a couple of bags in his hands. One held biscuits Wang had packed, it turned out, and the other contained jerky. It was extremely simple fare, but it would serve to keep their bellies from getting too empty.

"We got coffee, too," Elmer said, "but can't boil it up if we don't have a fire."

"We can make do one night without coffee," Duff said.

"Be easier with a swig or two from that flask."

Duff laughed. "Ye dinnae give up easily, do you, old friend?"

"Ain't in the habit of it." Elmer sighed. "But I don't want to be like ol' Pinky Jenkins, neither, always tryin' to cadge drinks from folks. We got plenty of water in our canteens to wash down these vittles."

Walter took one of the biscuits and hunkered on his heels in front of Ginny. "Here, I've got something for you to eat."

She lifted her head again. "Yeah? And how in hell am I supposed to eat anything when my hands are tied behind my back?"

"I can hold this biscuit for you, and you can take bites out of it."

"It'll be a cold day in hell before I do that, dirt-eater."

"But you must be hungry—"

"I wouldn't tell you if I was! Not if my stomach shriveled up to the size of a bean! Just get away from me."

"You're the most frustrating girl I ever met," Walter told her.

"An ugly string bean like you probably ain't ever been around girls much. If you were, they'd just laugh in your face."

"Have it your own way," Walter snapped as he straightened to his feet and turned away. He shook his head and blew an exasperated breath through his teeth.

Hearing Elmer chuckle quietly, Duff realized he was having a hard time not laughing, too. The situation in which they found themselves might be pretty serious overall, even dangerous, but the continued wrangling between Walter and Ginny was amusing. No denying that.

After they had finished their sparse meal, Elmer took a strip of jerky and a canteen over to the tree where Ginny was tied and gave it a try. "You ought to take a drink, anyway. Ain't no point in makin' yourself sick just 'cause you got took prisoner."

"Untie my hands and I'll eat and drink," she said. "Unless you're willin' to do that, go to hell."

"Duff, what do you think?"

"We'll risk it," Duff decided. "Stay at arm's reach away from her and I'll untie her wrists." He had to work by feel as he knelt beside the tree where Ginny was tied, but he had fashioned the knots to start with and had a deft touch. A length of rope went around her midsection and was still secured to the tree, so she couldn't really go anywhere.

When he freed her wrists, she pulled her arms back in front of her and started massaging her hands as best she could. A little whimper of pain escaped from her lips, which made Duff feel worse about what had happened. Of course, it could be just an act she was putting on, he warned himself, designed to play on his guilt and maybe open up some opportunity for her to escape. He wasn't going to let that happen.

She grabbed the canteen when Elmer extended it to her, took a long swallow of water, then accepted the strip of jerky. With strong teeth, she tore off a hunk and started chewing it, then said around the tough, dried meat, "I could use one of them biscuits, too, if the dirt-eater ain't gobbled 'em all down."

"Don't you get tired of using the same insult over and over again?" Walter asked her.

"Oh, there are plenty of other things I can call you," she shot back at him. Then her voice was a little softer as she added, "But gimme one of them biscuits, and I won't bother for now."

Walter took the biscuit over and held it out to her, staying far enough back all she could do was take it from him by stretching out her arm as far as it would go.

She laughed and said, "Look at you. Nearly a full-grown man, and you're scared of a girl. All of you are. Big, tough frontiersmen, you three are."

"We might trust ye more," said Duff, "if ye had acted the least bit trustworthy."

"Instead, you done your dadgum best to kill me," Elmer added.

Ginny just ate the biscuit and jerky and then asked for another drink from the canteen. Duff was about to give it to her when a hurried footstep sounded nearby. He straightened and turned, his hand dropping to the Colt on his hip.

Panting a little, Oliver came into the clearing quickly. "Fellas, it sounds like somebody's comin'!"

# CHAPTER 17

Knowing she was playing a hunch, Della led the other three girls toward the ridge that bulked ahead of them in the darkness. If she'd been looking for some place near the end of the Nightmare Trail that could be defended against possible pursuers, that ridge was where she would have gone. It was the closest high ground, the trees provided plenty of cover, and it commanded a good view in both directions.

The moon wouldn't be up for a while yet, meaning MacCallister and his friends wouldn't be able to see very well. Della counted on stealth to do the rest of the work and allow her and the others to approach near enough to hit their quarry before any of the men knew what was happening.

Even though she was confident her plan would work, Della winced a little every time a bit chain rattled or a horse stomped down a little too hard. It was next to impossible to lead horses through the night without them making *some* noise.

Near the foot of the ridge Della reached back to stop Lydia, who was following her. Lydia, in turn, stopped Patsy, who stopped Junie.

Della whispered for them to gather close around her, so they could hear. "We're gonna leave the horses here and go the rest of the way without them."

"What if we need to get away in a hurry?" asked Lydia.

"They'll still be close by. Anyway, there's no way we can take them up that slope in the dark without makin' so much noise people in Chugwater would hear us comin'."

"You don't even know for sure that bunch is up there."

Della heard the challenge in her cousin's voice. Lydia hadn't forgotten that slap from earlier. She likely never would, unless she got the chance to even the score. Well, Della might just give her that chance, one of these days, but it wasn't the time.

"Maybe they're not," she said. "If that's how it turns out, we'll look somewhere else. But if they *are* there, I don't want to give them a lot of warning and then go waltzin' right into a bunch of bullets."

Patsy whispered, "We'll do whatever you say, Della. What's the plan?"

"We'll go up the ridge as quiet as we can, then split up, two going one way and two the other. Stay low, don't make any noise, and listen for voices or horses movin' around or anything else that'll tip off the location of their camp. If you find them, back off and come back to the spot where we split up. We'll rendezvous there in an hour, whether we've found them or not."

A moment of silence went by.

Then Lydia said sullenly, "Fine. We'll do it that way. Sounds like it might even work. Who goes with who?"

"You're comin' with me," Della answered without hesitation. She didn't fully trust Lydia and wanted to keep her close. It wouldn't have surprised Della if Lydia argued with that decision, but the younger girl didn't say anything.

Della went on. "For now, all three of you stay right here with the horses. Tie 'em to some bushes or saplings so they can't wander off."

"What are you gonna do?" asked Patsy.

"Just scout ahead a little, maybe find the best route up the ridge. I've been here plenty of times, but it's been a while since the last time." Della pulled her Winchester from its saddle boot.

Cradling the rifle against her as she catfooted forward in the darkness, she felt her heart slugging hard in her chest and heard her pulse booming inside her head. She told herself she wasn't afraid. Hardcastles didn't know fear. They just forged ahead and did what needed to be done.

She hadn't worked out yet just what they would do if they found MacCallister's camp. Maybe stage some kind of distraction to get the men's attention and draw them off while she or one of the others slipped into the camp and freed Ginny.

It might even work out they could ambush the men without Ginny being in the line of fire. If that happened, they could cut down MacCallister and his friends before knowing they were in danger.

Of course, that would be cold-blooded murder, Della reminded herself. She had never killed a man, let alone shot one down from concealment.

As she had told her cousins, the men had brought their fate on themselves by riding up the Nightmare Trail in the first place. Whatever happened to them, they had it coming.

And maybe, just maybe, the next time some of the Hardcastle men rode out to rob a bank or hold up a train, they would take her with them. There was no reason she couldn't be an outlaw, too, Della told herself. She'd have blood on her hands . . . *She would have proven herself.*

That thought was so strong in her mind she was taken completely unaware when an arm snaked around her waist from behind and a hand clamped hard over her mouth.

\* \* \*

Cole told himself to take it easy. This was his own sister he had just grabbed, not some saloon gal. He didn't want to hurt her. As Della twisted and writhed in his grasp, he leaned his head forward, put his lips close to her left ear, and whispered, "Dang it, Della, stop fighting. It's Cole. I'm not gonna hurt you."

She went still, although she was still breathing hard from fright and exertion.

Cole waited a moment, then told her, "I'm gonna take my hand away from your mouth. Don't yell, all right?"

She jerked her head in a small nod.

Cole moved his hand and said, "You know who I am, right?"

"Yeah," she whispered back.

"So there's no reason for you to fight if I let go of you."

"I won't fight, Cole."

"Good. I'll whop you one if that's what it takes to settle you down. Don't think I won't." He stepped back a little to put some space between them as Della turned around.

In the thick darkness, he couldn't see her face very well, but he heard the irritation in her voice as she said, "You scared me out of ten years' growth! Why'd you grab me like that?"

"To keep you from hollering and warning whoever you're after that we're here. You and those other gals *are* tryin' to sneak up on somebody, aren't you?"

"Yeah," Della admitted with a sullen resentment in her tone. "And we would have done it, too, if you hadn't come along. Still will, if you'll just leave us alone."

"Answer me one question. Where's Ginny?"

Della hesitated for a second, then said, "MacCallister's got her."

"Duff MacCallister?"

"That's right. Him and that old-timer who runs with him

and a couple of sodbuster boys rode up the Nightmare Trail earlier. We tried to stop them, but they managed to ride off with Ginny as a hostage."

"They're here in the basin?"

Della nodded. "That's right."

In the back of his mind, Cole had figured something like that must have happened. Hearing the single shot that had sounded like it came from Longshot Basin, he had ridden in that direction to have a look around. Since nobody else at the home place seemed to have noticed the shot, he hadn't said anything or asked any of the others to come with him. He was confident whatever he found he could handle without any help.

Before he reached the spot where the trail started down into the basin, he had heard riders coming up behind him and had hidden in the rocks to see who they were. His sister Della and his cousins Lydia, Patsy, and Junie came up a short time later, reined in, and appeared to be waiting for darkness to fall. Cole wasn't close enough to overhear their conversation, but he could tell they were upset about something.

Ginny wasn't with them, so it was pretty easy to figure out she was involved in the trouble, whatever it was. Cole hoped she hadn't been hurt. He wasn't really close to anybody in the family except Della and Benjy, but he was a Hardcastle. Family loyalty was more important to him than almost anything else.

He had considered confronting Della and the others then and there, but he'd decided to wait and see what they were going to do. When they started down into the basin, he had given them enough of a lead so they wouldn't notice him and then followed them. They hadn't paid any attention to their back trail, which wasn't surprising considering their inexperience at such things and the fact they were girls.

When Della had started skulking around in the shadows by herself, he'd seen enough. It was time to find out what was going on. He had grabbed her, and in hasty, whispered conversation, he got the story out her. He felt a surge of anger at hearing a Hardcastle girl had been carried off as a prisoner, but at the same time, it sounded like MacCallister was trying to get out of the mess he and his friends had found themselves in without anybody getting hurt.

"You say there's a whole bunch of those sodbusters?" he asked Della.

"That's right. I don't know how many, exactly. But a big bunch of them, all related." She paused. "Kind of like us, I reckon."

"Except Hardcastles ain't sodbusters," Cole said dryly. "We haven't grubbed in the dirt since we left Arkansas, and that's the way it's gonna stay."

"Damn right. But that don't matter right now. We've got to get Ginny—"

"Ginny's fine," he interrupted her.

"How in blazes do you know that?" Della asked with a note of defiance in her voice.

"Because I've heard a heap about Duff MacCallister, and more than that, I've looked into the man's eyes. I'm not afraid of him, but I'd avoid a fight with him if I could. And I know he's not the sort to hurt a girl. He bluffed you, Della, plain and simple."

"I was afraid of that," she muttered, "but I didn't want to take a chance with Ginny's life."

"And you were right not to. Now we've got to figure out what to do next."

"I thought maybe we'd try some kind of distraction to draw off MacCallister and the others, so we can slip into the camp and get her loose. Either that, or . . . well . . . ambush them."

Even though it was probably too dark for her to see him, Cole shook his head. "You don't want to do that. You don't want cold-blooded murder on your conscience."

"I'm a Hardcastle," Della said, her voice getting hot with anger. "We don't give a damn about—"

"Trust me, you would. You'd give a damn about it, all right. Anyway, I don't think you could take MacCallister by surprise and it ain't likely he'd fall for any trick you might try to pull." Cole paused, thought for a moment, and sighed. "No, there's only one way to settle this."

"What's that?"

"We're gonna let them go."

"What did ye hear?" Duff asked Oliver after the young man hurried into camp.

"Horses, I think. It sounded like they were down below somewhere. I heard a little jingling noise, like the metal on harnesses, and maybe a hoofbeat or two."

Elmer said, "They're gonna try to slip up on us like Injuns, Duff. Only they ain't Injuns."

Duff heard a sharp intake of breath and looked around toward the tree where Ginny was tied. His instincts told him she was about to scream a warning to her cousins. Seeing Walter was the only one close to her, Duff snapped, "Walt, keep the girl quiet!"

Walter lunged at Ginny and went to his knees beside her. He clapped his hand to her open mouth and shut off the outcry before it could escape.

That brought his holstered gun within her reach, and her hands hadn't been tied again after she finished eating. Her left hand shot out and jerked the revolver from its holster.

Already moving, Duff kicked the gun out of her hand before she could pull the trigger.

She made a muffled sound of pain as the Colt flew out of her fingers. Clenching her other hand into a fist, she hammered it at Walter's head. He hunched his shoulders and hung on, absorbing the punishment she dealt out.

Duff moved behind the tree and reached around to grab Ginny's arms, pulling them back far enough to hold both her wrists in one hand while he used the other to tie her again, in what he feared was a more uncomfortable position.

It couldn't be helped, though.

He took his bandana from his pocket and wadded it into a ball, then told Walter to take his hand away from Ginny's mouth and Duff forced the gag between her lips before she could make a sound.

"Use your bandana to fasten it in place, lad," he told Walter, who followed the order as quickly as he could, even though it was awkward working in the dark. They managed to get it done without either of them losing a finger.

"Remember what I was sayin' about that wildcat, Duff?" Elmer asked.

"Aye, I thought of that very thing earlier. 'Tis a very apt comparison, I'm thinking."

With Ginny secured again and unable to cry out, Duff and Walter rejoined Elmer and Oliver near the edge of the trees.

Knowing Elmer's hearing was still extremely sharp despite his age, Duff whispered, "D' ye hear anything down there?"

"Yeah, the kid's right. I heard a horse or two. They're tryin' to sneak up on us, all right. If they figure on jumpin' us, they'll be in for a mighty big surprise . . . and an unwelcome one at that."

Duff's jaw tightened. The last thing in the world he wanted was a gun battle with the Hardcastles, especially a bunch of Hardcastle girls. The survey of Longshot Basin had been meant to be a peaceful mission, but it seemed as if that aim had been thwarted every step of the way.

"Don't start shooting unless they give us no other choice," he told his three companions. "I'd still like to try talking some sense into their heads."

"It ain't worked with that one back yonder," Elmer pointed out as he nodded toward Ginny. "I ain't holdin' out much hope—"

"MacCallister! Hey, MacCallister, you hear me?"

The shout that came up the slope to their ears took all four of them by surprise. The person who had hailed Duff was a man. Duff thought the voice was vaguely familiar.

"You gonna answer him?" whispered Elmer. "He might be tryin' to get you to pinpoint yourself, so's he can aim better."

"Aye," Duff replied. "But we can aim at the sound of his voice, too."

"Maybe it's a trick," Oliver suggested. "Some sort of distraction."

Duff considered that possibility.

Before he could reach a decision, the voice went on. "In case you don't remember me, this is Cole Hardcastle, MacCallister. I'm playin' square with you, I give you my word on that."

"Man's a known gunman and killer," Elmer said. "I don't know if you can trust him, Duff."

"I dinnae ken, either," Duff said, "but there be only one way to find out." Staying behind the cover of a tree trunk, he lifted his voice. "I hear ye, Hardcastle. What do ye want?"

"Just to talk, that's all. Hold your fire and let us come up there."

"Us?" repeated Duff.

"My sister Della and me. We both got things to say to you."

"And ye'll leave your guns down there where you are now?"

Cole laughed. "I think you know that ain't gonna happen, MacCallister. I feel plumb nekkid any time I'm not packing iron, and there are all these girls around. I'll swear to you, if anybody starts the ball, it won't be us."

"You'll be covered the whole way."

"Wouldn't expect any less."

Duff thought it over for a few more seconds, then called, "All right. The two of ye can come up. But if this is a trick, you'll be sorry ye tried to pull it."

"No tricks. Honest."

Elmer said, "I sure as blazes hope you know what you're doin', Duff."

"Aye, so do I." Duff lifted his Winchester to his shoulder and pointed it in the direction of the sounds he heard as someone approached up the ridge.

A few moments later, one figure appeared at the top of the slope, followed by a second one.

"That's far enough," Duff told them.

The first shape lifted his hands to elbow height and said, "Easy, MacCallister." Unmistakably, that was Cole Hardcastle, his voice dry and seemingly amused. "You can see my hands are empty. I'm not reachin' for a gun, and neither is my sister."

Della moved up alongside Cole in the starlight and followed his example, displaying open and empty hands.

"All right, Hardcastle, I see the two of ye. Speak your piece."

"First of all," Cole's tone grew serious, "is my cousin Ginny all right? Has she come to any harm? That's gonna go a long way toward determining how this conversation is gonna turn out."

"The lass is fine. I'll give *ye* my word on that. She's tied and gagged at the moment. I'll apologize for subjecting her to such discomfort and indignity, but she did try to kill my friend Elmer."

"Walloped me in the head with a rock," Elmer put in.

Cole chuckled. "Can't say as I'm surprised. Ginny always has been a bit of a spitfire. But if you say she's all right, MacCallister, I'll take your word for it. I've heard considerable about you, but never that you were a liar."

"Now that we've established the lass's condition, what else do ye want to know?"

"What'll it take to end this little standoff without any bloodshed?"

The question took Duff by surprise. "Is that what you're suggesting? All we've heard so far is we're all going to die for invading the Hardcastle domain."

"Well, it's true we don't care much for folks riding the Nightmare Trail and poking around Buzzard's Roost. Some of the family take it so unkind they might commence to shooting, but I don't reckon you and your friends meant any harm."

"That we did not," Duff replied. "Since you've talked to the lass with you, I suspect ye already ken we were simply checking out the condition of the trail."

"So you can bring a bunch of sodbusters in wagons over it."

"Longshot Basin does nae belong to your family. The Spencers have every right to homestead there. Would ye be so opposed to the idea if Thunder Canyon was still open and they did nae have to use the Nightmare Trail to reach the basin?"

Cole hesitated before replying, as if he had to think about

the question. Finally, he said, "That don't make any difference. We're not neighborly folks. Hardcastles don't like being crowded."

Walter spoke up. "We don't have any intention of crowding you, Mr. Hardcastle. We just want to be left alone to grow our crops."

"Who are you, boy?" Cole shot back.

"Walter Spencer, sir."

Duff would have preferred to keep this discussion between him and Cole, but he couldn't blame Walter for wanting to join in. It was the fate of Walter's family at stake, after all.

"How many of you are there?"

Walter glanced over at Duff, who nodded for him to answer. "Eight wagons, sir, and about thirty souls, all related. We're not troublemakers, Mr. Hardcastle, I promise you. We just want to make our homes in the basin and get along with everybody."

He certainly sounded sincere, thought Duff. Whether that would be enough to convince Cole, he didn't know. And even if Cole believed what Walter was saying, Duff wasn't sure it would make any difference in the long run.

At the moment, the short run was his primary concern, which meant getting out of the basin and back to Sky Meadow without a lot of bloodshed and death.

A few tense moments went by.

Duff heard Cole and Della whispering to each other but couldn't make out anything they were saying.

Finally, Cole turned to face the trees again and said, "Here's what we'll do, MacCallister. Turn Ginny over to us, and you and your friends can ride out."

"Turn the lass over and nothing be stopping ye from wiping us out, ye mean."

"Come on, MacCallister," Cole said, sounding amused

again. "We all know you're not going to hurt Ginny. That whole business about using her as a hostage was just a bluff. I can understand why you don't want to let her go. Tell you what . . . I'll take her place."

"Cole!" exclaimed Della. "What—"

He stopped her with a sharp word and then addressed Duff again. "How about it? Swap me for Ginny, and I'll ride with you all the way back over the Nightmare Trail. With me along, none of the rest of my family will bother you. Della will carry the word to them they're to leave you alone, that you and I have an agreement. Sounds fair, don't it?"

"And if this is some sort of double cross?"

"Well, then, I reckon you can shoot *me*. That wouldn't bother you near as much as if it was Ginny, would it?"

"Nae, 'twould not." Duff made up his mind. The risk seemed worth running to him. "All right. Keep your hands up and come ahead. Ye'll have to turn your weapons over to us until we're well away from Buzzard's Roost."

"Sure, I expected that much."

Cole ambled forward, keeping his hands lifted in plain sight.

"I hope you know what you're doin', Duff," said Elmer. "I know I said it before, but I still mean it."

"Aye, and 'tis still my hope as well," Duff agreed.

# CHAPTER 18

Duff waited until Cole Hardcastle came closer, then said, "Elmer, get his gun. Hardcastle, I'll have me rifle pointed at ye the whole time."

"I'll save you the trouble." Cole reached across his body with his left hand and carefully pulled his Colt from its holster. He extended it to Elmer butt-first. Then he bent slightly and slid a knife from its sheath inside his right boot. He handed that to Elmer as well, then took a two-shot derringer from his vest pocket and passed that over, too.

"Armed for bear, ain't you?" Elmer commented.

"You can check me over if you want, old-timer, and make sure I don't have any other hide-out guns."

"Reckon I'll do that very thing." Quickly, Elmer patted up and down Cole's lean body and then reported to Duff he didn't find any other weapons.

Duff said, "Walter, go back and free the lass from her bonds."

"Are you sure, Mr. MacCallister?" Walter sounded nervous. "She's liable to, uh, try to settle the score . . ."

Cole raised his voice a little and said, "Ginny, you leave this young fella alone, you hear? He's gonna turn you loose. Don't try to jump him or anything like that."

A few muffled noises came from the direction of the tree where Ginny was tied and gagged.

Cole chuckled and said to Walter, "I tried, young fella, but I'd keep a close eye on her if I was you."

Della said, "I can go help—"

"Stay right where ye are," Duff told her. "We dinnae want to put too much temptation for a double cross in your path, lass."

Della didn't say anything, and didn't budge from where she was.

A tense few minutes later, Ginny came stomping through the trees, trailed by Walter. Her gait was a little unsteady since she had been tied up for so long.

Della hurried forward to meet her and gripped her arm. "Are you all right?"

"Yeah, I reckon." Ginny practically spat, "They roughed me up some!"

"Now, is that strictly true?" Cole asked. "Or did they just do what they had to in order to make you behave?"

Della snapped, "What the hell is wrong with you? Why are you takin' their side over family?"

"I'm not taking anybody's side," Cole said. "I'm just trying to find out what happened. Once I know, I'll figure out what to do about it. So I'll ask you again, Ginny . . . did they actually mistreat you?"

"Well . . . no more than I forced 'em to, I reckon," she admitted with obvious reluctance. "But that don't mean I have to like it." Even in the darkness, they could tell she was glaring at Walter as she added, "I got some special scores to settle with that scrawny dirt-eater!"

"I didn't do anything—"

"Dinnae ye mind," Duff told him. "Ye will nae be convincing the lass to change her mind."

"Yeah, she's got it in for me," muttered Walter. His

younger brother patted him on the shoulder, but that was scant comfort.

Cole turned to his sister. "Della, take Ginny back down the hill to the others, and then y'all find a place to camp for the night. Nobody needs to be going back over the Nightmare Trail in full dark."

"We know that trail better than anybody, Cole," Della protested.

"Maybe so, but it still wouldn't be smart. Leaving will wait until morning."

Duff said, "By morning, the rest of your family will have heard what's going on and will have the trail blocked."

"More than likely," Cole allowed. "But as long as I'm with you, they won't try to stop you, especially if I tell them I made a deal with you. Hardcastles honor their bargains."

"So do MacCallisters."

"Yeah, so I've heard." Cole turned his head. "Della, do what I told you."

"All right, all right. Come on, Ginny."

"This ain't over," Ginny said darkly.

"For tonight, it is." Cole smiled at Duff in the starlight and went on. "Since you don't have to hide your camp anymore, I reckon you can have a fire and boil up a pot of coffee, right?"

Duff lowered his Winchester slightly but kept it where he could use it in a hurry if he needed to. "That sounds like a good idea," he agreed.


Duff had to admit, a cup of good, strong coffee made most things look better, even being trapped in an isolated basin by a clan of murderous outlaws. Cole Hardcastle had given his word not to try anything, so Duff didn't order that he be tied up. They sat on opposite sides of the small campfire Elmer had kindled, sipping the potent black brew from tin cups.

Oliver and Elmer were both nursing cups of coffee by the fire, too. Walter was standing guard at the edge of the trees, having relieved Oliver from that duty.

"I'm curious, MacCallister," Cole said. "What's your stake in all this?"

"The immigrants who want to settle here, ye mean?"

"That's right. You've got your own ranch to run, and it's a successful one, from what I hear. Why are you mixin' in this business?"

"I have no stake, as ye put it, other than wanting to help people who need help."

"But they're strangers to you, or at least they were when they first showed up in these parts."

Duff shrugged. "That does nae matter. They're still people in need of assistance."

"I can see givin' family a helping hand," Cole said with a puzzled shake of his head. "But something like this . . . you're a fool for taking a hand in the game."

Elmer snapped, "Ain't you never heard of doin' something just because it's the right thing to do?"

"I've heard about *you*," Cole replied with a quirk of an eyebrow. "Some of the gossip says you weren't much more than an owlhoot yourself, back in the old days."

Elmer glared at him in the firelight. "I done some things I ain't proud of, true enough, but it ain't always simple, like you're either an outlaw or you ain't."

"Aye," Duff put in. "For a time, I was considered an outlaw meself, back in Scotland."

"Is that so?" Cole said with a smile. "Sounds like it might be a good story."

"Perhaps I'll tell ye sometime . . . but not tonight. Tonight

I want to know what ye think your family will do, come morning."

"That's a pretty good question. Della said she sent one of the girls to tell Cousin Willie what happened."

"This Cousin Willie is the leader of your clan?"

"Well, he *thinks* he is, and honestly, most of the others go along with that."

Elmer said, "Sounds like you've got your eye on bein' the boss."

"Hell, no," Cole replied without a second's hesitation. "I'm not interested in running anything except my own life. But that don't mean I'm gonna go along with everything Willie says. There are a few others like me. Most of the family is willing to let him make the decisions, though. I suspect that come morning, he'll have men blocking the trail, since he knows it's your only way out of the basin."

"And they'll start shooting as soon as they lay eyes on us?"

"No, he'll wait to find out what's happened to me and those girls. Della and the others will start out for the home place at first light tomorrow, I'm thinkin'. By the time we come riding along, Willie will know what's goin' on. He'll know I'm your prisoner."

"And that will be enough to make them hold their fire?" Duff asked.

"Well . . . I'm sure hoping it is," Cole said with a smile. "Otherwise, I'm liable to be right in the way of a bunch of bullets."

"If I didn't know better," Duff said, "I'd say ye sound like ye really do want us to get out of here without any killing."

Cole drained the last of the coffee in his cup then regarded Duff solemnly. "I'll be honest with you, MacCallister. I know my brother Benjy snuck into town and scared your lady friend."

Duff's jaw tightened. "I have nae forgotten about that."

"But you didn't raise a posse and come after Benjy. You could've. Men have been lynched for doin' less than he did, especially fellas who ain't right in the head, like Benjy is."

"I'll not deny that I don't want him to have the chance to hurt Meagan, ever again. Her wrist was sore for a week, where he grabbed her."

"He doesn't know his own strength," Cole said. "That's the God's honest truth. He never meant to hurt her. I know that. He did what he did because he's smitten with her." Cole sighed. "Benjy may have the mind of a young'un, but when it comes to gals, he's a grown man. And there's a shortage of eligible females on Buzzard's Roost, let me tell you."

Oliver cleared his throat and asked, "How do you, uh, how do you get any wives up there, Mr. Hardcastle?"

Cole smiled indulgently. "I ain't sure that's something needs discussing with an innocent young lad like you. But since you brought it up . . . some of us venture out from the home place from time to time."

"On robbery sprees," Elmer said. "What do you do, kidnap women while you're away from there, drag 'em back, and then force 'em to marry up with you?"

"I reckon a man of your experience knows there are plenty of gals who work in saloons and road ranches and places like that who are glad for a chance to get out of that life. Things ain't always easy up on the Roost, I'll give you that much, but mostly it's an improvement over the way they've been living."

Duff figured there was some truth to what Cole was saying. Most soiled doves endured short, unpleasant existences because they believed they had no other alternative. Marrying into the Hardcastle clan might seem like a suitable escape from such an existence for some of them.

He was willing to bet some women were taken back to

Buzzard's Roost against their will, though. Sooner or later, a large enough posse, or perhaps even the army, might clean out that rat's nest. Maybe the Hardcastles were right to worry about immigrants settling in the basin. It might just speed up the inevitable.

Tonight, that wasn't Duff's concern. He steered the conversation back to what might happen in the morning. "Assuming your relatives do hold their fire when we ride up, do ye actually believe they'll allow us to pass?"

"I think so," Cole said. "Again, I'm betting my own life on that, aren't I? At this point . . . what else are you gonna do, MacCallister?"

"Aye, ye have a point there." Duff leaned forward and used a thick piece of leather to lift the coffee pot from where it sat at the edge of the crackling flames. "More coffee?"

Cole held his cup out with a smile. "Don't mind if I do."


Tension and weariness gripped the group as they rode up the Nightmare Trail the next morning. Nobody had gotten much sleep. Duff, Elmer, and Oliver had taken turns standing guard over the camp and keeping an eye on Cole Hardcastle.

To Cole's credit, he hadn't tried any tricks and had been cooperative in everything they had asked of him. He even seemed friendly enough, chatting with Oliver about the journey the group of immigrants had made so far. Then he had curled up in an extra blanket and gone to sleep.

Duff hadn't gotten in any hurry about making an early start. He wanted to give Della and the other girls enough time to get back to the home place, as Cole called the Hardcastle stronghold. Duff didn't want them caught in the middle, just in case any gunplay erupted.

He took the lead and motioned for Cole to ride beside

him on the outside of the trail so he couldn't lunge his horse to the side suddenly and force Duff off the trail. The two brothers came next, and Elmer brought up the rear.

Reaching the spot where the trail leveled off, Duff wasn't surprised to see a dozen heavily armed riders up ahead, crowding into the narrow passage between the mountainside and the rocky shoulder on the other side of the trail. The bottleneck was the perfect place to block the way out.

Duff didn't rein in. He continued walking his horse slowly toward the Hardcastles.

Cole was close beside him and said quietly, "That hombre with the little beard who's out in front is Cousin Willie."

"Aye, I figured as much."

"The mean-looking gent to his left is my cousin Ferris. He's the one who took a shot at you a couple of days ago when you were out here with some older fella."

"That older fellow was Waylon Spencer, the patriarch of the immigrants."

"I'm glad Ferris didn't kill either of you. If he got half a chance again, he wouldn't mind doing it. I don't like to speak ill of kinfolks, but I think he's got some snake blood in him, too."

"Some say the same of you," Duff pointed out.

"Just 'cause a fella's got a reputation don't mean *everything* about it is true." Cole paused, then added, "Your cousin Falcon ought to be proof enough of that."

Duff withheld comment on that and said, "I see your brother there, too."

Benjy was in the back of the group. He was so big, at least half a head taller than any of his companions, he wasn't hard to spot even in a crowd. He rose even taller and appeared to be standing up in his stirrups, looking for something . . . or someone.

Cole took off his hat and waved it over his head. Even from the distance, Duff could see the big grin on Benjy's face as he snatched off his hat and returned the wave.

"'Tis happy he is to see ye," he told Cole.

"Yeah, I reckon he was worried something might have happened to me. I've always taken care of Benjy. He's sort of like a big puppy. I ain't sure he'd be able to get along without me."

"For his sake, then, don't try any tricks or double crosses. If anything happens, 'tis ye I intend to shoot first."

"Don't worry, MacCallister. I gave you my word."

With less than twenty yards separating the two groups of riders, Duff let that distance close even more before he held up a hand in a signal to halt.

Willie Hardcastle glared across the intervening space and snapped, "What are you doing with these heathen invaders, Cousin Cole?"

"You know what I'm doing, Cousin Willie. I've promised them safe passage out of the basin, all the way to the other end of the Nightmare Trail."

"That was not your promise to make!"

"Seemed like the thing to do at the time," Cole drawled. "They were holding Ginny hostage."

Willie shook his head. "They would not have harmed her."

"Probably not, but I didn't want to take that chance. That's why I offered to swap places with her."

Willie raised his arm, pointed a finger at Duff, and said, "This man and his companions have come to our home uninvited. You know the penalty for that, Cousin Cole."

"I also know I don't want a bullet through me. Just let 'em go, Willie. Nobody has to get hurt."

Ferris spoke up. "Hardcastles never back down! What

the hell's wrong with you, Cole? You lost your spine or somethin'?"

Cole's eyes narrowed with anger. "I'm gonna pretend I didn't hear you say that, Ferris, since I know you must not be in your right mind just now. Otherwise you'd never say such a thing." He laughed humorlessly. "Hell, even Benjy's smarter than that."

"You hear that?" Benjy crowed. "Cole said I'm smart!"

Willie moved his horse forward a couple of steps. "If we allow these men to leave, they'll come back with the law."

Duff said, "So far, no real harm has been done, Mr. Hardcastle. I'd be for leaving it at that. No need to involve the law."

"He's lyin'," Ferris blurted out. "I say we kill 'em all right now!" His hand dropped to his right hip and clawed at the gun holstered there.

# CHAPTER 19

Willie Hardcastle had an old single-shot carbine in his left hand. Before Ferris could clear leather, Willie lashed out with the carbine and cracked the barrel across Ferris's right forearm. Ferris cried out in pain, opened his hand, and let his gun slide back into its holster.

"Stop that!" Willie said. "There'll be no shooting unless *I* give the order."

Ferris cradled his right arm against his chest. "Damn it, Cousin Willie—"

"And no cussing, either," barked Willie. "The Lord and I are still in charge here."

That was pretty bold of Willie, putting himself on equal footing with the Lord. But that was Willie's business—and the Lord's—not Duff's. He was just glad Willie had stopped Ferris from touching off a shoot-out.

Duff wouldn't have gone down without a fight. He had been ready to pull iron and return the Hardcastles' fire if they started shooting. Elmer would have done the same. And from what Duff had seen of Walter and Oliver, he figured the brothers would have gone down with guns blazing in their fists, too.

Glancing over at Cole, Duff saw a tiny muscle jumping

along the gunfighter's tightly clenched jaw. "'Twas a bit closer than I care for," he said quietly.

"Yeah, me, too," Cole agreed, and took a deep breath. "How about it, Cousin Willie? Are you going to let us pass? MacCallister said he wouldn't call in the law, and I'm willin' to take him at his word."

Willie frowned and didn't reply for a long moment. Finally, he said, "You intend to ride along with them, Cole?"

"That's right. As far as the end of the trail. MacCallister will let me go then."

"That was the deal we made," Duff put in.

"All right," Willie said. "We'll go along with it."

"Da—" Ferris began, then stopped himself before he finished uttering the curse. "Blast it, Willie, you can't trust anybody who's not family."

"I trust Cole. He's family."

"MacCallister's tricked him!"

Cole said, "I ain't fooled all that easy, Ferris. I'd say I'm a better judge of character than you are."

Ferris jutted out his jaw. "Yeah? What makes you think that?"

"I'm older than you, and I've been in a heap more scrapes. *And* I'm still alive." Cole made a scoffing sound. "You'd never have survived some of the places I've been, son."

Ferris continued glaring, and his face darkened with anger. But he didn't say anything else. He moved his horse back when Willie motioned for him to do so.

"We'll return to the home place," Willie told Cole, then he looked at Duff. "Go on your way in peace, MacCallister. But never return to Buzzard's Roost again. This safe passage holds today, and today only."

They would see about that, thought Duff, but he didn't

put the sentiment into words. The momentary truce was too fragile.

Willie, Ferris, and the other Hardcastles turned their mounts around carefully and started back along the Nightmare Trail toward the path that led to their home place higher on the mountain.

All except Benjy, who lingered and said, "When are you comin' home, Cole?"

"In a little while," Cole told him. "You go on along with Willie and the others."

Benjy pouted. "I want to ride with you. Don't want to go back to the home place with the rest of 'em."

Cole looked at Duff. "How about it, MacCallister? All right for Benjy to come with us?"

"Is he armed?" Duff asked.

"Yeah, he carries an old cap-and-ball pistol, but he's not much of a hand with it. And he'd never try to shoot anybody unless I told him to. I know you can't believe it because of what happened with Miss Parker, but Benjy really is a gentle soul."

Duff considered, then said, "I'll take a chance on him, but I'll be counting on you to make sure he behaves himself."

"Deal." Cole raised his voice. "All right, Benjy, you can come with us. But no trouble, all right? You have to be good."

"I will be, Cole, I promise." Benjy's moon face creased in a happy grin as he fell in with the others.

As they climbed the curving trail wasn't wide enough for Duff, Cole, and Benjy to ride side by side, so Duff kept Cole on his left and had Benjy take the next spot in line with Elmer riding beside him. Walter and Oliver moved to the rear. Benjy didn't seem to mind and chattered happily to Cole as they rode.

They passed the path to the home place. Duff was relieved to see none of the other Hardcastles were waiting there. He hadn't ruled out a change of heart on Willie's part.

It wasn't long before the trail sloped down again. Duff's gaze was always on the move as he scanned their surroundings and searched for any sign of an ambush. He barely trusted Cole Hardcastle, and that trust certainly didn't extend to Cole's cousins Willie and Ferris.

As angry as Ginny had been earlier, he wouldn't have put it past her to try to slip off and bushwhack them, either.

As they entered the trees on the lower slopes of Buzzard's Roost, Duff eyed the growth warily. They followed the twisting trail through it, but nothing happened. In late morning, they reached the spot where the Nightmare Trail merged with the main trail between Thunder Canyon and Chugwater.

All six men reined in. Cole crossed his hands on his saddle horn and leaned forward to ease his weary muscles. "You see, MacCallister? I promised you safe passage, and that's what you got."

"Aye, it seems as if ye have kept your word," Duff allowed. "Elmer, take the lads and head for Sky Meadow as quickly as ye can."

Elmer frowned and asked, "What about you, Duff?"

"I'll be staying here with Cole and his brother for a short spell. Just to make sure no treachery is involved."

Cole shook his head. "The Nightmare Trail's the only way down off Buzzard's Roost. No chance anybody got ahead of you and set up an ambush, if that's what you're worried about."

"An ounce of caution is better than a pound of careless-ness."

A burst of laughter came from Cole. "Is that an old Scottish proverb or something? I'll have to write that down."

"'Tis common sense, that's all. Once we were in the trees, your relatives could have circled around us without being seen. That's why we're going to wait here until my friends are well away."

"Sure," Cole said with a shrug. "I'm in no hurry to be anywhere. Are you, Benjy?"

"I'm in no hurry, Cole, as long as I'm with you," the big man said.

"All right. We'll go on," said Elmer. "But don't tarry too long, Duff. If you don't catch up to us after a while, I'll be comin' back lookin' for you."

"Not until ye have Walter and Oliver back with their people. And if you do have to come back, bring Wang with you."

Elmer jerked his head in a curt nod, then said to the brothers, "Come on, boys. Let's get you back to the wagons."

Duff and the two Hardcastles watched them ride away. Nothing was said until Elmer, Walter, and Oliver were out of sight.

Then Cole thumbed back his hat. "See? I told you nothing would happen."

"Let's give it some time," Duff suggested. "Meanwhile, I'd like to talk to ye about something else."

Cole's eyes narrowed. "Those sodbusters?"

"That's right."

Cole turned to his brother. "Benjy, why don't you ride on back up the trail a ways?"

"I'd rather stay with you, Cole," Benjy replied.

"You can stay in sight of me. I'm not gonna run off and leave you. Don't worry about that."

Benjy frowned. "You did last night. You went off somewhere, and when I woke up this mornin', you were gone. I didn't know if you were *ever* gonna come back!"

"I'll always come back, Benjy. I promise. Now, you ride on back up there toward the trees. Mr. MacCallister and I have to talk for a spell, but it won't be long."

Benjy still looked reluctant, but he nodded. "Well, all right. If you say so."

"I do."

Benjy turned his horse and loped toward the trees. Cole watched him go and sighed.

Duff said, "I'm not forgetting what happened with Miss Parker, but I'm starting to see what ye meant about him being a gentle soul. He's devoted to you, isn't he?"

"Yeah, I reckon he is."

"And ye have your hands full with him at times, I'll wager."

"That's the truth," Cole said. "Problem is, Benjy wants what he wants, when he wants it, and sometimes he gets carried away in goin' after it, like with Miss Parker. When you see her again, MacCallister, I wish you'd convey my apologies to her. I never should've let that happen."

Duff considered and then nodded. "Aye, I can do that. Especially if I have your word 'twill nae happen again."

"You do . . . to the best of my ability."

Duff looked at him intently. "Considering all I've heard about ye being a gunman and a killer and an outlaw, seeing how ye are with your brother is a bit odd."

"Like your friend Gleason said about his own past, it ain't always simple. Most folks are a mixture of good and bad."

"Your brother will be lost if anything ever happens to you."

Cole sighed. "I know. And don't think that doesn't weigh on my mind. But there's only so much I can do to protect him. If it was up to me, we'd just stay up there on Buzzard's Roost from now on and never come down . . . but the rest of the family has needs, too."

"Which ye take care of by robbing banks and holding up trains."

Cole's voice hardened as he said, "Don't go pokin' your nose any farther into Hardcastle business than you have to, MacCallister."

"Which brings us back to the Spencer family."

"The sodbusters."

"Aye."

Cole gestured toward the trail. "You want to take them to Longshot Basin."

"They have a right to settle there. 'Tis open range. And your family does nae own the Nightmare Trail. They have no legal right to stop anyone from using it."

"What'll you do if we try?"

"The authorities may have to be involved."

"You promised Cousin Willie you wouldn't do that," Cole said sharply.

"I promised I would nae report what happened yesterday and this morning . . . and I will not. But what happens in the future may be different. As your cousin himself said, safe passage was for today only."

Cole closed his eyes for a second and let out a groan. "Can't they just find some other place to homestead?"

"I suggested that. I wired the land office in Cheyenne about that very thing. But Waylon Spencer, the leader of the group, seems to have his heart set on the basin. Almost as if there's something special about it . . ." Duff's voice trailed off. He wasn't going to discuss his suspicions with Cole Hardcastle, but he remained convinced there was *something* Waylon Spencer hadn't told him.

"I'll talk to Willie and the others," said Cole. "Personally, I don't care if that bunch wants to settle there. I'm willing to live and let live, like they said. But I can't promise about the others. Hardcastles are standoffish, no denying that. They just don't want to have much truck with the outside world."

"If ye could convince 'em the Spencers mean no harm—"

"I said I'd talk to 'em, didn't I?" Cole snapped. "That's all I can promise you, MacCallister. If I can convince them to go along with what you want, I'll send word to you. But if you don't hear from me and those sodbusters start up the Nightmare Trail anyway . . . whatever happens is on their own heads."

The two men gave each other cold, hard stares for a moment, then Cole went on. "I've waited here long enough. Benjy and I are heading home."

Duff nodded. "Aye, go ahead. Enough time has passed."

"I wasn't askin' your permission. And I'll have my guns and my knife back now."

Duff leaned his head toward the south. "I'll leave them up the trail a bit. You can recover them later."

"I'm not a damn backshooter."

"As I said about your sister, best not to put temptation in your path."

Cole jerked his horse around and heeled it into motion toward the trees where Benjy waited for him a couple of hundred yards away. Cole didn't look back as Duff watched him go.

Duff didn't turn his horse toward Sky Meadow until the two Hardcastles were out of sight.

* * *

The Hardcastle home place was not one building but more than a dozen scattered over a broad bench that butted up against the base of a towering cliff. A spring bubbled out from the cliff, forming a pool and providing water for the clan. Enough grass grew so the horses had graze. Trees dotted the bench here and there, making lumber available, but all the houses were built of stone.

The main house was a sprawling structure of many rooms, built when Willie Hardcastle first led the family there from Arkansas and then added to numerous times over the years. Willie still lived there, along with Cole, Benjy, Della, Ferris, and several other Hardcastle cousins.

Other branches of the family had their own houses. The compound also included barns, corrals, a blacksmith shop, a smokehouse, and numerous storage buildings. Cole had seen wide-place-in-the-road settlements with fewer buildings and people than the Hardcastle home place.

As he and Benjy reached the top of the trail and rode out onto the bench, he saw a large group of people congregated in front of the main house. Cousin Willie was standing on the porch, evidently addressing the gathered clan. Cole could make out his cousin's powerful voice but not what Willie was saying.

Willie fell silent, however, as Cole and Benjy approached. He stared across the crowd's heads at the two riders, which prompted the assembled Hardcastles to swing around and look at them, too.

Cole thought he saw anger and accusation on many of the faces and wasn't surprised when he heard a familiar voice call out.

"There he is! The fella who turned his back on his family!" That was Ferris. The tall, rawboned man pushed through the throng until he broke out into the open and glared up at Cole and Benjy as they reined their horses to a halt.

"You'd better be careful about throwing around foolish words, Ferris," Cole said. "I might just take offense at them."

Ferris sneered. "I ain't afraid of you, Cole, especially after what you done today. Turnin' against your family and standin' with strangers!"

Cole leaned forward in the saddle and said, "You ain't afraid 'cause you figure I won't haul off and gun you down right in front of everybody. But just how sure are you about that?"

The veiled threat made Ferris pale a little under his tan. He had said too much to back down, though, so he swallowed and pressed on. "You think I was runnin' my mouth? What did I say that wasn't true? Didn't you take MacCallister's side when we tried to stop that bunch from leaving the basin?"

"I took the side of not getting any of my kinfolks killed."

That answer seemed to bolster Ferris's resolve. "There were twelve of us and four of them. We would've wiped 'em out! Or were you just scared of gettin' caught in the cross-fire?"

Through his teeth, Cole said, "I don't cotton to being called a coward, Ferris."

"You ain't answered my question!"

Everybody was looking at Cole, waiting for his response. With an effort, he kept a tight rein on his temper and said, "I didn't have to worry about getting caught in a crossfire. If you boys had slapped leather, MacCallister was going to shoot me first. He'd made that plenty clear. Duff MacCallister ain't a man who talks just to hear his gums flap . . . unlike others I could name."

Ferris's face turned brick red at the obvious insult.

"But that's not why I figured it'd be best to strike a deal with him and let him and his friends go," Cole continued. "Yeah, you had them outnumbered three to one. But you were facing Duff MacCallister and Elmer Gleason. I don't know anything about the young'uns, but MacCallister and Gleason have reputations as bad men to tackle in a fight. There's a mighty good chance before you managed to bring them down, they would've killed you, Cousin Willie, and probably four or five more. If those boys were able to do any damage at all, it might've been damn near a standoff."

"Don't curse," snapped Cousin Willie. "You're saying you acted the way you did to save *us?*"

Cole nodded. "That's right."

Ferris scowled. "You had no right. The family's honor always comes first, and they insulted it by comin' up here onto Buzzard's Roost. They had to die, and they would have if you hadn't turned yellow—"

The fury inside Cole bubbled up and boiled over. He kicked his feet out of the stirrups, launched himself out of the saddle at Ferris, and crashed into his cousin. Momentum drove them both to the ground.

# CHAPTER 20

Ferris yelled curses and slugged at Cole, who had landed on top. He tried to buck Cole off. Cole was lighter, but he clung stubbornly to his opponent with his left hand and used the right to pepper short, hard punches to Ferris's face. Ferris arched his back and finally writhed enough to throw Cole to the side.

As Cole rolled over, he heard the excited shouts coming from the crowd of his kinfolks. Hardcastles loved a fight. Blood roared so loudly in his head he couldn't understand the words, but he knew they were hollering.

He pushed up onto his hands and knees. Ferris lunged at him and threw a roundhouse punch that connected with Cole's jaw and jerked his head to the side. Stunned for a second by the blow, Cole sprawled belly-down on the ground.

Ferris came after him, eager to seize the advantage. He hooked a fist into Cole's ribs, then dug a knee into his back. Cole flung a hand up, reached back, and found Ferris's face. He clawed at the other man's eyes. Yelling in pain and anger, Ferris jerked his head away and lost his balance enough for Cole to surge up and ram an elbow into his chest. Ferris fell backward, and Cole was free again.

Both men scrambled to their feet and charged each other. They stood toe-to-toe, throwing punches and slugging it out as the roar of the crowd washed over them. Ferris was taller and had weight and reach advantages over Cole, but Cole was quicker and able to bob and weave out of the way of some of Ferris's punches. Ferris wasn't in as good shape, either, and would tire quicker.

Willie emerged from the crowd and walked toward them, waving his arms and shouting, "Stop that! Stop that, you men! Right now!" He was close enough to get hit by a wild punch.

Taking his eye off Ferris for a second, Cole glanced toward Willie, and Ferris's fist exploded on his jaw. Cole sailed backward and crashed down on his back. Ferris charged after him, ready to stomp him into the dirt—and mean enough to do it.

But before Ferris could reach Cole, a bellow like that of an enraged bull sounded, and massive arms caught him from behind. Ferris screeched in terror as Benjy grasped him by the back of the neck and the seat of his pants and lifted him high overhead in a feat of almost unbelievable strength.

From where he lay a few feet away, blinking his eyes rapidly to get the dust out of them, Cole looked up and saw his brother looming above him, with Ferris squirming but helpless in Benjy's grip. If Benjy slammed Ferris to the ground, as it looked like he was about to do, there was a good chance it would kill Ferris.

"Benjy, no!" Cole cried.

Benjy hesitated with Ferris poised above his head.

Cousin Willie moved in front of Benjy and said, "Don't harm your cousin, boy. It goes against the scriptures to murder a member of your own family."

Actually the Good Book said *Thou shalt not kill*, thought

Cole as he hurriedly got to his feet, but Cousin Willie had always had a tendency to pick and choose among the scriptures as to which ones the Hardcastles had to follow.

Benjy glared at Willie and said, "Ferris was gonna hurt Cole. He's got it comin'.'

Cole advanced toward Benjy and held out a hand to his brother, making gentle patting motions. "I'm all right, Benjy. See? Ferris and me were just scufflin'. I'm not hurt, and there's no harm done. You need to put him down now."

Benjy looked confused. "I thought you said for me not to put him down."

"I mean, set him back down on the ground easylike. Can you do that, Benjy?"

With obvious reluctance, Benjy swung his arms down in front of him and let go of Ferris, who still fell heavily on his face and belly. But being dropped like that was a lot better than what would have happened if Benjy had slammed him to the ground with full force. Ferris lay there breathing hard, pale with the knowledge of how close he had come to death.

"You can back off now, Benjy," Cole went on. "The fight's over. Ain't that right, Ferris?"

Ferris didn't respond.

Cole's voice hardened again. "I said, ain't that right, Ferris?"

"Y-yeah," Ferris panted. "Fight's . . . over."

"Well . . . all right," Benjy said.

"Why don't you go on inside the house?" Cole suggested. He spotted his sister in the crowd. "Della, take Benjy inside. Get him something cool to drink."

Della nodded and moved to Benjy's side. She took his arm and urged him toward the steps. "Come on with me, Benjy."

"Sure, Della," he rumbled. "I'll go anywhere with you, as long as Cole says."

Cole nodded and motioned for them to go on. Della led Benjy through the path that opened up in the crowd of Hardcastles.

Once Benjy was inside the house, Cole looked down at Ferris and said in a voice like ice, "Next time you call me a coward, Ferris, I'll kill you where you stand. No argument, no warning. I'll just shoot you dead. You got that?"

"Yeah," Ferris rasped. "I got it." He raised his head and gave Cole a look filled with pure hate, though.

He was going to have to keep an eye on Ferris, Cole told himself, and not let the hombre get behind him. Setting that aside for the moment he looked at Willie. "What's all this about?" He nodded toward the crowd.

"The family had a right to know what happened."

"So you harangued 'em and worked 'em up into a lather over what I did?"

"I spoke only the truth, as I always do," Willie insisted. "Many were not happy with your actions, including your cousin Ferris."

"That's what comes of making up your mind before you know all the facts."

"Facts?" Willie repeated with a frown. "What other facts can there be except that strangers came uninvited into the Hardcastle domain? The penalty for that is death, and you know it."

"Let's go inside. We need to have a talk, you and me."

Willie waved a hand at the crowd. "There are no secrets amongst a family."

"Maybe not, but there are some things it's better to talk out in private first."

Willie frowned at him for a long moment, then said, "Very well." He turned to the others and lifted his hands. "Go back to your homes. When there is a message to be delivered, I will bestow it upon you."

Quite a bit of muttering greeted his pronouncement. As Cole had told Duff MacCallister, Cousin Willie was the boss, but not everybody in the family agreed with everything he said. Willie was smart enough to know he ruled over the clan because neither Cole nor any of the others had challenged him. His grip on power was strong but not absolute.

As the horde of Hardcastles dispersed, Cole picked up his hat, slapped it against his thigh to get some of the dust off it, and went up the steps of the massive stone house with Willie. It was cooler inside due to the thick walls. Willie led him along oddly laid-out corridors to a small, windowless room he called his sanctuary.

Willie scraped a match to life on the sole of his left boot, then used the flame to light several candles. The wavering light revealed the room was plainly furnished with a couple of small tables, two ladderback chairs, and a stand on which an open Bible rested.

Willie swung around and said, "Tell me what is on your mind, Cousin Cole."

"Women," Cole said.

Willie's forehead creased in a frown. "What do you mean by that?"

Cole glanced over his shoulder to make sure the sanctuary door behind him was closed, then said, "That's why I wanted you to let MacCallister and the others go. I know the rule about how strangers are supposed to die for coming around Buzzard's Roost, but sometimes there are more important things than following the rules."

"And . . . women . . . are more important?"

"You're da—*dang* right." No point in irritating Willie any more than was necessary, thought Cole, so he'd bitten back the curse he'd been about to utter. "You know how

Benjy's been talkin' about how he wants to marry up with some gal."

"Your brother needs to learn how to control his animal urges," Willie snapped with a glare of disapproval.

"That's easy to say but not so easy to do. Whether you like it or not, Willie, most folks are human. They've got urges. And it's not just a romp and a little slap-and-tickle I'm talkin' about, either. Folks want families. Kids. Benjy's not the only one in need of a wife. Quite a few fellas up here are in that situation."

"*You* are unmarried," Willie pointed out.

"Yeah, I am, and I'm not hankering to get hitched, either. Benjy and the others are."

Willie drew in a deep breath, let it out in a sigh, then shrugged as he admitted, "There is some truth in what you say. But I fail to see what it has to do with allowing strangers to invade our land."

"There's a whole wagon train full of immigrants stopping at MacCallister's ranch," Cole explained. "Those two young fellas who were with him and Gleason belong to that bunch. I cozied up to one of 'em last night while they had me prisoner, and I found out a lot about them." Cole smiled. "He thought I was just tryin' to be friendly with all the questions I asked."

"These are the pilgrims who wish to homestead in Longshot Basin? Della and Ginny told me about them."

"That's right. There are five or six gals among them who are prime marryin' age, between fifteen and twenty. A couple more are younger but old enough, and four more are older but still young enough to bear more children. That's a dozen potential brides for Hardcastle men. That'd sure help with our problem, wouldn't it?"

Willie frowned and tugged at the short beard on his chin. "I had thought perhaps the next time you led a group out on . . . missionary work . . . you might persuade some women to return with you. Poor unfortunates who wish to be saved from a life of degradation, or young ladies who prefer not to spend years on the drudgery of farm labor—"

"Yeah, I know how it works," Cole broke in to his cousin's pretentious speech. "And *you* know those gals don't always want to come with us. But whatever you need to tell yourself so as not to feel too guilty—"

"Have a care, Cousin Cole," Willie interrupted. "Cast no aspersions on my motives."

"All right. Fine. We'll put that aside. It don't really matter, anyway. We don't have to go out and find any gals to marry up with our boys. They'll come to us if we just let them."

"The women you spoke of who belong to that wagon train."

"That's right."

"Are none of them already married? It seems as if some of the older ones would be, at least."

"All the older ones are," Cole admitted. "But widows are free to marry again, aren't they?"

"Nothing in the scripture forbids it," Willie said slowly. "A woman takes a husband until death do them part, and once that has occurred, she may take another husband."

Cole spread his hands and said, "Well, there you go. Simple as pie."

"The fathers of the unmarried females are unlikely to give their permission for their daughters to wed."

"That problem's got the same solution."

"So, you're saying . . ."

Willie was going to make him put it into words, thought Cole. Well, fine. He didn't care. He'd always liked plain talk, anyway.

"I'm saying we give those immigrants permission to use

the Nightmare Trail to get to Longshot Basin. Then we kill all the men, marry off all the older girls and women to the boys in our family who need wives, and take the kids into the family and raise 'em as Hardcastles."

Willie stared at him as seconds slipped past. Then he said, "Sometimes a sacrifice of blood is required to do the Lord's work. As long as it's not Hardcastle blood being spilled, I see nothing wrong with it." He paused and frowned. "But this man MacCallister . . . what if he accompanies them?"

"Then we'll just kill him, too," Cole said.

# CHAPTER 21

Elmer and Wang were waiting on the ranch house porch when Duff arrived at Sky Meadow.

Elmer rested his hands on the porch railing as he leaned forward and said by way of greeting, "Wang and me were just about to saddle up and come lookin' for you, Duff."

"It is good you appear to be unharmed," Wang added. "We were concerned."

"Aye, nothing else happened." Duff swung down from the saddle and gave the reins to one of the ranch hands who hurried up to take the horse. Duff stepped up onto the porch. "Nothing except Cole Hardcastle and I had a talk once we were alone."

"What did that snake-blooded varmint have to say for hisself?" Elmer wanted to know.

Duff thumbed back his hat. "He agreed to speak to the rest of his clan on behalf of the immigrants, claims he has nothing against them, personally, and has no objection to them settling in Longshot Basin."

Elmer's eyes narrowed in suspicion. "I wouldn't believe a damn thing that hombre has to say," he declared. "He's an outlaw and a killer."

"Aye. But he seems genuinely devoted to his family and does nae want a great deal of violence and bloodshed that would bring suffering to them. He was going to get them to agree to let the Spencers travel on the Nightmare Trail, and if he succeeds, he promised to send word to me. Otherwise"—Duff shrugged—"if they try to reach the basin without permission from the Hardcastles, there will be trouble."

"I wonder what they'd do if we sent word to the army and got a cavalry escort to travel up yonder to the basin with the Spencers. You reckon you could arrange that, Duff?"

Duff was on a friendly basis with several army officers and had done favors for the military before, as well as selling them cattle for beef rations. What Elmer suggested was a possibility, but it might take some time to work out the details. Duff didn't mind if the immigrants remained at Sky Meadow for as long as was necessary to ensure their safety, but more than once, he had sensed Waylon Spencer was in a hurry to reach Longshot Basin.

He just didn't know *why* Spencer felt that way.

"I'll look into it—"

"A rider comes," Wang interrupted.

Duff looked around and spotted the figure on horseback heading toward Sky Meadow's headquarters. The rider was still several hundred yards away, but Duff's eyesight was keen enough he quickly recognized her. "'Tis Meagan. I wonder what brings her out here." He frowned. "'Tis not trouble, I'm hoping."

"Could be she just come to see you," Elmer suggested. "The gal *is* sweet on you, you know."

Duff grinned. "Aye. And the feeling be mutual. Still . . . Meagan is the sort of lass who generally has a good reason for everything she does."

The three men waited on the porch as she continued riding toward the ranch. Although anxious to talk to Waylon Spencer about what had happened during the journey to

Longshot Basin, Duff was sure Walter and Oliver would have told quite a bit to the Spencer family patriarch already. It would have to wait until Meagan told what brought her to Sky Meadow.

Capable of several different methods of riding, Meagan sometimes wore a dress, used a sidesaddle, and was very elegant. Other times she donned a split skirt and rode astride. Other times she pulled on a pair of men's trousers, tucked her hair up under her hat, and hit the saddle like a forty-a-month-and-found cowpuncher. More than once, she had helped Duff drive herds of cattle or horses, and she could eat dust and cuss a balky steer with the best of them.

Dressed like a cowboy told Duff she had a certain urgency to her errand, whatever it was.

She rode up to the porch, reined in, and said, "Hello."

"And good afternoon to you," Duff replied. "Come up here and sit down."

Wang said, "There is cool lemonade. I will bring the pitcher and glasses."

"That sounds wonderful," said Meagan. "It's a dusty ride out here."

The same ranch hand who had taken Duff's horse earlier came out of the barn and hurried over to take charge of Meagan's mare. "Want me to unsaddle her, Miss Parker?" the young cowboy asked. "Are you gonna be here for a spell?"

"I may be," Meagan told him with a smile as she handed over the reins.

"Well, don't you worry, I'll take good care of her."

"'Tis obliged to you we are, Len," Duff told him. He held out a hand and took Meagan's arm as she came up the steps.

A moment later, Duff, Meagan, and Elmer were seated in wicker chairs on the porch. Not much of a breeze was blowing, but in the shade the heat wasn't oppressive. Meagan took off her hat and let her blond, wavy hair tumble around her shoulders and a short distance down her back.

Duff felt a slight tightening in his chest. Her beauty always affected him. "'Tis very glad I am to see ye, as always, but what brings ye out here today?"

"I came to see if those immigrants are still camped here, or if they've moved on to Longshot Basin already."

Duff and Elmer exchanged a glance, then Duff said, "They're still here."

"I know. I saw their wagons next to the trees as I was riding in."

Before Duff could ask her what her interest was in the Spencers, Wang came out of the house carrying a tray with a pitcher of lemonade and four empty glasses on it. He set the tray on a small table and filled the glasses with the cool, sweet drink, then handed them to the others and took the remaining empty chair himself.

"You were discussing the Spencer family," he said, proving he had overheard that much of the conversation as he was coming out of the house.

"Has something happened regarding them?" Duff asked Meagan.

"Some men arrived in Chugwater yesterday evening. They rode in just as I was closing up the shop, and their leader saw me and spoke to me." She paused. "They're looking for those immigrants."

Duff took a sip of the lemonade and kept his face impassive, but inside, Meagan's news didn't surprise him. All along, he had sensed more to the story than Waylon Spencer had revealed. The mysterious strangers Meagan spoke of had to be part of it. "Did this fellow say what they wanted?"

Meagan shook her head. "Not really. He did tell me his name. Major Thomas Kingman."

"A military man, he was? 'Twas a cavalry patrol that rode in?"

"No, they were all civilians, including Major Kingman. He explained that he still used the rank, even though he hasn't actually held it since the end of the war."

Elmer grunted. "So he served in the Late Unpleasantness, did he? He happen to say what outfit he rode with?"

"No, but from the way he acted, and the way the men with him followed his orders, I think he must have been their commander."

Elmer looked over at Duff. "When the war was over, some fellas either stuck together or got back together with their old outfits after goin' home and findin' civilian life not to their likin'." He shrugged. "That's how it was with some of the hombres I rode with."

"And some of those groups became desperadoes, as well," Duff observed. To Meagan, he said, "The men ye saw, did they strike ye as outlaws?"

"I honestly don't know, Duff. They were all hard, capable-looking men, including Major Kingman. But their goal, their motive, I can't really say what that might be. All I know is . . . when I looked at them, I got the feeling I needed to be careful around them."

Duff trusted Meagan's instincts almost as much as he trusted his own. He asked her, "What exactly did this fellow Kingman say to ye?"

"He asked if a group of immigrants named Spencer had come through Chugwater recently. I think he already had a pretty good idea they had."

"Trailin' 'em," Elmer said.

"And what did ye tell him?" Duff asked.

"I thought about lying and saying the Spencers hadn't been there, but I realized that probably wouldn't do any good. So many people in town know about them. I figured

Major Kingman wouldn't just accept what I told him and would keep asking around about them, so I told him the truth—that they'd been there and moved on."

"Did ye tell him they were out here at Sky Meadow?"

"That bit of information I kept to myself," said Meagan. "I just told him I didn't know where they had gone. There's a very good chance Kingman will find out where they are, of course. It was no secret they were coming out here to Sky Meadow. But it might take him a while. It was obvious Kingman and his men had been doing some hard traveling. They took rooms at the hotel and put their horses in the livery stable to rest. I thought you needed to know about it, so I came out here today to tell you as soon as I was able to get away from the shop."

Elmer said, "It sounds to me like this fella Kingman has trouble in mind. I never heard tell of a bunch of hard-lookin' hombres trailin' somebody when they *weren't* looking to rob 'em or settle some kind of score with them."

"That seems likely to me as well," said Wang, "given what I know of human nature."

"Aye," Duff agreed. "And there be one man who should be able to give us an answer."

"Waylon Spencer," said Elmer.

Duff nodded. "'Tis time I have another talk with him."

Meagan accompanied Duff as he walked toward the immigrant camp. Ahead of them, children ran and played around the wagons, women hung up washing on lines they had strung between trees, and men mended harness, greased wagon wheels, and worked on other chores needing to be done before the group set out again on their journey.

A couple of dogs saw Duff and Meagan coming and ran toward them, barking. That got the attention of Waylon Spencer, who strode out to meet them along with his son

Grady and brother Burl. Spencer had been working on his wagon and wiped his hands with a rag as he approached.

"Afternoon, Mr. MacCallister," he said with a nod. "And Miss Parker, isn't it?"

"That's right," Meagan told him.

"What can I do for you?" Without waiting for Duff to answer, Spencer went on. "My sister-in-law is rather upset about all those, ah, adventures her boys got into while they were with you, Duff. But she's grateful you brought them back safely."

"'Twas always my intention to do so." Since he didn't know when Kingman and the other men might show up at the ranch, he figured it was best to get right down to business. "We need to have a talk, Mr. Spencer."

The man frowned, seemingly surprised by Duff's stern attitude. "What about? Is there some problem with us staying here at your ranch? We're getting ready to move out and head for Longshot Basin as soon as possible. I know from talking to Walter and Oliver those Hardcastles may give us trouble, but I'm sure we can talk sense into their heads. They can't be completely unreasonable."

Duff wouldn't count on that, but at the moment, the outlaw clan wasn't the problem. "'Tis not the Hardcastles worrying me right now. 'Tis Major Thomas Kingman and his friends." Duff pitched his voice low enough only Spencer, Grady, and Burl could hear him.

All three men reacted instantly to his words, catching their breath and standing up straighter. A dark, angry flush stole across Waylon Spencer's face. His brother Burl looked angry, too. Grady just frowned in concern.

"Where did you hear that name?" Spencer snapped.

Meagan said, "Major Kingman introduced himself to me yesterday evening, right after he and twenty men rode into Chugwater."

Burl burst out, "Blast it, Waylon. You said they'd never be able to trail us all the way up here. You just don't know how stubborn that crazy son of a"—he stopped short for a second, glanced at Meagan, and then finished. "How stubborn Kingman is."

Duff said, "'Twould be wise for ye to tell us what that is all about, Mr. Spencer."

"What happened to calling me Waylon?" Spencer asked with a scowl.

"I think until we find out exactly what's going on here, I'd prefer to call ye Mr. Spencer."

"What you're asking about is family business. Personal and private—"

"If trouble is about to follow ye onto my ranch, that makes it *my* business," Duff broke in, his voice flat, brooking no argument.

Grady said, "He's right, Pa. Mr. MacCallister's helped us a lot and risked his own life to do it. You need to tell him the truth."

"And you need to stop telling your elders what to do," Spencer said.

"You ain't that much elder than *me*," said Burl, "and I reckon you owe MacCallister the truth, too. Besides, we got to think about how we're gonna deal with this. You know good and well Kingman ain't gonna stop if he's got our scent. The man's a bloodhound!"

Spencer looked around, meeting the worried frowns from his son and brother, the stern, intent look Duff gave him, and the frank curiosity on Meagan's face. Finally, he nodded and said, "All right. I suppose you do have a right to know the story, since you've extended your hospitality to us like this, Duff."

"Come on over to the house," Duff invited, leaning his

head in that direction. "Wang has lemonade. That might keep your voice lubricated and help ye talk."

"It'll take something stronger than lemonade," Spencer said. He glanced at Grady and Burl. "Not a word of this to the others just yet, you understand? We'll figure out what to do next before we tell them."

"All right," Burl agreed. "But you better figure it out pretty quick, Waylon. No tellin' when Kingman'll show up, and you know as well as I do that when he does, he'll have death in his hand."

# CHAPTER 22

"All this goes back to the war," Waylon Spencer said a few minutes later when they were all seated on the front porch. Wang had given the older man his chair and was perched on the porch railing.

"I ain't surprised," Elmer responded. "That blasted war casts a mighty long shadow, and ain't no tellin' when it'll stop. You'd think folks could just say it's over and done with and get on with their lives, but too many people just can't seem to do that."

"No true Scotsman is likely to forget Culloden any time soon," Duff pointed out. "So I ken how ye feel, Mr. Spencer. Who is Major Thomas Kingman?"

"He is . . . was . . . the commanding officer of the cavalry unit I rode with. From what Miss Parker says, he still has a good number of the men with him."

"What unit was that?" asked Elmer.

Spencer laughed, but there wasn't even a trace of humor in the sound. "We didn't have an actual military designation. We called ourselves the Buckeye Brigade, because we were from Ohio."

"Irregulars," Elmer breathed.

Spencer nodded. "That's right. And it probably won't surprise you to know some in Kansas, Missouri, and Tennessee called us by another name."

"Good Lord!" Elmer exclaimed before Spencer could go on. "You rode with the Buckeye Butchers!"

Spencer sighed. "That's right. So did Burl and Leon. We're not proud of it, and to this day, we all wish we'd never thrown in with them. But the things they did to get that name . . . we never had any real part in those. I give you my word on that."

"That's what most fellas say who rode with bunches like that." Elmer made a face. "I know that from experience. I was part of an irregular outfit on the other side."

Meagan said, "I don't know much about any of that. Are you saying you weren't actually in the Union army, Mr. Spencer?"

"That's right, ma'am. We fought on the side of the Union, but we were . . . well . . ."

"Outlaws," Elmer said. "Raidin' towns that supported the Confederacy, robbin' banks, lootin' and burnin' and killin'—"

"The ones on the other side did the same thing in the border country," snapped Spencer. "How many settlements supporting the Union were wiped out and burned to the ground?"

"I ain't denyin' it happened. Reckon there was plenty of wrong-doin' on both sides." Elmer grimaced again. "Lord knows I was part of plenty of things I wouldn't mind takin' back now, if only I could. But ain't no changin' the past."

"No, there sure isn't. I've wished the same thing many times."

Duff said, "So how does that explain this Major King-man coming to Chugwater looking for you? I'm assuming major wasn't his official rank?"

Spencer shook his head. "No, none of us had official ranks. We elected our officers. Kingman was in charge, and he might as well have called himself a general for all it really meant. The only thing that counted was that he gave the orders . . . and nobody wanted to cross him."

"A bad hombre?" asked Elmer.

"As bad as I've ever come across. He was smart. Went to college and was even a professor for a little while before the war broke out. Claimed he knew all about history and warfare, and I have to give him credit. He was good at it. He said the quickest way to make an enemy quit was to hurt those he cared about. That's why he tried to avoid engagements with the Confederate forces when he could and hit their towns instead." A hollow note had come into Spencer's voice as he spoke.

Duff figured the awful memories playing in the older man's mind were what put it there.

Spencer continued. "'Put them to the sword,' Major Kingman said. It didn't matter if they were women and children. They were rebels, and so they deserved to die. They brought their own fates down on their heads because of the evil they supported. That was his standing order—put them to the sword."

Spencer paused and looked down at the glass of lemonade in his hand, which was shaking slightly. He lifted the glass and downed the liquid in one swallow. Duff could understand why the man had said it might take something stronger than lemonade to get this story told.

Spencer looked at Meagan and said, "I'm truly sorry for talking about such ugliness in front of a lady, Miss Parker."

"That's all right, Mr. Spencer. Under the circumstances, it's more important to get the truth out than it is to worry about some arbitrary standards of propriety."

"I appreciate that, ma'am."

"Go on," Duff said. "Why is Kingman following ye, and how long has this been going on?"

"In a way, ever since the war, like I said. Ever since what

happened at Hungry Dog Creek." He looked across the yard and remembered that day.


*Tennessee, 1865*

*The war was going to be over any day now. That was what most of the boys said. Waylon Spencer didn't know if he believed it or not, but the end of the fighting couldn't come too soon to suit him. He just wanted to get home, back to his wife and boys. The last letter he'd gotten from Edith, more than a month ago, she'd said she was trying to keep the farm going, but it wasn't easy with only Grady and Robert to help her. There were so many things that little boys just couldn't do . . .*

*If he ever made it back, he wanted to forget about everything he had seen the last four years. All the blood, all the dying, all the misery human beings could inflict upon one another.*

*But he was afraid those experiences were going to haunt his dreams forever.*

*His brothers rode beside him in the cold, drenching rain. If the temperature dropped much more, the rain was going to turn to ice pellets. Waylon wasn't sure what was worse, a muddy road or an icy one.*

*"I sure wish those Johnny Rebs would just go ahead and give up," Leon said. Like the other two, he rode with his head tipped forward so the rain would run off the front of his hat brim. "Don't they know they're whipped? It's just a matter of time."*

*"Why don't you tell the major that?" suggested Burl. "The Rebs are beat, so we might as well turn around and go on home, hadn't we? Our little bunch ain't gonna make any difference on how the war turns out."*

*Waylon said, "For the major, it's not about winning the war, and we all know it."*

*His brothers didn't say anything to that, but they understood exactly what he meant.*

*To Major Thomas Kingman, the conflict no longer had anything to do with strategic, political, or moral considerations. Kingman was there to kill Rebs, plain and simple, and any loot he managed to accumulate in the process was just gravy.*

*At the moment, Kingman and the rest of the Buckeye Brigade were about half a mile behind the Spencer brothers, who were scouting the road between the settlements of Rosedale and Lettsburg. Early this morning, the Brigade had paid a visit to Rosedale. Because of the cold January rain, they hadn't been able to set fire to the buildings, but they had left a good number of Southern sympathizers dead in the streets and had cleaned out the businesses of money and supplies.*

*The war had been going on for so long and had been so hard on the Confederacy and its supporters there really wasn't a lot left to steal, but every loaf of bread they took, every Reb they killed, meant the war would end that much sooner, the major always said.*

*Waylon and his brothers usually managed to volunteer for other chores, like scouting or tending to the horses, whenever a raid was going to take place. The other members of the Brigade were happy to let them do that. The Spencers were older, all of them married and family men, so the young firebrands were glad to shove them aside. More glory, more loot . . . more killing . . . for them. Waylon and his brothers had thought they were just doing their part to preserve the Union by joining up with the Buckeye Brigade.*

*That was before they had known what war was really like, and especially, what Major Thomas Kingman was like.*

*As Waylon rode, he recalled the clash he'd had with Kingman the day before. He had tried to convince the major Rosedale didn't have any strategic importance and wasn't likely to be very lucrative as far as foraging and pillaging went.*

*"You're just making excuses because you want to spare those filthy traitors, Spencer!" Kingman had flared at him as they stood outside the major's tent. The rain hadn't started yet, and the glow from a nearby campfire painted Kingman's face with a red glare. "This isn't the first time you've spoken up in defense of the Rebels. If I didn't know better, Spencer, I'd say that maybe you actually feel sorry for them!"*

*"No, sir," Waylon had said, shaking his head vehemently. "I want to beat the Confederacy and preserve the Union just as much as you do."*

*"I doubt that," Kingman had snapped. Jabbing an accusatory finger at Waylon's face, he went on. "You'd better just watch yourself, mister. You don't have what it takes to be a member of the Buckeye Brigade! If you and your brothers sympathize with the Rebels, maybe you should just go fight on their side!"*

*That was the major. Laughing, charming, easy-going one minute, red-in-the-face, spitting furious the next. Waylon had known better than to say anything to him but had done it anyway. Anything less than the pure, unbridled hatred Kingman felt for the Confederates was regarded as betrayal and was likely to set the major off on one of his tirades. Waylon just hadn't been thinking when he suggested they ride around Rosedale and leave the town and its inhabitants alone.*

*That was just too bad for those folks, he thought as he*

*rode through the rain with his brothers. War was loose in the land, and it swung its bloody scythe at anyone unlucky enough to be in the way.*

Leon reined in and pointed ahead of them as Waylon and Burl brought their mounts to a halt, as well.

"Creek's up a mite, from the looks of it," Leon said.

"How do you know?" asked Burl. "We've never been here before."

"Yeah, but you can see it's nearly bank full. We'll have to be careful crossing it."

Waylon said, "That's Hungry Dog Creek."

Both of his brothers looked at him.

"How do you know that?" Leon wanted to know.

"I saw the map Major Kingman has. It's the only creek between Rosedale and Lettsburg. The major said it originally had some Cherokee name nobody could pronounce, but the words meant Hungry Dog Creek, so that's what everybody started calling it."

"When'd you sit around talkin' about creeks with the major?" Burl asked.

"Yesterday. Before he got so mad."

"Before you poked him like you would a bear, you mean," Leon said.

"Reckon I'd rather poke a bear," Burl added.

"Let's just go have a look," Waylon said as he impatiently kneed his horse forward.

The three men rode to the edge of Hungry Dog Creek. Even running bigger than usual because of the rain, it wasn't a very big stream. Twenty feet wide, maybe. Waylon could only guess at the depth, but he didn't figure it was more than two or three feet. The horses ought to be able to ford it without having to swim, he thought. "I'll check it out. You boys stay here."

"We can come with you—" Leon began.

"No. I just said stay here."

They might have grumbled a little; Waylon couldn't tell for sure because of the rain. But they stayed where they were on the northern bank as he started across.

Waylon felt the current tugging at his horse's legs, but the animal didn't have any trouble staying upright. It splashed right on through the water, which, as Waylon had speculated, was only a couple of feet deep. He came out on the other bank, turned, and waved at his brothers.

"Go on back and tell the major to come ahead," he called to them over the sluicing sound of the rain. "I'll wait here."

They lifted their hands to acknowledge the order and turned to ride back to the rest of the brigade. Waylon sat with his shoulders slumped and his head drooping as water poured off his hat. He wished he had a slicker, but in a downpour like this, it probably wouldn't have done much good anyway.

After a moment, he lifted his head and looked one way and then the other along the stream. Brush crowded up close to the banks and the road on both sides. He ought to take a look around, he told himself, make sure nothing was amiss . . .

But what was the point? Nobody else would be out in miserable weather like this, and besides, the war was going to be over any day now. Everybody said so.

Waylon lowered his head, sighed, slipped into a half stupor.

He didn't rouse from it until he heard the riders approaching on the other side of the creek. The Buckeye Brigade numbered approximately seventy-five men. Even in a hard rain, on a muddy road, that many horses made a racket as they loped along. Waylon saw Leon and Burl out *in front of the others by fifty feet. They slowed as they reached the creek and started across.*

Behind them, Major Kingman rode in the forefront of the main group. He had one of the few slickers in the outfit. The dark blue garment made him a little hard to see in the gloom. He lifted a gloved hand and waved the men on.

Leon and Burl emerged from the creek and joined Waylon.

"See anything?" Burl called to his brother.

"Nothing." Waylon watched as Kingman's horse entered the creek and high-stepped across in an arrogant, haughty fashion. Like rider, like horse, thought Waylon.

More men started into the water behind Kingman. Nobody wanted to get in too much of a hurry fording the stream. There was still a chance a horse could step in a hole and break a leg or start floundering around. It was pretty unlikely a rider tossed off in two feet of water, even fast flowing water, would drown, but stranger things had happened. The brigade bunched up a little and spread out as more men rode into Hungry Dog Creek.

The volley of gunfire slammed through the air like thunder, but was no thunderstorm. It was a bullet storm . . . and it swept right through the Buckeye Brigade.

Waylon Spencer gasped in pure shock as men jerked in their saddles and clapped their hands futilely to blood-spouting holes in their bodies. Several toppled from their horses and landed in the creek. The water began to turn pink around them. Even in the overcast, the grisly spectacle was visible.

Men and horses screamed as shot after shot roared. Half the saddles were empty already, Waylon realized in stunned amazement. Next to him, Burl yelped.

Waylon jerked his head toward his brother and shouted, "Are you hit?"

*"No, but one just came mighty damn close!"*

The next second, Waylon heard what sounded like a bee hum past his left ear—a bullet from an ambusher's gun. He whipped his head back and forth, saw clouds of smoke spurting from the bushes on both sides of the creek. Had to be at least forty or fifty Rebs hidden there, he thought wildly.

And he had told his comrades to come ahead without ever checking for an ambush. That realization hollowed out his guts and his soul. Men were dying, and it was his fault. They weren't his friends, not really; he had no friends among the Buckeye Brigade except his brothers. But he had fought at their side and he felt their deaths keenly. He jerked his rifle to his shoulder, aimed at a spot where he had just seen a muzzle flash in the brush, and pulled the trigger.

The hammer snapped harmlessly. The powder charge had gotten wet. He wasn't sure how the Confederates had kept their powder dry enough to carry out the attack. They must have loaded extra rifles and wrapped the breeches in oilcloth.

A high-pitched yell split the air. Riders emerged from the curtains of rain upstream and charged through the water at the battered, bloody remnants of the brigade. Say what you wanted about the Rebs, they had damn good cavalry. The saber-wielding riders in gray smashed into the confused Northern irregulars. Cold steel flashed as more men died with their throats slashed by swift, sweeping blows or were transfixed by powerful thrusts that drove blades all the way through them. It was a ghastly scene. Slaughter, pure and simple.

Gray-clad soldiers burst from the brush, yelling and carrying rifles with fixed bayonets. They splashed into the creek, jabbing right and left, ripping open horse's bellies, making sure any brigade member who toppled out of the *saddle died in the stream. The water wasn't pink any longer; it was red—dark red—as if it had turned completely to blood.*

*One howling Reb ran toward the Spencer brothers. Leon dug a pistol out from under his rain-sodden coat and leveled it. The cap sparked when the hammer fell, and the charge detonated, causing the pistol to go off with a boom. The lead ball plowed into the Confederate soldier's chest and flung him backward like a giant fist. He dropped his rifle in the mud and didn't stir again.*

*A man on horseback lunged out of the creek onto the road and thundered past the still-stunned Spencers. Waylon caught only a glimpse of his face but recognized him as Hank Beauchamp, one of Major Kingman's lieutenants. Beauchamp was fleeing wildly, but Waylon couldn't blame him. The brigade had lost half its number in the opening volley, and many more had been killed already. There was nothing to do except flee.*

*Hacking frenziedly left and right with his own saber, Kingman reached the bank on his horse. As he broke free, he pointed the blade at Waylon and screamed, "You did this!"*

*For a second, Waylon thought Kingman meant his failure to sniff out the ambush. With guilt filling him, he would have agreed with that.*

*But then Kingman went on. "You betrayed us to the Rebels! Traitor! Traitor!"*

*Kingman believed Waylon had double-crossed them and set up the ambush? That was crazy! He never would have done such a thing.*

*Despite that, Kingman charged the brothers, clearly intent on killing all of them.*

*His horse had taken only a couple of lunging strides when its front legs folded up underneath it. The mount crashed to the ground, throwing Kingman over its head into the muddy road. Shouting in their blood lust, Rebel soldiers ran toward him, bayonets poised to stab and rend.*

*Kingman ignored the threat and raised his head to screech at Waylon, "I'll find you, Spencer! I'll kill you . . . if I have to come back from Hell to do it!"*

*As the Rebs closed in around Kingman, Burl grabbed Waylon's arm, tugged on it, and yelled, "Let's get out of here!"*

*The three did just that while they had the chance. Wheeling their horses while bullets still sang around them, they galloped away over the muddy road to Lettsburg and left Hungry Dog Creek and the bloody massacre of the Buckeye Brigade far behind them.*

# CHAPTER 23

"We figured Kingman was dead, of course," Spencer said as he sat on the front porch of the ranch house at Sky Meadow, the empty lemonade glass still in his hand. "With all those Confederate soldiers surrounding him, about to bayonet him, no way he could have survived."

"Then how did he?" asked Elmer.

"We found out later a Confederate general rode up just then and ordered a halt to all the killing," Spencer explained. "One of the Rebs had already stabbed Kingman with his bayonet, but it wasn't a fatal wound. He and all the others of the brigade who were still alive were taken prisoner. They were actually pretty lucky, if you stop to think about it. They were held in a temporary prisoner of war camp, but the war was over only a few months later. They were never shipped off to one of the really bad camps."

Spencer sighed. "But it was bad enough where they were, I reckon. They didn't get much medical care, and the Confederacy wasn't able to feed its own soldiers by that point, so Yankee prisoners just about starved. But like I said, during the spring it was all over and the boys were able to go home."

"Including Major Kingman," Duff said.

"That's right. He was in pretty bad shape from his

wound. I heard he was laid up for more than a year before he recovered."

Meagan said, "He seemed healthy enough when he talked to me yesterday evening."

Spencer nodded. "It took him even longer to get back to normal, but I suppose he is . . . at least physically."

"Still holding a grudge against ye, though, I'll wager," said Duff.

"You know, for a while, I hoped he wouldn't. And it appeared that might be the case. After my brothers and I heard a rumor he was still alive, we looked into it and found out he'd gone back to his hometown in Ohio, just like the three of us had done, and had gone back to teaching once he was healthy enough again. He was married before the war started, and his wife's the one who took care of him and nursed him back to what he had been. Along the way, they had some kids. Three kids, two boys and a girl."

Spencer looked around as if he were searching for a place to put the empty glass. Wang slid from the porch railing, took it from him, and carried it over to the table. Spencer murmured his thanks, then resumed the story.

"About a year ago, Kingman's wife and children were on a train bound for Kansas City—going to visit her folks, who had moved there. The train derailed and went off a trestle into a gulch. Nobody's fault, really. Just a fluke, but Mrs. Kingman and the youngsters were all killed in the crash. I reckon they were all that had kept the major's hate from taking over him. With them gone, he didn't care anymore about teaching or anything else. He just wanted to settle that old grudge against me."

"So he has nae actually been searching for you ever since that ambush," Duff said.

"Not really, although it feels that way sometimes because

that's where it all started. He's hated me and my family for that long. It's just that his own family kept the hate at bay."

"How do you know all this?" asked Meagan.

"He told me some of it himself," Spencer said. "He caught up with me at a church social in our hometown and might have killed me right then and there, if some of the fellas hadn't grabbed him and dragged him away when he started yelling and raving at me.

"I heard more about it not long after that, from mutual acquaintances, I reckon you'd say. Men who served in the brigade during the war. They told me the major had contacted them about getting the unit back together. His letters hinted they were going to come after me and the rest of my family, and then, once that score was settled, they'd go on and resume what they'd been doing during the war."

"Bein' outlaws," Elmer said.

"That's right. Only it would be strictly for the loot, and it wouldn't be confined to towns that sympathized with the Confederacy."

Duff said, "So he recruited a gang from among yer old comrades, but some turned him down and warned you, instead?"

"That's right. If they hadn't, we might not have been able to leave Ohio in time to avoid being attacked. Kingman might well have taken us by surprise and wiped us all out."

Meagan said, "I'm surprised he found twenty men willing to leave their regular lives behind and follow him on a . . . a mission of vengeance like that."

"I ain't," Elmer said. "There's a heap of fellas who've been restless, missin' somethin', ever since the war ended. You go through all that boredom and hardship and misery, and the only thing that breaks it up is little surges of killin' and bein' scared outta your wits that *you're* about to die. That does somethin' to a man's mind.

"The lucky ones, the strong-willed ones, the ones who have somethin' else to live for are able to put that out of their heads and live like regular folks again. Sounds like Kingman even did that for a while, but when he lost the anchor holdin' him in place, he drifted off into bein' loco."

"That's it all right," said Spencer. "That's exactly what happened."

"And some of those boys he called on," added Elmer, "well, they was probably owlhoots to start with. Lots 'o fellas wound up that way after the war."

Duff rested his hands on his knees and said, "So ye got your family together and left Ohio in the hopes of avoiding a showdown with Kingman."

Spencer frowned. "That makes it sound like we ran away. I'm not afraid of Kingman, not any more than I would be of any other lunatic, but the rest of the family . . . my boys and their wives and kids, and Leon's and Burl's grandkids, and all the others . . . they didn't have one thing to do with what happened. They don't deserve to be hurt. But I know Kingman would never stop with just me and my brothers."

Spencer's voice grew hollow again. "'Put them to the sword,' that's what he'd say. 'Kill them all.'" He looked around at the others on the porch. "I swear, if I believed he'd be satisfied with just taking my life, I'd go to him today and tell him to go ahead and kill me, just leave the rest of my family alone." He shook his head. "But that's not what he'd do."

Duff had never met Thomas Kingman, but he had a hunch Spencer was right.

Meagan said, "After talking to the man yesterday evening and looking into his eyes, I agree with you, Mr. Spencer. He was friendly, charming, and well-spoken. But something in the way he looked when he asked about you and your family just made me feel cold inside."

Nodding, Spencer said, "That's the way he is, all right."

"So that's why you're in a hurry to reach Longshot Basin," said Duff. "Ye want to get there before Kingman can catch up to you."

"We just wanted a place to settle, and I hoped the major would never be able to find us. But when I heard about Longshot Basin, it seemed perfect. Enough good land for us to homestead, and a place easy to defend if it ever came to that. After all, as far as I knew then, there was only one way in and out of the basin. If Kingman came for us, we would stop him at Thunder Canyon."

"But now Thunder Canyon is gone, or useless for reaching the basin, at any rate."

"Even better," said Spencer. "This so-called Nightmare Trail . . . Kingman could never get his gang over it. We could hold it forever with half a dozen men."

"If 'twas not for the Hardcastles."

Spencer sighed. "That's a problem, all right." He brightened slightly. "But if we can reach the basin, the Hardcastles won't want Kingman's bunch using the trail, either, will they?"

Elmer said, "There's no tellin' what a bunch of hillbilly owlhoots like that'll do. You don't want to be puttin' any faith in them, Waylon."

"But what else can we do?" Spencer asked with a bleak note in his voice.

Duff said, "I might be able to prevail upon the army to provide ye with a cavalry escort to the basin. I dinnae believe the Hardcastles would want to take on the United States army."

"How long would that take?"

Duff spread his hands. "I dinnae ken. A couple of weeks, perhaps, or a month?"

"We can't wait that long. If Kingman's in Chugwater, he'll find out in a day or two we're here on your ranch, Duff, if he doesn't know already. As soon as he's sure, he'll come gunning for us."

Elmer clenched a fist. "We'll give him a mighty hot welcome if he does, by grab!"

Spencer made a slashing motion in the air with his right hand. "No! I'm not going to put you or anybody else in danger. We're going to Longshot Basin, and if it comes to a battle, we'll fight it there." He drew in a deep breath. "The Spencers have run far enough. Longshot Basin will be where we make our stand!"

There was no talking Spencer out of it. It was much too late in the day for the immigrants to start to Longshot Basin, but Spencer insisted they would pull out the next morning.

"Not by yourself, you won't," Elmer declared. "I'm comin' with you, Waylon. I'll do my best to see you and your family make it to where you're goin'."

Wang said, "I will accompany your wagons as well, Mr. Spencer. I would like to see this Nightmare Trail and Longshot Basin for myself."

"I appreciate that, fellas." Spencer looked over at Duff. "You've done more than your share to help us already, Duff. I want you to stay here at Sky Meadow instead of tangling with the Hardcastles again."

Meagan laughed.

Spencer looked puzzled as he asked, "What did I say that's funny, Miss Parker? If you don't mind my asking."

"It's just the idea of someone telling Duff MacCallister to remain behind and stay out of trouble," Meagan said. "I'm not sure I've ever heard anything more unlikely in my life."

Duff grinned. "Ye make it sound as if I'm a wee bit foolhardy."

"No, it's just that MacCallisters and trouble go together, and there's no way of keeping them apart."

"Ye may well be right about that," Duff told her with a shrug. He looked at Spencer. "I'll be coming with ye as well. I'll not go so far as to say the three of us are a match for the Hardcastles, but Elmer, Wang, and meself have tackled some pretty high odds in the past."

"And we've always come out on top," Elmer added.

"Although, logically speaking, any outcome must eventually have its initial occurrence," said Wang.

"Meanin' there's a first time for everything?" Elmer asked him.

"Exactly."

"I'll take them odds. I got a hunch my luck ain't gonna run out yet."

Duff hoped that was true for all of them.

After Spencer had returned to the immigrant encampment to tell them to get ready for the next morning's departure, and Elmer had tagged along with him, and Wang had gone back into the house, Duff and Meagan were left alone, sitting on the porch.

"Am I going to have to tell ye that ye cannae go along on the trip to Longshot Basin?" he asked her.

"Since when do you have a great deal of success telling me what I can and can't do, Mr. MacCallister?"

"Oh, I ken, I ken," he assured her. "Ye have a mind of your own, and an independent streak a mile wide. But I honestly believe 'twould not be a good idea for ye to accompany us on this journey."

"Well, you're not going to have to argue with me," she said, "because it just so happens I agree with you this time."

His tawny eyebrows rose in surprise as he looked at her. "Ye do?"

"Yes, I do. Under the circumstances, it's possible you'll be in danger from two different directions at once."

"The Hardcastles and this gang of Major Kingman's."

"Right. And while you sometimes seem to have eyes in the back of your head, I think even the great Duff MacCallister would have trouble looking *three* directions at once, and that's what you might have to do if you were trying to keep up with me, too."

"Ye always say you can take care of yourself."

"And so I can," Meagan asserted, "but just because I know that, it doesn't mean you wouldn't get distracted because you were worried about me. So that would mean you'd be running an even greater risk for yourself, and I don't want that."

Duff considered what she said and slowly nodded. "Ye really have been thinking this through, haven't ye?"

"I've learned a lot from you about how to handle trouble, Duff. Of course, that's probably because you wind up getting in so much of it . . ."

He shrugged in acknowledgment of her point.

"But at the same time, I know there are things you're much better suited for than I am," she went on. "I'm happy I've been able to help you out at times in the past—"

"You've saved me life on numerous occasions, ye mean, including the very first time we met."

"Aye, tha' be true," she said, smiling to show her mockery of his Scottish burr was good-natured. "I just think it might be better for me to sit this one out."

"Well, to tell ye the truth, 'tis a real load off me mind knowing ye feel that way. And 'twill probably be safer in the long run if I'm able to concentrate all me efforts on getting the Spencers to Longshot Basin."

"I make no promises about the next time some ruckus comes calling, though," she said with a laugh. "I may be bound and determined to get right in the middle of that one."

Duff reached over and took her hand. "A finer ally no man ever had, in life's troubles and in its joys."

"Thank you, Duff," she said softly.

If they hadn't been sitting next to each other in separate chairs, he might well have put his arms around her and kissed her at that moment . . . but there was something to be said for just sitting there in quiet, affectionate companionship and holding hands.

After a few minutes of silence went by, however, Duff grinned. "I ken there are many reasons why ye would feel that way, but why in particular did ye refer to me just then as 'the great Duff MacCallister'?"

"Well, it certainly wasn't because of your modesty!" Meagan told him with another laugh.

# CHAPTER 24

The immigrant camp was on high alert that night, just in case Kingman had discovered their whereabouts and was already making plans to strike against them. Guards were posted all night.

Duff added to that security by having several members of his crew standing watch, as well. He got up several times during the night to step out onto the porch and look and listen intently, making sure that everything was all right.

During one of those times, he ran into Elmer doing the same thing.

"Everything's quiet," the old-timer reported. "Kingman must not have found out where the Spencers are yet."

"Either that, or he believes he'll have better luck waiting to attack them after they've left the ranch and are out on the open range."

Elmer nodded. "You could be right about that. I've talked to Waylon enough about the war to know Kingman had a reputation as a pretty good field commander. He was plenty nervy, but didn't mind waitin' for a better time to strike if he thought it was possible."

Duff rested his hands on the porch railing and leaned forward to peer out into the darkness. "I've been thinking about that ambush—the one on Hungry Dog Creek during the war."

"Waylon blames himself for that, sure enough."

"But he insists he had nothing to do with setting it up," Duff went on. "'Tis unlikely that many Confederate forces would be lying in wait, just on the off chance the Buckeye Brigade would ride along that road. Remember what Mr. Spencer said. The Confederates had a good number of riflemen hidden in the brush, plus a group of cavalry waiting for just the right moment to strike."

In the shadows, Elmer rasped his fingers over grizzled stubble as he stroked his chin in thought. "You're sayin' the Rebs *knew* ahead of time Kingman's bunch was gonna be comin' along that road."

"That seems the most likely explanation to me."

"If that's true, then *somebody* sold 'em out," Elmer said with anger in his voice. "Nothin' puts a burr under my saddle faster than somebody who's supposed to be on your side goin' over to the enemy."

"In that case, while some of the guilt Mr. Spencer feels is justified, the true responsibility for all those deaths lies elsewhere."

"On the fella who betrayed 'em to the Rebs."

"Aye."

Elmer shook his head. "Even if we're right in our speculatin', after all this time, whoever was to blame is probably dead. And even if he ain't, how would you ever know?"

"Proving anything is unlikely, I'll admit," Duff said. "But I thought I would broach the subject with Mr. Spencer anyway and perhaps ease his mind, if only a bit. With the threats looming over them, he needs to be as clear-headed as possible."

"Ain't that the truth." Elmer paused, then added, "What

do you think the chances are of them makin' it to Longshot Basin?"

"I dinnae ken," Duff said, "but 'tis certain I am that I would nae be wagering a brand new tam o' shanter on it."

Despite being awake several times during the night, Duff was up early the next morning. Wang was up even earlier and had coffee brewing and breakfast cooking when Duff came into the kitchen.

"Did ye sleep any?" Duff asked.

"Of course. A clear mind promotes restful sleep, and I try to banish disturbing thoughts, especially before I seek slumber."

"A wise course for everyone to follow, I'm thinking. But sometimes difficult to do."

"One can only try." Wang checked the biscuits baking in the oven, then went on. "I looked up toward the immigrant encampment a short time ago. They appear to be moving around and getting ready for departure. Their cook fires were burning."

"I'll walk up and see them in a bit . . . as soon as the coffee's ready."

Duff waited until he had a tin cup of the strong, black brew, then took it with him as he strolled toward the camp. The dogs noticed him coming, of course, and ran out to greet him with raucous barks. He saw men getting the wagons ready to roll, women preparing coffee and food, and children stumbling around, knuckling sleepy eyes.

Waylon Spencer strode out from the camp and said, "Good morning, Duff."

"Mr. Spencer." Duff nodded.

"I can understand why you wouldn't want to call me

Waylon, after everything I told you yesterday about how I got all those men killed . . ."

"Hold on a bit," Duff said as Spencer's voice trailed off miserably. "I'd like to talk to ye about that very thing, if ye dinnae mind."

"If you've changed your mind about coming with us—"

"Nae, 'tis not that at all. Ye said Major Kingman accused ye of conspiring with the Confederate forces?"

Spencer frowned in the reflected light from the cooking fires. "That's right. But I didn't do it. I was guilty of being careless, I'll not deny that, but I would never betray the men I rode with."

"Aye. Even knowing ye as little as I do, I have no doubt of that. And the guilt you speak of, surely that's tempered by the circumstances. You were exhausted, and as ye said, the war was nearly over."

Spencer grunted. "That didn't make any difference to the men who were killed that day, or the ones taken prisoner. There's no excuse for what I did . . . or rather, failed to do."

"How many men escaped from that ambush?"

"Well . . . there was so much confusion, it's hard to say . . . but I never heard of anybody getting away except me and my brothers."

"There was one other," Duff reminded him. "Ye mentioned his name. Hank Beauchamp."

Spencer nodded. "Yes, of course, Lieutenant Beauchamp. I'd forgotten about him. I suppose he got away. He rode past us and was heading hell-for-leather toward Lettsburg the last time I saw him."

"So, he managed to make it out of the creek while all the shooting was going on."

"That's right. He was lucky." Spencer frowned and

cocked his head a little to the side. "What are you getting at, Duff?"

"Just thinking," Duff said. "Was there anything . . . different . . . about Lieutenant Beauchamp that day?"

"No, he acted the same as he always did." Spencer scratched at his jaw, and Duff could tell from the look on his face he was thinking back to that bloody day again. "I just don't remember—*Wait*. There was one thing. I don't reckon I've thought about it in years, but that moment when he bolted past is pretty well etched in my mind. The lieutenant had this red bandana he wore sometimes, but that day, it wasn't around his neck. It was tied around his upper right arm."

Duff nodded. He had put this theory together on the fly, but Spencer's recollection when right along with what Duff was thinking. He said, "Did ye ever ask yourself why he might have done that?"

Spencer's eyes widened. He was smart enough to grasp the implication of Duff's words right away. "It was a signal!" he exclaimed. "Good Lord! That bandana could have been like a . . . a warning flag. A sign that the Rebs weren't supposed to shoot at him . . ."

"Because he's the one who got word to the Confederates ye and the others would be riding along that road on that day. I dinnae ken exactly how he managed it, but he must have, Waylon. 'Tis the only thing that makes sense."

Spencer looked shocked for a moment, then he raised a hand and scrubbed it over his face wearily. "All these years," he muttered. "All these long years, I've believed it was completely my fault. And there's still no excuse for my failure. But it wouldn't have happened if we hadn't been betrayed. No one else could it have been." He looked up at Duff.

"Kingman was right. We did have a traitor in the brigade. But it wasn't me."

"What happened to Beauchamp?"

Spencer shook his head. "I have no idea. I never heard anything about him after the war. He might as well have fallen off the face of the earth."

"'Tis probably what he wanted to do. He would nae want his perfidy being discovered. More than likely, he avoided Kingman and the other survivors."

"Maybe I should go to Kingman, tell him the truth—"

"And what are the odds he'd believe ye?" Duff broke in. "After all these years of blaming you and nursing his hate, do ye think he'd give it up on the basis of a theory ye cannae prove?"

"Well . . . probably not," admitted Spencer. "Besides, Kingman and Beauchamp were friends. They always got along well. Kingman wouldn't want to believe the lieutenant would betray him, even though it must be what happened."

"Aye. We'll never know why. But it explains the red bandana on Beauchamp's arm and the fact he made it out when none of the others in the creek did."

Spencer reached out, grasped Duff's shoulder, and squeezed it for a second. "Thank you, Duff," he said, his voice taut with emotion. "It doesn't absolve me, but perhaps it lightens the load a little."

"As well it should, Waylon."

The older man's brief smile indicated he'd noticed Duff was using his given name again. "We'll be ready to go as soon as it's light enough. Would you like to have breakfast with us?"

"I appreciate the invitation, but Wang will have breakfast ready at the house for him and me and Elmer by the time I get back." Duff drank the last of the coffee in his cup and nodded. "At sunup, we ride."

\* \* \*

Being able to rest for a few days had made a difference in the group of immigrants. When they'd arrived in Chug-water and then at Sky Meadow, weariness had gripped them visibly. Faces were gray with more than just trail dust, and shoulders had slumped. They shuffled tiredly when they walked.

As they set out there was a fresh spring in their steps, and eyes were lit up with hope and anticipation. Duff heard laughter and eager talk as he rode along the line of wagons with Elmer and Wang.

The respite had even helped the livestock. The heads of the mules and oxen didn't droop as much.

The eastern sky was awash with gold, although the orange orb of the sun hadn't yet put in an appearance. It wasn't far below the horizon, though.

Duff and his companions reined in alongside the first wagon. Waylon Spencer was on the seat with his wife Edith. Like all the others, they looked eager to get started.

Two riders waited on the other side of the lead wagon. Walter and Oliver Spencer were mounted on different horses from the ones they had taken on the scouting trip to Longshot Basin.

"Morning, boys," Duff greeted them over the backs of the wagon team.

"Hello, Mr. MacCallister," Walter said.

In his obvious excitement, Oliver blurted out, "Uncle Waylon said we could ride out front!"

"That's right," Spencer said. "You fellows have covered the ground before, so it makes sense for you to lead the way." He glanced at Duff. "If that's all right with you. I mean, you know where we're going even better than my nephews do."

"'Tis fine with me," Duff assured him. "They're good lads, and I'll be proud to have them riding with us."

"Darn right," added Elmer. "They handled theirselves real well on that little jaunt."

"All right, then." Spencer untied his team's reins from the brake lever. "I suppose we're ready to roll out."

"You give the signal, Waylon," Duff told him.

Spencer nodded and stood up on the driver's box, turning so he could look back along the line of wagons. He raised his arm and then waved it to motion them forward as he bellowed the universal command of all wagon masters.

*"Wagons . . . hoooo!"*

# CHAPTER 25

"How long will it take to get there?" Oliver asked as he and his brother rode alongside Duff. "We'll be in Longshot Basin before dark, won't we?"

From behind them, Elmer said, "You're gettin' a whole heap ahead of yourself, boy. We made a lot better time when it was just us ridin' horseback. With those wagons followin' us, we'll be doin' good today to make it as far as where the Nightmare Trail forks off."

"Is that right, Mr. MacCallister?" asked Walter.

"Aye," Duff said. "And 'twill require most of the day tomorrow to follow the trail around the mountain and down into the basin."

"But it's not that far," Oliver protested.

"Perhaps not as the crow flies. But ye saw that trail. Wagons cannae be hurried over it. 'Twill be a slow, steady process, with the wagons spread out a good distance apart."

"And that's if we don't run into any trouble from those Hardcastle varmints," Elmer added.

Walter said, "That fella Cole promised to talk to the rest of his family, didn't he, Mr. MacCallister? He was gonna try to persuade them to leave us alone?"

"That's what he said. Whether or not he had any success, I cannae say."

It would been best if they could have waited for Cole Hardcastle to get word to him before leaving Sky Meadow, thought Duff. Cole was supposed to let him know if it was safe for the wagon train to proceed.

Unfortunately, the arrival of Major Thomas Kingman in Chugwater, along with the dregs of what had been the Buckeye Brigade, had changed everything. The Spencers couldn't afford to wait. Duff would have been willing to let them remain camped at Sky Meadow for as long as was necessary, but he had to admit, it would be easier for the immigrants to defend Longshot Basin from an attack. As Waylon Spencer had said, it was built to hold off an army.

Unfortunately, the reverse was true, too. Once in the basin, the immigrants would be bottled up. If Kingman decided to seal off the Nightmare Trail, he could keep them trapped in the basin indefinitely.

And a lot of wild cards were in this game—namely, the Hardcastles. Duff wished he knew whether Cole had had any luck convincing his family to leave the pilgrims alone.

The wagons kept up a steady pace and by midday had covered half the distance to Buzzard's Roost, Thunder Canyon, and Longshot Basin. Waylon Spencer called a halt to allow the teams to rest. The people could use a break, too. They would eat leftovers from breakfast for their lunch, but a couple of the women built a small fire to boil several pots of coffee.

Duff, Elmer, and Wang gave their horses water, then turned the animals loose to graze. Duff was standing near the wagons, a grass stem in his mouth, gazing toward Buzzard's Roost which was visible in the distance, when he spotted a rider heading toward them from that direction.

He spat out the grass stem and called softly, "Elmer." The old-timer was only a few yards away, talking to Waylon

Spencer. When he looked around, Duff nodded toward the man approaching on horseback and said, "Rider coming."

Elmer and Spencer looked in that direction, and both stiffened as they saw the rider.

"Can you tell who it is?" asked Spencer.

"Not yet," Duff said. "I've a spyglass in me saddlebags, though." He stepped over to the horse and brought out the telescope. After extending it and lifting it to his right eye, Duff peered through the lenses. He needed a moment to find what he was looking for, but when he did, a familiar lean figure leaped into sharp relief. "'Tis Cole Hardcastle," he told Elmer and Spencer.

"Is he alone?" asked Elmer.

Duff moved the spyglass, shifting his view back along the trail and then up onto the thickly wooded lower slopes of Buzzard's Roost. "It appears he is. I see no signs of other riders."

Spencer said, "Then he can't be much of a threat to us, can he?"

"I would nae ever say that about a man such as Cole Hardcastle," Duff replied as he lowered the telescope. "A man like this is always dangerous, as long as he draws breath . . . if he wants to be. But aye, alone as he is, he does nae appear to pose much of a threat to us. We'll have to wait and see what he has to say for himself."

"You reckon we ought to go meet him, Duff?" Elmer suggested. "Away from the wagons, I mean."

"So there'll be less likelihood of innocents coming to harm if gunplay were to break out?" Duff nodded. "'Tis not a bad idea, but I want ye to stay here, Elmer, and Wang, as well. I'll brace Hardcastle on me own."

Elmer frowned. "I don't know if that's a good idea. I mean, no offense, Duff, but even though you're a heap faster on the draw than you were when you got to Wyoming, you ain't as slick as Hardcastle. He's got a rep as bein' mighty fast."

"If a shootout was what he wanted, he had chances before now. I'll risk it." Duff took hold of his horse's reins, put a foot in the stirrup, and swung up onto the animal's back. "Stay here."

The firm tone of his voice didn't leave any room for argument on Elmer's part.

Duff rode away from the wagons. As he put distance behind him, he felt eyes following him. Word of Cole Hardcastle's approach must have spread, as well as the news that Duff was riding out to meet him. Naturally enough, the immigrants would be intensely curious about what was going to happen next.

Duff wanted to find that out, himself.

He intercepted Cole about half a mile from where the wagons had stopped. Both men reined in when approximately twenty feet separated them.

Cole had a smile on his face as he rested his hands on the saddle horn and leaned forward. "Mornin', MacCallister. Although I reckon it's afternoon by now, ain't it?"

"As of a short time ago, aye. So 'tis good afternoon I'll be bidding ye, Hardcastle, and I hope ye have brought good news with ye."

"I think it is, but I suppose we'll have to wait and see. I'll get right to it. My family has agreed those immigrants can use the Nightmare Trail to get to Longshot Basin."

Relief went through Duff, but he cautioned himself not to get carried away just yet. "And they'll allow the Spencers to settle in the basin unmolested?"

"Don't reckon they would have agreed to let the sod-busters use the trail if they didn't intend for 'em to homestead the basin."

"Probably not," said Duff, "but I'd like to hear it spoken anyway."

"All right," Cole said, sounding a little irritated. "They can settle in the basin. Satisfied?"

"Aye." Duff's eyes narrowed. "Would ye be willing to ride with us, just to insure that?"

Cole glared at him for a second but then laughed abruptly. "Volunteer to be a hostage again, you mean? Well, hell, sure, why not? I don't have anything to be afraid of."

"'Tis glad I am to hear it. Come on."

They rode side by side toward the wagons. That ought to be a signal in itself that things were all right, at least for the moment, thought Duff.

Elmer and Waylon Spencer rode out to meet them. Elmer eyed Cole warily but gave him a civil nod after they had all reined in.

Duff said, "You fellows haven't actually met. Waylon Spencer, this is Cole Hardcastle."

"I'm pleased to meet you, Mr. Hardcastle," Spencer said, "as long as you've brought good news for us."

"I reckon I have, Mr. Spencer," drawled Cole. "My family has decided it's all right for you folks to travel over the Nightmare Trail to Longshot Basin and settle there, if that's what you've made up your minds to do."

"It is. I assume you spoke up on our behalf?"

"I just laid out the situation the best I could and let folks make up their own minds. Can we count on your bunch not causing trouble for *my* family?"

"We've no reason to hunt trouble with anybody," Spencer declared. "All we want is to be left alone to work our farms and live our lives."

Cole nodded and said, "Sounds like we're in agreement, then."

Walter and Oliver had been drifting closer on their horses as the men talked.

Cole grinned at them. "Howdy, boys. Glad to see you both made it back."

"Yes, sir, Mr. Hardcastle," Walter replied. "Do you mind if I ask you a question?"

"Go ahead."

"Miss Ginny . . . how's she doing?"

Cole chuckled. "You mean, is she over bein' mad at you? I wouldn't count on that, son. From what I've heard, the two of you had a pretty good scrap, and Ginny, well, she's the sort to hold a grudge. Maybe not as much as Lydia, though."

Oliver said, "I was just going to ask you about her, sir."

"You're the one who tossed her in the brambles, right?"

Oliver looked down and muttered, "Yes, sir."

"She might forgive you for that if you both live long enough. Like, say, in a hundred years or so."

"She's all right, though, isn't she? I mean, she wasn't scratched up so bad she won't heal up, was she? I swear, I never really meant to do her any harm. I just wanted to get her to quit fightin' me . . ."

"She's fine," Cole assured him. "My sister took good care of her."

"I'm glad to hear it."

Duff said, "We'd better be moving on. We need to get to the fork in the trail today and maybe on up to the lower slopes of Buzzard's Roost. Might be better camping spots in the trees."

"That's a fact," Cole said. "If you're willing to take my advice, I can find you a good place to stop for the night."

"We'd appreciate that, Mr. Hardcastle," said Spencer. "You know these parts a lot better than any of us do."

"That's true. If we're gonna be neighbors, nothing wrong with giving each other a helping hand, is there?"

"Not at all."

Cole turned his horse and motioned to Walter and Oliver. "Come on, boys. Why don't you ride with me?"

They looked at Duff, who nodded. They were all going to be in plain sight, so he didn't think it was likely Cole would try any sort of trick, especially if he and Elmer weren't far behind them.

As the two fell in side by side about fifty feet behind Cole and the two young men, Elmer asked quietly, "You trust that snake-blooded varmint, Duff?"

"Not entirely. He seems friendly enough, but 'twould be a good idea to keep an eye on him, I'm thinking."

"And a mighty close eye it's gonna be, too," Elmer agreed with a scowl.


The wagons reached the spot where the Nightmare Trail veered off toward Buzzard's Roost and swung left to follow it. They were still traveling close together and wouldn't have to spread out until they were higher on the mountain, where the truly nightmarish part of the trail began.

By late afternoon, they had almost reached the lower slopes. The trail led straight up a gentle incline in front of them and entered the trees about a quarter of a mile away. Small ridges flanked the route on both sides. Duff, riding beside the lead wagon with Waylon Spencer at the reins, turned his head to look back and forth. Boulders that had tumbled down from higher on the mountain littered both ridges. The rocks were worn and rounded, indicating they had been there for a long time, possibly centuries.

Duff felt a faint prickling on the back of his neck. He didn't see anything unusual or threatening, though.

Cole Hardcastle was still riding ahead of the wagons with Walter and Oliver. Duff nudged his mount to a faster pace and soon caught up with them. Cole looked back over his shoulder with a frown as Duff rode up, and Duff could tell something was worrying him, too.

"MacCallister, I was just telling these boys something's giving me the fantods," Cole said. "You haven't seen anything amiss, have you?"

"Nae," Duff replied, "but I dinnae mind telling ye, I feel the same—"

The crack of a rifle shot interrupted him. Cole Hardcastle's hat flew off his head as the gunfighter yelped a surprised curse. His horse started to rear, spooked by the shot and Cole's reaction to it. Cole pulled the reins tight to bring the animal under control.

"Get back to the wagons!" Duff shouted at Walter and Oliver as he whirled his horse and searched for the source of the shot. That sudden movement probably saved his life. He felt as much as heard the wind-rip of a bullet pass his ear as another rifle cracked somewhere not too far off.

Duff spotted a gray puff of powder smoke from one of the boulders on the ridge to the left of the trail. Another slug whipped past him from the other direction.

Bushwhackers were hidden up behind those rocks on both sides of the trail, he realized. He didn't figure any of the Hardcastles would come so close to blowing out the brains of one of their own, so that left only one other explanation for the ambush.

Major Thomas Kingman and what was left of the Buckeye Brigade had gotten in front of the wagon train and laid a trap for their quarry. And they were doing their best to live up to their other nickname—*the Buckeye Butchers.*

"Come on!" Duff yelled to Cole as he hauled his horse around and galloped toward the wagons.

Cole fell in alongside him and both men leaned forward in their saddles over the necks of their mounts to make themselves smaller targets. Dirt and grass spurted into the air as bullets struck the ground ahead of them and to both sides. Being good riders, they veered their horses back and forth slightly to throw off the aim of the men shooting at them.

Ahead of them, Walter and Oliver were riding hell-for-leather toward the wagons . . . but that didn't mean they would be safe once they got there. The bushwhackers would target the rest of the immigrants, too, as they tried to take their revenge on Waylon Spencer.

The wagons had jolted to an abrupt halt as the gunfire blasted. Men yelled for their wives and children to get into the wagon beds and lie down between the thick sideboards, which would stop at least some of the bullets. Lead whistled through the air. As Duff came closer, he saw some of the arching canvas covers on the vehicles jerking as bullets ripped through them.

Elmer and Wang had both dismounted to return the fire. Elmer stood beside the second wagon in line, which belonged to Burl Spencer. The red-bearded, barrel-chested immigrant knelt on the driver's box and cranked off rounds from the Winchester he had tucked against his shoulder.

Duff spotted another red head sticking out through the opening in the canvas at the front of the wagon bed as Burl's granddaughter Becky joined the fight. The pretty teenager had a Winchester, too, and coolly peppered the rocks on the left-hand ridge.

Farther back along the line of wagons, Wang fired slowly and methodically with a rifle. Duff knew he was waiting each time until he had a clear shot at one of the bushwhackers, even if that target was nothing more than an inch or two of flesh as a would-be killer peered around a boulder. Wang was an incredibly dangerous fighter at close range with shuriken, nunchuks, or just bare hands and feet, but he was also a deadly shot with a rifle when he needed to be.

The rest of the Spencer men had reacted quickly and were putting up a stout defense, laying down heavy fire on both ridges which Duff was sure had the bushwhackers diving for cover often enough to blunt their attack. He saw all of that instantly, his keen brain taking in the situation in the blink of an eye.

But he also knew the ambushers had the high ground and quite possibly a numerical advantage, while the defenders had only the cover of the wagons. Things didn't look good in the long run for the immigrants.

He pulled his feet from the stirrups, yanked his Winchester from its saddle boot, and dropped from the saddle while his horse was still moving. Duff landed running and levered a round into the rifle's chamber while he was catching his balance.

A few yards away, Cole Hardcastle did likewise. He dropped to one knee beside the left front wheel of Waylon Spencer's wagon and brought the Winchester to his shoulder. The rifle cracked and spurted flame. He worked the lever and fired again toward the ridge to the right of the trail.

Duff ran around the mule team and knelt beside the other front wheel. He spotted a bushwhacker leaning out from behind a rock to draw a bead and snapped a shot at the man. The slug missed, but it struck the boulder only inches from the bushwhacker's face and make him jerk back involuntarily.

The man's feet must have gotten tangled up. Still holding his rifle, he waved his other arm wildly in the air and toppled into plain sight. As he lay there, he made the fatal mistake of trying to bring his rifle into play rather than scuttling back behind cover as fast as he could.

Duff, who had already worked his rifle's lever, put a

round through the bushwhacker's head. Duff saw him jerk and then roll onto his back, where he didn't move again.

Duff fired at another man but missed. He was thinking about crawling underneath the wagon and continuing the fight from there, when he heard something and turned to look toward the trees.

A line of ten riders swept out of the pines and galloped toward the wagons, the horses lunging and surging, powder smoke erupting from the guns in the riders' hands as they charged toward the immigrants.

Even though Duff had never laid eyes on the fellow before, he knew the grim-faced leader could be only one man.

*Major Thomas Kingman.*

# CHAPTER 26

So many bullets kicked up dust as they struck the ground it looked like a wave washing toward Duff. He twisted and dived underneath the wagon. Slugs ricocheted off the iron tires bound around the outside of the wheels and chewed splinters from the spokes.

Cole Hardcastle rolled under the wagon from the other side. As he came to a stop on his belly, he raised his head, stared at Duff, and exclaimed, "What the hell, MacCallister! Who are those skunks? I swear, it's not my family!"

"I ken that," Duff told him. "'Tis a long story, Hardcastle. Old enemies of Waylon Spencer."

"So they want to kill him and wipe out his whole family?"

Duff nodded. "That's right."

"Well, damned if we're gonna let that happen!"

The ferocity of that response surprised Duff a little. Cole sounded like he had a real stake in this, in addition to saving his own skin after getting caught in the ambush.

Cole had dropped his rifle when he threw himself under the wagon, but he drew his revolver and quickly crawled behind one of the wheels. As the pounding hoofbeats grew louder, Cole aimed through the wheel spokes and began firing.

Duff did the same on the other side of the vehicle. The riders raced along both sides of the wagon train, firing into the vehicles. Duff heard howls of pain and knew the immigrants were suffering casualties. Anger filled him as he tilted his gun up and snapped a shot at one of the riders flashing past.

The man yelled, dropped his gun, and flung his hands in the air. He pitched out of the saddle, landed hard, and rolled a couple of times before coming to a stop in a bloody heap. Duff saw that his bullet had taken the man under the chin and angled up through his brain before blowing out through a fist-sized hole in the back of his skull.

"Got one!" Cole exulted.

Duff looked over his shoulder and saw a man lying facedown several yards from the wagons on that side. If the immigrants had managed to kill or wound another one or two of them, that would have whittled down the odds considerably.

But bushwhackers were still up on the ridges. Duff had accounted for one of them, and he hoped Elmer and Wang had downed some, too. The immigrants were far from out of danger, but at least they and their allies were putting up a good fight.

Duff came up on hands and knees and crawled out from under the wagon. The riders who had charged out of the trees had galloped past the wagons and were wheeling around and regrouping for another attack. Duff did a quick head count and saw six were left.

One of them was Kingman, and with a shout and a wave of the hand holding a gun, he ordered his men forward again.

At the same time, the half dozen ambushers who were still in the fight left the cover of their boulders and bounded down the slopes toward the wagons, shouting and firing their rifles as they came.

Duff squeezed off a shot and blew another of the Buckeye Butchers out of the saddle. He swung the Colt to the right and tried to draw a bead on Kingman, but just as he triggered the gun, one of the other riders cut in front of his target. That man slumped forward, clutched at his saddle horn but missed, and then rolled off his horse to land in the limp sprawl of death.

Kingman reached the lead wagon and vaulted out of the saddle in a daring leap that carried him onto the driver's box. He was no longer a young man, but his insane hatred must have given him strength and coordination belying his years, to finally be confronting his longtime enemy.

Duff saw Kingman make that leap and knew the major was going after Waylon Spencer. Duff had his hands full at the moment and couldn't help. One of the bushwhackers was practically in his face, screaming curses and driving the butt of his rifle at Duff's head.

Duff triggered the Colt in his hand, but the hammer fell with a harmless snap. The gun was empty. He twisted aside desperately and avoided the blow aimed at his head, but the bushwhacker crashed into him with such force he was knocked backward off his feet. The bushwhacker fell, too, but kept trying to slam the rifle's stock into Duff's face.

Duff jerked his head aside. The rifle butt hit the ground only inches from his left ear. He smashed the empty Colt in his hand against the left side of the bushwhacker's head. The man sagged, but his hat, held on his head by a taut chin strap despite the collision, blunted the blow's force that he wasn't knocked out. With both hands gripping the rifle, he thrust the breech against Duff's throat and bore down on it.

Duff knew the man would crush his windpipe if he kept up the terrible pressure for more than a few seconds. He flipped the Colt around in his hand and struck with the butt, hammering it against the man's head three times as fast as he could. He felt bone crack and then shatter under the on-slaught. Blood welled from the bushwhacker's nose and mouth. The outlaw let go of the rifle and slid down until he was lying stretched out on top of Duff, dead weight.

Grimacing, Duff rolled the corpse off him and turned onto his left side. He raised his head, looked around, and saw that the battle had deteriorated mostly into hand-to-hand combat up and down both sides of the wagon train.

Except in the case of Wang. He used his feet as well as his hands as he took on three of Kingman's men. A spinning kick that carried Wang high off the ground crushed the jaw of one man and laid him out. The move brought Wang around so that he landed lightly on one foot and a knee, a position from which he exploded upward to slash a side-hand blow across the throat of the second man. A short, sharp punch to the belly of the third man doubled him over and put him in perfect position for Wang to dispose of him with another side-hand blow, this time to the back of the neck. The whole thing had taken less than five seconds, oc-curring almost too fast for Duff's eye to follow the action.

Not far away, Elmer crouched with a gun in each hand. Duff didn't know where the old-timer had picked up the second revolver, but watched him put it to good use. He fired both guns at the same time, the booming reports blending into one loud peal of gun-thunder, and two of Kingman's men flew backward as the heavy rounds punched through their bodies.

Those were the final shots of the conflict. Duff heard grunts of effort and the meaty smack of fists striking flesh and followed them around the lead wagon to see Waylon Spencer and Thomas Kingman slugging it out, trading ter-rific blows that had the men staggering back and forth and breathing hard. Blood dripped from cuts on their battered, swollen faces.

Duff looked along the line of wagons, saw that the rest of Kingman's men appeared to be down, either dead or at least out of the fight. The Spencer men, including Walter and Oliver, hurried toward Duff. Some of them looked a little the worse for wear, with bloodstains on their clothes from various wounds, but none appeared to be hurt too badly.

Cole Hardcastle came up to Duff and said, "Looks like it's over, MacCallister."

"Not quite," replied Duff with a nod toward the battle still going on between Waylon Spencer and Thomas Kingman.

Elmer and Wang joined them, as well.

"Nobody on our side was killed," Elmer reported. "And mighty doggone lucky that was, too."

"How many of Kingman's men are still alive?" asked Duff.

"Three or four, but they're shot up bad enough they ain't gonna give us no more trouble."

"Best keep an eye on them anyway, just to be sure. Ye dinnae want to be shot by a man ye considered harmless."

"Nor by anybody else," Elmer agreed with a grim chuckle. "All right, I'll post guards over 'em. Be a good job for them two boys who rode with us before. They're cool-headed." He nodded toward Spencer and Kingman. "You reckon we ought to give Waylon a hand?"

"Not unless he needs it," Duff said. "I'm thinking he'd want to end this fight himself . . . and he's close to doing it."

That was true. Spencer and Kingman were close to the same age, but Spencer appeared to have more strength and stamina. He wasn't completely steady on his feet, but Kingman was reeling around and wildly missing with most of his punches.

One such errant blow brought him within reach of a roundhouse right from Spencer that caught Kingman on the jaw with a sound like an ax biting deep into a tree stump. Kingman's momentum kept him stumbling forward for a couple more steps, then he went down hard on his face. He struggled to rise but slumped down again, unable to do it.

Spencer backed off. He lifted his right arm in a torn, crimson-streaked shirt sleeve and dragged the back of his trembling right hand across bloody, swollen lips.

His wife Edith climbed down from the wagon and ran toward him, crying, "Waylon! Oh, Waylon!"

He caught her with his left arm and pulled her against him, muttering, "It's all right, Edith, it's all right now. It's over."

Kingman recovered from his stupor enough to push himself onto his side and then flop over onto his back. His eyes were still closed as he groaned. His chest rose and fell in a deep, ragged manner.

Finally, as Spencer and Edith stood nearby watching him, Kingman managed to open his eyes and raise his head. He gazed around unfocused for a moment then his eyes lit on Spencer and hatred kindled in them again.

With a struggle almost painful to watch, he pushed himself to a sitting position. "Did I . . . Did I hear you say . . . this was over . . . you damn traitor?" he rasped. "Because it . . . isn't. It never will be . . . until you're dead . . . like all those good men . . . you betrayed at . . . Hungry Dog . . . Creek!"

Spencer let go of Edith and took a step toward Kingman, putting himself between the two of them. "You're insane, Kingman. You were wrong then, and you're wrong now. I never told the Rebs we were going to be on that road that day. It was Beauchamp!"

Kingman's eyes widened. "Beauchamp! Hank was . . . my friend . . . Why would he . . ."

"I don't know why. But he was the only one who made it out of that creek alive. That red bandana he always wore was tied around his arm that day. A sign for the Rebs not to shoot him! You should ask *him* why he did it, if you know where he is."

"Hank is . . . dead." Kingman's breathing was settling down to a more normal rate. "He hanged himself . . . in Santa Fe . . . two years after the war was over."

Spencer asked, "You ever ask yourself why he'd do such a thing? Maybe because he felt too much guilt over what he'd done?"

"He wouldn't . . . He wouldn't . . ."

Duff thought he caught a glimpse of realization in Kingman's eyes as the man muttered the denial. Despite not wanting to believe it, Kingman knew what Spencer had said made sense. Of course, there was no way to prove any of it, but at least Kingman knew a much more reasonable explanation for what had happened on that cold, rainy winter day back in '65.

Kingman looked down, his eyes shrouded with hate again, muttered something unintelligible and moved to climb to his feet. Waylon Spencer just shook his head in disgust and contempt and turned away.

Duff started to call out to him not to do that, to warn him that he was giving Kingman too tempting a target, but it was too late. With his hatred giving him one last burst of strength, Kingman surged to his feet, yanked a short-barreled pistol from under his shirt, and swung it up toward Waylon Spencer's back.

Three shots rang out, blending into one, before Kingman could pull the trigger. All three slugs smashed into his chest, striking in a space small enough to be covered by the breast pocket of his shirt. The impact knocked Kingman backward. He tripped and fell, landing on his back with his arms flung out to the sides. The gun he had pulled slipped unfired from his fingers as he drew in one breath. It came out of him in a grotesque rattle that testified he was dead.

Duff, Elmer, and Cole Hardcastle lowered their pistols. All three weapons had wisps of powder smoke curling from their muzzles. Duff was glad he had reloaded while Spencer and Kingman were talking. He hadn't trusted the former major to accept defeat. Not one bit.

At the roar of the shots, Spencer had clutched Edith to him, shielding her with his own body. He kept her pressed against him as he looked at Duff, Elmer, and Cole and said hoarsely, "Thank you, men. He just couldn't give it up, even though I think he knew, there at the end, that I was right and he was wrong."

"Aye," said Duff. "There be an old saying. 'If ye feed the wolf of hate for too long, sooner or later he consumes *ye*, too.'"

# CHAPTER 27

As Elmer had said, the handful of Kingman's men who had survived the battle were in no shape to cause more trouble. They were able to ride, although some were wounded badly enough they had to be tied into their saddles. Duff asked Wang to take them back to Chugwater and turn them over to Marshal Jerry Ferrell, who could hold them, get them medical attention, and go through his reward posters to see if any of them were wanted in Wyoming.

"You do not believe you will need my assistance in the rest of the journey?" asked Wang.

"Oh, I'm not saying that at all," Duff replied. "I dinnae ken what may happen once we get up there on the Nightmare Trail. I considered asking Elmer to take the prisoners back—"

"But he knows the route you are taking better than I do and so might be more helpful," Wang broke in. "That is an entirely logical approach to take, Duff. While I am somewhat disappointed not to see the journey through to the end, your plan is the best available option." He nodded. "Of course I will do it."

Duff clapped a hand on the smaller man's shoulder. "'Tis thanking ye I am for your understanding, Wang. Once we have the Spencers settled in Longshot Basin, nothing will be stopping ye from visiting them any time ye please."

"Other than the Hardcastles," Wang pointed out. "They have agreed to allow the Spencers to use the trail this time, but they may not want anyone else coming and going over it."

Elmer was listening to the conversation and put in, "Hell, once they've broken their own rule once, what's the point of enforcin' it after that? If you ask me, they ought to live and let live, give up their outlaw ways, and be good neighbors to the Spencers. That way, they won't have near as much trouble in the future."

"You think that, do you, Gleason?"

The soft voice came from behind Elmer. He looked back over his shoulder and saw Cole Hardcastle standing there, thumbs hooked in his gun belt and an unreadable expression on his face.

The Good Lord had never put much backup in Elmer Gleason. He met Cole's eyes squarely. "Yeah, that's the way I see it, but I ain't one to tell other folks how to carry on their own business."

"Sounded to me like that's what you were just doing."

Elmer shook his head. "No, sir. I was expressin' an opinion to friends, which I got every right to do. I didn't come find you and tell you how to act, did I?"

Cole shrugged. "I reckon not. You can think whatever you want, I suppose, but that ain't always wise if you don't know all the facts."

"Well, why don't you tell me the facts, then?" Elmer asked with a challenging note in his voice.

A smile spread slowly across Cole's face. "No, we'll just leave it at that. Like you said, you've got a right to your opinion." He turned and strolled away.

"I don't trust that varmint," Elmer muttered. "He's got too much snake blood in him to suit me."

"He fought bravely on our side when Kingman attacked," Duff said. "But I know what ye mean, Elmer."

Duff wasn't going to fully trust Cole or any of the Hardcastles until the Spencers were safe in Longshot Basin.

The idea of camping in the trees on the lower slopes of Buzzard's Roost had to be abandoned. Fighting off Kingman's attack had delayed the wagon train too long, and the immigrants needed time to patch up their wounds and rest.

Also, with all the bullets flying around, several mules and oxen had been wounded fatally. The group had brought extra stock with them so they could switch out teams on their long journey, which left them with enough animals for all the wagons to make it the rest of the way. A couple of the dead oxen were butchered for fresh meat.

Also a consideration was the matter of burying Thomas Kingman and the men with him who had been killed. Spencer had insisted it was the only decent thing to do and his brothers agreed.

"We rode with all those fellas durin' the war," Burl Spencer said with a grim look on his bearded face. "Some of 'em might've been bad anyway, but Major Kingman led some of 'em into it. They never would've come after us if he hadn't been goadin' 'em on."

"That's right," Leon Spencer agreed. "We had to fight them to protect our families, but I can't bring myself to feel good about them bein' dead. I'm just glad it wasn't any of us or ours."

They dug graves and laid the men to rest as the last of the light faded from the western sky. It was a solemn group around the campfires that night. Quite a few bandages were visible, reminders of the desperate fight that had taken place only a short time earlier.

Even though several of the men were wounded, no one was hurt badly enough he was unable to stand guard on his regular shift. The hours of darkness passed quietly.

Everyone was up early the next morning, getting ready for the wagons to roll again. With any luck, they would reach their new home in Longshot Basin before the day was over.

Cole Hardcastle came to Duff and said, "MacCallister, you and me need to ride out front today. I told my kinfolks I'd be leading the wagons. If they see the two of us together, they'll know everything's all right and going according to the agreement we made."

Duff nodded. "'Tis acceptable, and a good idea."

A few minutes later, the group was ready to get moving.

Duff and Cole mounted up and rode out ahead of the wagons. Waylon Spencer shouted the command to roll, and the vehicles lurched into motion as the teams strained against their harness. Elmer rode alongside the lead wagon. Walter and Oliver, instead of scouting ahead, took up the rear guard along with two of their second cousins, Harry and Gilbert. In their middle teens, only slightly younger than the other pair.

The pace was slower because so much of the route was uphill. After the losses in the battle the day before, the Spencers couldn't afford to push their stock. Stops to rest the teams were frequent.

During those halts, Duff and Cole ranged a little farther ahead of the wagons. In the trees, Duff's keen vision searched among the pines for any sign of potential trouble.

Cole grinned at him. "Anybody who didn't know better would think you didn't trust me, MacCallister."

"Caution is a habit of mine," Duff explained. "I've needed it to stay alive this long."

"You are preaching to the choir, old son," said Cole. "There's no such thing as being too careful."

"And there are plenty of places in these trees where ambushers could conceal themselves, as your sister and her cousins did."

Cole chuckled. "Yeah, after that little ruckus, I'm not sure how soon Cousin Willie will let those girls stand guard again, if he ever does. Plenty of the boys figure gals shouldn't be toting guns and watching the trail. They didn't like the idea of them being out here to start with."

"Such as your cousin Ferris, if I'm recalling his name correctly."

"You are," said Cole. "And to be fair, Ferris don't like much of anything. Him and me have never gotten along that well. But"—Cole shrugged—"he's a Hardcastle."

"And that says it all, does it not?"

"I reckon it does."

Duff didn't spot anything threatening and the journey continued.

Moving through the trees and up the lower slopes took several hours, but because of the early start, it was still only mid-morning when he and Cole came to the spot where the section of the route deserving to be called the Nightmare Trail actually started. They reined in and waited for the wagons to catch up.

Once everyone was there, Duff gathered the immigrants together and went over the plan one more time. No one would ride on the wagons, not even the children. If one of the wagons went off the trail, only the goods and supplies would be risked, not any lives. The men and the older boys would lead the teams. One man or boy would follow each wagon, and his only job would be to watch the wheels on the right side. If they came too close to the edge, the follower would call out a warning, and everything would stop while the situation was assessed.

When the procession started up again, the leaders would urge the team closer to the rock wall rising on the left, away from the brink. The journey would be harrowing, no doubt about that, but if everyone did their job, the wagons stood a good chance of making it safely to Longshot Basin.

The wagons would be separated by approximately a hundred yards. Groups of women and children would walk between them, keeping fifty yards back from the one in front of them.

"With that much distance between ye and the wagons in front of and behind ye, everybody ought to be safe," Duff stressed.

The most important thing was getting everybody over the mountain and then down into the basin.

"Cole Hardcastle and I will go first," he concluded. "Does everyone understand what you're supposed to do?"

Nods and calls of agreement came from the group.

"Then we're ready to start." Duff went on. "The stock has rested enough while we were talking. Everyone get to your places, and Mr. Spencer"—this to Waylon—"ye can lead off whenever you're ready."

"Thanks, Duff." Spencer hugged his wife Edith, gave her a quick kiss on the forehead, and went to the head of his mule team. His grandson Harry, who would be the other leader, joined him there. Harry's younger brother Gilbert would be following the wagon and watching the wheels.

Duff and Cole rode a short distance along the trail and then stopped and turned their horses to look back. They sat there for less than a minute before Spencer and Harry tugged on the harness and the mules leaned into the task. The wagon began to move.

"Here we go," said Duff.

He and Cole rode at an easy pace up the trail. The almost sheer stone wall rose on their left. The wooded slope fell away dizzyingly on their right. Duff rode closest to the wall, with Cole on the outside. Cole had suggested that arrangement. As he'd explained, he knew the trail better than Duff and wouldn't be likely to stray too close to the edge. His horse was also more familiar with it.

After they had gone a hundred yards or so, they stopped and hipped around in their saddles again to look back down the trail at the lead wagon. Waylon Spencer and his grandson trudged along, each holding the harness of the mules at the front of the team. Progress was grindingly slow, but as far as Duff could see from where he was, the wagon seemed to be in good position. The front and back wheels on the right were about a foot and a half from the trail's edge.

"Looking good, looking good," Harry's brother Gilbert sang out from behind the wagon. His voice sounded clearly through the mountain air, so not only his brother and grandfather were able to hear it, but Duff and Cole farther up the trail, as well.

"Looks like it's gonna work," Cole commented. "It's gonna be a long day, though."

"Aye, on both those counts," Duff agreed.

They resumed the trek.

Because of the mountainside's curve and the way the vehicles were spread out, Duff could see only the first two or three wagons each time he and Cole stopped to check on the immigrants' progress. Although they still had a long way to go, no mishaps had occurred, and the wagon train's progress, while slow, was steady. At that rate, it would take most of the day.

And it was all right with Duff. As long as they got down and into Longshot Basin by nightfall was all that mattered.

He regarded it as a milestone of sorts when they came in

sight of the cleft where the smaller trail branched off and sloped up toward the Hardcastle stronghold. *The home place*, Cole called it. Only a short distance past that, the trail leveled off, which meant the going would be easier for the wagon teams. If they could get all the wagons on the level stretch, Duff intended to call a halt and let the livestock rest for a short time.

With that thought in mind, he grinned. "'Tis a good omen we've made it this far, I believe."

"You know, MacCallister, a part of me wishes I could agree with you."

Duff heard and recognized the soft whisper that followed Cole's oddly foreboding words. It was the sound of gun metal sliding on leather. Duff twisted in the saddle and reached for his own Colt as he saw Cole's gun coming up. Two bitter realizations struck him like a potent left-right combo of fists.

Cole had double-crossed him after all. And there was no way in hell Duff could beat the gunfighter's draw.

# CHAPTER 28

Duff had managed to wrap his fingers around his revolver's walnut grips before Cole's gun came level.

Peering over the barrel, Cole said, "Don't do it, MacCallister. I can put a bullet through your head before you clear leather, and you know it."

Duff drew in a deep breath. "Aye, I suppose ye can," he admitted. "But would ye? I believed we had a certain respect between us, if not friendship."

"That's because you're a decent man and have a good heart. Me?" Cole shrugged. "I'm a Hardcastle. That ought to be answer enough for you."

"Aye," Duff said, nodding slowly. "Aye, 'tis enough." He lifted his hand away from his gun. "What happens now?"

"You'll find out."

The ominous words had barely left Cole's mouth when Duff heard the sharp crack of shots from somewhere back along the trail. He stiffened in the saddle and turned his head to gaze behind him.

Waylon Spencer must have seen Cole holding a gun on Duff, because he had given the order to stop the wagons. Harry was squeezing between the lead wagon and the cliff, getting behind cover as his grandfather waved him back.

Spencer turned and stood ramrod-straight in front of the team, watching to see what Cole would do next as echoes from the three or four rapid shots rolled across the landscape and slowly diminished.

Duff stared stonily at Cole and said in a flat voice, "If you're responsible for any of these good people being hurt, ye might as well go ahead and pull that trigger now, Hardcastle. Because if ye don't, I'll hunt you down and kill you."

"From anybody else except you, I'd think that was just bluster, but I believe you, MacCallister. The smart thing to do would be to kill you, like you say. But not just yet."

The lack of any more shots was slightly encouraging. If it had sounded like a big battle at the other end of the wagon train, Duff would have worried Elmer or some of the Spencers might have been killed. It was still possible, of course, but maybe there weren't too many casualties.

Anger smoldered inside Duff. He liked to believe he was a good judge of character. While he had never fully trusted Cole Hardcastle, he had been convinced the man wouldn't try to double-cross them. He had accepted Cole's word that the Hardcastles had agreed the immigrants could use the Nightmare Trail and settle in Longshot Basin.

But it appeared Cole had been lying the whole time. Duff felt like a fool.

Hoofbeats and the rattle of rocks made him look toward the passage leading up to the stronghold. Willie Hardcastle came into view, riding along the cleft with Ferris and several other men behind him. Willie's expression was hard and unyielding. He carried a Winchester across the saddle in front of him, as did his companions.

Willie led the group the short distance down the trail to where Duff and Cole waited. As he reined in, he turned his baleful glare toward Cole and said, "You should have killed him. This man is too dangerous to the family to leave alive."

"I agree with you, Cousin Willie," drawled Cole. "But we said we wouldn't kill any of these pilgrims right off the bat unless they didn't give us any other choice."

"*You* were the one who suggested wiping them out in the first place, except for the ones we want," snapped Willie. "I'm still not sure why you suddenly changed your mind and then argued for mercy."

"It ain't mercy. It's common sense. We might be able to get some use out of some of the others. For one thing"— Cole nodded toward Duff—"MacCallister here owns a pretty successful ranch, and a bunch of his relatives are rich, too. Lawyers and politicians and businessmen and such. They might pay a tidy little sum to keep him alive."

Duff stared at Cole for a moment and then burst out with a hearty laugh.

Cole glared at him. "What's so damned funny?"

"Ye actually believe 'twould be a good idea to demand ransom from Falcon and the rest of the MacCallister clan for my safe return?"

"Don't your kinfolks value your life?" demanded Willie.

"Aye, perhaps they do. But they're not the sort to knuckle under to outlaws and kidnappers." Duff shook his head. "All ye'd be doing is taking hold of a hornet's nest and hugging it to your bosom."

Ferris said, "Then you ought to go ahead and shoot him, Cole. Damned if he don't sound like he's tryin' to talk you into it!"

"No, I reckon he's just telling it straight," said Cole. "Well, we're already in this up to our necks. We might as well carry on with it. MacCallister, Willie's gonna take your gun. Don't try anything or I *will* shoot you, whether I want to or not. Keep those hands up where I can see 'em."

Outnumbered and outgunned as he was, and in this precarious location to boot, Duff figured getting himself killed would just leave him unable to help the Spencers. He lifted his hands in plain sight and remained motionless while Willie brought his horse closer, leaned over, and snagged Duff's Colt from its holster. A bitter, sour taste filled Duff's mouth at being disarmed.

Cole said, "Now tell Spencer to come on up here, and bring those two youngsters with him. Some of my cousins will be herding the rest of them up the trail from below."

"Ye had them hidden, just waiting for all of the wagons to pass by and get onto the trail," Duff said.

"That's right."

Duff cocked his head a little to the side. "Did ye ken Major Kingman and his men were going to attack us?"

"Now, how in the hell would I know that? That was as big a surprise to me as it was to you, MacCallister. By then, I had my own plans for you. I couldn't very well sit out that fight and let Kingman slaughter your whole bunch. I was glad I was there to lend a hand."

Duff shook his head slowly and said, "I cannae figure ye out, Hardcastle."

"Then don't waste your time trying." Cole motioned curtly with the gun he held. "Come on, get moving. It's time you saw the Hardcastle home place."

Della was standing on the front porch of the big house when Ginny and Lydia came out and joined her. All three girls watched the spot on the other side of the bench where the trail came out. Della's nerves and muscles were taut with anticipation. She had heard the shots a short time earlier and knew Cole and the others had put the plan into play.

"You reckon they killed 'em all?" Ginny asked with a nervous edge in her voice.

Della snorted. "Not with four shots, they didn't."

Lydia said, "I hope they didn't have to shoot that fat boy Oliver. I've still got a score to settle with him."

Della looked over at her cousin. Lydia sounded as sullen and truculent as ever, but Della thought she saw worry lurking in the younger blonde's eyes.

Lydia had talked a lot about Oliver Spencer since their encounter a few days earlier. Mostly she went on about the score she had to settle with him. But she didn't always sound angry or vengeful. Neither did Ginny when she talked about Walter, although she did still refer to him scornfully as "dirt-eater" and make fun of how scrawny he was. She had said something more than once, though, about wondering what he was doing.

It was unusual for Lydia and Ginny to be thinking about any boys that much. Which wasn't really surprising, since the only boys around were either their brothers or cousins.

Della felt the same way . . . which was why she had gone to Cole before he left to join the wagon train and talked him into sparing *all* the immigrants, not just the women and children.

"You're loco," Cole had said as he frowned at her in surprise at the suggestion. "We can't take those young fellas into the family. It's one thing when you're talkin' about getting women and girls to marry up with our boys—"

"You reckon the Hardcastle girls aren't interested in getting hitched, too?" Della had interrupted him. "Blast it, Cole, the prospects for us aren't any better than they are for the boys."

"Second or third cousins ain't so bad," Cole had argued.

"Hell, in a pinch even a first cousin will do. Willie will go along with that."

"I'm not talking about what he will or won't go along with. It's not that simple, Cole, and you know it. This whole family's been stuck up here on Buzzard's Roost for too long. We need more new blood than hauling a few girls back from a raid will bring in."

"Maybe you're right," Cole had admitted, although he didn't sound convinced. "Thinking we can convince some of the young men from that wagon train to throw in with us just won't work, though. What are we gonna do? Put guns to their heads and make them marry you and Lydia and Ginny . . ." His voice had trailed off as he stared at her. "That's exactly what you're thinking, isn't it?"

Della had shrugged. "The girls you bring back from raids aren't exactly volunteering to get hitched to our boys, are they? They just know they don't have any choice. If it works one way, it ought to work the other."

Cole just shook his head in amazement. "You've got the craziest way of thinking of any female I ever did see."

"All I'm asking is that you don't kill all the men and boys right away. You can always shoot them later if you need to. That's fair enough, ain't it?"

"I suppose so." Cole squinted at her in sudden suspicion. "Tell me you haven't gone soft on that damned MacCallister."

With a toss of her head, Della had snapped, "Of course I haven't. I haven't gone soft on anybody."

"Yes, you have," Cole had said. "I can tell by looking at you. Don't forget, Della, I'm your big brother. I know how you think."

"You don't know a damned thing about me."

"You're just wasting your time," Cole had told her. "MacCallister's a stiff-necked do-gooder. He'd never throw in with a sorry bunch like the Hardcastles, even if he didn't already have a girl back in Chugwater . . . which he does. A mighty pretty girl, too. Owns a dress shop. She's the one Benjy was sweet on and got himself shot over. You might, too, if you set your cap for Duff MacCallister."

"You've got it all wrong," Della had muttered. "Now, will you do like I asked or not?"

"Well . . . I think we'll still wind up having to shoot most of them and drop their carcasses in a ravine. But I suppose there's a chance a few of them might want to save their own skins, even if it means marrying hellcats like Lydia and Ginny." Cole had given her a penetrating stare. "If you're not after MacCallister, then that's what this is really about, ain't it? Those two boys y'all tangled with before. Lydia and Ginny are mad at them, but they're a mite taken with them, at the same time." Cole laughed. "All their cousins know better than to stand up to those two. Walter and Oliver, they're dumb enough they just might do it, and that makes them interesting."

"So you'll go along with it?"

"For now," Cole had allowed. "And as long as they don't give us too much trouble. But our main goals are still to stop those pilgrims from settling in Longshot Basin, and to rustle up some brides for our boys at the same time."

"Fine." Della had turned to stalk about, but not before throwing over her shoulder, "But you're wrong about me and that MacCallister fella. You couldn't be more wrong."

But was he, Della thought as she waited for Cole, Willie, Ferris, and the others to return with their prisoners? Was there a chance he was right about Duff MacCallister? The man was big and handsome and capable, and a lot better than any prospects Della might have at the home place.

Convincing MacCallister of that would be a formidable challenge, though. She had been around him enough to know how stubborn he was. He wasn't likely to abandon his ranch and his friends . . . and that gal in Chugwater . . . to join up with an outlaw clan, even with Della herself as an added inducement to the offer. He'd tell them all to go to hell, and Cole would put a bullet in his head.

# CHAPTER 29

Duff watched intently as the party of immigrants gathered in front of the stopped wagon train. It was a slow process. They were herded at gunpoint up the Nightmare Trail and had to slip between the vehicles and the cliff one by one. Finally, everyone was there. Elmer and the two boys, Walter and Oliver, brought up the rear just as they had before the double cross.

Duff heaved a sigh of relief as he saw Elmer and realized his old friend looked unharmed. Evidently, no one had been killed in the brief flurry of gunfire right after Cole got the drop on him, although Waylon's grandson Grady Jr. and cousin Ezekiel Kelly sported bloodstained bandages. Grady Junior's was on his right leg, Zeke's on his upper left arm. They had been winged but didn't appear to be badly hurt.

They were mad and scared, though, just like all the other prisoners.

"You see, MacCallister, I told you nobody would be killed as long as they cooperated," Cole said. "No matter what you think of us, we're not cold-blooded murderers."

Duff grunted. "I believed ye before. 'Tis not a mistake I'm likely to be making again any time soon."

"Suit yourself," Cole said with a shrug. He motioned with the gun in his hand. "Get moving."

Duff and Cole led the way up the passage to the Hardcastle stronghold. Willie and Ferris weren't far behind them. The other mounted Hardcastle men covered the prisoners every step of the way. The ambushers who had been posted in hiding until all the wagons had passed, came last, riding the horses they also had concealed deep in the trees.

The plan had been well thought out, mused Duff. He was confident Cole had come up with it. None of the other Hardcastles he had met were cunning enough to work out such an effective scheme.

It took about a quarter of an hour to climb to the bench where the Hardcastle home place was located.

Leaning on the porch railing, Della caught her breath and tightened her grip on the rail as she caught sight of hats rising into view at the top of the trail. Mounted figures loomed up and came toward the house, followed by a large group of men, women, and children trudging along on foot. More riders brought up the rear, herding the captured immigrants along like they were livestock . . . which, in a way, they were, where the Hardcastles were concerned.

The two men in the lead were instantly recognizable to Della. One of them was her brother Cole, who held a gun pointing in the general direction of the man beside him . . . who was none other than Duff MacCallister.

When the trail topped out and Duff could see the assortment of buildings, he was impressed in spite of his anger at the situation.

The clan had themselves a veritable settlement of sorts. No businesses, of course, but everything else they needed to survive. They would have to bring in some supplies from outside, which explained what Cole and Benjy had been doing on the way to Chugwater the day Duff first encountered them.

"So this is home to the Hardcastles, then," he commented.

"Yep. Has been for more than twenty years, ever since the family came up here from the Ozarks."

Duff shook his head and said, "'Tis still surprising to me I never heard of ye until recently."

"We're modest folks. We don't like to call attention to ourselves," Cole responded dryly. He waved a hand, taking in all their surroundings from Buzzard's Roost across the basin to the rugged badlands beyond, and added, "Besides, there ain't really much up here in these parts that interests folks . . . or at least, there wasn't until recently."

Duff knew he was referring to the Spencers planning to settle in Longshot Basin. And Cole was right. If a group of people wanted to hide away from the world, it was a pretty good place to do it.

They headed for a big, sprawling house that must have been the original dwelling. Duff spotted several figures waiting on the porch, and as they came closer, he could tell they were all female. Blond hair shining in the sun made him think two of them were Della and Lydia.

He hoped briefly that Lydia wouldn't shoot Oliver Spencer in retaliation for him tossing her into the briar patch. But then, *all* of their lives were in danger as long as the Hardcastles had them, Duff reminded himself.

As they came to a stop in front of the house, Duff recognized not only Della and Lydia but also Ginny and the other girls who had been with the bunch they had clashed with a few days earlier. In addition, a dozen other young women were gathered there. They gazed with avid eyes at the prisoners . . . almost like cattle buyers sizing up a herd.

That thought made Duff's forehead crease momentarily

in a frown. Just what did the Hardcastles have in mind for their captives, anyway?

He had a pretty good idea what the young men wanted. They had gathered on both sides of the newcomers, forming a gauntlet of sorts through which the prisoners walked nervously. The Hardcastle men eyed all the Spencer women and girls of marriageable age.

Realization burst on Duff's brain. The Spencers had been rounded up for matrimonial purposes!

At first glance, that idea was almost humorous. But then cold, deadly reality soaked in. Most of the female prisoners had husbands. Those men would have to be disposed of, so their wives would turn into widows. Willie Hardcastle, hypocritical though his attitude might be, wasn't going to allow adultery to run rampant in the clan he commanded.

Clearly, however, the Hardcastle "ladies" were in need of husbands, too, Duff realized. Perhaps Willie would grant all the married Spencers divorces, in order to bring an infusion of new blood into the clan. Duff had heard of shotgun weddings plenty of times . . . but never shotgun divorces!

Della moved onto the top step and asked her brother, "Have you told them what's going to happen, Cole?"

"No, I left that for you to do," he said. "Seeing as how it was your idea and all."

Willie Hardcastle rode up and demanded, "Someone had better tell me what's going on here. You said we might be able to make use of these men, Cole, but I'm blessed if I see how!"

"Della was just about to explain that, Cousin Willie," drawled Cole as he grinned mockingly at his sister. "Well, go ahead, Della."

She glared at him and tossed her blond curls defiantly. "We're just going to do what the Good Lord commands of us, Cousin Willie. We're going to marry, be fruitful, and multiply."

Willie's eyes got bigger. He jerked a hand toward the prisoners and exclaimed, "With . . . with these heathens?"

"If their women are good enough for our boys to marry up with, the men ought to be good enough for the Hardcastle girls who need husbands."

"That's preposterous!" Willie glared at Cole. "That's why you had us bring them up here? Because of some ridiculous scheme to bring them *all* into the clan?"

Waylon Spencer stepped up, ignoring the menacing guns that swung in his direction. "That's insane. No one in my family is going to marry into a bunch of bloodthirsty outlaws!"

Cole looked at him and said, "This bloodthirsty outlaw risked his life helping you fight off those . . . what was it you called them? The Buckeye Butchers?"

"Because ye wanted to save us for your own nefarious purposes," Duff pointed out.

Elmer made his way to the front of the group of captives, waved his arms, and yelled, "This whole thing is plumb crazy!"

Ferris moved his horse closer to Elmer and suddenly kicked the old-timer in the back. Elmer cried out and sprawled on the ground. Ferris pointed his gun at him and said, "Nobody wants to marry you, you old pelican, so you're just a waste of space."

Duff was about to lunge his horse at Ferris in the hope of distracting him before he could pull the trigger, when Cole shouted, "Damn it, Ferris, holster that iron! Right now!"

Ferris didn't follow the command, but he didn't fire. Instead, he glared at Cole and said, "I don't like this mouthy old codger. He's no good to us, and you know it, Cole."

"We agreed there wouldn't be any killing until we'd hashed it all out."

Waylon Spencer said, "There won't be any hashing it out. None of us will go along with this crazy scheme."

"You speak for every member of your group, Mr. Spencer?" Cole looked at Burl Spencer's redheaded grand-daughter Becky and moved his horse closer to her. "How about you, little lady? You'd rather die than marry some big, strapping Hardcastle boy?"

Becky's little brother Teddy was standing beside her. Suddenly, he darted in front of her and glared up at Cole. "You get away from my sister," he yelled. "Nobody's gonna bother her while I'm around!"

Becky put her hands on the boy's shoulder and held him back. "Stop it, Teddy. You're just going to get yourself in trouble."

Cole grinned down at him. "You've got a lot of fire in you, don't you, son? I like to see that. Means you'll make a good Hardcastle when you grow up, even though you'll be an adopted one."

"No, sir! I'm a Spencer! I'll never be no dadgum Hard-castle!"

With weariness in his voice, Willie said, "That's enough. Take all the women and girls into the house and have them guarded. Put the men and boys in the smokehouse and the blacksmith shop. Those places ought to be big enough to hold all of them. And bar the doors so they can't get out!" He frowned at Cole. "You and I will go into the house and discuss this, cousin. We'll pray about it, too. We need to figure out what the Lord wants us to do here."

"I can tell you that," said Cole. "He wants us to keep the family going, no matter what it takes."

Willie snorted. "We'll see." He waved an arm at the prisoners. "Lock them up! And if any of them try to escape . . . well, you can take *that* as a sign the Lord wants them dead!"

The smokehouse was the more secure of the two makeshift jails, so the Hardcastles made sure to lock Duff and Elmer in there, along with Waylon Spencer and his brothers and several of the younger men, including Walter and Oliver. The confines were cramped, but the prisoners were able to sit down on the hard-packed dirt floor. Not much light penetrated into the thick-walled structure, so a thick gloom cloaked all of them.

Waylon Spencer sighed. "I really hoped with that lunatic Kingman dead, we'd be able to settle down peacefully at last."

"Maybe once Kingman was done for, all of you should've turned around and gone back where you came from," Elmer suggested.

"It was too late for that," Spencer said. "We'd all sold our farms and sunk almost everything into this journey. We couldn't turn back. All that was left was to go ahead, no matter what the obstacles." He sighed again. "Now my determination to make a fresh start is going to cost all our lives, and the women will be forced into a life of degradation and slavery!"

"Unless we go along with this crazy idea of joining the Hardcastles," said Walter.

Oliver swallowed hard. "Did you see how those girls were looking at us?"

"You mean Ginny and Lydia?" Walter asked.

"Yeah. I'm not sure they want to marry us . . . or torture us!"

Elmer said, "Could be some of both, I reckon."

Waylon Spencer said, "There's no point in talking about it. It'll never happen. I forbid it."

Duff wasn't sure the other Spencers were going to go along with that. Some of them might be willing to take a chance in order to save their lives, especially the unmarried males like Walter and Oliver.

The older men, the ones with wives and families, were less likely to cooperate. They wouldn't want to see their wives turned over to other men, the children taken to be raised as Hardcastles. They would put up a fight . . . and then the Hardcastles would murder them and take what they wanted, anyway.

Unless Duff could figure a way out.

# CHAPTER 30

Della tried to follow Cole and Willie into Willie's sanctum, but her cousin turned back and barred her entrance.

"This discussion is for the men," Willie intoned, almost in his hellfire-and-brimstone voice but not quite.

"The Hardcastle women have a stake in this, too," argued Della.

"Once we have made our decision, we will share it with the women, as always."

"You mean you'll tell us what to do."

"As is only fitting and proper."

From behind Della, Ferris said, "Yeah, that's right, so get out of the way and let the men through."

Della would have turned around and lit into him, but at that moment Cole appeared in the doorway and said quietly, "Go on, Della. You got things this far. There's nothing else you can do."

Seething, Della glared at her brother for a second, but she knew Cole was right. None of the men would allow themselves to be budged. All she and the other women could do was hope for the best. "All right. But you make sure we're treated fairly, Cole."

Willie said, "Fair has nothing to do with it. Only the will

of the Lord, and subordinate to that, the will of the family, has any meaning."

"And by the will of the family, you mean weasels like Ferris."

Ferris's face turned red with anger, but before he could snap back at her, Cole said wearily, "Just go on, Della."

"Fine." Still fuming, Della turned and stalked away from the door.

Behind her, Ferris and half a dozen other men filed into Cousin Willie's sanctum. It was going to be crowded in there, but it probably wouldn't take them long to reach a decision. Most of the men went along with whatever Cousin Willie wanted. Cole was the most likely to defy his wishes . . . but only if he wanted to. Sometimes Cole's aims and Willie's aligned.

Della had no idea if that was going to be the case this time.

As soon as she stepped out onto the porch, Lydia, Ginny, Patsy, and several of the other girls and young women flocked around her.

"What did they say?" Lydia demanded. "Do we get to keep any of those fellas or not?"

"They haven't decided. They're talking it over."

Ginny shorted in derision. "You mean Cousin Willie's tellin' them what they're going to do."

Della shrugged. "He *is* the head of the family. He's been taking care of us for a long time."

"That don't mean he's always right," said Lydia. Frowning, she added bluntly, "I don't want him killin' that fat boy Oliver."

"Why not?" Della asked her, equally plainspoken. "You just called him fat. And he threw you in that mess of brambles, remember?"

"I ain't likely to forget! Some of those scratches still hurt. But he ain't really all *that* chubby, I reckon. And at least he don't run off with his tail tucked betwixt his legs like a whipped dog if you look at him sideways, like some of the fellas around here do."

"And that Walter put up a decent fight," added Ginny. "For a beanpole dirt-eater, that is."

Della sighed and shook her head. Those two were gone on the Spencer boys. Though if anybody accused them of it, they would deny it up one way and down the other.

"All right," she said. "I'll slip back in there and see if I can listen at the door and hear what they're sayin'. That won't change anything, though."

"At least we'll know what they're gonna do," Ginny said.

Della nodded and went back into the house. She was worried Cousin Willie might have posted guards at the door and they would run her off if she tried to eavesdrop, but it wasn't the case. The corridor outside the door to Willie's sanctum was empty.

But it didn't matter. Just as she walked up, the door opened and Cole came out.

Della caught her breath at the look on her brother's face. It was hard as stone. As her heart dropped, she knew he hadn't argued in favor of what the women wanted at all.

"Cole . . . ?" she said.

"Sorry, Della," Cole said.

She could tell he didn't mean it.

He went on. "Come morning, we're going to get rid of those Spencer men and the boys older than fifteen. Cousin Willie and the rest of the fellas think it's just too dangerous to keep them around here, and I agree with them."

Ferris came out of the room and said in a surly voice, "If

we're gonna get rid of them, I don't understand why we don't just go ahead and do it now."

Willie stepped into the corridor and said, "Because even men doomed by their own foolishness deserve a chance to make things right between themselves and the Lord. The prisoners will have tonight to do that."

Della plucked at his sleeve. "But Cousin Willie—"

He jerked his arm away and interrupted her protest. "It has been decided, girl," he intoned with a glare, his voice like an Old Testament prophet declaring judgment. "In the morning, they all die."

Even though it was mostly dark inside the smokehouse, the blackness thickened when night fell. If Duff had been of a mind to waste the time and effort doing it, he could have waved his hand in front of his face without seeing it.

"Reckon they're gonna feed us?" Elmer asked.

"I dinnae ken." Duff chuckled, but there wasn't much humor in the sound. "I suppose that depends on whether they've decided if we live or die. No point in wasting good food on men who won't live long enough to get all that hungry."

"Speak for yourself," Elmer growled. "My belly already figures my throat's been cut, and it don't care how much longer we've got."

From the other side of the smokehouse, Walter asked, "Mr. MacCallister, do you reckon they're gonna kill us?"

Duff could tell the youngster was trying to be brave, but his voice held a slight quaver.

"I dinnae ken what they intend to do, Walter, but the intention is nae always the reality."

"We're still alive, son," Waylon Spencer said, "and Spencers don't give up hope."

"I know, Uncle Waylon, but some of those Hardcastles"— Walter's voice dropped as if he was afraid someone might be eavesdropping—" act like they're crazy!"

Nobody trapped in the stygian hole was going to disagree with him.

A few more minutes dragged by, seeming longer than they actually were, and then Duff sat up straighter as he heard footsteps approaching the smokehouse. They stopped just on the other side of the door.

"You prisoners in there, listen to me." The solemn voice belonged to Willie Hardcastle. "The leaders of our clan have talked and prayed and come to a decision as to your fate. Tomorrow morning, at sunup, those of you above the age of fifteen will be taken from this place to another, and there you will be shot and your bodies disposed of."

Duff heard several sharply indrawn breaths inside the smokehouse, but kept his own jaw clamped shut.

Beside him, Elmer muttered, "Damn."

"Buck up, boys," Waylon Spencer said quietly. "Don't give that man the satisfaction of hearing you cry."

On the other side of the door, Willie went on. "We take no satisfaction in this."

"That's a damned lie." Another mutter from Elmer.

"The sanctity of our family must be protected at all costs," Willie continued. "The whole world has always turned its hand against the Hardcastles, and we have no reason to believe you would be any different. All men outside the clan are treacherous and cannot be trusted. Therefore, we have no other choice.

"However, you are still human and deserve a chance to make your peace with God, so you have tonight. I suggest you spend it humbling yourselves in prayer."

Willie stomped away, leaving most of the captives in a state of shocked horror.

Not surprising, Elmer spoke first into the stunned silence. "That ol' boy's crazier 'n an outhouse rat."

"Not by his lights," said Duff. "But by ours, aye, the man's a bit of a fanatic. However, he has his family on his side and believes he is doing right by them." He paused. "So that leaves us with tonight."

"To . . . to pray?" asked Oliver.

"Nay, lad, not in the way you're likely thinking. Ask the Lord to give us quick brains and strong arms, so we can figure a way out of this smokehouse."

He had already poked around their prison when he and the others were first herded in there, but he redoubled his efforts, standing up and running his fingers over every inch of the walls. As the men moved out of his way, he searched for any gap or weakness, any spot where he might create an opening and then enlarge it.

If he had his knife, it would have been easier, but the Hardcastles had taken that blade, along with all their other weapons.

Even so, when his fingers probed a soft area in one of the vertical boards on the back wall, right under the place where it joined the roof, he felt a surge of excitement and dug harder with his fingernails. Taking off his belt, he used the tongue on the buckle to gouge out more of the wood. A little rain had gotten in at some point in the past, he speculated, and caused rot to set in.

"You been standin' still for a spell, Duff," Elmer said in the darkness. "You find somethin'?"

"Perhaps," Duff replied. He hadn't said anything because he didn't want to get the others' hopes up. It might turn out to be nothing . . . as it still certainly could.

The chance was out in the open, though, so he went on.

"There's a small rotten place at the top of one of the boards. If I can make it big enough to get my hand in there, I might be able to work it back and forth and loosen it."

"One board won't be enough to get us out of here," Waylon Spencer said.

"Nae, 'twill nae," Duff agreed. "But with one board out, we'd have a much better chance of working another one loose."

Walter said eagerly, "We can help, Mr. MacCallister. Just tell us what to do."

"For now, just don't lose hope, lad." Duff went back to work with the belt buckle.

If they had been just sitting in the dark with the thought of their impending deaths weighing heavily on their minds, the time probably would have dragged by in torturous fashion. As it was, with even the slightest sliver of hope, the hours raced past.

Finally, when Duff estimated it was after midnight, he had a big enough opening at the top of the board he was able to slip all his fingers through the gap and grasp the thick board. He pushed on it with all his strength.

Nothing happened. The board didn't budge.

Duff didn't give up. He took a deep breath and tried again, grunting with the effort he put into it. Still no movement. "Elmer, come over here. Follow my voice."

A moment later, Elmer's shoulder bumped into Duff's. "What do you want me to do?"

"Give me your hand."

Duff reached out, felt Elmer's arm, and clasped the old-timer's wrist. He positioned Elmer's hand on the board he was trying to move.

"Put your other hand on there, too, and when I say *push*, shove on it as hard as ye can."

"All right." Elmer was still quite strong for his age, having been toughened up by an adventurous life spent mostly working outdoors.

Hoping Elmer's added strength would be enough, Duff said, "Ready? Push!"

Duff gripped the top of the board, placed his other hand flat underneath that spot, and he and Elmer shoved, pitting their muscle power against the nails holding the board in place. Once again, Duff thought the stubborn thing wasn't going to move even a fraction of an inch . . .

And then it did.

"Feel that?" Elmer asked excitedly. "We budged it. Let's go again—"

"Wait," Duff interrupted him. "Give me a moment."

The amount of play they had created was tiny, but Duff pushed and pulled, working the board back and forth as much as he could, hoping to loosen the nails some more. He did that for a minute or so, then said to Elmer, "Now, let's push again."

They strained against the board, and again, after a few maddening seconds, it moved slightly.

"Are you getting it?" asked Waylon Spencer.

"It appears we may be," Duff said, "but we're still far from being out of here."

"Let us help," Spencer suggested. Several of the other men seconded that.

"Keep your voices down," Duff cautioned. "There may be a guard outside the door. We dinnae want to alert him anything is going on in here." An idea occurred to him. "Some of you lads sing "Amazing Grace" or some other hymn. If anyone is listening, they'll believe we're trying to get right with the Lord, as Willie said, and will nae hear what we're really talking about."

In whispers while they others were singing, several of them worked out the arrangement. Waylon Spencer got on his knees and placed his hands against the board. His brother Burl reached over his shoulders and got ready to push, as well. Duff still had hold of the top of the board, with Elmer's hands just below his.

"Let's give it a try," Duff said quietly.

The four men pushed. The board moved almost immediately.

Duff heard a faint squealing sound and whispered urgently, "Stop!"

"What is it?" Waylon Spencer asked.

"The nails are going to make noise when they pull loose. Take it slow and easy, lads."

Carefully, the men pushed and the board loosened more. When they stopped, Duff worked it back and forth. He estimated the board was about six inches wide. If they were able to get it off, the opening wouldn't be big enough for any of them to fit through . . . but if they could loosen another board and remove it, at least one of the prisoners could slip through the gap. He was confident Walter Spencer could do it.

Leverage made all the difference. After half an hour of work, being careful not to make too much noise, the board came loose and Duff turned it so he could bring it into the smokehouse. Elmer took it and leaned it against one of the side walls.

With the board removed, the light from the moon and stars coming through the opening seemed bright after the thick shadows had enclosed them for so long. Duff could dimly see the figures around him and noticed six nails held the vertical boards in place, two each at the top and bottom and two in the middle. He could also see the single cross board positioned about four feet off the ground. The structure had been built tight to keep smoke in, but it hadn't been built to contain prisoners. The hams that normally hung up in there weren't any threat to break out.

"All right, lads, let's get back at it," he said when they had all caught their breath. "We have only a few hours left until daylight."

And they all knew what was waiting for them when the sun came up in the morning . . .

# CHAPTER 31

The slight graying of the light penetrating into the smoke-house gave Duff a renewed sense of urgency as he pulled the second board they had taken loose inside the building. He leaned it against the wall and said, "Walter, see if ye can slide through there."

Walter got down on his knees so he could work his way under the brace board that ran from one rear corner to the other. Once an arm and shoulder were through, he ducked his head so it would clear, and sucked in his stomach as much as he could.

"He's gonna make it!" Elmer whispered excitedly as Walter's back and chest cleared the boards on either side of the gap.

Walter stretched out on his side and pulled his hips and legs through. He was completely outside.

"Wish we had Wang with us," Elmer said. "He could wiggle through there with no trouble, and he could take care of any guards out front."

"Aye," Duff agreed, "but Wang is nae here." He put his face in the opening and said to Walter, who had gotten to his feet, "Take a look around the corner, lad, but be very careful about it when ye do. We need to know the odds we're facing."

Walter nodded. Duff could tell how nervous he was,

but Walter had shown in the past that he could remain coolheaded in times of danger. Duff hoped it was still the case.

Staying close to the wall, Walter slid along it to the corner and then out of sight. Despite his own icy nerves, Duff's heart was beating pretty fast by the time Walter came back.

"There's only one man standing guard," he reported, "and he looks like he's half asleep."

"And there's no lock on the door, only a bar across it, as I recall from when they put us in here," Duff said. "So ye can lift it off of there . . . if ye can deal with the guard."

Walter took a deep breath and said, "Hand me one of those boards."

"Are ye sure, lad?"

"I'm sure. He's not even holding his rifle. It's leaning against the wall beside him. And *he's* leaning on the wall, too, with his arms crossed."

Duff passed one of the boards out through the opening and said, "Ye must strike quickly. No hesitation. And accurately, as well."

Oliver leaned in and said, "You can do it, Walt."

"Thanks, Ollie. I won't let you down." Walter hefted the board and moved it around a little to get familiar with the balance of it. Then he nodded to the men watching him through the opening and headed for the front of the smokehouse.

Duff and the others moved quickly over to the other side of their prison and listened intently at the door. The tension in the shadowy room increased.

Then they heard the guard mutter, "Wha—," followed immediately by a heavy thud.

No shots roared out, and the guard didn't yell. Those were the things Duff had been the most worried about.

Another few seconds passed before another thud sounded. Walter was making sure the sentry wasn't going to wake up any time soon.

The rasping noise of the door bar being lifted off its brackets was the sweetest sound they had heard in a while. The latch rattled and then the door swung open.

Oliver was the first one out. He threw his arms around his older brother and hugged Walter. "I knew you could do it! I just knew it."

Duff stepped out next. The guard lay facedown a few feet away. Duff didn't know if Walter had killed the man, and didn't care. He bent and pulled the guard's Colt from its holster then handed the gun to Elmer, who had followed him out of the smokehouse.

Duff spotted the Winchester leaning against the wall and picked it up. It felt good to be armed again.

"The rest are supposed to be locked in the blacksmith shop," he whispered to Waylon Spencer. "Since no alarm is being given, whoever is on guard there must not have noticed what's going on over here. I'll go have a look around—"

"That won't be necessary," a new voice said nearby. "Hold your fire, MacCallister."

A slender figure stepped out of the shadows, holding a rifle. Based on the newcomer's size and lean build, Duff might have thought it was Cole Hardcastle who had spoken. But the starlight on fair hair and the higher pitch of the voice told Duff Della was the one confronting them.

She didn't threaten them with the rifle, however, and a second later, more shapes appeared, following her out of the darkness.

"Here's the rest of your bunch," said Della. "We broke them out of the blacksmith shop."

"We?" Duff repeated.

"Me and the girls. Lydia, Ginny, Patsy, and Junie. We're gonna turn you loose so you can get out of here. Best hurry. There's not much time."

"What about our wagons and teams?" Waylon Spencer asked.

"They're still down on the trail," Della said. "Willie plans to take all the valuables out of the wagons, tumble them down the mountain, and bring the teams up here later. You'll have to leave them. Go on back down the Nightmare Trail. Maybe you can get away on foot. That's the best we can do."

Duff said, "Cole and Willie and the others will never let that happen, and ye ken that already. They'll run us down as soon as 'tis light and kill us then."

"Well, do you have a better idea?" Della demanded angrily.

"Give us the guns that ye and your cousins have, so we'll at least have a fighting chance when they come after us."

"Then you'd kill some of our family," Della said. "We don't want that . . ."

"Ye cannae have it both ways," Duff told her. The sky had lightened enough he could see Della's face, and he could tell just how much her emotions were warring inside her. The same was true of the other girls.

Another new voice made Duff catch his breath.

"MacCallister's right, Della. You got to make a choice . . . and so do I." Cole Hardcastle appeared on Duff's right, holding a gun.

Duff started to turn in that direction, which would have brought the Winchester he was holding to bear, but Cole went on. "Don't do it, amigo. I don't want to kill you."

"Ye were quick enough to condemn us last night," Duff said.

"I played along with Willie and Ferris," snapped Cole.

"And to tell you the truth, I had a mighty hard time makin' up my mind. The whole thing kind of gnawed at my guts all night and didn't let me sleep. I finally decided to come and set you boys free . . . only to find my little sister had already done it."

"Cole!" Della exclaimed with a note of hope. "You're going to let them go?"

"I still think it's a mighty dumb thing to do, but . . . yeah, I reckon I am. Like you said, MacCallister, the problem will be getting away from the rest of our bunch. When Willie and Ferris find out you're gone, they're gonna be mad enough to chew nails. They'll track you down—"

"Cousin Cole," Willie Hardcastle roared. "What treachery is this? Have you taken the side of evildoers?"

"Dadgum it," muttered Elmer. "This is like the Fourth of July with a whole crowd showin' up!"

"You can tell Cole's double-crossed us!" Ferris was jabbing a pistol toward the former captives. "I knew he would. That's why I've been keepin' an eye on him. I told you we couldn't trust him, Cousin Willie. He let the prisoners loose! Kill him! Kill 'em all!" The gun in Ferris's hand spouted flame.

Duff heard the slug whistle past him.

That shot was enough to start the ball. Willie Hardcastle and the others with him opened fire as well.

Duff shouted to Waylon Spencer and the other unarmed men, "Hit the dirt, lads!" He brought the Winchester to his shoulder and hoped it was fully loaded.

As Cole moved closer to Duff, Ferris fired again. Cole grunted and took a step back but didn't fall. His gun flamed again and again. A couple of the men with Willie and Ferris staggered and then crumpled to the ground.

Willie charged toward Duff, shouting incoherently. He triggered the gun in his hand, but he was so caught up in his rage his shots went wild. Coolly, Duff lined his sights on the leader of the Hardcastle clan and stroked the Winchester's trigger. The rifle cracked.

Willie jerked back, stumbled, and his gunhand began to sag. "No!" he cried. "This can't be! I . . . I . . ." He dropped the gun and pitched forward on his face.

Cole staggered as Ferris drilled him again. Della screamed her brother's name and swung her rifle up toward Ferris, but before she could pull the trigger, a huge shape loomed up behind him. Enormous hands wrapped around Ferris's neck and lifted him off the ground. Ferris's legs kicked wildly.

"You hurt Cole!" bellowed Benjy. "You hurt Cole!" He shook Ferris like a dog shaking a rat.

Ferris's body whipped back and forth. With Benjy's hands clamped around his neck, his spine snapped like a rotten branch. When Benjy finally dropped him lifelessly to the ground, Ferris's head sat at a grotesquely unnatural angle on his shoulders.

Cole had fallen, too. Della dropped to her knees beside him and took hold of his shoulders, lifting him and propping him against her.

"Cole, damn it, you went and got yourself shot," she moaned.

The sun still wasn't up, but the sky was plenty light enough for Duff to see the large bloodstains on the front of Cole's shirt. He saw, as well, the way the gunman's mouth quirked wryly as he looked up at Della.

"Yeah, I . . . I reckon I did," Cole said. "And by . . . another Hardcastle . . . at that."

"Ferris was never worthy of the name," Della told him. "He was never any better than a mongrel dog!"

With Willie and Ferris and several of the other men dead, the survivors from Willie's group had thrown down their guns and lifted their hands as Duff and Elmer covered them. The old-timer had scored during the brief but deadly fight, too, dropping one of the Hardcastles. Another man was down but just unconscious, not dead, crowned by the board Walter had swung during the fracas.

Off to the side, the four Hardcastle girls stood holding rifles, looking uncertain what they should do next.

Duff glanced at them and said, "Ladies, 'tis time to make up your minds whether ye want to take a hand in this battle or not."

Uncertain, they stood there for a long moment, and then Lydia threw her rifle onto the ground. "The hell with it. Oliver, are you all right?"

"Yeah, I . . . I reckon I am," he replied as he stood up from the ground where he'd dived when Duff yelled to hit the dirt. He brushed himself off and answered, "Yeah, I'm fine."

"Good." Lydia pointed a finger at him. "Because I ain't done with you yet."

Ginny put her rifle on the ground. "How about you, Walter? I saw you swingin' that board around. Pretty good fightin' for a beanpole."

Walter gestured toward the open door of the smokehouse. "If I wasn't a beanpole, I never would have been able to break our boys out of that place."

"You did that?"

Walter nodded. "I sure did."

As the other two girls put their rifles on the ground, Ginny moved closer to him and they just stood there looking at each other.

Duff figured they would work out whatever needed to be worked out. He handed the Winchester to Waylon Spencer and said, "Help Elmer keep an eye on those other fellows. And some of our lads should get those rifles the lasses put down. I suspect we'll have no more trouble with the Hardcastles, but ye never know."

Spencer nodded grimly.

Duff knelt on Cole's other side. "'Tis thanking ye I am for coming to our aid. I'm sorry ye wound up paying the price."

"That . . . that's all right," Cole rasped. "I hate . . . goin' against family . . . but Willie and Ferris . . . were wrong. The time was . . . comin' to an end . . . when our family could . . . hide out up here. It was never gonna . . . last forever." Cole found the strength somewhere to lift a hand and clutch Duff's arm. "MacCallister . . . Ferris and me . . . we were the ones . . . who went out on those raids . . . just us two . . . you understand? Nobody else from the family . . . needs to go to jail . . . for what we done."

Duff knew that wasn't true. There had been more outlaws among the Hardcastle clan than just Cole and Ferris.

But if Cole wanted the two of them to take all the blame, Duff supposed it wouldn't hurt anything . . . on one condition. "I can tell that to the law, but no one will believe it if there are any more raids," Duff said.

"There . . . won't be." Cole's eyes sought his sister. "You hear me, Della? The way we used to live . . . it's over."

"I hear you, Cole," she said as tears ran down her cheeks. "Benjy and me, we'll see to that."

"There are some good folks . . . among them Spencers. If you . . . let them live in peace . . . in Longshot Basin . . . I reckon there's a good chance . . . there'll be some marryin' between the clans . . . anyway . . ." Cole leaned his head back and smiled. "It'd sure make me happy . . . if things turned out . . . that way . . ."

His eyes slowly closed, and he sighed. He was gone, and Duff and Della knew it. Della lowered her head, sobbed, and held Cole's bloody form against her.

"'Tis truly sorry I am, lass," Duff told her.

"He . . . he was a good man. He didn't always do good things, but he was a good man."

"Aye. 'Tis true of most of us, sometimes more than we'd like to admit." Duff rested a hand on her shoulder. "And we can honor him by respecting his wishes . . . about what we tell the law, and about letting the Spencers settle in Longshot Basin."

"We'll talk about it later, but . . . I agree." Della drew in a deep, ragged breath. "Maybe it's time we all tried to be good neighbors for a change."

Wang was waiting on the porch at Sky Meadow when Duff and Elmer rode in a few days later, which was no surprise, but Duff hadn't expected to see Meagan. She went down the steps to meet him when he dismounted.

He took her in his arms, held her gratefully for a long moment, then brushed a kiss across her forehead. "'Tis good to see ye, lass."

"And I'm glad to see you," she told him.

"What brings ye to Sky Meadow today?"

"You know, I'm not sure." Meagan smiled. "When I got up this morning, I just had a feeling you might be back today, so I decided to ride out and see if my instinct was right."

"Feminine intuition usually is."

From the porch, Wang said, "Souls that are connected always have a sense of each other."

Meagan nodded. "That's true, too. I've been worried, Duff. I had a feeling there might be some trouble going on."

Elmer had also swung down from his saddle. He grunted and said, "When *ain't* there trouble goin' on whenever there's a MacCallister around?"

"Aye," Duff said with a laugh. "It does seem that way, does it not?" He slipped an arm around Meagan's shoulders, but as he did, the image of another blonde appeared for an instant in his thoughts.

Then he put that away and started up the steps to the porch with Meagan. "Come on. I'll tell ye all about it."

*Keep reading for a special bonus!*

**WILLIAM W. JOHNSTONE**
**and J.A. Johnstone**

**BRANNIGAN'S LAND**
**MEAN AND EVIL**

**Ex-lawman turned cattle rancher Ty Brannigan**
**loves his wife and children.**
**And may Lord have mercy on those who would harm**
**them—because Ty Brannigan will show none.**

No one knows their way around a faro table, bank vault,
or six-shooter more than Smilin' Doc Ford.
When he's not gambling or thieving, he's throwing lead.
If he's feeling especially vicious, he's slitting throats
with his Arkansas toothpick. Roaming the west with Doc
is a band of wild outlaws including a pair of hate-filled
ex-cons and the voluptuous Zenobia "Zee" Swallow,
Doc's kill-crazy lady.

The gang have been on a killing spree, leaving a trail of
bodies near Ty Brannigan's Powderhorn spread in
Wyoming's Bear Paw Mountains. U.S. marshals want Ty
to help them track down Smilin' Doc's bunch. But when
the hunt puts the Brannigan clan in the outlaws' sights,
Ty and his kin take justice into their own hands—
and deliver it with a furious, final vengeance.

*Look for* **MEAN AND EVIL** *on sale now!*

# CHAPTER 1

"I declare it's darker'n the inside of a dead man's boot out here!" exclaimed Dad Clawson.

"It ain't dark over here by the fire," countered Dad's younger cow punching partner, Pete Driscoll.

"No, but it sure is dark out here." Dad—a short, bandy-legged, gray-bearded man in a bullet-crowned cream Stetson that had seen far better days a good twenty years ago—stood at the edge of the firelight, holding back a pine branch as he surveyed the night-cloaked, Bear Paw Mountain rangeland beyond him.

"If you've become afraid of the dark in your old age, Dad, why don't you come on over here by the fire, take a load off, and pour a cup of coffee? I made a fresh pot. Thick as day-old cow plop, just like you like it. I'll even pour some of my who-hit-John in it if you promise to stop caterwaulin' like you're about to be set upon by wolves."

Dad stood silently scowling off into the star-capped distance. "Did you hear that?" he asked quietly, raspily, turning his head a little to one side.

"Hear what?"

"That." Dad turned his head a little more to one side. "There it was again."

Driscoll—a tall, lean man in his mid-thirties and with a thick, dark-red mustache mantling his upper lip—stared across the steaming tin cup he held in both hands before him, pricking his ears, listening. A sharpened matchstick drooped from one corner of his mouth. "I didn't hear a thing."

Dad turned his craggy, bearded face toward the younger man, frowning. "You didn't?"

"Not a dadgum thing, Dad." Driscoll glowered at his partner from beneath the broad brim of his black Stetson. He'd been paired with Clawson for over five years, since they'd both started working at the Stevens' Kitchen Sink Ranch on Owlhoot Creek. In that time, they'd become as close as some old married couples, which meant they fought as much as some old married couples. "What's gotten into you? I've never known you to be afraid of the dark before."

"I don't know." Dad gave his head a quick shake. "Somethin's got my blood up."

"What is it?"

Dad glowered over his shoulder at Driscoll. "If I knew that, my blood wouldn't be up—now, would it?"

Driscoll blew ripples on his coffee and sipped. "I think you got old-timer's disease. That's what I think." He sipped again, swallowed. "Hearin' things out in the dark, gettin' your drawers in a twist."

Dad stood listening, staring out into the night. The stars shone brightly, guttering like candles in distant windows in small houses across the arching vault of the firmament. Finally, he released the pine bough; it danced back into place. He turned and, scowling and shaking his head, ambled back over to the fire. His spurs chinged softly. On a flat, pale rock near the dancing orange flames, his speckled tin coffee pot, which owned the dent of a bullet fired long ago by some cow-thieving Comanche bushwhacker in the Texas Panhandle, gurgled and steamed.

"Somethin's out there—I'm tellin' ya. Someone or some-*thing* is movin' around out there." Dad grabbed his old Spencer repeating rifle from where it leaned against a tree then walked back around the fire to stand about six feet away from it, gazing out through the pines and into the night, holding the Spencer down low across his skinny thighs clad in ancient denims and brush-scarred, bull-hide chaps.

Driscoll glanced over his shoulder at where his and Dad's hobbled horses contentedly cropped grass several yards back in the pines. "Horses ain't nervy."

Dad eased his ancient, leathery frame onto a pine log, still keeping his gaze away from the fire, not wanting to compromise his night vision. "Yeah, well, this old coot is savvier than any broomtail cayuse. Been out on the range longer than both of them and you put together, workin' spreads from Old Mexico to Calvary in Alberta." He shook his head slowly. "Coldest damn country I ever visited. Still got frost bite on my tired old behind from the two winters I spent up there workin' for an ornery old widder."

"Maybe you got frostbite on the brain, too, Dad." Driscoll grinned.

"Sure, sure. Make fun. That's the problem with you, Pete. You got no respect for your elders."

"Ah, hell, Dad. Lighten up." Driscoll set his cup down and rummaged around in his saddlebags. "Come on over here an' let's plays us some two-handed—"

He cut himself off abruptly, sitting up, gazing out into the night, his eyes wider than they'd been two seconds ago.

Dad shot a cockeyed grin over his shoulder. "See?"

"What was that?"

Dad cast his gaze through the pines again, to the right of where he'd been gazing before. "Hard to say."

"Hoot owl?"

"I don't think so."

The sound came again—very quiet but distinct in the night so quiet that Dad thought he could hear the crackling flames of the stars.

"Ah, sure," Driscoll said. "A hoot owl. That's all it was!" He chuckled. "Your nerves is right catching, Dad. You're infecting my peaceable mind. Come on, now. Get your raggedy old behind over here and—"

Again, a sound cut him off.

Driscoll gave an involuntary gasp then felt the rush of blood in his cheeks as they warmed with embarrassment. The sound was unlike anything Dad or Pete Driscoll had ever heard before. A screeching wail? Sort of cat-like. But it hadn't been a cat. At least, like no cat Dad had ever heard before, and he'd heard a few during his allotment. Night-hunting cats could sound pure loco, fill a man's loins with dread. But this had been no cat.

An owl, possibly. But, no. It hadn't been an owl, either.

Dad's old heart thumped against his breastbone.

It thumped harder when a laugh vaulted out of the darkness. He swung his head sharply to the left, trying to peer through the branches of two tall Ponderosa pines over whose lime-green needles the dull, yellow, watery light of the fire shimmered.

"That was a woman," Driscoll said quietly, his voice low with a building fear.

The laugh came again. Very quietly. But loudly enough for Dad to make out a woman's laugh, all right. Sort of like the laugh of a frolicking whore in some whorehouse in Cheyenne or Laramie, say. The laugh of a whore mildly drunk and engaged in a game of slap 'n' tickle with some drunken, frisky miner or track layer who'd paid downstairs and was swiping at the whore's bodice with one hand while holding a bottle by the neck with his other hand.

Dad rose from his log. Driscoll rose from where he'd been leaning back against his saddle, reached for his saddle ring Winchester, and slowly, quietly levered a round into the action. He followed Dad over to the north edge of the camp.

Dad pushed through the pine branches, holding his own rifle in one hand, his heart still thumping heavily against his breastbone. His tongue was dry, and he felt a knot in his throat. That was fear.

He was not a fearful man. Leastways, he'd never considered himself a fearful man. But that was fear, all right. Fear like he'd known it only once before and that was when he'd been alone in Montana, tending a small herd for an English rancher, and a grizzly had been prowling around in the darkness beyond his fire, occasionally edging close enough so that the flames glowed in the beast's eyes and reflected off its long, white, razor-edged teeth that it had shown Dad as though a promise of imminent death and destruction.

The cows had been wailing fearfully, scattering themselves up and down the whole damn valley . . .

But the bear had seemed more intent on Dad himself.

That was a rare kind of fear. He'd never wanted to feel it again. But he felt it now, all right. Sure enough.

He stepped out away from the trees and cast his gaze down a long, gentle, sage-stippled slope and beyond a narrow creek that glistened like a snake's skin in the starlight. He jerked with a start when he heard a spur trill very softly behind him and glanced to his right to see Driscoll step up beside him, a good half a foot taller than the stoop-shouldered Dad.

Driscoll gave a dry chuckle, but Dad knew Pete was as unnerved as he was.

Both men stood in silence, listening, staring straight off down the slope and across the water, toward where they'd heard the woman laugh.

Then it came again, louder. Only, this time it came from Dad's left, beyond a bend in the stream.

Dad's heart pumped harder. He squeezed his rifle in both sweating hands, bringing it up higher now, slipping his right finger through the trigger guard, lightly caressing the trigger. The woman's deep, throaty, hearty laugh echoed then faded. Then the echoes faded, as well.

"What the hell's goin' on?" Driscoll said. "I don't see no campfire over that way."

"Yeah, well, there's no campfire straight out away from us, neither, and that's where she was two minutes ago."

Driscoll clucked his tongue in agreement.

The men could hear the faint sucking sounds of the stream down the slope to the north, fifty yards away. That was the only sound. No breeze. No birds. Not even the rustling, scratching sounds little animals made as they burrowed.

Not even the soft thump of a pinecone falling out of a tree.

It was as though the entire night was collectively holding its breath, as though anticipating something bad about to occur.

The silence was shattered by a loud yowling wail issuing from behind Dad and Driscoll. It was a yapping, coyote-like yodeling, only it wasn't made by no coyote. No, no, no. Dad heard the voice of a man in that din. He heard the mocking laughter of a man in the cacophony as he and Driscoll turned quickly to stare back toward their fire and beyond it, their gazes now cast with terror.

The crazy, mocking yodeling had come from the west, the opposite direction from the woman's first laugh.

Dad felt a shiver in Driscoll's right arm as it pressed up against Dad's left one.

"Christalmighty," his partner said. "They got us surrounded. Whoever they are!"

"Toyin' with us," Dad said, grimacing angrily.

Then the woman's voice came again. Only, this time, it issued from its original direction, straight off down the slope and across the darkly glinting stream. Both men grunted their exasperation as they whipped around again and stared off toward the east.

"Sure as hell, they're toyin' with us!" Driscoll said tightly, angrily, his chest expanding and contracting as he breathed. "What the hell do they want?" He didn't wait for Dad's response. He stepped forward and, holding his cocked Winchester up high across his chest, shouted, "*What the hell do you want?*"

"Come on out an' show yourselves!" Dad bellowed in a raspy voice brittle with terror.

Driscoll gave him a dubious look. "Sure we want 'em to do that?"

Dad only shrugged and continued turning his head this way and that, heart pounding, as he looked for signs of movement in the deep, dark night around him.

"Hey, amigos," a man's deep, toneless voice said off Dad and Driscoll's left flanks. "Over here!"

Both men whipped around with more startled grunts, extending their rifles out before them, aiming into the darkness right of their fire, looking for a target but not seeing one.

"That one's close!" Driscoll said. "Damn close!"

Now the horses were stirring in the brush and trees beyond the fire, not far from where that cold, hollow voice had issued. They whickered and stumbled around, whipping their tails against their sides.

"That tears it!" Pete said.

He moved forward, bulling through the pine boughs, angling toward the right of his and Dad's fire which had burned down considerably, offering only a dull, flickering, red radiance.

"Hold on, Pete!" Dad said. "Hold on!"

But then Pete was gone, leaving only the pine boughs jostling behind him.

"Where are you, dammit?" Pete yelled, his own voice echoing. "Where the hell are you? Why don't you come out an' show yourselves?"

Dad shoved his left hand out, bending a pine branch back away from him. He stepped forward, seeing the fire flickering straight ahead of him, fifteen feet away. He quartered to the right of the fire, not wanting its dull light to outline him, to make him a target. He could hear Pete's spurs ringing, his boots thudding and crackling in the pine needles ahead of him, near where the horses were whickering and prancing nervously.

"What the hell do you want?" Pete cried, his voice brittle with exasperation and fear. "Why don't you show yourselves, dammit?"

His boot thuds dwindled in volume as he moved farther away from the fire, spurs ringing more softly.

Dad jerked violently when Pete's voice came again: "There you are! Stop or I'll shoot, damn you!"

A rifle barked once, twice, three times.

"Stop, dam—" Pete's voice was drowned by another rifle blast, this one issuing from farther away than Pete's had issued. And off to Dad's left.

Straight out from Dad came an anguished cry.

"Pete!" Dad said, taking one quaking footstep forward, his heart hiccupping in his chest. "*Pete!*"

Pete cried out again. Running, stumbling footsteps sounded from the direction Pete had gone. Dad aimed the rifle, gazing in terror toward the sound of the footsteps growing louder and louder. A man-shaped silhouette grew before Dad, and then, just before he was about to squeeze the Spencer's trigger, the last rays of the dying fire played across Pete's sweaty face.

He was running hatless and without his rifle, his hands clamped over his belly.

"Pete!" Dad cried again, lowering the rifle.

"Dad!" Pete stopped and dropped to his knees before him. He looked up at the older man, his hair hanging in his eyes, his eyes creased with pain. "They're comin', Dad!"

Then he sagged onto his left shoulder and lay groaning and writhing.

"*Pete!*" Dad cried, staring down in horror at his partner.

His friend's name hadn't entirely cleared his lips before something hot punched into his right side. The punch was followed by the wicked, ripping report of a rifle. He saw the flash in the darkness out before him and to the right.

Dad wailed and stumbled sideways, giving his back to the direction the bullet had come from. Another bullet plowed into his back, just beneath his right shoulder, punching him forward. He fell and rolled, wailing and writhing.

He rolled onto his back, the pain of both bullets torturing him.

He spied movement in the darkness to his right.

He spied more movement all around him.

Grimacing with the agony of what the bullets had done to him, he pushed up onto his elbows. Straight out away from him, a dapper gent in a three-piece, butternut suit and bowler hat stepped up from the shadows and stood before him. He looked like a man you'd see on a city street, maybe wielding a fancy walking stick, or at a gambling layout in San Francisco or Kansas City. The dimming firelight glinted off what appeared a gold spike in his rear earlobe.

The man stared down at Dad, grinning. He was strangely handsome, clean-shaven, square-jawed. At first glance, his smiling eyes seemed warm and intelligent. He appeared the kind of man you'd want your daughter to marry.

Dad looked to his left and blinked his eyes, certain he wasn't seeing who he thought he saw—a beautiful flaxen-haired woman with long, impish blue eyes dressed all in black including a long, black duster. The duster was open to reveal that she wore only a black leather vest under it. The vest highlighted more than concealed the heavy swells of her bosoms trussed up behind the tight-fitting, form-accentuating vest.

The woman smiled down at Dad, tipped her head back, and gave a cat-like laugh.

If cats laughed, that was.

More movement to Dad's right. He turned in that direction to see a giant of a man step up out of the shadows. A giant of a full-blooded Indian. Dressed all in buckskins and with a red bandanna tied around the top of his head, beneath his low-crowned, straw sombrero. Long, black hair hung down past his shoulders, and two big pistols jutted on his hips. He held a Yellowboy repeating rifle in both his big, red hands across his waist.

He stared dully through flat, coal-black eyes down at Dad.

Dad gasped with a start when he heard crunching foot-steps behind him, now, as well. He turned his head to peer over his shoulder at another big man, this one a white man, step up out of the shadows, holding a Winchester carbine down low by his side. He was nearly as thick as he was tall, and he had a big, ruddy, fleshy face with a thick, brown beard. His hair was as long as the Indian's. On his head was a badly battered, ancient Stetson with a crown pancaked down on his head, the edges of the brim tattered in places.

He grunted down at Dad then, working a wad of chaw around in his mouth, turned his head and spat to one side.

Dad turned back to the handsome man standing before him.

As he did, the handsome man, lowered his head, reached up, and pulled something out from behind his neck. He held it out to show Dad.

A pearl-handled Arkansas toothpick with a six-inch, razor-edged blade.

To go along with his hammering heart, a cold stone dropped in Dad's belly.

The man smiled, his eyes darkening, the warmth and intelligence Dad had previously seen in them becoming a lie, turning dark and seedy and savage. He turned and walked over to where Pete lay writhing and groaning.

"No," Dad wheezed. "Don't you do it, you devil!"

The handsome man dropped to a knee beside Pete. He grabbed a handful of Pete's hair and jerked Pete's head back, exposing Pete's neck.

Pete screamed.

The handsome man swept the knife quickly across Pete's throat then stepped back suddenly to avoid the blood geysering out of the severed artery.

Pete choked and gurgled and flopped his arms and kicked his legs as he died.

The handsome man turned to Dad.

"Oh, God," Dad said. "Oh, God."

So this was how it was going to end. Right here. Tonight.

Cut by a devil who looked like a man you'd want your daughter to marry. Aside from the eyes, that was . . .

As though reading Pete's mind, the handsome man grinned down at him. He shuttled that demon's smile to the others around him and then stepped forward and crouched down in front of Dad.

The last thing Dad felt before the dark wing of death closed over him was a terrible fire in his throat.

# CHAPTER 2

"You think those rustlers are around here, Pa?" Matt Brannigan asked his father.

Just then, Tynan Brannigan drew his coyote dun to a sudden stop, and curveted the mount, sniffing the wind. "I just now do, yes."

"Why's that?" Matt asked, frowning.

Facing into the wind, which was from the southwest, Ty worked his broad nose beneath the brim of his high-crowned tan Stetson. "Smell that?"

"I don't smell nothin'."

"Face the wind, son," Ty said.

He was a big man in buckskins, at fifty-seven still lean and fit and broad through the shoulders, slender in the hips, long in the legs. His tan face with high cheekbones and a strawberry blond mustache to match the color of his wavy hair which hung down over the collar of his buckskin shirt, was craggily handsome, the eyes drawn up at the corners. The eyes were expressive, rarely veiling the emotions swirling about in his hot Irish heart; they smiled often and owned the deeply etched lines extending out from their corners to prove it.

Ty wasn't smiling now, however. Earlier in the day, he and Matt had cut the sign of twelve missing beeves as well as the horse tracks of the men herding them. Of the long-looping devils herding them, rather. Rustling was no laughing matter.

Matt, who favored his father though at nineteen was not as tall and was much narrower of bone, held his crisp cream Stetson down on his head as he turned to sniff the wind, which was blowing the ends of his knotted green neckerchief as well as the glossy black mane of his blue roan gelding.

He cut a sidelong look at his father, and grinned. "Ah."

"Yeah," Ty said, jerking his chin up to indicate the narrow canyon opening before him here in the heart of west-central Wyoming Territory's Bear Paw Mountains. "That way. They're up Three Maidens Gulch, probably fixin' to spend the night in that old trapper's cabin. The place has a corral so they'd have an easy time keeping an eye on their stolen beef."

"On *our* beef," Matt corrected his father.

"Good point." Ty put the spurs to the dun and galloped off the trail they'd been on and onto the canyon trail, the canyon's stony walls closing around him and Matt galloping just behind his father. The land here was rocky so they'd lost the rustler's sign intermittently though it was hard to entirely lose the sign of twelve beeves on the hoof and four horseback riders.

A quarter mile into the canyon, the walls drew back and a stream curved into the canyon from a secondary canyon to the east. The stream, glistening in the high-country sunlight and sheathed in aspens turning yellow now in the mountain fall, their wind-jostled leaves winking like newly minted pennies, hugged the trail as it dropped and turned hard and flinty then grassy as it bisected a broad meadow, the stream now hidden from Ty and Matt's view by heavier pines on their right.

The forest formed the shape of an arrow as it cut down from the stream toward Ty and Matt. That arrow point crossed the trail a hundred yards ahead of them.

They followed the trail through the forest fragrant with pine duff and moldering leaves.

At the edge of the trees, Ty drew the dun to a halt. Matt followed suit, the spirited roan stomping and blowing.

Ty gazed ahead at a rocky saddle rising before them a hundred yards away. Rocks and pines and stunted aspens stippled the rise and rose to the saddle's crest.

"The cabin's on the other side of that rise," Ty said, reaching forward with his right hand and sliding his Henry repeating rifle from its saddle sheath.

Both gun and sheath owned the marks of time and hard use. Ty had used the Henry during his town taming years in Kansas and Oklahoma, and the trusty sixteen-shot repeater had held him in good stead. So had the stag-butted Colt .44 snugged down in a black leather holster thonged on his buckskin-clad right thigh.

The thong was the mark of a man who used his hogleg often and in a hurry, but that was no longer true. Ty had been ranching and raising his family in these mountains for the past twenty years, ever since he'd met and married his four childrens' lovely Mexican mother, the former Beatriz Salazar, sixteen years Ty's junior.

He no longer used his weapons anywhere near as much as when he'd been the town marshal of Hayes or Abilene, Kansas or Guthrie, Oklahoma. Only at such times as now, when rustlers were trying to winnow his herd, or when old enemies came gunning for him, which had happened more times than he wanted to think about. At such times he always worried first and foremost for the safety of his family.

His family's welfare was paramount.

That's what he wanted to talk to Matt about now . . .

He turned to his son, who had just then slid his own Winchester carbine from its saddle sheath and rested it across his thighs. "Son," Ty said, "there's four of 'em."

"I know, Pa." Matt levered a round into his Winchester's action then off-cocked the hammer. He grinned. "We can take 'em."

"If this were a year ago, I'd send you home."

Again, Matt grinned. "You'd try."

Ty laughed in spite of the gravity of the situation he found himself in—tracking four long-loopers with a son he loved more than life itself and wanted no harm to come to. "You and your sister," Ty said, ironically shaking his head. He was referring to his lovely, headstrong daughter, MacKenna, who at seventeen was two years younger than Matt but in some ways was far more worldly in the ways that seventeen-year-old young women can be more worldly than boys and even men.

Especially those who were Irish mixed with Latina.

Mack, as MacKenna was known by those closest to her, was as good with a horse and a Winchester repeating rifle as Matt was, and Matt knew it. Sometimes Ty thought she was as good with the shooting irons as he himself was. Part of him almost wished she were here . . .

"You're nineteen now," Ty told Matt.

"Goin' on twenty," Matt quickly added.

"Out here, that makes a man." Ty jerked his head to indicate the saddle ahead of them. "They have a dozen of our cows, and they can't get away with them. They have to be taught they can't mess with Powderhorn beef. If we don't teach 'em that, if they get away with it—"

"I know, Pa. More will come. Like wolves on the blood scent."

"You got it." Ty narrowed one grave eye at his son. "I

want you to be careful. Take no chances. If it comes to shootin', and we'd best assume it will because those men likely know what the penalty for rustling is out here, remember to breathe and line up your sights and don't hurry your shots or you'll pull 'em. But for God sakes when you need to pull your head down, pull it down!"

"You know what, Pa?" Matt asked, sitting up straight in his saddle, suddenly wide-eyed, his handsome face showing his own mix of Irish and Latin, with his olive skin, light brown hair which he wore long like his father, and expressive, intelligent tan eyes.

"What?"

"A few minutes ago, I wasn't one bit scared," Matt said. "In fact, I was congratulatin' myself, pattin' myself on the back, tellin' myself how proud I was that I was out here trackin' long-ropers with the great Ty Brannigan without threat of makin' water in my drawers. But now I'm afraid I'm gonna make water in my drawers! So, if you wouldn't mind, could we do what needs doin' before I lose my nerve, pee myself, an' go runnin' home to Ma?"

He kept his mock-frightened look on his father for another three full seconds. Suddenly, he grinned and winked. Trying to put the old man at ease.

Ty chuckled and nudged his hat up to scratch the back of his head. "All right, son. All right. I just had to say that."

"I know you did, Pa."

Ty sidled his mount up to Matt's handsome roan, took his rifle in his left hand and reached out and cupped the back of Matt's neck in his gloved hand, pulling him slightly toward him. "I love you, kid," he said, gritting his teeth and hardening his eyes. "If anything ever happened to you . . ."

Feeling emotion swelling in him, threatening to fog his eyes, he released Matt quickly, reined the dun around, and booted it on up the trail.

Matt smiled after his father then booted the roan into the dun's sifting dust.

Ten minutes later, father and son were hunkered down behind rocks at the crest of the saddle. Their horses stood ground-reined twenty feet down the ridge behind them.

Ty was peering through his spyglass into the valley on the saddle's other side, slowly adjusting the focus. The old trapper's cabin swam into view—a two-story, brush-roofed, age-silvered log hovel hunkered in a meadow on the far side of a creek rippling through a narrow, stony bed.

The cabin was flanked by a lean-to stable and a pole corral in which all twelve of his cows stood, a few chewing hay, others mooing nervously. Five horses milled with the cattle, also eating hay or munching grass that had grown high since the place had been abandoned many years ago. That fifth horse might mean five instead of four men in the cabin. One man, possibly whoever was buying the stolen beef, might have met the others here with the cows. Ty would have to remember that.

A half-breed named Latigo He Who Rides had lived here—an odd, quiet man whom Ty had met a few times when he'd been over here looking for unbranded mavericks that had avoided the previous roundup.

Ty had never known what had happened to He Who Rides. One year on a trek over to this side of the saddle he'd simply found the cabin abandoned. It had sat mostly abandoned ever since except when rustlers or outlaws on the run used it to overnight in. It was good and remote, and known by only folks like Ty himself who knew this eastern neck of the mountains well.

Rustlers had moved in again, it looked like. Ty had a

pretty good idea who they were led by, too. A no-account scoundrel named Leroy Black. His brother Luther was probably here, as well. They were known to have rustled in the area from time to time, selling the stolen beef to outlaw ranchers who doctored the brands or to packers who butchered it as soon as the cows were in their hands.

Knowing the Blacks were rustling and being able to prove it, however, were two separate things.

The Black boys were slippery, mostly moved the cattle at night. They were probably working with their cousins, Derrick and Bobby Dean Barksdale. The Blacks and Barksdales made rustling in the Bear Paws and over in the nearby Wind Rivers a family affair. That they were moving beef in the light of day meant they were getting brash and would likely get brasher.

Ty grimaced, his cheeks warming with anger.

Time to put them out of business once and for all.

Ty handed the spy glass to Matt hunkered beside him, staring through a separate gap between the rocks.

"Have a look, son. Take a good, careful look. Get a good sense of the layout before we start down, and note the fifth horse in the corral. The odds against us likely just went up by one more man. We'll need to remember that."

"All right, Pa." Matt took the spyglass, held it to his eye, and adjusted the focus.

He studied the cabin and its surroundings for a good three or four minutes then lowered the glass and turned to his father, frowning. "They don't have anyone on watch?"

Ty shook his head. "Not that I could see. They've gotten overconfident. That works in our favor."

"We gonna wait till dark? Take 'em when they're asleep?"

Ty shook his head. "Too dangerous. I like to know who I'm shooting at." He glanced at the sun. "In about an hour, the sun will be down behind the western ridges. It'll be dusk in that canyon. That's when we'll go. Knowing both the Blacks and Barksdales like I do, they'll likely be good and drunk by then."

Matt nodded.

Ty dropped to his butt and rested back against one of the large rocks peppering the ridge crest. He doffed his hat, ran a big, gloved hand brusquely through his sweat-damp hair. "Here's the hard part."

"The hard part?"

"Waiting. Everyone thinks lawdogging is an exciting profession. Truth to tell, a good three-quarters of it is sitting around waiting for something to happen."

"Good to know," Matt said. "In case I ever start thinkin' about followin' in my old man's footsteps."

"Forget it," Ty said, smiling. "You're needed at the Powderhorn. That's where you're gonna get married and raise a whole passel of kids. We'll add another floor to the house." Suddenly, he frowned, pondering on what he'd just said. "That is what you'd like to do—isn't it, Matt?"

A thoughtful cast came to Matt's eyes as he seemed to do some pondering of his own. Finally, he shrugged, quirked a wry half-smile, and said, "Sure. Why not?"

Ty studied his oldest boy. He'd always just assumed, since Matt had been a pink-faced little baby, that the boy would follow in Ty's footsteps. His ranching footsteps. Not his lawdogging footsteps.

Now he wondered if he'd made the wrong assumption. His own father had assumed that Ty would follow in Killian Brannigan's own footsteps as a mountain fur trapper and hide hunter. That they'd continue to work together in the Rockies, living in the little cabin they shared with Ty's hard-working mother halfway up the Cache la Poudre Canyon near La Port in Colorado. Killian Brannigan had been hurt when Ty had decided to go off to the frontier army and fight the Indians and then, once he'd mustered out, pin a badge to his chest. One badge after another in wide-open towns up and down the great cattle trails back when Texas beef was still being herded to the railroad hubs in Kansas and Oklahoma.

Those years had been the heyday of the Old Western gunfighter, so Ty, too, had had to become good with a gun.

Despite what Ty had said to Matt about lawdogging being three-quarters boredom, it had been an exciting time in his life. While he'd visited his parents often, he'd never regretted the choice he'd made. Being a mountain man and working in tandem with his mountain woman, Ciara Brannigan, pronounced "Kee-ra," had been his father's choice. Killian and Ciara had both been loners by nature and had preferred the company of the forests and rivers to that of people. While Ty had loved his parents and enjoyed his childhood hunting and trapping and hide-tanning alongside his mother and father, he'd been ready to leave the summer he'd turned seventeen.

And leave he had.

Now he realized he should have known better than just to assume that his own son would want to follow in his own ranching footsteps. It wasn't a fair assumption to make. And now Ty wondered, a little skeptically as he continued to study his son, if he'd been wrong. He hoped he wasn't, but he might be. If so, like his own father before him, he'd have to live with the choice his son made. That time was right around the corner, too, he realized with a little dread feeling like sour milk in his belly.

He just hoped Matt didn't make Ty's own first choice. He didn't want his son to be a lawman. He wanted him to stay home and ranch with Ty and the boy's mother, Beatriz.

* * *

Time passed slowly there on the top of that saddle.

The sun angled westward. Deep purple shadows angled out from the western ridges. Bird song grew somnolent.

Ty kept watch on the cabin. While he did, two of the four men came outside, separately and at different times, to make water just off the dilapidated front stoop. Another came out to empty a wash pan. That man came out the cabin's back door a few minutes later to walk over to the corral and check on the cattle that were still mooing and grazing uneasily. That was one of the Barksdale brothers clad in a ragged broadcloth coat and floppy-brimmed felt hat. He wore two pistols on his hips and held a Winchester in his hands.

On the way back to the cabin, he took a good, long, cautious look around. Then he reentered the cabin through the back door.

While Ty kept watch, Matt rested his head back against a rock, tipped his hat down over his face, and dozed.

Finally, Ty put his spyglass away and touched his son's arm. "Time to go, son," he said. "Sun's down."

He picked up his rifle and looked at Matt, who yawned, blinking his eyes, coming awake. He wanted to tell the kid to stay here, out of harm's way, but he couldn't do it. Matt wouldn't have listened, and he shouldn't have. He wasn't a kid anymore. He was almost twenty and he was part of a ranching family. That meant he, like Ty, had to protect what was his.

Ty hoped like hell they got through this all right. If anything happened to that kid, his mother would never forgive Ty and Ty would never forgive himself.